THE NOVELLINO OR ONE HUNDRED ANCIENT TALES

ROUTLEDGE LIBRARY OF MEDIEVAL LITERATURE
VOLUME 105A

Advisory Board

THE NOVELLINO OR ONE HUNDRED ANCIENT TALES

AN EDITION AND TRANSLATION BASED ON THE 1525 GUALTERUZZI *editio princeps*

EDITED AND TRANSLATED BY
JOSEPH P. CONSOLI

NEW YORK AND LONDON

First Published 1997 by Garland Publishing Inc.

Transferred to Digital Printing 2010 by Routledge
2 Park Square, Milton Park, Abingdon, Oxon OX14 4RN
711 Third Avenue, New York, NY 10017, USA

Routledge is an imprint of the Taylor & Francis Group, an informa business

First issued in paperback 2016

Library of Congress Cataloging-in-Publication Data

Novellino. English & Italian.

The novellino, or, One hundred ancient tales : an edition and translation based on the 1525 Gualteruzzi editio princeps / edited by Joseph P. Consoli.

p. cm. — (Garland library of medieval literature ; v. 105A)

Includes bibliographical references and index.

ISBN 978-0-8153-1080-8 (hbk)
ISBN 978-1-138-97732-7 (pbk)

1. Short stories, Italian—Translations into English. 2. Italian fiction—To 1400—Translations into English. I. Consoli, Joseph P., 1949– II. Series.

PQ4253.A4E5 1997
853'.0108—dc20 96-41562
CIP

Publisher's Note
The publisher has gone to great lengths to ensure the quality of this reprint but points out that some imperfections in the original may be apparent.

Preface of the General Editors

The Garland Library of Medieval Literature was established to make available to the general reader modern translations of texts in editions that conform to the highest academic standards. All of the translations are originals, and were created especially for this series. The translations usually attempt to render the foreign works in a natural idiom that remains faithful to the originals, although in certain cases we have published more poetic versions.

The Library is divided into two sections: Series A, texts and translations; and Series B, translations alone. Those volumes containing texts have been prepared after consultation of the major previous editions and manuscripts. The aim in the edition has been to offer a reliable text with a minimum of editorial intervention. Significant variants accompany the original, and important problems are discussed in the textual notes. Volumes without texts contain translations based on the most scholarly texts available, which have been updated in terms of recent scholarship.

Most volumes contain introductions with the following features: (1) a biography of the author or a discussion of the problem of authorship, with any pertinent historical or legendary information; (2) an objective discussion of the literary style of the original, emphasizing any individual features; (3) a consideration of sources for the work and its influence; and (4) a statement of the editorial policy for each edition and translation. There is also a select bibliography, which emphasizes recent criticism on the works. Critical writings are often accompanied by brief descriptions of their importance. Selective glossaries, indices, and footnotes are included where appropriate.

The Library covers a broad range of linguistic areas, including all of the major European languages. All of the important literary forms and genres are considered, sometimes in anthologies or selections.

The General Editors hope that these volumes will bring the general reader a closer awareness of a richly diversified area that has for too long been closed to everyone except those with precise academic training, an area that is well worth study and reflection.

James J. Wilhelm
Rutgers University

Lowry Nelson, Jr.
Yale University

This text is dedicated to the memory

of

Elide Macchietti Paganini

TABLE OF CONTENTS

INTRODUCTION

Critics concur that *The Novellino* is "the first collection of short stories [to appear] in Italian literature" (Lo Nigro 9). While earlier collections written in Italian did exist, such as *I conti di antichi cavalieri* and *Il libro dei sette savi*, these were primarily redactions, revisions and translations from extant French and Latin collections. *The Novellino* is the first collection to be composed specifically for an Italian audience. Most scholars now place the date of composition sometime between 1281 and 1300. While the work's originality assured it a place in the canon of Italian literature, until recent times its position in relation to critical interest remained marginal at best. For over two hundred years after its composition, *The Novellino* suffered from benign neglect.

To date only seven manuscripts produced before the *editio princeps* have been discovered which contain substantial portions of *The Novellino*, and the number of novellas found in each one varies significantly. Only the *editio princeps* of 1525, prepared by Carlo Gualteruzzi (**Gz**) and its "twin" manuscript, Biblioteca Apostolica Vaticana 3214 (**V**), penned by Giulio Cammillo Del Minio for Pietro Bembo in 1523, contain exactly one hundred novellas.

Researchers agree that no autograph, original or exact copy of the original manuscript exists today. While diagrams of the relationships among these manuscripts and the *editio princeps* vary greatly, virtually all paleographic studies divide these into two fundamental categories: those that follow the content and order of the *editio princeps*, and those that do not. Of the six remaining manuscripts, five of these, all of which are either mutilated or abridged, follow the ordering of the novellas found in the *editio princeps*. These include:

1. The Palatino 566 (**A**), located in the Biblioteca Nazionale in Florence, penned in the first half of the 14th century. It contains 42 complete novellas and 7 incomplete from the Gualteruzzi edition.
2. The Gaddiano rel. 193 (**G**), located in the Biblioteca Mediceo-Laurenziano in Florence, penned sometime after 1315. It contains 30 novellas from the Gualteruzzi edition.
3. The Magliabechiano-Strozziano, class XXV, n. 513 (**S**), located in the Biblioteca Nazionale in Florence, penned at the end of the 14th century or the beginning of the 15th century. It contains 53 novellas from the Gualteruzzi edition.
4. The Codex Pluteo 90 sup. 89 (**L**), located in the Biblioteca Mediceo-Laurenziano in Florence, penned in the late 15th century. It contains only two novellas from the Gualteruzzi edition.
5. The Panciatichiano-Palatino 32, Section II, already numbered 138 (**P**^{2}), located in the Biblioteca Nazionale in Florence, penned around the middle of the

14th century. This second half of a manuscript contains 27 novellas which follow the Gualteruzzi edition.

The most controversial manuscript, primarily because of its early creation and the fact that it diverges significantly from the Gualteruzzi ordering, is the first section of number 5 mentioned above.

1. The Panciatichiano-Palatino 32, Section I, already numbered 138 (**P**[1]), located in the Biblioteca Nazionale in Florence, penned at the end of the 13th century or the beginning of the next. This manuscript entitles the work *Libro di novelle e di bel parlar gentile* (*Book of Tales and of Lovely Gentile Speech*). It is comprised of 85 novellas which follow a different order from the Gualteruzzi edition. There are also novellas not found in Gualteruzzi and others which have been significantly altered.

The first person to demonstrate a serious interest in *The Novellino* was the humanist Cardinal Pietro Bembo, who most probably came across an ancient manuscript containing the novellas, and realizing the importance of such a work, had a personal copy prepared for himself in 1523 by Giulio Cammillo Del Minio. This was destined to become the Vatican 3214 codex. In a letter to Del Minio, the Cardinal writes, "I have received from the hand of M. Romulo the example of the ancient tales which you had written for me in the best hand, and as I can see very well corrected, along with the rhymes of the poets from those times (Biagi cxli)." It comes as no surprise that this humanist scholar, who dedicated so much of his time to the study of the vernacular, should be the first to realize the importance of this first collection of Italian vernacular tales.

Two years later, Carlo Gualteruzzi edited the first printed edition of *The Novellino* at the Benedetti presses in Bologna. While no documentation exists which states explicitly that Pietro Bembo was responsible for Gualteruzzi's interest in *The Novellino*, it is common knowledge that the two were intimate friends and that Gualteruzzi served as the translator for some of Bembo's Latin works. It seems most probable that Gualteruzzi was introduced to the collection of tales by Bembo, and most probably the editor utilized the same manuscript to produce the *editio princeps* that Del Minio used to copy his manuscript.

While Bembo's participation remains equivocal, it is known for certain that another humanist-poet, Giovanni Della Casa, was actually involved in encouraging and financing Gualteruzzi's project. In a letter to the editor, dated July 25, 1525, Della Casa writes, "Concerning the money that you intend to return to me, I would like to say that it would please me to offer it to you as a gift...moreover, I beg you, if you love me (as you surely do), to keep the money as I have no use for it whatsoever, as you can imagine, and you might have need of it for the printing of *The Novellino*, or some other need of yours (Moroni 2)."

Gualteruzzi entitled his work *Le Ciento Novelle Antike* (*One Hundred Ancient Tales*). Della Casa's letter is important not only for its verification of the author's involvement in Gualteruzzi's text, but most importantly because it is the first time that the collection is called *Il Novellino*. Over three hundred years will pass before Della Casa's label is accepted as the permanent title for the collection of novellas.

As an artifact the *editio princeps* leaves much to be desired. Published on 40 numbered and 6 unnumbered leaves, using a crude type face, the book includes no woodcuts, engravings or embellishments of any kind. Distancing between letters is not uniform nor are the lines regimentally aligned. Rubrics are not distinguished by typeface or bolding from the novella texts, and errors in composition require an extensive *errata* listing at its conclusion.

The only direct information concerning Gualteruzzi's reasons for publishing the text is found in the dedication which he addresses to his benefactor, Goro Gherio, Bishop of Fano and Vicelegate of Bologna. What excited the editor most was the originality of the text, as well as the pleasure he anticipated it would give to its readers.

> "Having come into my hands the present work of one hundred novellas, which of all things written in vernacular prose that up to this day have come to my attention, I judge to be the most ancient. It came to my soul to place these before all men so that the pleasure and profit that these have rendered me can also be rendered to whomever it pleases to read them."

For Gualteruzzi the publication of the collection was not just a literary exercise, but more like a passionate, archeological quest--an unearthing of a national treasure, conceding to the novellas their natural right "to adapt to the full light their delicate fruits which for so long have remained behind and been held oppressed and suffocated by the cruel oblivion of time." He emphasized the importance of these tales "without an author" and "without a title" to the Italian literary tradition by acknowledging the fact that the "very graceful M. Giovanni Boccaccio had woven together old flowers from this field and new ones from every other collection, marvelously and without airs, to delightfully produce a canvas of his forever beloved novellas."

Gualteruzzi could not have been more correct in his assessment of the importance of this find, as well as the enormous impact that this genre would have on the development of Italian literature. Unfortunately, the *editio princeps* met with a rather tepid reception, and, to add insult to injury, this first edition, having been prepared during the Inquisition, was quickly eclipsed by the more "politically correct" second edition brought forward by Vincenzo Borghini at the Giunti presses of Florence in 1572.

Borghini is better known for his rewriting of *The Decameron* in 1573. This conservative enterprise was destined to failure since the public never allowed Borghini's rendition to supplant Boccaccio's original. *The Novellino*, alas, had no crown of Florence gracing its title page. A text, lacking an original title, significant critical history and, more importantly, authorial pedigree, Gualteruzzi's rustic, sometimes raucous

edition was readily transplanted by the graceful, elegant, but never improper Borghini variant. The Florentine version would maintain supremacy until the appearance of the accurate reprinting of the *editio princeps* by Tosi (Colombo) in 1825, and even afterwards, editors, until recently, would effortlessly substitute proper Borghini selections for the more risqué novellas of Gualteruzzi.

Borghini's *Novellino* is now considered by all critics as a "corrected edition." He removed seventeen tales from the *editio princeps* and included eighteen different stories. By entitling the first novella as the *Proemio* and removing it from his numbering scheme, he maintained the desired number of one hundred novellas in his edition. Five tales were removed because of what he must have considered their salacious nature. Other novellas were withdrawn which might have seemed compromising to contemporary life, faith and religion (Biagi clxviii). He also liberally edited many remaining novellas, removing any mention of Jesus Christ or any displaying of clergy or religious figures in what might be construed as a negative light. At times his editing was so severe that it completely altered the plot and the essence of the novella. The novellas which he extracted from the Gualteruzzi collection are numbers 6, 7, 12, 16, 17, 18, 36, 37, 39, 54, 57, 62, 75, 86, 87, 91, and 93.

Cesare Segre appropriately describes *The Novellino* as a collection of "delicious novellas." Before the twentieth century, these stories were minimized, described as sketches, notes about tales and little yarns, of interest only for historical purposes, or as artifacts on which a great tradition, the Italian novella, eventually developed. The appearance of Boccaccio's masterpiece less than a century later pushed *The Novellino* into even deeper obscurity (even though he incorporated eight of *The Novellino* tales into *The Decameron*). To compare these works in a general manner is unfortunate, since they differ significantly in form, structure and narrative intent. Joan Hall adeptly characterizes the situation when she describes *The Decameron* in relation to *The Novellino* as "Wonderful to read, but something else (p.18)."

It is obvious from the selection of tales found in *The Novellino* that the composer(s) intended it to represent the variety and richness of short prose pieces available to the medieval Italian reader. In this sense it serves as a cento, a prosaic *crestomazia*, which illustrates the diversity of themes from a plethora of sources, penned in varying degrees of detail and completeness, representing the complex nature of this ignored but quite developed literary genre.

"In the beginning was the Word" and the word was made poetry. By the end of the thirteenth century, lyrical composition was flourishing and highly regarded in Italy. The Scuola Siciliana poets had already established an impressive array of lyrical works, focusing on the canzone, with the accomplishments of such authors as Rinaldo d'Aquino, Pier delle Vigne, Guido delle Colonne and Giacomino Pugliese. Even the Emperor Frederick II, the most prominent character in *The Novellino*, contributed to this body of poetry. Giacomo da Lentini, il Notaro, created the first sonnet, the love genre which would spiritually and lyrically soar to wondrous eminence in the later works of Petrarch and Shakespeare. And the rest of Italy did not lag behind, with the poetic achievements

of such figures as Guittone d'Arezzo and Bonagiunta da Lucca. By this time, the Bolognese, Guido Guinizelli had already completed the first poems on which the famous Dolce Stil Novo school would build. It was as if the Italians had resurrected David's harp and created secular songs, inspired by the psalms of the Old Testament. Verse was truly the literature of choice in the thirteenth century.

During the same period only one other significant prose work was prepared, *Il libro de' vizi e delle virtudi* (*The Book of Vices and Virtues*) by Bono Giamboni, but the originality of this Prudentius offspring has been questioned by some critics. It seems logical, therefore, to assume that the author(s) of *The Novellino* prepared the work in order to advance the cause of prose, to inform the public that there was a prose tradition in Italy, to elevate the genre to an appropriate status, declaring it complementary to poetry and, like its sister art, worthy of study and masterful production.

The first tale found in *The Novellino* functions as the text's prologue. It is particularly peculiar, yet profoundly significant, that this predominantly secular work, in its very first sentence evokes the figure of Jesus Christ: "When our Lord Jesus Christ spoke to us in human form, among His words, He said that the tongue speaks from the abundance of the heart." This reference to the importance of speech for the Savior elevates the status of narrative and direct address from a singularly communicative means to an artistic medium. By naming the protagonist of the New Testament in its initial lines, *The Novellino* seems to be selecting the parables and gospels of the Christian Bible as its literary ancestors, rather than the lyrical songs, hymns and psalms of the Old Testament. The "novel" then in the "novella" is not derived solely from a magnification of subject matter concerned with contemporary protagonists, as some critics suggest (Piccoli Addoli 6), but also because of this new initiative aimed at assisting the coming of age of narrative as an acceptable art form.

While lyrical compositions traditionally focused on the aesthetics and mysteries of love, narrative, as *The Novellino* demonstrates, exploded the potentials of creative writing by broadening the scope of subjects investigated to include a myriad of other human emotions, virtues and appetites. Many critics, such as Favati, Segre and Hall, divide the one hundred novellas into ten distinct categories, in an attempt to make *The Novellino* the prototype for *The Decameron*. Joan Hall, in her article "The Organization of *The Novellino*," develops the following categories:

Novelle	**Categories**
1-10	truth, propriety, justice
11-20	generosity
21-30	exposure of vice and virtues
31-40	ambiguity, demystification, non-communication, misapprehension

41-50	ambiguity, equivocation, illusion, displacement
51-60	exposure, manipulation
61-70	reversal, trickery
71-80	failure, misadventure, loss, reproof
81-90	greed, unrealistic expectations
91-100	reversal, frustrations

Whether one agrees with the precise definitions prescribed by any of these critics is less important than the fact that they all exhibit a wide variety of subjects, most of which were not apparent in the verse tradition. Interestingly, love receives only minimal exposure in *The Novellino*, appearing as a primary subject in only four percent of the tales (Hall 14).

Gualteruzzi's mentor chose the perfect number of novellas to comprise his collection. This selection of precisely one hundred stories was in no way serendipity. In fact, the author(s) took great pains to ensure this outcome, occasionally combining different tales into one in order to achieve the desired outcome. One hundred is the perfect medieval number, based on the mystical figure of the Trinity; three (3) times thirty-three (33), plus one (1) for perfection: a number designating universality, totality and closure. Dante, just a few decades later, would select the same number to characterize the total Christian supernatural universe.

The Novellino, of course, does not pretend to the auspicious heights of *The Divina Commedia*, but it was intended as a representation of the universe of the narrative world of the short story. The sources from which the novellas spring are multiple and varied, geographically spanning the known world from Europe to the Middle East, culled from a multitude of languages and transcribed from a variety of genres. The author's intent was to demonstrate the magnitude of the short story legacy, to include the lengthy and the brief, the domestic and the exotic, the good and the bad, thereby constructing a narrative Noah's Ark of the short story tradition, what Alessandro D'Ancona described as an "embryonic" study.

D'Ancona's detailed study of the sources of the novellas accentuates the vast array of texts and traditions from which these stories came. The literary historian enumerates earlier literary and historical origins for sixty-eight of the Gualteruzzi novellas which produce an impressive and multicultural miscellany, including works from the Provençal *vidas*, the French *nouvelles*, tales from the Latin vulgate, classical and oriental legends and historical accounts, the Crusades, the chivalric cycles and, of course, Christian tradition and the *Bible*. Interestingly, Biblical themes are restricted to the Old Testament and concentrate on regal protagonists, and the only mention of Jesus Christ as a character (83) is unquestionably apocryphal and taken from an oriental source (D'Ancona 136-38). The original author(s) intentionally avoided retelling any tales from the New Testament, treating it as the Divine Autograph of the Novella tradition, and as such, already perfect and inappropriate and ludicrous to replicate.

Mixed among these "lovely" cultural "courtesies and responses" are contemporary stories, many most probably written by *The Novellino* author(s), concerned with Italy and, in particular, Florence. These Italian novellas are truly "flowers of speech," since they were predominantly procured from the oral tradition (Mulas 153-55) and their concentration on minor predicaments of the quotidian citizenry adds a novel genus to this medieval narratological garden. The inclusion of stories exclusively concerned with things Italian secured a position for short Italian prose in the narrative tradition, proudly placing it alongside other more recognizable representatives from the genre's universal lineage.

The first half of *The Novellino* substantiates the commonly held belief that its author(s) was most probably a Florentine of the Ghibelline persuasion. Twenty-two of the first fifty novellas are concerned with the exploits, education and proper comportment of kings, and another sixteen tales center around members of the court, primarily knights, barons and minstrels. The greatest and most wondrous rulers from throughout world history and literature are granted space among the stories of *The Novellino*. Biblical regents are well represented by the appearances of David (6) and Solomon (7). The heroic kings of the classical world are exemplified by another father and son team of tales concerned with Philip of Macedonia (3) and Alexander the Great (4). From England there are stories about King Henry (19, 20) and Richard the Lion-Hearted (76), and from France there unfold accounts concerning Saint Louis (25, 60) and Raymond Berenguer (42, 64). From the romance cycles two potentates, Charlemagne (18, 60) and Arthur (82), appear in the pages of *The Novellino*, and even Eastern sovereigns receive proper coverage, as in the tales involving Prester John (2) and the Sultan (9, 25, 61, 73, 76).

Such a coterie of kings ingeniously prepares the landscape for the introduction of a new literary character, an Italian monarch who heretofore had not graced the fictional stage: the Emperor Frederick. Our anonymous author(s) discarded the principal, traditional heroes of feudal literature, none of whom was Italian, and focused on this Sicilian Emperor as the primary character of his collection. The author(s) of *The Novellino*, intentionally or otherwise, melded the figures of Frederick II and his grandfather, Frederick Barabarossa, in an attempt to create a fictional personality of mythic proportions. If there is a protagonist of *The Novellino* it would have to be the Emperor Frederick, for he appears in more stories than any other character. Nine novellas are concerned with a variety of his exploits (2, 21, 22, 23, 24, 30, 59, 90, 100) and reveal significant aspects of his fictive personality. The author(s) deliberately placed tales concerning the Emperor at the strategic locations of the beginning (2) and the end (100) of the collection. There is no doubt that one of the intentions of *The Novellino* was to depict a series of scenes concerning the Emperor to be used "almost like a mirror" by future writers so that they might celebrate the feats of Italian rulers in time to come.

All of these stories are decidedly secular; even those taken from the *Bible*, where celestial beings often appear, are more concerned with demonstrating the human qualities required by a ruler, rather than portraying examples of spiritual might. One must

acknowledge, however, that novellas 2 and 21 indicate that our author(s) maintained a healthy respect for the supernatural. Even in this decisively feudal first half of the text, *The Novellino* begins to entertain stories concerned with the new developing classes of the urban, civic and merchant worlds, of which many critics believe our author(s) was a member. Tales begin to unfold where doctors, lawyers and professors replace the chivalric enterprises of knights and barons.

In the second half of the collection interest in phenomena concerning these novel classes escalates. At first, the stories in the second half oscillate between two traditional, high-profile groups of literary protagonists: well-known classical figures and knights. Classical figures concentrate on Roman rulers (67, 69, 71) and philosophers (71, 72) whose presence evokes the greatness of the Empire. While Greek philosophers are also represented in this section (61, 66, 68), the author(s) never identifies them as Greek, as he often does for the Romans: such as, "Papirius was a very powerful and wise Roman man (67)," or "Cato the philosopher was a very great Roman (72)." Under such circumstances, the misidentification of Socrates as "a noble Roman philosopher (61)" seems more like wishful partisanship than unpardonable ignorance.

While Tristan (65), Lancelot (82) and the sons of Priam (81) appear in this second section of *The Novellino*, in general the knights and lords who occupy these novellas do not represent the traditional literary feudal characters, nor are their actions the expected chivalric feats. The author(s) introduces the reader to French (60, 62) and Provençal (64), but primarily Italian (58, 77, 80, 84, 88, 89) knights and lords who were never among the fashionable members of the Carolingian and Arthurian cycles. Once again *The Novellino* composer(s) reminds his readers that there are countless figures outside of the established romance and epic traditions who are worthy of literary attention and that Italian characters should cease to be ignored.

The actions of these novel figures are not what the readers were accustomed to experiencing in medieval literature. Here there are no knife-bridge crossings, no slaying of dragons or rescuing of demure demoiselles in distress; instead one encounters obscene gesturing (58), hoseless horsemen (77), steeds advancing into battle buttocks first (32), and the coarse diminution of womanhood (80). These stories can often seem vulgar, rude, unsophisticated and unchivalrous; and, to an extent, so they were meant to be. This new genre was never intended as a prose version of what already existed in verse.

No novella better exemplifies the new in the collection than number 45. The early scenes from this adventure could have been copied directly from the manuscript of some romance canto: two knights errant, on horseback, sword in hand, come across one another in a wood by a fountain and naturally a contest ensues. After a while, following traditional chivalric custom, the two agree to a brief respite and exchange pleasantries, during which one, Alibon, learns that he is battling none other than the great Lancelot, and "once he realized that his adversary was Lancelot, the knight began to fear his abilities." The tale does not go on to tell its readers who won the fray, nor what wounds each hero endured or how valiantly they conducted themselves in battle. *The Novellino* is not interested in touting the feats of chivalrous knights, or showing who is mightier,

stronger or more valorous. Its primary interest is in the word, in demonstrating how the intelligent use of the tongue, a word, phrase or sentence exercised in the right place and at the right time can psychologically debilitate the most heroic adversary and win the day for even the most common of individuals. This new prose genre celebrates the power of words, elevating them to equal status with deeds, forcing readers, at this point, to go back and possibly lend less credence to Prester John's chide of the Emperor Frederick, when he said "he was very wise in word but not in deed (2)." This value placed on rhetorical virtue no doubt prepared the literary soil for the fabulous fruits found in Day VI of *The Decameron*.

The principal innovative aspect of *The Novellino* is its inclusion of everyday people into the ranks of its protagonists. Before this collection, representatives from the non-privileged classes were invisible to the literary world, relegated to a place not unlike Dante's vestibule to the Inferno where readers were cautioned, "Let us not speak of them, but look, and pass." *The Novellino*, particularly in the later stories, grants literary citizenship to the rank and file. Tales are dedicated to figures from all walks of life: common citizens, local priests, peasants, merchants and the overly ingenuous. In these pages the minstrel shifts from talking about people to the person who is talked about. Prostitutes and ladies of loose morals appear in comic relief rather than exemplary chastisement. These are the tales that have generated the more negative responses from the literary establishment who describes them as sketches, dirty little stories and semi-literary texts.

The fact is that *The Novellino* does not merely dress up traditional chivalric characters in popular medieval costumes, but instead presents the reading public with stories that were circulating among the members of the emerging urban classes and the peasantry. This in no way diminishes or debases the status of literature, but enriches and enlarges its scope by preserving and presenting to posterity the legends of social strata which up to that point had been unceremoniously ignored. The style displays the culture in question: brevity reflects the reduction of leisure time allotted to these classes; repetition reminds one of the oral roots of literature among the *illiterati*; and colloquialisms expose the variations in speech patterns, idiomatic expressions and vocabulary selection among the differing social groups. While contemporary critics may find these stories less than satisfying, the same cannot be said for literary luminaries of the time, for Boccaccio might never have created the monk of Lunigiana (*Dec.* I,4) without the parish priest Porcellino (54) as a guide, and Andreuccio might never have been duped so wonderfully in the magic city of Naples (*Dec.* II,5) if his ancestor, the village oaf, had never gone shopping in Florence (95). Here one encounters new varieties of verbal flowers, buds that prosper in city streets, blooms that spread through the peasant countryside, and blossoms that unfold in the provincial parish churches--new species of "flowers of speech"; one might even describe them as "wonderful to read, but something else."

Women appear to have a more substantial role as active participants in the tales of *The Novellino* when compared to the sedentary situations they occupied in earlier

Italian poetry. In thirty-six of the novellas women characters contribute to the development of the plot. Unfortunately this increase in exposure does not translate into a more sophisticated appreciation of or investigation into the complexities of the female personality in the Middle Ages. Contemporary readers will be disappointed in the ignorance of things concerning women demonstrated by our author(s). The majority of these tales are concerned with the results of sexual situations where women are portrayed as diabolical seducers of innocent men (15, 36, 87), or as the passive or accepting receptacles of male sexual energy (3, 49, 54, 88). Such stories only accentuate the limited and negative views concerning women held by many medieval men. The author(s) exacerbates the situation by taking the only attribute considered affirmative and unique to women, beauty, and transforming it into a mysterious and dangerous energy, "What a thing is the tyranny and beauty of woman (14)!"

It is not only in sexual situations that women are represented as deficient and limited. There are novellas where women are displayed as silly, stupid creatures (33, 96), or as totally vain and selfish (26). In these tales one finds frightening females of vicious character, void of charity (59, 70), as well as those who can be relied upon to divulge secrets and disperse gossip (67). The representation of women in *The Novellino* cannot be considered one of the constructive novelties of the collection. In fact, this inimical attitude towards women reaches its outrageous zenith with the raucous, rude hysterics of a group of knights at the hatefully vulgar description of the scent of women by Master Migliore delli Abbati as "pike past its prime (80)."

There are a few novellas, however, which break from this mean tradition and present more positive and engaging female characters. The practical "little lady" who lives in a cottage and saves the great philosopher Melisus from drowning in a "silly, water-filled little ditch (38)" intimates that men, who habitually have the luxury of keeping their heads in the clouds, repeatedly rely upon the knowledge of sensible women to survive. The seemingly silly risqué remarks of Lady Agnesina (57) and her friends at their garden party might seem superficial, but actually constitute one of the first literary views into the Italian medieval mystery world of women in the company of women. And here one encounters ladies sophisticated and comfortable in their understanding of sexuality, and a strong suggestion that these acts might not have been as distasteful and burdensome to them as medieval readers were previously led to believe. The Lady of Shalott (82) reminds readers that women can suffer the pains of love as much as men, and can also react to the malady of love in tragic and heroic ways. The Gascon Lady (51) proves that not only men are capable of manipulating the power of language and effectively formulating "fine replies." Her actions suggest that the "gentle and noble hearts" called to creative, lexical action in the first novella must include women as well as men. Unfortunately these strivings towards a better understanding of women in the Middle Ages are all neutralized by Seneca's words in novella 71 where he proclaims a woman worthy and capable of ascertaining sophisticated logic and rhetoric for the sole reason that she resembles a man. "If you were a woman as all others, I would not speak to you as I do. For, although you are a woman, you have a man's intelligence, as so I

speak to you as follows." Critics undeniably will have to wait for the appearance of *The Decameron* before any debate concerning changing attitudes towards women can begin.

There is no question that *The Novellino* deserves the recognition it has received from critics for initiating the novella tradition in Italy, which through the centuries has produced some of the culture's greatest literary achievements, from the stories of Boccaccio to Pirandello, from Sercambi and Basile to D'Annunzio and Verga. But the collection is much more than a historical curiosity and warrants closer scrutiny from the literary community. *The Novellino* draws examples from a myriad of international prose sources which have influenced Italian culture and rewrites them in a distinctly Italian manner. It presents a new literary genre based upon narrative writing and direct address. The collection expands traditional literary subjects to include a wider range of human emotions and invites a broader section of citizens to participate in the literary experience. In a sense, *The Novellino* realizes the power of speech and transforms it into an art which can be appreciated by a larger audience. The collection expands the selection in the literary flower shop and praises the crocus and daffodil as much as the rose.

SELECTED BIBLIOGRAPHY

Editions

Biagi, Guido. *Le Novelle antiche dei codici Panciatichiano-Palatino 138 e Laurenziano-Gaddiano 193. Introduzione di Guido Biagi*. Florence: Sansoni, 1880.

Borghini, Vincenzo. *Libro di novelle, et di Bel Parlar Gentile*. Florence: Giunti, 1572.

Di Francia, Letterio. *Le Cento novelle antiche o libro di novelle e di bel parlar gentile detto anche il Novellino. Introduzione e note di Letterio Di Francia*. Turin: UTET, [1794] 1970.

Favati, Guido. *Il Novellino: Testo critico, introduzione e note a cura di Guido Favati*. Genoa: Bozzi, 1970.

Gualteruzzi, Carlo. *Le Ciento Novelle Antike*. Bologna: Benedetti, 1525.

Lo Nigro, Sebastiano. *Novellino e Conti del Duecento*. Turin: UTET, 1964.

Piccoli Addoli, Pia. *Il Novellino. Le ciento novelle antike. Introduzione di Pia Piccoli Addoli*. Milan: BUR, 1957.

Segre, Cesare. *Il Novellino*. IN *La Prosa del Duecento*. Milan: Ricciardi, 1959, pp. 793-881.

Sicardi, Enrico. *Il Novellino e altre novelle antiche*. Livorno: Giusti, 1919.

Storer, Edward. *Il Novellino, the Hundred Old Tales, translated from the Italian by Edward Storer*. New York: Dutton, 1925.

Criticism

Aruch, A. "Frammenti del *Novellino*." *Giornale storico della letteratura italiana*, 63 (1916): 179.

Aruch, A. "Il manoscritto Marciano del *Novellino*." *Bibliofilia X, disp*. 8: Florence, 1908.

Battaglia, Salvatore. "Premesse per una valutazione del *Novellino*." *Filologia romanza*, 2 (1955): 279-.

Crespo, Roberto. "Il 'don contraignant' nel *Novellino*." *Medioevo Romanzo*, 15 (1990): 353-63.

Cuomo, Luisa. "La novella del tempo perduto." IN Raimondo, Ezio (ed.). *Dal Novellino a Moravia: Problemi della narrativa*. Bologna: Mulino, 1979, pp. 23-47.

Cuomo, Luisa. "La novella dell'amore ritrovato ovvero Narciso e lo specchio della verità." *Studi e problemi della critica testuale*, 21 (1980): 123-53.

Cuomo, Luisa. "Sillogizzare motteggiando e motteggiare sillogizzando: Dal *Novellino* alla VI giornata del *Decameron*." *Studi sul Boccaccio*, 13 (1981-1982): 217-65.

D'Ancona, Alessandro. "Del *Novellino* e delle sue fonti." *Studi di critica e storia letteraria*, 2 (1912): 1-163.

Dardano, Maurizio. "Varianti della tradizione del *Novellino*." IN *Studi in onore di Alfredo Schiaffini*. Rome: Edizione dell'Ateneo, 1965, pp. 284-400.

Favati, Guido. "La novella LXIV del *Novellino* e Uc de Saint Circ." *Lettere italiane*, 9 (1959): 133-73.

Frank, Amy Lynne. *Telling Tales: The 'Libro di novelle e di bel parlar gentile' and the Appearance of Literature*. Stanford: Stanford University Dissertation, 1993.

Genot, Gerard and Paul Larivaille. *Étude du Novellino, I. Repertoires des structures narratives*. Nanterre: Université de Paris X, 1987.

Genot, Gerard and Paul Larivaille. "Style narratif, rhetorique, tradition: Sur le *Novellino*." *Revue Romane*, 19 (1984): 284-97.

Hall, Joan. "'Bel parlare' and Authorial Narration in the *Novellino*." *Italian Studies*, 44 (1989): 1-18.

Hall, Joan. "The Organization of the *Novellino*." *Italian Studies*, 39 (1984): 6-26.

Hall, Joan. "Words and Deeds in the *Novellino*: An Analysis of the First Tale." *The Modern Language Review*, 77 (1982): 63-73.

Monteverdi, Angelo. "Che cos'è il *Novellino*?" *Studi e saggi sulla letteratura italiana dei primi secoli*. Milan: Ricciardo, 1954, pp. 125-65.

Moroni, Ornella (ed.), *Corrispondenza: Giovanni Della Casa, Carlo Gualteruzzi*. Rome: SEAM, 1994.

Mulas, Luisa. *Lettura del Novellino*. Rome: Bulzoni, 1984.

Paolella, Alfonso. "Strategie discorsive e retoriche: La novella dei tre anelli nel *Novellino* e nel *Decameron*." *Lingua e stile*, 16 (1981): 297-315.

Raimondi, Ezio and Bruno Bastile. *Dal Novellino a Moravia: Problemi della narrativa*. Bologna: Mulino, 1979.

Richardson, Brian. "Criteri editoriali nella prima stampa del *Novellino*." *Lingua nostra*, 53 (1992): 4-7.

Russo, Vittorio. "La tradizione retorica nel *Novellino*." *Filologia romanza*, 6 (1959): 401-22.

Schiaffini, Alfredo. *Tradizione e poesia nella prosa d'arte italiana dall latinità medievale a Giovanni Boccaccio*. Rome: n.p., 1943.

Segre, Cesare. "Due racconti del *Novellino* nel *Llegar en ocasión* di Lope de Vega." *Travaux-de-Linguistique-et-de-Littérature*, 16 (1978): 483-87.

Segre, Cesare. "Sull'ordine delle novelle nel *Novellino*." IN *Miscellanea di studi in onore di Vittore Branca. I. Dal medioevo al Petrarca*. Florence: Olschki, 1983, pp. 129-39.

Simpson, Roger. "Costello's 'The Funeral Boat': An Analogue of Tennyson's 'The Lady of Shalott'." *The Tennyson Research Bulletin*, 4 (1984): 129-31.

Thomas, A. "Richard de Barbezieux et le *Novellino*." *Giornale di filologia romanza*, 3 (1880): 12-17.

Travi, A. "Dal *Libro di novelle e di bel parlar gentil a Le cento novelle antiche*." *Miscellanea del Centro di studi medievali*, ser. II, n.s. 62 (1958): 209-63.

Varnhagen, H. "Uber die Abhängigkeit. Der vier ältesten Drucke des *Novellino* von einander." IN *Miscellanea di studi critici edita in onore di Arturo Graf*. Bergamo: Istituto italiano d'arti grafiche, 1903, pp. 507-.

Vutano, G. *L'Elemento storico del Novellino*. Palermo: n.p., 1934.

METHODOLOGY

The Italian text is a direct translation of the 1525 *editio princeps*, copied from an original located in the Biblioteca Palatina in Parma, Italy (no. 13247). While this edition is not universally accepted as the closest example of the original, it is believed to be so by a majority of critics. This edition was selected also because it is the basis for most of the literary criticism produced concerning *The Novellino*.

Carlo Gualteruzzi was far from a systematic editor; his spelling, punctuation, use of abbreviations, hyphenation, capitalization, word frequency, sentence composition and paragraphing are anything but uniform. In order to present the text as closely as possible to the original for those interested in reading the Italian, only a minimum of editorial intrusions have been applied. These include the introduction of accents and apostrophes, the imposition of uniformity of spelling and capitalization, when it becomes obvious, within each novella, and the expansion of abbreviations. Since the original text makes no distinction between direct and indirect address, a comma has been inserted before dialogue to provide the reader with an appropriate pause. I have respected the editor's minimal use of commas, which were obviously applied by hand to the original printing. I have also honored Gualteruzzi's orthographic idiosyncracies and regionalisms, which include the parsimonious and awkward use of the letter "*h*" before vowels, the insertion of a "*n*" immediately preceding "*gn*", a predilection for the letter "*k*" as a substitute for "*ch*" before an "*i*" or an "*e*". The only nod to modernity is the fitting substitution of the letter "*u*" with the letter "*v*", which was not in use at the time.

Unless otherwise indicated, the notes to the Italian edition are taken from the 1612 *Vocabolario della Crusca*. The Gualteruzzi edition served as a source of examples for this early dictionary.

The English translation remains as true to the original as possible. The object of the translation is not to subjectively produce the most beautiful rendition, but rather to approximate the original so that its readers might participate, to some extent at least, in the original intentions of the author. In order to achieve this, no radical emendations have been made. Readers of the translation will notice significant variations in sentence, as well as novella length, an intense interest in repetition, and a penchant for introducing sentences with a conjunction or adverbial form. In general the language found in *The Novellino* might be described as concentrated, where much is said with a minimum of words; but because translation cannot be accomplished solely on the word level, occasionally sentences have been combined or split to accommodate the peculiarities of the English language. Modern colloquialisms have been used sparingly, and only when the dialogue in a tale is obviously intended to be contemporary and informal.

The results of the translation may seem at times awkward to readers of our epoch, but these sometimes unwieldy, sometimes simplistic forms are indispensable to a better understanding of the construction of Italian medieval prose at its inception.

Extensive notes accompany this translation, providing readers with brief descriptions of historical figures, events and periods. Many of the characters and situations discussed require explanations, since they are not easily recognizable to an English speaking audience. Every attempt was made to utilize English language materials so that those who so desire may consult sources directly to obtain even more information; when this was not possible, foreign language quotes were translated into English to facilitate understanding. All sources are listed in the *Bibliography to the Notes*. When no source is mentioned, the information was selected from a general work, usually *The Encyclopaedia Britannica*, or the *Encarta* CD-Rom encyclopedia. All translations of quoted sources found in the *Introduction* are my own.

I would like to take this opportunity to thank the Rutgers University Research Council for awarding me a grant to travel to Parma in order to consult the *editio princeps*. Rutgers University Libraries provided a semester sabbatical during which I was able to complete the first draft of the translation. I wish to thank Professor Franca Nardelli who instructed me in the basic principles of medieval transcription. The late Professor Lowry Nelson, Jr. added grace to my initial, clumsy attempts, which were further cultured by my medieval mentor, Professor James J. Wilhelm.

Joseph P. Consoli
Rutgers University

The Novellino or One Hundred Ancient Tales

AL REVERENDISSIMO MONSIGNOR GORO GHERIO VESCOVO DI FANO ET DIGNISS. VICELEGATO DI BOLOGNA SIGNORE ET BENFATTOR SUO SINGOLARISSIMO.

Io stimo Reverendissimo et da me sempre osservandissimo Monsignore gratioso ufficio per colui usarsi, il quale a suo potere s'ingegna essere ad infiniti huomini o, di lor bene, o di lor diletto cagione. Per la qualcosa essendomi alle mani venuta la presente opera delle cento novelle, la quale di tutte le cose in prosa volgare scritte, che insino a questo dì sono alla mia notitia pervenute; giudico essere la più antica; m'è caduto nell'animo di quella porre nel cospetto de gli huomini: affine, che il piacere et pro che essa a me ha renduto; possa etiandio rendere a chiunque di leggerla piacerà. Alla qualcosa fare come che & questa & altre simiglianti ragioni mosso m'habbiano; nondimeno niuna ve n'ha, che con più acuto stimolo m'habbia sospinto, che il pensare di sommamente dovervi in ciò piacere. Conciosiacosa, che io sappia troppo bene voi niuna cura havere maggiore, che di giovare altrui; et non pur a quegli, che vivono; ma a coloro altresì che mentre vivono fecero la loro età fiorire, riducendo in chiara luce gli loro dilicatissimi frutti stati lungamente per lo adietro dalle crudeli ombre della dimenticanza aduggiati et soffocati tenuti. Perchè come volenteroso servidore il quale senza il comandamento dal suo Signore aspettare quelle cose operando, che suo piacere crede, che sieno quello con ogni sollecitudine s'ingegna di prevenire; a fuori mandare questa presente opera mi sono dato. Oltre acciò non possendo io di tanta benignità verso di me quanta è sempre stata la vostra, quelle gratie rendere, che si converrebbe a dovervene io bastevolmente ringratiare; ho voluto in questa guisa almeno poscia che altrimenti non posso mostrarmivi grato. Appresso questo perciochè ella senza titolo e senza nome d'Auttore si truova estimai ben fatto, quella col raggio della vostra singolar virtù illuminare. Acciochè dalle tenebre togliendola ove in fino a questo tempo miseramente è giaciuta sotto la chiarissima insegna del vostro nome, lucente e bella si dimostri a' riguardanti. Senza che essendo (come manifestamente appare) il Facitore di lei stato Thoscano, dicevole cosa m'è paruta, che quegli honori, che ad esso rendere non si possono, alla gentilissima Patria di lui, come aproducitrice di così nobile pianta, almeno si rendano. Et a cui potre' io acciochè questo avenisse più convenevole indirizzarla, che a voi? Che luce dirittamente siete della Thoscana gloria. Il quale non ad ammassar denaro come molti altri fanno, ma a Magnificenza usare vi siete dato. La qual virtù, sì come il Sole è del cielo chiarezza et lume, così è ella di ciascuna altra ornamento et splendore. Il che se per sè stesso in voi manifesto non fosse, io producerei molte provincie in mezzo, et cittadi et popoli, li quai per benefici da voi ricevuti tranquillissima et lieta menano la lor vita. Che più Bologna stessa ne potrebbe hoggimai ampissima testimonianza rendere: la quale, vostra buona mercé, tutta giuliva et tutta festante si vive.

TO THE MOST REVEREND MONSIGNOR GORO GHERIO BISHOP OF FANO AND THE VERY DIGNIFIED VICE-LEGATE OF BOLOGNA LORD AND MOST EXCEPTIONAL BENEFACTOR.

I esteem the very Reverend and always most respected Monsignor who utilizes his gracious office and his power as the reason for the goodness and the pleasure of an infinite number of men. For this reason, having come into my hands the present work of one hundred novellas, which of all things written in vernacular prose, that up to this day have come to my attention, I judge to be the most ancient. It came to my soul to place these before all men so that the pleasure and profit that these have rendered me can also be rendered to whomever it pleases to read them. And in order to do this thing, this and other similar reasons moved me, but not less than these, what prompted me with an even fiercer incentive, was the thought that you might derive pleasure from this venture. Since I know too well that you have no greater want than to be of use to others, and not just to those who exist, but to those who likewise make their age flower, because they live to adapt to the full light their delicate fruits which for so long have remained behind and been held oppressed and suffocated by the cruel oblivion of time. Because, just like the most willing servant who, without the expressed wishes of his master, waits for things to appear which he believes will bring him pleasure and arranges the anticipation of such things with all speed, so I allow myself from the outside to send the present work to you. Since I have never been in possession of as much kindness as I have always received from you, having had such pleasure given to me, it is only right that I should show sufficient gratitude in some way, and so I wished to do so in the following way, otherwise I would not have been able to express my appreciation. Since this work finds itself without a title and named author, I sincerely believe that it can only be illuminated by the beam of your exceptional virtue, so that it might be removed from the shadows where until now it has miserably remained, and be placed under the most elucidating sign of your name, so that it might appear sparkling and beautiful to all who gaze upon it. Without a doubt (as is obviously apparent) it is not possible to render to the maker of this work the honors which he deserves, so a suitable idea occurred to me, that one could at least render these honors to the most gentle fatherland of the producer of such a noble plant. And to whom could I more readily address this so that it might come to pass, other than you? For you are a candid light which comes from the glory of Tuscany, which you use not to amass money as many others do, but for the magnificence of your land. Just as the sun is the clarity and light of the heavens, so is this the ornament and splendor of each and every other virtue. Which, if by itself were not made manifest, I would produce many provinces, and in the middle, cities and people who, because of

Renderannosi a voi adunque gli honori et le gratie, che a così fatto merito si confanno da coloro, a quai queste Novelle gioverà haver lette. Li quali per mio aviso saranno infiniti. Perciochè come che a prode et a piacere di coloro, che non sanno et disiderano di sapere il loro Componitor le facesseano per tanto è da dire, che ella di gran lunga più aggradire non debbano a coloro, che con più sottile intelligenza le leggeranno. Conciosiacosa, che veggendo essi quanto maestrevolmente il vostro leggiadrissimo M. Giovanni Boccaccio habbia, vecchi fiori di questo prato, et nuovi d'ogni altro raccolti tessendo insieme, maravigliosa et senza modo dilettevole renduta la tela delle sue sempre care novelle, ad un'hora l'une per l'altre sieno loro più profittevoli e più care. Et chi dirà, che il vedere la scrittura di que' tempi, la quale io quanto per me s'è potuto il più, mi sono d'osservare ingegnato (nè altrimenti havrei potuto fare; se io quella della sua propia forma trarre non havessi voluto) non renda altrui nello scrivere per innanzi et più giudicoso et più accorto? Certo, che io creda niuno. restami adunque humilemente et reverentemente pregarvi ad essere contento di lietamente et con buon viso ricevere la detta operetta: povero dono nel vero alla vostra grandezza et a gl'infiniti obbrighi, che io a voi tengo, ma forse non isconvenevole all'humile stato mio. Nel quale non possendo io altro fare; mi darò a continuamente pregare Dio, che in lunga felicità a commune bene de gli huomini vi conservi.

Fedelissimo Servidore
Carlo Gualteruzzi

kindnesses received from you, now lead lives full of great tranquillity and joy. Who more than Bologna herself could render ample testimony today, she who because of your good mercy, lives in complete gladness and bliss. They will render to you, then the honors and the gratitude, which I estimate to be infinite, for such a meritorious thing suits those who have derived pleasure from the reading of these novellas. Since their composer made these for the profit and pleasure of those who do not know but desire such knowledge, that is to say, not only for those who for a longer period of time have enjoyed them for they have read them using a more subtle intelligence. Since, after having seen these how masterfully the very graceful M. Giovanni Boccaccio had woven together old flowers from this field and new ones from every other collection, marvelously and without airs, to delightfully produce a canvas of his forever beloved novellas, and at any given hour now some now others seem the most profitable and the most cherished. And who would say that the sight of writings from those times, which I have contrived to observe as many as possible (nor would I have been able to do otherwise, nor wished to, had I not drawn from the original form) does not render that writing to others from this time forward as more judicious and sagacious? For certainly I believe that no one would do so. It remains for me, therefore, to humbly and reverently beg you to be happy and pleased, and to receive this little book with a contented countenance: such a poor gift in truth when I consider your liberality and the infinite number of obligations for which I am indebted to you; but perhaps not unbecoming to my humble station. And since I can do no more, I will give myself over to continuous prayer so that God may keep you and thereby prolong the happiness of the common good of all men.

Your Most Faithful Servant,
Carlo Gualteruzzi

Qui appresso scriveremo per nome le *Novelle* cioè le ***Robrike*** per meglio ritrovarle sanza troppo ciercarne.

Here below we will write the ***Novellas*** by name, that is, the ***Rubrics*** in order to better locate them without too much trouble.

Novella I.

Questo libro tratta d'alquanti fiori di parlare di belle cortesie, e di be' risposi, e di belle valentie e doni secondo ke per lo tempo passato anno fatto molti valenti uomini.

Quando lo nostro singniore Giesù Cristo parlava umanamente con noi infrall'altre sue parole ne disse, ke dell'abondanza del quore parla la lingua. Voi k'avete i quori gentili e nobili infralli altri acconciate le vostre menti e le vostre parole nel piaciere d'iddio, parlando, onorando, e temendo, e laudando quel singniore nostro, kenn'amò prima, ke elli ne criasse, e prima kennoi medesimi ci amassimo. E se in alcuna parte non dispiaciendo allui si può parlare per rallegrare il corpo, e sovenire, e sostentare, facciasi con più onestade, e con più cortesia, ke fare si puote. Et acciò kelli nobili e gentili sono nel parlare e nell'opere quasi com'uno specchio appo i minori, accioké il loro parlare e più gradito però ke escie di più dilicato stormento, facciamo qui memoria dal quanti fiori di parlare, di belle cortesie, e di belli risposi, e di belle valentie, di belli donari, e di belli amori, secondo ke per lo tempo passato anno fatto già molti. E ki avrà quore nobile & intelligentia sottile sille potrà somigliare per lo tempo, ke verrà per innanzi, et argomentare e dire e raccontare in quelle parti, dove avranno luogo a prode & a piaciere di coloro, ke non sanno e disiderano di sapere. E se i fiori, ke proporremo fossero mischiati intra molte altre parole non vi dispiaccia, kel nero è ornamento dell'oro, e per un frutto nobile e dilicato piacie talora tutto un orto, e per poki belli fiori tutto uno giardino. Non gravi a' leggitori, ke sono stati molti, ke sono vivuti grande lunghezza di tempo, & in vita loro anno appena tratto un bel parlare od alcuna cosa da mettere in conto fra' buoni.

Novella II.

Della ricca ambascieria, la quale fecie lo presto Giovanni al nobile Imperadore Federigo.

Presto Giovanni nobilissimo singniore indiano mandoe ricca e nobile ambascieria al nobile e potente Imperadore Federigo, a colui, ke veramente fu specchio del mondo in parlare & in costumi, & amò molto dilicato parlare, & istudiò in dare savi risposi. La forma ella intentione di quella ambascieria fu solo in due cose, per volere alpostutto provare, sello'mperadore fosse savio in parlare & in opere. Mandolli per li detti ambasciadori tre pietre nobilissime, e disse loro, donatelle allo'mperadore, e ditelli dalla parte mia, kevvi dica quale èlla migliore cosa del mondo, elle sue parole e risposte serberete & aviserete la corte sua e costumi di quella, e quello, ke inverrete, raccontarete a me sanza niuna mancanza. Furo allo'mperadore, dove erano mandati per lo loro

Novella I.

This book is concerned with certain flowers of speech, lovely courtesies and responses, and lovely aptitudes and gifts, as they were set forth by many worthy men in times past.

When our Lord Jesus Christ spoke to us in human form, among His words, He said that the tongue speaks from the abundance of the heart.[1] You who, among all others, have gentle and noble hearts, adjust your minds and words to the pleasure of God, speaking, honoring, fearing and praising that Lord of ours who loved us before He created us and before we loved one another. And if it does not displease Him in any way, one may speak to hearten, assist and sustain the body, doing so as honestly and politely as possible. Since the noble and courteous are in word and deed almost like a mirror for those of lesser standing, because their speech is more agreeable, as it issues from a more delicate instrument; here let us remember certain flowers of speech, lovely courtesies and responses, and lovely aptitudes and gifts, and lovely love stories as they were set forth by many in times past. And may he who has a noble heart and subtle intellect attempt to imitate these in times to come, and to discuss, tell and relate these stories wherever he may find himself, for the profit and pleasure of those who do not know but desire such knowledge. And if the flowers we propose are mingled with many other words, do not be displeased, for black may be embellished by gold, just as an entire orchard gives pleasure from one noble, delicate fruit, or an entire garden with but a few beautiful flowers. Do not burden yourselves with blame, readers, for there have been many who have lived exceedingly long lives, yet during their lives have hardly uttered a courteous word, or accomplished anything worthy of placing them among the good.

Novella II.

Concerning the rich embassy which Prester John[1] sent to the noble Emperor Frederick.[2]

Prester John, a noble Indian lord,[3] sent a rich and noble embassy to the noble and powerful Emperor Frederick, he who was truly the mirror of the world in words and manners, and who loved very much delicate speech and was well-versed in preparing wise replies.[4] The form and intent of that embassy consisted of only two things, a desire, above all else, to test if the emperor was wise in both words and works. He sent, with the mentioned ambassadors, three very precious stones,[5] and said to them, "Give these to the emperor and ask him, on my behalf, to tell you what is the finest thing in the world. Heed his words and answers, and observe his court and its customs, and that which you find, relate to me omitting nothing." They were in the presence of the emperor to whom they had been sent by their lord. They greeted him in a manner befitting his rank and, on behalf of their above-named lord, they gave the previously mentioned stones to him. He took them and asked nothing about their virtues. He had

singniore salutaronlo siccome si convenia per la parte della sua Maestade, e per la parte dello loro soprascritto singniore. Donaronli le sopra dette pietre, quelli le prese, e non domandò dilloro virtude fecielle riporre, e lodolle molto di grande bellezza. Li ambasciadori feciero la domanda loro, e videro li costumi ella corte. Poi dopo poki giorni addomandaro commiato. Lo'mperadore diede loro risposta, e disse, ditemmi al singnor vostro, kella miglior cosa di questo mondo si è misura. Andaro li ambasciadori e rinuntiaro e raccontaro ciò, k'aveano veduto & udito, lodando molto la corte dello'mperadore ornata di bellissimi costumi, el modo de' suoi cavalieri. Il presto Giovanni udendo ciocké raccontaro li suoi ambasciadori lodò lo'mperadore e disse, ke era molto savio in parola, ma non in fatto, acciocké non avea domandato della virtù di così care pietre. Rimandolli ambasciadori & offerselli selli piaciesse, kel farebbe siniscalco della sua corte. E fecielli contare le sue ricchezze, elle diverse ingenerationi[a] de' sudditi suoi & il modo del suo paese. Dopo non gran tempo pensando il presto Giovanni, kelle pietre, k'avea donate allo'mperadore avevano perduta loro virtude, dapoi, ke non erano per lo'mperadore conosciute. Tolse uno suo carissimo lapidaro, e mandollo cielatamente alla corte dello'mperadore e disse, alpostutto metti lo'ngiegnio tuo kettu quelle pietre mi reki, per niun tesoro rimanga. Lo lapidaro si mosse guernito di molte pietre di gran bellezza, e cominciò presso alla corte allegare sue pietre. Li Baroni e cavalieri veniano a vedere di suo mestiero. L'uomo era molto savio, quando vedeva alcuno k'avesse luogo in corte, non vendeva, ma donava, e donò anella molte, tanto, kella lode dillui andò dinanzi allo'mperadore. Lo quale mandò per lui, e mostrolli le sue pietre. Lodolle ma non di gran vertude. Domandò se avesse più care pietre. Allora lo'mperadore fecie venire le tre care pietre pretiose, k'elli disiderava di vedere. Allora il lapidaro si rallegrò e prese l'una pietra e misellasi in mano e disse così. Questa pietra Messere vale la migliore città ke voi avete. Poi prese l'altra e disse. Questa Messere, vale la miglior provincia ke voi avete. E poi prese la terza e disse. Messere questa vale più ke tutto lo'mperio, e strinse il pungno con le soprascritte pietre. La vertude dell'una il cielò, ke nol potero vedere, e discese giù per le gradora[b], e tornò al suo singniore presto Giovanni, e presentolli le pietre con grande allegrezza.

Novella III.

D'un savio Greco, k'uno Re teneva in pregione, come giudicò d'uno destriere.

Nelle parti di Grecia ebbe un singniore, ke portava corona di re & avea grande reame, & avea nome Filippo, e per alcuno misfatto tenea un savio Greco in pregione. Il quale era di tanta sapientia, ke nello'ntelletto suo passava oltr'alle stelle. Avenne un giorno, ke a questo singniore fu appresentato delle parti di Spagna un nobile destriere

them taken away, and praised very much their great beauty. The ambassadors asked their question and observed the customs of the court. Then, after a few days, they asked for permission to take their leave. The emperor answered them by saying, "Tell your lord for me that the greatest thing in this world is moderation."[6] The ambassadors left; they went home and narrated what they had seen and heard, praising greatly the court of the emperor adorned with the beautiful customs and manners of his knights. Prester John, hearing what his ambassadors said, praised the emperor and said that he was very wise in word but not in deed, since he had not asked about the virtues of such precious stones. He sent his ambassadors back, offering one of them, if it was pleasing to the emperor, as seneschal[7] to the court. And he had him count all the emperor's riches and note the diverse ancestries of his subjects and the customs of his country. After a short time, thinking that the stones he had given to the emperor had lost their powers, since the emperor did not understand their value, Prester John selected one of his best loved lapidarians[8] and secretly sent him to the court of the Emperor saying, "Apply your knowledge in every conceivable way and return those stones to me so that none of the treasure remains." The lapidarian went furnished with many stones of exceptional beauty, and, when near the court, he began to work at setting his stones. The barons and knights came to see him practice his craft. The man was very wise. When he saw someone attached to the court, he did not sell to him, but instead gave freely; and he gave away many rings, so many that his praise reached the ears of the emperor, who sent for him and displayed his own stones to the man. The lapidarian praised them, but did not acknowledge them as having powerful virtues. He asked if the emperor had any more precious stones. Finally the emperor had the three very precious stones that he wished to see brought forward. At last the lapidarian became delighted and took one stone in his hand and said, "This stone, Sire, is worth the greatest city that you possess." Then he took another, and said, "This, Sire, is worth the greatest province that you possess." And then he took the third one, and said, "Sire, this one is worth more than your entire empire." And he clenched his fist around the above mentioned stones. The power of one concealed him so that he could no longer be seen,[9] and he descended the staircase and returned to his lord, Prester John, and presented the stones to him with great delight.

Novella III.

Concerning a wise Greek, whom a king kept imprisoned, and how he appraised a steed.

Somewhere in Greece there was a lord who wore the crown of a king and had a great realm. He was called Philip[1] and he had imprisoned a wise Greek[2] for certain misdeeds. This Greek was extremely sagacious, possessing an intellect which passed far beyond the stars.[3] One day it happened that a noble steed of great strength and beauty, from somewhere in Spain, was presented to this lord. He asked his lord marshal to

di gran podere, e di bella guisa. Addomandò lo singniore mariscalki per sapere la bontà del destriere, fulli detto, ke in sua prigione avea lo sovrano Maestro intendente di tutte le cose. Fecie menare il destriere al campo, e fecie trarre il Greco di prigione e disselli. Maestro avisa questo destriere, kemmi è fatto conto, ke tusse' molto saputo. Il Greco avisò il cavallo, e disse. Messere lo cavallo è di bella guisa, ma cotanto vi dico, kel cavallo è nutricato a latte d'asino. Lo Re mandò in Ispagna ad invenire come fu nodrito, & invennero, kella destriera era morta, & il puledro fu notricato a latte d'asina. Ciò tenne il Re a grande maraviglia, & ordinò, k'elli fosse dato un mezzo pane il dì alle spese della corte. Un giorno avenne kello Re adunoe sue pietre pretiose, e rimandoe per questo prigione Greco e disse, Maestro tusse' di grande savere, e credo, ke di tutte le cose t'intendi, dimmi, sett'intendi delle virtù delle pietre, qual ti sembra di più ricca valuta? Il Greco avisò e disse, Messere, voi quale avete più cara? Lo Re prese una pietra intrall'altre molto bella e disse. Maestro questa mi sembra più bella e di maggior valuta. Il Greco la prese e miselasi in pugno e strinse, e puoselasi all'orecchie, e poi disse, Messere qui a un vermine.[a] Lo Re mandò per maestri e feciela spezzare, e trovaro nella detta pietra un vermine. Allora lodò il Greco d'oltre mirabile senno & istabilio, ke uno pane intero li fosse dato per giorno alle spese di sua corte. Poi dopo molti giorni lo Re si pensò di non essere legittimo Re. Mandò per questo Greco & ebbelo in loco sacreto e cominciò a parlare e disse. Maestro di grande scientia ti credo e manifestamente l'oe veduto nelle cose, in k'io t'o domandato. Io voglio ke tummi diki cui figliuolo io fui. Il Greco rispose, Messere, ke domanda mi fate voi? Voi sapete bene ke foste figliuolo del cotale padre. Ello Re rispose, non mi rispondere a grado, dimmi sicuramente il vero, e se nol mi dirai, io ti farò di mala morte morire. Allora il Greco rispose, Messere io vi dico ke voi foste figliuolo d'uno pistore.[b] Ello Re disse, vogliolo sapere da mia madre, e mandò per la madre, e constrinsela con minaccie feroci. La madre confessò la veritade. Allora il Re si chiuse in una camera con questo Greco, e disse, maestro mio grande prova o veduto della tua sapientia, priegoti, ke tummi diki come queste cose tulle sai. Allora il Greco rispose, Messere io lo vi dirò. Il cavallo conobbi a latte d'asino esser nodrito per propio senno naturale, acciok'io vidi ke avea li orecchi kinati, ecciò non è propia natura di cavallo. Il verme nella pietra conobbi però kelle pietre naturalmente sono fredde & io la trovai calda. Calda non puote essere naturalmente se non per animale lo quale abbia vita. Emme come conoscesti essere figliuolo di pistore? Il Greco rispose, Messere quando io vi dissi del cavallo cosa così maravigliosa, voi mi stabiliste dono d'un mezzo pane per dì, e poi quando della pietra vi dissi, voi mi stabiliste un pane intero, pensate, k'allora m'avidi cui figliuolo voi foste. Ke se voi foste suto figliuolo di Re vi sarebbe paruto poco di donarmi una nobile città onde a vostra natura parve assai di meritarmi di pane sì come vostro padre faciea. Allora il Re, riconobbe la viltà sua, e trassello di prigion e donolli molto nobilemente.

determine the worth of this steed. He was told that in his prison he had the consummate teacher, knowledgeable in all things.[4] He had the steed led to a field and had the Greek brought from prison. He said, "Master, examine this steed for it has been told to me that you are a very learned man." The Greek examined the horse and said, "Sire, the horse is beautiful in appearance, but this much I can tell you, that the horse was nurtured on the milk of an ass." The king sent to Spain to determine how it had been raised, and he discovered that the mare had died and her colt had been nursed with the milk of an ass. The king was greatly amazed by this and ordered a half-loaf of bread, at the expense of the court, be given to him each day. One day it happened that the king gathered together all his precious stones. Once again he sent for this Greek prisoner and said, "Master, you are a man of great knowledge, and I believe you understand all things. Tell me if you are familiar with the virtues of stones. Which of these seems to you the most valuable?" The Greek examined them and said, "Sire, which one is dearest to you?" The king selected a very beautiful one from among the others and said, "Master, this seems to me the most beautiful and the most valuable." The Greek took it in his fist and clenched it tightly and raised it to his ear; then he said, "Sire, inside there is a maggot." The king sent for his own masters and had them break it open, and inside said stone they found a maggot. He then praised the Greek for such wisdom beyond wonder and decreed that an entire loaf of bread, at the expense of the court, be given to him each day. Then, many days later, the king began to suspect that he was not a legitimate king. He sent for this Greek, and brought him to a secret place and began to speak, saying, "Master, I believe you possess great abilities. This I have seen you prove in the things that I have asked of you. I wish you to tell me whose child I am." The Greek replied, "Sire, what kind of question is this? You know very well that you are the son of your father." And the king answered, "Don't patronize me, but tell me, with all certainty, the truth. And if you do not, I will make you die a most horrible death." And so the Greek replied, "Sire, I tell you that you are the son of a baker." And the king said, "I wish to learn this from my mother." And he sent for his mother and forced her with ferocious threats. His mother confessed the truth. Then the king locked himself in a room with this Greek and said, "My master, great proof have I seen of your intellect, I pray you tell me how you came to know all these things." Then the Greek replied, "Sire, I will tell you everything. I knew that the horse had been nurtured with the milk of an ass by using natural wisdom, for I saw that his ears were bent and this is not natural for a horse. I knew the maggot was inside the stone because stones are naturally cold, yet I found this one warm. It could not be warm naturally unless a living animal were present." "And me, how did you know I was the son of a baker?" The Greek answered, "Sire, when I told you such a wondrous thing about the horse, you decreed for me a gift of a half-loaf of bread per day, and then when I told you about the stone, you granted me an entire loaf. You must understand that it was then that I realized whose son you were. For if you were really the son of a king, it would have seemed but little to grant me a noble city, whereas to your nature a loaf of bread, just as your father might have made, seemed an appropriate recompense. Then the king realized his meanness and led the Greek out of prison and rewarded him in a most noble manner.

Novella IIII.

Come uno Giullare[a] si compianse dinanzi ad Alexandro d'un cavaliere al quale elli avea donato per intentione kel cavaliere li donerebbe ciò ke Alexandro li donasse.

Stando Alexandro alla città di Giadre[b] con moltitudine di gente ad assedio, un nobile cavaliere era fuggito di prigione. Et essendo poveramente ad arnese misesi ad andare ad Alexandro ke donava larghissimamente sopra gli altri singniori. Andando per lo cammino trovò uno uomo di corte[c] nobilemente ad arnese. Domandollo dove andava lo cavalier rispose. Vo ad Alexandro, kemmi doni acciok'io possa tornare in mia contrada onoratamente. Allora il Giullare rispose e disse, ke vuoli tu, k'io ti doni ettu mi dona ciò ke Alexandro ti donarà? Lo cavaliere rispose. Donammi cavallo da cavalcare e somiere, e robbe, e dispendio convenevole arritornare in mia terra. Il Giullare li le donò & in concordia cavalcaro ad Alexandro lo quale aspramente avea combattuto la città di Giadre, era partito dalla battaglia e facieasi sotto un padiglione disarmare. Lo cavaliere ello Giullare si trassero avanti. Lo cavaliere fecie la domanda sua ad Alexandro umile e dolcemente. Alexandro non li fecie motto nèlli fecie rispondere. Lo cavaliere si partì dal Giullare e misesi per lo cammino arritornare in sua terra. Poco dilungato il cavaliere li nobili cittadini di Giadre recaro le chiavi della città ad Alexandro, con pieno mandato d'ubbidire allui siccome allor singniore. Alexandro allora si volse in verso e' suoi baroni e disse, dove è kimmi domandava k'io li donasse. Allora fu trammesso per lo cavaliere, k'addomandava il dono. Lo cavaliere venne & Alexandro parlò e disse. Prendi nobile cavaliere le chiavi della nobile città di Giadre kella ti dono volontieri. Lo cavaliere rispose, Messere non mi donare cittade, priegoti ke tummi doni oro o argento o robbe come sia tuo piaciere. Allora Alexandro sorrise e comandò k'elli fossero dati due mila marchi[d] d'argento. E questo si scrisse per lo minore dono, ke Alexandro donò mai. Lo cavaliere prese i marki e donolli al Giullare. Il Giullare fu dinanzi ad Alexandro, e con grande stantia[e] addomandava k'elli faciesse ragione, e fecie tanto ke fecie restare lo cavaliere. Ella domanda sua si era di cotale maniera dinanzi ad Alexandro. Messere io trovai costui in cammino, domandalo ove andava, e perkè. Dissemmi, ke ad Alexandro andava perk'elli donasse. Con lui feci patto. Donali, & elli mi promise di donare ciò ke Alexandro li donasse. Onde elli a e rotto il patto, k'a rifiutato la nobile città di Giadre e preso li marki. Perk'io dinanzi alla vostra singnioria addomando, kemmi facciate ragione, e sodisfare quanto vale più la città ke marki. Allora il cavaliere parlò, e primamente confessò i patti, poi disse. Ragionevole singniore, que', kemmi domanda è Giucollare[f] & in quore di Giullare non puote discendere singnioria di cittade, il suo pensero fu d'argento e d'oro. Ella sua intentione fu tale. Et io o pienamente fornita la sua intentione. Onde la tua singnioria proveggia nella mia diliveranza, secondo ke piacie al tuo savio consiglio. Alexandro e' suoi baroni prosciolsero il cavaliere, e comendaronlo di grande sapientia.

Novella IIII.

How a jester[1] complained before Alexander[2] about a knight, to whom he had made a gift, with the understanding that the knight would give to him all that Alexander bestowed upon the knight.

While Alexander was laying siege to the city of Gaza[3] with a multitude of men, a noble knight escaped from prison. And being poorly equipped, he went in search of Alexander, who gave very liberally to other gentlemen.[4] While on the road, he met a man of the court[5] nobly equipped. The man asked him where he was going. The knight responded, "I am going to Alexander so that he might give to me that which I need to return honorably to my homeland." The jester then spoke, and said, "Do you wish me to give you what you need? And then you can give to me all that Alexander bestows upon you." The knight replied, "Give me a horse to ride, a packhorse and clothing and enough money to return to my land." The jester gave these things to him, and together they rode off to Alexander, who had been bitterly fighting the city of Gaza and had left the battlefield and was having his armor removed under a pavilion.[6] The knight and jester presented themselves before him. Humbly and sweetly the knight made his request of Alexander. Alexander said not a word, not giving a reply. The knight left the jester and began his journey back home. After the knight had traveled only a short way, the noble citizens of Gaza brought the keys of the city to Alexander with the unconditional mandate to obey him as their lord.[7] Alexander then turned toward his barons and said, "Where is he who asked gifts of me?" Then the knight who had requested gifts was sent for. The knight came and Alexander spoke and said, "Noble knight, take the keys to the noble city of Gaza, for I give it to you willingly." The knight answered, "Sire, do not give any city to me; I beg you, give me gold, or silver or clothing, as it may please you." Then Alexander smiled and commanded that he be given two thousand silver marks.[8] And it is written that this was the smallest gift ever given by Alexander. The knight took the marks and gave them to the jester. The jester presented himself to Alexander and with great insistence demanded justice, and he made such a ruckus that the knight was restrained. And his request to Alexander was as follows, "Sire, I found this man traveling along the road; I asked him where he was going and why. He told me that he was going to Alexander seeking gifts. I made an agreement with him. I gave him what he needed and he promised to give to me everything that Alexander gave to him. But he broke our agreement when he refused the noble city of Gaza, and took the marks instead. And so I ask in the presence of my lord that you grant me justice and compensate me in marks equal to the worth of the city minus the marks already received." Then the knight spoke, but first he confessed to the agreement and then said, "Just lord, he who asked this of me is a juggler,[9] and in the heart of a jester, the lord of a city cannot reside. His thoughts were on gold and silver, and his intentions were the same, and I have completely satisfied his intentions. And so, my lord, provide for my deliverance, as it may please your wise counsel." Alexander and his barons released the knight and commended his great wisdom.

Novella V.

Come uno Re conmise una risposta a un suo Giovane figliuolo la quale dovea fare ad ambasciadori di Grecia.

Uno Re fu nelle parti di Egitto, lo quale avea un suo figliuolo primogenito, lo quale dovea portare la corona del Reame dopo lui, questo suo padre dalla fantilitade[a] si cominciò e feciello nodrire intra savi uomini di tempo, sì ke anni avea quindici giamai non avea veduto niuna fanciulezza. Un giorno avenne, kello padre li conmise una risposta ad ambasciadori di Grecia. Il Giovane stando sull'Arringhiera per rispondere alli ambasciadori. Il tempo era turbato e piovea, volse gli occhi per una finestra del palagio e vide altri giovani, ke accoglievano l'acqua piovana, e facevano pescaie e mulina di paglia. Il Giovane vedendo ciò lasciò stare l'Arringhiera e gittossi subitamente giù per le scale del palagio & andò alli altri giovani, ke stavano a ricievere l'acqua piovana, e cominciò affare le mulina e le Bambolitadi.[b] Baroni e cavalieri lo seguirono assai e rimenaronlo al palagio, chiusero la finestra el Giovane diede sufficiente risposta. Dopo il consiglio si partio la gente. Lo padre adunò filosofi e Maestri di grande scientia, propuose il presente fatto. Alcuno de' savi riputava movimento d'omori, alcuno fievolezza d'animo, ki diciea infirmità di cielabro, ki diciea una e ki diciea un'altra secondo le diversità di loro scientie. Uno filosofo disse, ditemi come lo Giovane è stato nodrito, fulli contato come nodrito era stato con savi e con uomini di tempo lungo da ogni fanciullezza. Allora lo savio rispose, non vi maravigliate sella natura domanda ciò k'ella a perduto, ragionevole cosa è bamboleggiare in giovanezza & in vecchiezza pensare.

Novella VI.

Come a David Re venne in pensero di volere sapere quanti fossero i sudditi suoi.

David Re, essendo Re per la bontà d'iddio, che di peccoraio l'avea fatto singniore, li venne un giorno pensero di volere alpostutto sapere quanti fossero e' sudditi suoi, acciò fu atto di vanagloria, onde molto ne dispiacque a dio, e mandolli l'Angelo suo e fecielli così dire. David tu a' peccato, così ti manda a dire lo singnior tuo, o vuolitu stare tre anni in inferno, o tre mesi nelle mani de' nemici suoi cioè tuoi, o stare al giudicio delle mani del tuo singniore? David rispose, nelle mani del mio singniore mi metto, faccia di me ciò, kelli piacie. Or ke fecie iddio, punillo secondo la colpa, ke quasi la maggior parte del popolo suo li tolse per morte, acciok'elli si vanagloriò nel grande novero, così lo scemò & appicciolò il novero. Un giorno avenne ke cavalcando David vide l'Angelo

Novella V.

How a king entrusted a reply to his young son, who was to give it to the ambassadors of Greece.

There was a king from somewhere in Egypt who had a first-born son, who was to wear the crown of the realm after him. From infancy, this father began to have him raised in the company of wise old men, so that, at fifteen years of age he still had not experienced childhood. One day it happened that his father entrusted him with a reply for the ambassadors of Greece. The youth was standing at a railing, responding to the ambassadors. The weather was turbulent and rainy; he turned his eyes toward a palace window and saw other young people gathering up rain water and constructing weirs and water-mills of hay. The young man, seeing this, left the railing and immediately rushed down the palace stairs and went out among the other young people who had gathered to capture the rain water, and he began to make water-mills and do other childish things. The barons and knights quickly followed him and led him back into the palace and closed the window. The young man continued with his sufficient reply. After the council, everyone went on their way. The father gathered together philosophers and teachers of great learning and presented the facts of the situation to them. Some of the wise men attributed them to movements of the humors,[1] others to a feebleness of the soul; still others believed it to be a disease of the brain. Some said one thing, others something else, according to the diversity of their learning. One philosopher said, "Tell me how the young man was raised." It was explained that he was raised by wise men and elders, and kept far away from all other children. Then the wise man answered, "Don't be surprised if nature asks for that which it has lost; it is a reasonable thing to play in youth and to think in old age."

Novella VI.

How the thought came to King David[1] to desire to know the number of his subjects.[2]

To King David, who became king because of the goodness of God, who, from a shepherd made him lord,[3] one day it came to mind to wish, above all else, to know the number of his subjects. And this was an act of pride which was greatly displeasing to God.[4] And He sent one of his angels to him and had him say thus, "David, you have sinned. Your Lord sends me to say this to you. Do you wish to remain three years in hell, or three months in the hands of His enemies, that is yours; or will you allow judgment to rest in the hands of Your Lord?" David replied, "I place myself in the hands of My Lord. May He do with me as He pleases." So what did God do? He punished him according to his guilt, so that almost half of his people were taken by death. Since he had experienced such pride in the great number of his people, so He diminished and

d'iddio con una spada igniuda k'andava uccidendo, comunque elli volle colpire uno, e David smontoe subitamente, e disse. Messere mercie perdio non uccidere li innocenti, ma uccidi me cui è la colpa. Allora per la dibonarità di questa parola Dio perdonò al popolo e rimase l'uccisione.

Novella VII.

Qui conta come l'Angelo parlò a Salamone e disse ke torrebbe Domenedio il Reame al figliuolo per li suoi peccati.

Leggiesi di Salamone, ke fecie un altro dispiaciere addio onde cadde in sententia di perdere lo Reame suo, l'Angelo li parlò e disse così. Salamone per la tua colpa tusse' dengnio di perdere lo Reame. Ma così ti manda lo nostro singniore, ke per li meriti della bontà di tuo padre, elli nol ti torrà nel tuo tempo, ma per la colpa tua lo torrà a figliuolto. E così dimostra i guidardoni del padre meritati nel figliuolo, elle colpe del padre punite nel figliuolo. Nota ke Salamone studiosamente lavorò sotto'l sole con ingiengnio di sua grandissima sapientia. Fece grandissimo e nobile rengnio. Poi k'ell'ebbe fatto providessi, ke non voleva, kel possedessero aliene rede, cioè strane rede, fuori del suo lengniaggio. Et accioe tolse molte mogli e molte amike per avere assai rede, e dio provide, quelli ke è sommo dispensatore, sì, ke tra tutte le mogli & amike ke erano cotante, non ebbe se non un figliuolo. Et allora Salamone si provide, di sottoporre & ordinare sillo Reame sotto questo suo figliuolo, lo quale Roboam avea nome, k'elli rengniasse dopo lui certamente. Ke fecie dalla gioventudine infino alla senettute ordinare la vita al figliuolo con molti ammaestramenti, e con molti nodrimenti. E più fecie, ke tesoro li ammassoe grandissimo e misello in luogo sicuro. E più fecie, ke incontanente poi si brigò, ke in concordia fu con tutti li singniori, ke confinavano con lui, & in pace ordinò e dispose sanza contentione tutti e' suoi baroni. E più fecie kello dottrinò del corso delle stelle, & insengniolli avere singnioria sopra i domoni. E tutte queste cose fecie perkè Roboam rengniasse dopo lui. Quando Salamone fue morto, Roboam prese suo consiglio di gente vecchia e savia, propose e domandò consiglio in ke modo potesse riformare lo popolo suo. Li vecchi l'insengniaro, ragunerai il popolo tuo e con dolci parole dirai, kettu li ami siccome te medesimo, e k'elli sono la corona tua e kesse tuo padre fu loro aspro, kettu sarai loro umile e beningnio, e dove elli li avesse faticati, kettu li soverrai in grande riposo. Esse in fare il tempio furo gravati, tulli agievolerai. Queste parole l'insengniaro i savi vecchi del rengnio. Partissi Roboam & adunò uno consiglio de' giovani, e fecie loro somigliante proposta. E quelli li addomandaro, quelli con cui prima ti consigliasti, come ti consigliaro? E quelli irracontò loro a motto a motto. Allora li giovani dissero. Elli t'ingannano, percioké i rengni non si tengono per parole ma per prodezza e per franckezza. Onde settu dirai loro dolci parole parrà kettu abbia paura del popolo, onde esso ti soggiogherà e non ti terrà per singniore, e non ti ubbidiranno. Ma fae per nostro senno, noi siamo tutti tuoi servi el singniore può fare de' servi quello kelli piacie. Onde dilloro con vigore e con ardire, k'elli sono tutti tuoi servi e kinnon t'ubbidirà tullo punirai

minimized their number. One day it happened that, while riding, David saw the angel of God with a naked sword going about killing his people. And just as he was about to strike one, David quickly dismounted and said, "Sire, by God, have mercy! Don't kill these innocents, but kill me, who am at fault." Then, because of the goodness of these words, God pardoned the populace and stayed the execution.

Novella VII.

Here is told how the angel spoke to Solomon,[1] *and said that God would take the realm from his son because of Solomon's sins.*

It is written that Solomon once again displeased God, in a manner that would result in the loss of his realm.[2] The angel spoke to him and said, "Solomon, your guilt has earned you the loss of your realm. But our Lord sends this message to you that, because of the goodness of your father, He will not take it during your lifetime; but because of your misdeeds, He will take it away from your son."[3] And in this way, God demonstrated how the rewards of a father are merited by his son, and how the sins of a father are visited upon his son. It is known that Solomon studiously toiled from sunup to sundown and utilized the genius of his great wisdom to create a very great and noble realm. After he had done so, he made provisions so that his realm would not fall into the hands of strangers, that is, foreign rulers outside of his bloodline. To accomplish this, he took many wives and lovers so that he might have many descendants.[4] But God, who is the ultimate provider and dispensor, from all of Solomon's wives and lovers, who numbered many, allowed only one son to be born. And then Solomon arranged to subject and order his realm under this son, whose name was Roboam,[5] so that he would certainly rule after him. He did this by organizing the boy's life, from infancy through old age, with much nurturing and instruction. And he did more. He amassed a very great treasure and stored it in a secure place. And he did more. Immediately he conspired to live in harmony with all the lords whose realms bordered on his lands, and he ordered and enjoined all his barons to live in peace without contention. And he did more. He indoctrinated his son concerning the movements of the stars and he taught him to have dominion over demons. And all these things he did so that Roboam might rule after him. When Solomon died, Roboam took counsel from the old, wise men.[6] He proposed questions and sought advice concerning the ways in which he should reform his people. The elders instructed him, "Gather together your people, and with sweet words tell them that you love them as you love yourself and that it is they who are your crown. And where your father had been severe with them, you instead will be humble and mild; and where he forced them to toil arduously, you will direct them with great tranquillity. And if they were heavily burdened in the construction of the temple,[7] you will ease their plight." These words were the instructions of the wise elders of the realm. Roboam left them and called the young men to counsel and made a similar request of them. And these men asked of him, "Those from whom you first sought counsel, how did they advise

secondo la tua aspra leggie. Esse Salamone li gravò in fare lo tempio, ettulli graverai setti verrà in piaciere. Il popolo non t'avrae per fanciullo, tutti ti temeranno, e così terrai lo Reame ella corona. Lo stoltissimo Roboam si tenne al giovane consiglio. Adunò il popolo e disse parole feroci. Il popolo s'adirò. I Baroni si turbaro. Feciero pusture[a] e leghe. Giuraro insieme cierti baroni sì ke in trentaquattro dì dopo la morte di Salamone perdè delle dodici parti le dieci del suo Reame per lo folle consiglio de' giovani.

Novella VIII.

Come un figliuolo d'uno Re donò a un re di Siria scacciato.

Uno singniore di Grecia lo quale possedea grandissimo Reame & avea nome Aulix, avea uno suo Giovane figliuolo al quale faciea nodrire & insegniare le sette arti liberali e faciealli insengniare vita morale cioè di be' costumi. Un giorno tolse questo Re molto oro e diello a questo suo figliuolo, e disse, dispendillo come ti piacie. E commandò a' baroni, kennon l'insegniassero spendere, ma solamente avisassero il suo portamento, el modo k'elli tenesse. I baroni seguitando questo Giovane un giorno stavano con lui alle finestre del palagio. Il Giovane stava pensoso vide passare per lo cammino gente assai nobile secondo l'arnese e secondo le persone. Il cammino correa a piè del palagio, comandò questo Giovane, ke fossero tutte queste genti menate dinanzi dallui, fue ubbidita la sua volontade, e vennero i viandanti dinanzi dallui. Ell'uno k'avea lo quore più ardito, ella fronte più Allegra si fecie avanti e disse. Messere, kenne domandi? Il Giovane rispose, domandotti onde se'? E di ke conditione? & elli rispose. Messere, io sono d'Italia e mercatante sono molto ricco, e quella rickezza k'i'o, noll'o di mio patrimonio. Ma tutta l'oe guadangniata di mia sollecitudine. Il Giovane domandò il seguente, il quale era di nobili fattioni[a] e stava con peritosa[b] faccia e stava più in dietro, kell'altro, e non così arditamente, quelli disse, kemmi domandi Messere? Il Giovane rispose, domandotti d'onde se', e di ke conditione? Et elli rispose. Io sono di Siria e sono Re & o sì saputo fare, kelli sudditi miei m'anno cacciato. Allora il Giovane prese tutto l'oro e diello a questo scacciato. Il Grido andò per lo palagio. Li Baroni e cavalieri ne tennero grande parlamento, e tutta la corte sonava della dispensagione di questo oro. Al padre furono raccontate tutte queste cose elle domande elle risposte a motto a motto. Il Re incominciò a parlare al figliuolo udenti molti Baroni, e disse. Come dispensasti? Ke pensero ti mosse? Quale ragione ci mostri, ke a colui, ke per sua bontà avea guadangniato non desti, & a colui, k'avea perduto per sua colpa e follia tutto desti? Il Giovane savio rispose. Messere non donai a ki non m'insengnioe, nè a neuno donai. Ma ciò k'io feci fu Guidardone e non dono. Il mercatante non m'insengniò neente, nolli era neente tenuto. Ma quelli, ke era di mia conditione figliuolo di Re, e ke portava corona di Re, il quale per la sua follia avea sì fatto, ke i sudditi suoi l'aveano cacciato,

you?" And he repeated their advice, word for word. Then the young men said, "They have deceived you, for realms are not held by words, but by courage and candor. Whereby, if you speak sweet words to them, it will seem that you are afraid of the people. Then they will subdue you and not recognize you as lord and not obey you. But listen to our wisdom; we are all your servants and a lord may do as he pleases with his servants. So, with vigor and ardor, tell them that they are all your servants, and he who does not obey you will be punished according to your harsh laws. And, if Solomon burdened them with the construction of the temple, so will you burden them, if it pleases you. The people will not take you for a child; everyone will fear you, and in this way you will maintain your realm and your crown." Foolhardy Roboam took the young men's advice. He gathered together his people and spoke to them using ferocious words. The people became enraged. The barons became agitated. They formed secret alliances and leagues. Certain barons swore allegiances among themselves, so that, thirty-four days after the death of Solomon, because of the foolish counsel of young men, Roboam lost ten of the twelve divisions of his realm.[8]

Novella VIII.

How the son of a king gave a gift to an outcast King of Syria.

A Greek gentleman, who possessed a very great realm, and was called Aulix,[1] had a young son whom he had nurtured and instructed in the seven liberal arts,[2] and taught to lead a moral life, that is, to be well behaved. One day this king withdrew a great deal of gold and gave it to his son, and said, "Distribute it as you please." And he charged his barons not to instruct the boy in its allocation, but only to observe his comportment and the manner in which he conducted himself. Following this youth, one day the barons found themselves with him at the windows of the palace. The young man was deep in thought; he saw people pass by on the road below who, from their dress and persons, seemed very noble indeed. The road ran to the foot of the palace. The young man demanded that all these people be brought before him. His wish was obeyed, and the travelers came before him. And the one who had the most daring heart and the most cheerful aspect came forward, and said, "Sire, what do you ask of us?" The young man replied, "I ask you, from where do you come and from what station?" And he answered, "Sire, I am from Italy, and I am a very rich merchant. I did not inherit my riches, but I earned them using my own abilities." And the young man questioned the next traveler, who was of noble aspect, and remained timid of expression and kept himself further back than the other one, and not so brazenly he said, "Sire, what do you ask of me?" The young man replied, "I ask you, from where do you come and from what station?" And he answered, "I am from Syria, and I am a king, and I knew how to act so well that my subjects expelled me." Then the young man took all the gold and gave it to this exile. A cry went up throughout the palace. The barons and knights engaged in a great debate concerning this matter, and the entire court buzzed about the dispensing of this gold. All

m'insengniò tanto ke i sudditi miei non caccieranno me. Onde picciolo dono diedi allui di così ricco insengniamento. Udita la sententia del Giovane, il padre elli suoi Baroni il comendaro di grande sapientia diciendo, ke grande speranza ricievea della sua giovenezza, ke nelli anni compiti sia di grande valore. Le lettere corsero per li paesi a' singniori & a' Baroni e furonne grandi disputationi tralli savi.

Novella IX.

Qui si ditermina una quistione e sententia, ke fu data in Alexandria.

In Alexandria, la quale è nelle parti di Romania, accioké sono dodici Alexandrie, le quali Alexandro fecie in marzo dinanzi, k'elli morisse. In quella Alexandria sono le rughe,[a] ove stanno i saracini, li quali fanno i mangiari a vendere e cierca l'uomo la ruga per li piue netti mangiari, e più dilicati siccome l'uomo fra noi cierca de' drappi. Un giorno di lunedì un quoco saracino, lo quale avea nome Fabrac, stando alla cucina sua. Un povero saracino venne alla cucina con uno pane in mano, danaio non avea da comperare da costui, tenne il pane sopra il vasello e ricievea lo fumo kenn'uscia, & innebriato il pane del fumo, kenn'uscia del mangiare, e quelli lo mordea e così il consumò di mangiare. Questo Fabrac non vendeo bene questa matina, recolsi a ingiuria & annoia e prese questo povero saracino e disselli, pagammi di ciò, kettu ai preso del mio. Il povero rispose, io non'o preso della tua cucina altro, ke fumo. Di ciò k'ai preso del mio mi paga, diciea Fabrac. Tanto fulla contesa, ke per la nova quistione e rozza e non mai più avenuta, n'andaro le novelle al Soldano. Il Soldano per molta novissima cosa raunò savi, e mandò per costoro. Formò la quistione. I savi saracini comminciaro a sottigliare e ki riputava il fumo non del quoco diciendo molte ragioni. Il fumo non si può ricievere e torna ad alimento e non a sostantia nè propietade, ke sia utile, non dee pagare. Altri dicievano, lo fumo era ancora congiunto col mangiare, era in costui singnioria e generavassi della sua propietade, e l'uomo sta per vendere di suo mestiero, e kinne prende è usanza ke paghi. Molte sententie v'ebbe. Finalmente fu il consiglio, poi k'elli

these things were told to his father, the questions and the answers were related word for word. The king began to speak to his son within the hearing of many barons, and he said, "How did you distribute the gold? What thoughts moved your actions? What reason can you demonstrate to us that to him, who through his own fine abilities had earned much, you gave nothing; and to him, who lost all through his own fault and foolishness, you gave all?" The wise young man replied, "Sire, I gave nothing to him who taught me nothing; in reality I gave to no one. For that which I supplied was a reward and not a gift. The merchant taught me nothing and he received nothing in return. But he who was of my station, a king's son, one who wears a king's crown, who through his own foolishness did such things that forced his subjects to cast him out, he taught me much, so that my subjects will not cast me out. And so I gave him a little gift for such a rich lesson." Having heard the opinion of the young man, the father and his barons commended him for such great wisdom, saying that they had received great hope from such a youth who had achieved such great wisdom in so few years. Letters coursed through the territories to all the lords and barons and there were great disputations among the wise men concerning this matter.

Novella IX.

Here is decided a question and resolution which was given in Alexandria.

In Alexandria, which is found somewhere in Romania,[1] given that there are twelve Alexandrias which Alexander founded during the March before he died.[2] In that Alexandria there are streets where the Saracens live and prepare food for sale and where men search these streets for the purest and most delicate edibles, just as men among us search for fabrics. On a given Monday, a Saracen cook, whose name was Fabrac, was standing at his kitchen when a poor Saracen approached the kitchen with a loaf of bread in hand. He had no money to buy from the cook; he held his bread over a pot on the stove and received the smoke that issued forth. In this way his bread became saturated with the rising smoke from the cooking food. Then he bit into the bread and, in this manner, consumed his food. This Fabrac had not sold very much that morning. He was filled with injury and irritation. He grabbed this poor Saracen and said, "Pay me for that which you have taken from me." The poor man replied, "I have taken nothing but smoke from your kitchen." "For that which you have taken, pay me," said Fabrac. The quarrel was so unique and tactless, such a one had never occurred before, that the news eventually reached the Sultan.[3] For such an uncommon situation, the Sultan gathered together his wise men. He sent for them and formulated the question. The wise Saracens began to argue subtly, employing many justifications; some affirmed that the smoke did not belong to the cook, "Smoke cannot be retrieved and returned to an aliment. It has no substance and no useful properties. The man need not pay." Others said, "The smoke was still enjoined to the food which maintained dominion over it, and from which it generated its properties. The cook was selling according to his trade and

sta per vendere le sue derrate,[b] tu & altri per comperare, dissero. Tu giusto singnore fa', kel facci giustamente pagare la sua derrata secondo la sua valuta. Sella sua cucina ke vende dando l'utile propietà di quella, suole prendere utile moneta & ora k'a venduto fumo, ke èlla parte sottile della cucina, fae singniore sonare una moneta, e giudica, kel pagamento s'intenda fatto del suono k'escie di quella e così giudicò il Soldano ke fosse osservato.

Novella X.

Qui conta d'una bella sententia, ke die lo schiavo di Bari tra uno Borghese & uno pellegrino.

Uno Borghese di Bari andò in Romeaggio[a] e lasciò trecento bisanti[b] a un suo amico con queste conditioni e patti. Io andrò siccome addio piacierà, ess'io non rivenissi darali per l'anima mia, ess'io rivegno a cierto termine daramene quello, kettu vorai. Andò il pellegrino in Romeaggio rivenne al termine ordinato, e raddomandò i bisanti suoi. L'amico rispose, conta il patto. Lo Romeo lo contò a punto, bendicesti, disse l'amico. Te dieci bisanti ti voglio rendere i dugento novanta mi tengo. Il pellegrino cominciò addirarsi diciendo, ke fede è questa? Tu mi tolli il mio falsamente, ell'amico rispose soavamente, io non ti fo torto ess'io lo ti fo síanne dinanzi alla singnioria. Richiamò ne fue. Lo schiavo di Bari ne fu giudice. Udio le parti. Formò la quistione. Onde nacque questa sententia e disse così a colui ke ritenne i bisanti. Rendi i dugento novanta bisanti al pellegrino el pellegrino ne dea atte dieci, ke tulli ai renduti, po' kel patto fue tale, ciò kettu vorai mi renderai, onde i dugentonovanta ne vuoli rendilli, e i dieci kettu non volei prendi.

Novella XI.

Qui conta come maestro Giordano fu ingannato da un suo falso disciepolo.

Uno Medico fu, lo quale ebbe nome Giordano, il quale avea uno disciepolo. Infermò uno figliuolo d'uno Re. Il maestro v'andò, e vide ke era da guarrire. Il disciepolo, per torre il pregio al maestro, disse al padre. Io veggio k'elli morrà certamente, e contendendo col maestro, si fecie aprire la bocca allo'nfermo e col dito stremo li vi puose veleno mostrando molta conoscenza, in sulla lingua. L'uomo morio. Lo maestro se n'andò, e perdeo il pregio suo, el disciepolo il guadangniò. Allora il maestro giurò di mai non medicare se non Asini, e fecie la fisica delle bestie e di vili animali.

anyone taking from him is acting in a manner requiring payment." Many assertions were proffered. Finally an agreement was reached. "Since this man was selling his merchandise for you and others to buy," they said, "You, just man, must pay justly for his merchandise according to its worth. If it is edibles which he sells and to which he gives useful properties, then he must be used to receiving useful payment in kind. And now that he has sold smoke, which is the subtle component of cooking; you Sir, make a coin ring and be it resolved that payment is perceived to have been made by the sound which rises from that coin." And so it was observed how the Sultan decreed.

Novella X.

Here is told of a splendid opinion which the Slave of Bari[1] *formulated between a citizen*[2] *and a pilgrim.*

A citizen of Bari went on pilgrimage to Rome and left three hundred bezants[3] with a friend under the following conditions and agreement, "I will go, as it pleases God, and if I never return, give this money for the good of my soul. But if I return within a prescribed period of time, return to me that which you wish." The pilgrim went on pilgrimage to Rome and returned within the prescribed time, and he asked for the return of his bezants. His friend replied, "Recount to me our agreement." The Roman pilgrim repeated it exactly. "You have told it well," said the friend; "Here, I wish to give you ten bezants and I will keep two hundred and ninety." The pilgrim became outraged, saying, "What faith is this? You have taken falsely from me." And the friend suavely replied, "I have done you no wrong; and if I have, let us present this case to the seignory."[4] Eventually they were called to the court where the Slave of Bari was presiding. He listened to both sides and formulated the question from which he generated this opinion. He said the following to the man who had kept the bezants, "Return two hundred and ninety bezants to the pilgrim and the pilgrim will give you the ten which you returned to him. This is because the agreement was as follows, 'that which you wish, you will return to me.' Since you wished for the two hundred and ninety; return them, and the ten which you did not want; take them."

Novella XI.

Here is told how Master Giordano[1] *was deceived by a false disciple of his.*

There once was a doctor named Giordano, who had a disciple. The son of a king fell ill. This teacher went to him and realized that he could cure him. The disciple, in order to steal all prestige from his master, said to the father, "I can see that your son will surely die." And, disagreeing with his teacher, and acting as one of great learning, he opened the sick man's mouth and, using his little finger, deposited some poison on the man's tongue. The man died. The teacher went away and lost all of his prestige, which was gained by his disciple. From that moment on the teacher swore that he would only attend to asses, and so began his practice of administering to wild beasts and dumb animals.

Novella XII.

Qui conta dell'onore ke Aminadab fecie al Re David suo naturale singniore.

Aminadab conducitore[a] e Mariscalco del Re David andò con grandissimo essercito di gente per commandamento del Re David ad una città de' filistei. Udendo Aminadab kella città non si potea più tenere e kell'avrebbe di corto. Mandò al Re David kelli piaciesse di venire all'oste con moltitudine di gente perkè dottava[b] del campo. Il Re David si mosse incontanente & andoe nel campo. Aminadab, suo Mariscalco, domandoe, perkèmmicci ai fatto venire? Aminadab rispose. Messere però kella città non si può tenere più & io volea kella vostra persona avesse il pregio di così fatta vittoria anzi kell'avess'io. Combatteo la città e vinsella ello pregio ell'onore n'ebbe David.

Novella XIII.

Qui conta come Antinogo[a] riprese Alexandro, perk'elli si facieva sonare una cietera a suo diletto.

Antinogo conducitore d'Alexandro, faciendo Alexandro un giorno per suo diletto sonare, il sonare era una cietera. Antinogo prese la cietera e ruppella e gittolla nel fango e disse ad Alexandro cotali parole. Al tuo tempo & etade si conviene rengniare e non cieterare, e così si può dire. Al corpo e rengnio vil cosa èlla lussuria, e quasi a modo di cietera. Vergonissi dunque ki dee rengniare in vertude e diletta in lussuria. Re Porro il quale combattè con Alexandro, a un mangiare fecie tagliare le corde della cietera a un cieteratore e disse queste parole. Meglio è tagliare ke sviare, kè a dolcezza di suono si perdono le vertudi.

Novella XIIII.

Come uno Re fecie nodrire uno suo figliuolo dieci anni in luogo tenebroso e poi li mostrò tutte le cose e più li piacque le femine.

A uno Re nacque un figliuolo i savi Strologi providero k'elli stesse anni dieci, kennon vedesse il sole. Allora il fecie notricare e guardare in tenebrose spelonke. Dopo il tempo detto lo fecie trarre fuori, & innanzi allui fecie mettere molte belle gioie, e di molte belle donzelle tutte cose nominando per nome e dettolli le donzelle essere domoni, e poi li domandaro quale d'esse li fosse più gratiosa. Rispose, i domoni. Allora lo Re di ciò si maravigliò molto dicendo, ke cosa è tirranía e bellore di donna.

Novella XII.

Here is told of the honor which Aminadab[1] *gave to King David, his natural lord.*

Aminadab, leader and marshall for King David, went with a very great army, on King David's command, to a Philistine city.[2] Aminadab, hearing that the city could not hold out any longer and that it would soon be his, sent to King David asking him, if it pleased the king, to come to his army with a multitude of men, for Aminadab feared the impending battle. King David immediately made preparations and went to the battlefield. He questioned Aminadab, his marshall, "Why have you made me come here?" Aminadab replied, "Sire, even though the city cannot hold out any longer, I wanted you, in person, to gain the glory of this ready-made victory, rather than myself." The battle was fought and the city won, and the merit and honor were bestowed upon David.

Novella XIII.

Here is told how Antigonus[1] *reprimanded Alexander,*[2] *who played a cithara for his personal pleasure.*

One day Antigonus, a commander for Alexander, happened upon Alexander who was playing an instrument for his personal pleasure;[3] the instrument was a cithara.[4] Antigonus seized the cithara, smashed it, and threw it into the mud, and said these words to Alexander, "At your age and time of life, it is more appropriate to rule than to play the cithara." And so, it can be said that, to both the body and the kingdom, lasciviousness, almost like the playing of a cithara, is a vile thing. Thus he who should reign in virtue, but instead delights in lasciviousness, should be ashamed. Once, at a repast, King Porus,[5] who fought with Alexander, had the strings of a musician's cithara cut, and said these words, "It is better to cut these strings than to be diverted, for one may lose all virtue to the sweet sounds of music."

Novella XIIII.

How a king had his son raised for ten years in a tenebrous place, and then he displayed all things to him, and he liked women the most.[1]

A son was born to a king. His wise astrologers advised him that the boy must stay ten years without seeing the sun. And so he had the boy raised and guarded in shadow-filled caverns. After the prescribed time, he had the boy brought out into the open air, and had many lovely jewels and many beautiful young women brought before him. Everything was identified by name, and the young women were said to be demons.[2] Then the boy was asked which of these things he found most gracious. He replied, "The demons." Then the king, hearing this, was greatly amazed, and said, "What a thing is the tyranny and the beauty of woman!"

Novella XV.

Come uno Rettore di terra fecie cavare un occhio asse & uno al figliuolo per osservare giustitia.

Valerio Maximo nel libro sesto narra ke Calogno essendo Rettore d'una terra ordinò ke ki andasse a moglie altrui dovesse perdere li occhi. Poco tempo passante vi cadde uno suo figliuolo. Lo popolo tutto li gridava misericordia & elli pensando ke misericordia era così buona cosa & utile, e pensando kella giustitia non vole perire ell'amore di suoi cittadini kelli gridavano mercie lo stringea providessi d'osservare l'uno ell'altro cioè giustitia e misericordia. Giudicò e sententiò kal figliuolo fosse tratto l'uno occhio, & asse medesimo l'altro.

Novella XVI.

Qui conta della gran misericordia ke fecie San Paolino vescovo.

Beato Paolino vescovo fu tanto misericordioso, ke keggiendolli una povera femina misericordia per un suo figliuolo ke era in prigione, e Beato Paolino rispose. Non o diketti sovenire d'altro. Ma fa' così. Menammi alla carciere dov'è'l tuo figliuolo. Menolvi. Et elli si mise in prigione in mano de' tortori, e disse. Rendete lo figliuolo a questa buona donna, emme ritenete per lui.

Novella XVII.

Della grande limosina ke fecie uno Tavoliere[a] *per dio.*

Piero Tavoliere fu grande uomo d'avere e venne tanto misericordioso, ke prima tutto lo avere dispese a' poveri per dio. E poi quando tutto ebbe dato & elli si fecie vendere & il prezzo diede a' poveri tutto.

Novella XVIII.

Della vendetta ke fecie Iddio d'uno Barone di Carlo Magno.

Carlo Magno essendo ad oste sopra i Saracini, venne a morte, fecie testamento, intrall'altre cose giudicò suo cavallo e sue arme a' poveri. E lasciolle a un suo Barone kelle vendesse e desselle a' poveri. Quelli si tenne e non ubbidio. Carlo tornò allui e disse, otto generationi[a] di pene m'ai fatte sofferire in purgatorio per die per lo cavallo

Novella XV.

How the chancellor of a land had one of his eyes removed and one from his son, in observance of the law.

Valerius Maximus,[1] in Book Six,[2] narrates that Calognus,[3] as chancellor of a land, decreed that whoever goes with the wife of another should forfeit his eyes. A short time later, one of his sons fell guilty to the decree. The entire population cried out to him for mercy. And he, believing that mercy was a very fine and useful thing, yet thinking that justice must not perish, was affected by the love of his citizens who cried out to him for mercy. And so he made provisions to observe both one side and the other, that is, justice and mercy. He judged and passed sentence that one eye should be removed from his son, and the other from his own person.

Novella XVI.

Here is told of the great mercy displayed by Saint Paulinus the Bishop.[1]

Blessed Paulinus the Bishop was so merciful that a poor woman asked him for mercy for her son, who was in prison.[2] And Blessed Paulinus replied, "I have no other means by which to help you. But do the following. Lead me to the jail where your son is." She took him there. And he placed himself in prison into the hands of the torturers, and said, "Restore this good woman's son to her and keep me in his stead."

Novella XVII.

Concerning the great charity which a moneylender[1] *demonstrated for God.*

Piero the moneylender was a man of great means who became so merciful that first he distributed all his possessions in God's name. And then, when he had given everything away, he had himself sold and gave all the proceeds to the poor.

Novella XVIII.

Concerning the vengeance which God effected on a baron of Charlemagne.[1]

Charlemagne met his death while waging war with his army against the Saracens.[2] He prepared his last will and testament and, among other things, bequeathed his horse and his arms to the poor. And he left them with one of his barons, directing him to sell these things and donate the proceeds to the poor. But this man kept these things and did not obey him. Charles returned to him and said, "Eight forms of punishment you have made me suffer in Purgatory for each day that you have retained my horse and

ell'arme ke ricievesti. Ma gratia del singniore mio io ne vo purgato in cielo, e tulla comperrai amaramente. Ke udenti centomila genti venne un trono[b] da cielo & andonne con lui in abisso.

Novella XIX.

Della grande libertà e cortesia del Re Giovane.

Leggiessi della bontà del Re Giovane guerreggiando col padre per lo consiglio di Beltramo. Lo quale Beltramo si vantò k'elli avea più senno ke niuno altro. Di ciò nacquero molte sententie delle quali ne sono qui scritte alquante. Beltramo ordinò collui. K'elli si faciesse dare al padre la sua parte di tutto lo tesoro. Lo figliuolo il domandò tanto kell'ebbe. Quelli li fecie tutto donare a' gentili genti et a' poveri Cavalieri, sì ke rimase a neente e non avea ke donare. Un uomo di corte[a] li addomandò kelli donasse. Quelli rispose k'avea tutto donato, ma tanto mi è rimaso ancora, k'i'o nella bocca un laido dente, onde mio padre a offerti duo mila Marki[b] a kimmi fa sì pregare, k'io l'o diparta da gli altri, va a mio padre e fatti dare li Marki & io il mi trarrò di bocca alla tua rikiesta. Il Giullare andò al padre e prese li Marki et elli si trasse il dente. Et un altro giorno avenne k'elli donava a uno gentile dugento Marki. Il Siniscalco overo Tesoriere prese quelli Marki e mise uno tapeto in una sala e versollivi suso & uno luffo di tapeto mise di sotto perkè il monte paresse maggiore. Et andando il Re Giovane per la sala li le mostrò il Tesoriere diciendo, or guardate Messer come donate. Vedete quanti sono dugento Marki kelli avete così per neente. E quelli avisò e disse. Picciola quantitade mi sembra a donare a così valente uomo. Daraline quattrocento ke troppo credeva, ke fossero più i dugento Marki ke non mi sembrano a vista.

Novella XX.

Della grande libertà e cortesia del Re d'Inghilterra.

Lo giovane Re d'Inghilterra spendeva e donava tutto un povero cavaliere avisò un giorno un coperchio d'uno nappo d'ariento. E disse nell'animo suo. Se io posso nascondere quello la Masnada[a] mia ne potrà stare molti giorni. Misessi il coperchio dell'ariento sotto il Siniscalco allevare le tavole riguardò l'ariento. Trovaronlo meno. Cominciaro a metterlo in grido, et a ciercare i cavalieri alla porta. Il Re giovane avisò costui kell'avea e venne allui sanza romore, e dìsselli ketissimamente. Mettillo sotto amme k'io non sarò cierco. Ello cavaliere pieno di vergongnia così fecie. Il Re giovane li le rende fuor della porta. E miselli di sotto, e poi lo fecie chiamare e donoli l'altra partita. E più di cortesia fecie ke poveri cavalieri una notte entrarono nella camera sua, credendo veramente kello Re giovane dormisse. Adunaro li arnesi elle robbe a guisa di furto. Ebbevene un ke mal volentieri lasciava una ricca coltre, kel Re avea sopra presella

arms. But, thanks to my Lord, I have been purified and am going to heaven. But you will pay bitterly for this." Then, a clap of thunder came from heaven that was heard by a hundred thousand people and carried him with it into the abyss.

Novella XIX.

Concerning the grand liberality and courtesy of the young king.[1]

Here one reads of the goodness of the young king who warred against his father with the counsel of Beltram.[2] This Beltram boasted that he was wiser than all others.[3] From this many questions were born, some of which are written down here. Beltram ordered the king to force his father to give him all of his part of his father's treasure. The son asked so persistently that he finally received it. He then distributed it all to gentlemen and poor knights so that nothing remained and he had no more to give. A minstrel requested a gift from him. He replied that he had given away everything. "But enough still remains from which my father has offered two thousand marks[4] to whoever can convince me to remove an unsightly tooth from the others I have in my mouth. Go to my father and make him give you the marks, and, to honor your request, I will extract it myself from my mouth."[5] The minstrel went to his father and received the marks and the king extracted his own tooth. And another day it happened that he had bestowed two hundred marks on a gentleman. The seneschal,[6] or rather his treasurer, placed a carpet on the floor of a room, took those marks and poured them onto it. He placed a cotton flock under the carpet so that the mound would appear larger. And when the young king entered the room, the treasurer exhibited the mound to him, saying, "Now, Sire, see how much you are giving away. See how much two hundred marks is, that you believed to be nothing." And the king observed the mound and said, "It seems such a meager amount to give to such a valiant man. Give him four hundred. For I believed two hundred marks to be a much greater amount, until I actually saw them."

Novella XX.

Concerning the great liberality and courtesy of the King of England.[1]

The young king of England spent and gave away everything. One day a poor knight espied the cover of a silver goblet.[2] And, deep within his very soul, he said to himself, "If I could conceal that cover, my family could survive for many days." He then placed the silver cover under his cloak.[3] The seneschal[4] inventoried the silver while clearing the tables. He found one piece missing, began to cry out in alarm and to search each knight at the door. The young king had observed what this poor man had done. Silently he went up to him and whispered, "Put it under my cloak, for I will never be searched." And the knight, full of shame, did just so. The young king returned it to him outside the door and placed it under his cloak. He then called for the knight and gave

e cominciò attirare. Lo Re, per non rimaner scoperto, prese la sua partita e teneva siccome que' tirava, tanto ke per fare più tosto li altri vi puosero mano. Et allora lo Re parlò. Questa sarebbe rubberia e non furto cioè a torre per forza. Li cavalieri fuggiro quando l'udiro parlare ke prima credevano ke dormisse. Un giorno lo Re vecchio padre di questo Re giovane lo riprendea forte diciendo, dove è tuo tesoro? Et elli rispose. Messer io n'o più ke voi non avete, quivi fu il sì el no. Ingaggiarsi le parti. Aggiornaro il giorno, ke ciascuno mostrasse il suo tesoro. Lo Re giovane invitò tutti i baroni del paese, ke a cotal giorno fossero in quella parte. Il padre quello giorno fecie tendere uno ricco padiglione e fecie venire oro et ariento in piatte e vasella et arnese assai, e pietre pretiose infinite e versò in su i tapeti, e disse al figliuolo, dove è il tuo tesoro? Allora il figliuolo trasse la spada del fodero. Li cavalieri adunati trassero per le vie e per le piazze. Tutta la terra parea piena di cavalieri. Il Re non poteo riparare. L'oro rimase alla singnioria del giovane. Lo quale disse a' cavalieri, prendete il tesoro vostro. Ki prese oro, ki vasello, ki una cosa, ki un'altra, sì ke di subito fu distribuito. Il padre ragunò poi suo sforzo per prenderlo. Lo figliuolo si richiuse in uno castello e Beltramo dal Bornio con lui. Il padre vi venne ad assedio. Un giorno, per troppa sicurtà, li venne un quadrello per la fronte disaventuratamente, kella contraria fortuna kel seguitava l'uccise. Ma innanzi k'elli morisse vennero allui tutti i suoi debitori et addomandaro loro tesoro ke allui aveano prestato. Il Re giovane rispose, singniori a mala stagione venite kel vostro tesoro è dispeso. Li arnesi sono donati. Il corpo è infermo non avrete omai di me più buono pengnio. Ma fe' venire uno Notaio e quando il Notaio fu venuto disse quello Re cortese, scrivi k'io obbrigo mia anima a perpetua prigione infino attanto ke voi pagati siate. Morio questi. Dopo la morte andaro al padre suo e domandaro la moneta. Il padre rispose loro aspramente diciendo, voi siete quelli ke prestavate al mio figliuolo, ond'elli mi faciea guerra, et impero, sotto pena del quore e dell'avere, vi partite di tutta mia forza. Allora l'uno parlò e disse. Messer, noi non saremo perdenti kennoi avemo l'anima sua in prigione. Ello re domandò in ke maniera, e quelli mostraro la carta. Allora il Re s'umiliò e disse, non piaccia addio kell'anima di così valente uomo stea in prigione per moneta, e conmandò ke fossero pagati e così furo. Poi venne Beltramo d'Albornio in sua forza, e quelli lo domandò e disse. Tu diciesti k'avei più senno ke uomo del mondo or ov'è tuo senno? Beltramo rispose, Messere, io l'o perduto. E quando l'ai perduto? Messere quando vostro figliuolo morio. Allora conobbe lo Re kel senno k'elli avea sì era per bontà del figliuolo, silli perdonò e donolli molto nobilemente.

him the other part of the goblet. And he was so full of courtesy that one night a band of poor knights entered his chambers, truly believing that the young king was asleep. They gathered up all his clothes and arms, intending to commit theft. There was one most reluctant to leave behind a lavish blanket which was covering the king. He grabbed it and began to pull. The king, so as not to remain exposed, grabbed his side and held firmly as the other man pulled, until the other knights were summoned to lend a hand. And then the king spoke, "This is not just thievery, but robbery, that is, the act of taking by force." When they heard him speak, whom they originally believed to be asleep; the knights fled. One day the old king,[5] father of the young king, strongly reprimanded him, saying, "Where is your treasure?" And he replied, "Sire, I have a greater treasure than you." And from this a yes and no battle of words ensued.[6] The day dawned when each was to show the other his treasure. The young king invited all the barons in the land to gather at that place on the specified day. That day his father had a rich pavilion erected, and had gold and silver in plates and vases brought forward, and weapons aplenty, as well as an infinite number of precious stones. He spilled all his treasures onto carpets and said to his son, "And where is your treasure?" Then the son unsheathed his sword from its scabbard. The assembled knights secured all the roads and squares. The entire land seemed full of knights. The king could not defend himself. The gold remained the property of the young man, who said to his knights, "Take this, for the treasure is yours." One took gold, another a vase. One took one thing, another something else, until it was all quickly distributed. Then the father regrouped his forces to vanquish his son who had shut himself up in a castle with Bertran de Born.[7] The father stormed the castle. The young king became overconfident, and one day, by sorry chance, a blunted arrow pierced his brow.[8] And so misfortune, which had begun to follow him, finally killed him. But before he died, all his creditors came and demanded reparation for the treasures they had lent him. The young king replied, "Gentlemen, you have come at a bad time, for your treasures have been dispersed. Even my arms have been given away. My body is sick, and you can no longer expect me to make good my pledges." But he summoned a notary, and when the notary came, this courteous king said, "Write down that I obligate my soul to perpetual prison until all of you have been properly paid." Then he died. After his death, they went to his father and demanded money.[9] The father replied bitterly, saying, "You are the men who lent my son the means to wage war against me. Leave this place for I swear with all my power that you risk the loss of your hearts and your possessions." Then one man spoke up and said, "Sire, we will not be the losers here, for we have your son's soul in prison." And the king asked how this could be possible, and they showed him the document. Then the king was humiliated, and said, "It cannot please God to have the soul of such a valiant man remain in prison for money." He commanded that they be paid, and so they were. Then Bertran de Born fell to the king's forces, and the king asked him, "You claimed to be the wisest man in the world. Where now is your wisdom?" Bertran replied, "Sire, I lost it." "And when did you lose it?" "Sire, when your son died." Then the king understood that this man's wisdom was the product of his son's goodness. He pardoned him and bestowed many noble gifts upon him.[10]

Novella XXI.

Come tre maestri di nigromantia vennero alla Corte dello'mperadore Federigo.

Lo'mperadore Federigo fue nobillissimo singniore ella gente k'avea bontade venia allui da tutte parti perkè l'uomo donava volontieri e mostrava belli sembianti a ki avesse alcuna spetiale bontà. Allui venieno Sonatori, Trovatori, e belli Favellatori, Uomini d'arti, Giostratori, Skermitori d'ogni maniera gente. Stando lo'mperadore Federigo e faciea dare l'acqua le tavole coverte, si giunsero allui tre Maestri di Nigromantia con tre schiavine[a] salutaronlo così di subito et elli domandò, quale è il maestro di voi tre? L'uno si trasse avanti e disse. Messer io sono. Ello'mperadore il pregò ke giuocasse cortesemente. Et elli gittaro loro incantamenti e feciero loro arti. Il tempo incominciò atturbare, ecco una pioggia repente e' tuoni, e' fulgori, e' baleni, e parea ke fondesse una grangniuola ke parea copelli d'acciaio. I cavalieri fuggiendo per le camere ki in una parte ki in una altra. Rischiarossi il tempo. Li maestri chiesero commiato e kiesero guidardone. Lo'mperadore disse, domandate. Que domandaro? Il Conte di S. Bonifatio era più presso allo'mperadore. Que dissero? Messere conmandate a costui ke venga in nostro soccorso contra li nostri nemici. Lo'mperadore li le comandò molto teneramente. Misessi il Conte in via colloro. Menaronlo in una bella cittade, cavalieri li mostraro di gran paraggio, e bel destriere, e belle arme li apprestaro, e dissero, questi sono atte ubbidire. Li nemici vennero a battaglia. Il Conte li sconfise e francò lo paese. E poi ne fecie tre delle battaglie ordinate in campo. Vinse la terra. Diedelli moglie. Ebbe figliuoli. Doppo molto tempo tenne la singnioria. Lasciaronlo grandissimo tempo, poi ritornaro. Il figliuolo del Conte avea già bene quaranta anni. Il Conte era vecchio. Li maestri tornaro e dissero ke volevano andare a vedere lo'mperadore ella corte. Il Conte rispose. Lo'mperio sia ora più volte mutato, le genti siano ora tutte nuove, dove ritornerei? E' maestri dissero, noi vitti volemo al postutto menare. Misersi in via camminaro gran tempo. Giunsero in corte. Trovaro lo'mperadore e' suoi Baroni k'ancor si dava l'acqua la quale si dava, quando il Conte n'andò co' maestri. Lo'mperadore li faciea contare la novella que la contava. I'o poi moglie. Figliuolo k'anno quaranta anni. Tre battaglie di campo o poi fatte il mondo è tutto rivolto come va questo fatto? Lo'mperadore li le fa raccontare con grandissima festa a' Baroni et a' Cavalieri.

Novella XXI.

How three masters of necromancy[1] came to the court of the Emperor Frederick.[2]

The Emperor Frederick was a very noble lord and gifted people came to him from all over the world because the man gave most willingly and welcomed most heartily anyone who had a special talent.[3] To him came musicians, troubadours,[4] tellers of beautiful tales, men trained in the arts, jousters and fencers; people with every imaginable skill. One day, while at table, the Emperor Frederick was having water poured,[5] when three masters of necromancy, dressed in pilgrims' gowns,[6] arrived. They greeted him immediately and he asked, "Which of you three is the master?" One man stepped forward and said, "Sire, I am he."[7] And the Emperor asked courteously if he would demonstrate his powers. And they began to conjure enchantments and to practice their arts. The weather became turbulent, sudden rains arrived with thunder, lightning and flashes of light. Suddenly hail appeared which seemed like molten steel poured from cupels. All the knights fled to their rooms, one went one way, others went another. The weather cleared and the masters asked permission to leave, requesting recompense. The Emperor said, "Ask what you will." What did they ask for? The Count of Saint Boniface[8] was seated closest to the Emperor. These necromancers said, "Sire, command that man to come to our aid against our enemies." The Emperor, most tenderly, ordered him to go. The count set out on the road with them. They led him to a beautiful city. Knights of noble lineage were presented to him and they prepared him with a handsome steed and fine armor. And they said, "These knights owe allegiance to you." The enemy came to battle. The count defeated them and liberated the country. And then he went out into the field and conducted three battles and won over the entire land. He was given a wife and had children. After much time he became lord of the land. The masters had left him for much time and then returned. The count's son was now well over forty years old and the count himself had grown old. The masters returned and said that they wished to go to see the Emperor and his court. The count replied, "The Empire must have changed many times by now. The people must all be new. What would I be returning to?" And the masters said, "Above all else we wish to lead you back there." They set out and traveled for a long time. Finally they arrived at the court. They found the Emperor and his barons still having water poured, just as they had been doing when the count had left with the masters. The Emperor asked him to tell his tale, and this he did. "I now have a wife. My children are in their forties. I have fought three battles in the field. The world has been turned upside down. How can this be?" The Emperor had him retell his tale with great pomp and circumstance to his barons and knights.

Novella XXII.

Come allo'mperadore Federigo fuggì un Astore dentro in Melano.

Lo'mperadore Federigo, stando ad assedio a Melano, silli fuggì un suo Astore e volò dentro a Melano. Fecie Ambasciadori errimandò per esso. La potestade ne tenne consiglio. Arringatori v'ebbe assai. Tutti dicieano ke cortesia era arrimandarlo più k'a tenerlo. Un Melanese vecchio di gran tempo consiglio alla podestà[a] e' disse così. Come ci è l'Astore così ci fosse lo'mperadore, kennoi lo faremmo disentire di quello k'elli fa al distretto di Melano. Perk'io consiglio kennon lissi mandi. Tornaroli Ambasciadori e contaro allo'mperadore siccome consiglio n'era tenuto. Lo'mperadore udendo questo disse, come può essere? Trovossi in Melano niuno ke contradiciesse alla proposta? Risposero li Ambasciadori, messer sì. E ke uomo fu? Messere fu uno vecchio. Ciò non può essere, rispose lo'mperadore, ke uomo vecchio diciesse sì grande villania. Messere pur fue. Ditemmi, disse lo'mperadore, di ke fattione e di ke era vestito? Messere era canuto e vestito di vergato. Ben può essere, disse lo'mperadore, da ke è vestito di vergato k'elli è un matto.

Novella XXIII.

Come lo'mperadore Federigo trovò un Poltrone[a] a una fontana e chieselli bere e poi li tolse il suo Barlione.[b]

Andando lo'mperadore Federigo a una caccia con veste verdi siccome era usato, trovò un Poltrone a una fontana in sembianti, et avea distesa una tovaglia biankissima insull'erba verde et avea suo Tamericie[c] con vino e suo Mazzero[d] molto polito. Lo'mperadore giunse e chieselli bere. Il Poltrone rispose, con ketti dare io bere? A questo nappo non porrai tu bocca. Settu ai corno[e] del vino ti do io volentieri. Lo'mperadore rispose, prestammi tuo Barlione et io berrò per convento ke mia bocca non vi apprestarà. Ello Poltrone li le porse e tennelli lo convenente. E poi non li le rendeo anzi spronò il cavallo e fuggì col Barlione. Il Poltrone avisò bene ke de' cavalieri dello'mperadore fosse. L'altro giorno andò alla corte. Lo'mperadore disse alli uscieri, secci viene un Poltrone di cotal guisa fatelmi venire dinanzi e non li fermate porta. Il Poltrone venne. Fu dinanzi allo'mperadore. Fecie il compianto di suo Barlione. Lo'mperadore li fecie contare la novella più volte in grande solazzo. Li Baroni l'udiro con gran festa. Ello'mperadore disse, conoscieresti tu tuo Barlione? Sì Messere. Allora lo'mperador si trasse lo Barlione di sotto per dar adiveder k'elli era suto. Allora lo'mperadore per la nettezza di colui li donò molto riccamente.

Novella XXII.

How a goshawk[1] *of the Emperor Frederick*[2] *fled into the city of Milan.*

The Emperor Frederick was attacking Milan,[3] when one of his goshawks fled from him and flew into the city of Milan. He sent ambassadors, asking for the return of this bird. The podesta[4] called together a counsel. Haranguers attended aplenty. Everyone stated that chivalry required the return of the hawk, rather than retaining it. An old Milanese, who had served for many years as counsellor to the podesta, spoke thus, "The goshawk came to us as if it were the Emperor, so that we could make him repent for all the distress he has caused Milan. For this reason I recommend that we do not send the bird back to him." The ambassadors returned and recounted everything to the Emperor, just as it had occurred at counsel. The Emperor, hearing this, said, "How can this be? Was there anyone to be found in Milan that went contrary to our proposal?" The ambassadors replied, "Yes, Sire." "And who was this man?" "Sire, he was an old man." "This cannot be," replied the Emperor, "that an old man should utter such great villainy." "Sire, and yet it happened just so." "Tell me," said the Emperor, "What did he look like and how was he dressed?" "Sire, his hair was white and his dress was striped." "This I can believe," said the Emperor, "for only madmen are dressed in stripes."[5]

Novella XXIII.

How the Emperor Frederick[1] *came across a lazy idler at a fountain and asked him for a drink and then took his belt flask.*[2]

One day, while out hunting dressed in customary green,[3] the Emperor Frederick came across a man at a fountain, who appeared to be a lazy idler. The man had spread out a spotless white tablecloth on the green grass, along with a tamarisk flagon filled with wine and a clean, long loaf of corn-cob bread. The Emperor approached him and asked for something to drink. The idler replied, "With what can I give you to drink? You will not place your mouth on my goblet. If you had a horn flask, I'd give you some wine willingly." The Emperor replied, "Lend me your belt flask and I swear that I will drink from it in such a way that my mouth never comes near to it." And the idler handed it to him and the Emperor kept his promise. But afterward, he did not return it, but spurred his horse away and fled with the flask. The idler understood well that he was a knight of the Emperor. The next day he went to the court. The Emperor said to his bailiffs, "If a man who appears to be an idler comes here, have him brought to me and don't bar the gate to him." The idler came. He was brought before the Emperor. He complained about his flask. For his enjoyment, the Emperor had him retell his tale many times. The barons listened with great amusement. And then the Emperor said, "Would you recognize your flask?" "Yes, Sire." Then the Emperor reached down and brought up the flask for all to see that it was there. Then the Emperor rewarded this man most richly for his cleanliness.[4]

Novella XXIIII.

Come lo'mperadore Federigo fecie una quistione a duo Savi e come li guidardonò.

Messere lo'mperadore Federigo si avea duo grandissimi Savi; l'uno avea nome Messer Bolgaro ell'altro Messer M. Stando lo'mperadore un giorno tra questi Savi, l'uno si era dalla destra parte ell'altro dalla sinestra. Ello'mperadore fecie loro una quistione e disse. Singniori secondo la vostra leggie poss'io a' sudditi miei a cui io mi voglio torre ad uno e dare ad un altro sanza altra cagione? Acciò ke io sono singniore. E dicie la leggie kecciò ke piacie al Singnior si è leggie intra i sudditi suoi. Dite se io lo posso fare poi kemmi piacie. L'uno de' duo Savi rispose. Messere ciò ketti piacie puoi fare de' sudditi tuoi sanza colpa. L'altro rispose e disse. Messer amme non pare. Però kella leggie è giustissima elle sue conditioni si vogliono giustissimamente osservare e seguitare. Quando voi togliete si vuole sapere perkè. Et a cui date. Perkè l'uno ell'altro Savio diciea vero ad ambi due donoe. All'uno donò capello scarlatto e palafreno bianco. Et all'altro donò ke faciesse una leggie a suo senno. Di questo fu quistione intra Savi a cui avea più riccamente donato. Fue tenuto ke a colui k'avea detto, ke poteva dare e torre come li piaciea donasse robbe e palafreno come a Giullare perkè'll avea lodato. A colui ke seguitava la guistitia si diede affare una leggie.

Novella XXV.

Come il Soldano donò a uno dugento marki, e come il Tesoriere li scrisse veggiente lui ad uscita.

Saladino fu Soldano nobilissimo Singniore prode e largo. Un giorno donava a uno dugento marki kell'avea presentato uno paniere di rose di verno ad una stufa. Il Tesoriere suo dinanzi dal lui si scrivea ad uscita scorselli la penna e scrisse trecento. Disse il Saladino, ke fai? Disse il Tesoriere, Messere errava e volle dannare il sopra più. Allora il Saladino parlò. Non dannare scrivi quattro cento. Per mala ventura s'una tua penna sarà più larga di me. Questo Saladino al tempo del suo Soldanato ordinò una triegua trallui e' Cristiani e disse di voler vedere i nostri modi e selli piaciessero diverebbe cristiano. Fermossi la triegua. Venne il Saladino in persona a veder la costuma de' Cristiani. Vide le tavole messe per mangiare con tovaglie bianchissime lodolle molto. E vide l'ordine delle tavole ove mangiava il Re di Francia. Partito dall'altre lodollo assai. Vide le tavole ove mangiavano i maggiorenti lodolle assai. Vide come li poveri mangiavano in terra umilmente. Questo riprese forte e biasimò molto kelli amici di lor Singniore mangiavano più vilmente e più basso. Poi andaro li Cristiani a veder la costuma loro. Videro ke i Saracini mangiavano in terra assai laidamente. Il Soldano

Novella XXIIII.

How the Emperor Frederick[1] posed a question to two wise men[2] and how he rewarded them.

The Lord, Emperor Frederick had two very great wise men, one named Mister Bolgaro[3] and the other Mister M.[4] One day the Emperor stood between these two wise men, one on his right side and the other on his left.[5] And the Emperor posed a question to them, saying, "Gentlemen, according to your law, can I take, if I so wish, from one of my subjects and give to another, without any other reason except that I am a lord? And the law says that what is pleasing to the lord is law among his subjects. Tell me if I may do so, when it pleases me."[6] One of the two wise men replied, "Sire, you can do anything you please to your subjects, without blame." The other replied saying, "Sire, to me it does not seem so. Since the law is extremely just, its conditions must be most justly observed and followed. When you take from someone, he will wish to know why and to whom you are giving." Since both wise men spoke the truth, he rewarded both of them. To one he gave a scarlet hat and a white palfrey. And to the other he gave the opportunity to use his intellect to effect a law. From this, discussion ensued among the wise men, who debated which man was more richly recompensed. It was decided that to him who had said that the Emperor could give and take as he pleases, clothes and a palfrey were given, as to a minstrel who had flattered him. To him who followed justice, he gave the ability to make law.[7]

Novella XXV.

How the Sultan[1] gave two hundred marks[2] to a man, and how his treasurer wrote it down as he watched.

Saladin[3] was the Sultan, a very noble lord, valiant and generous.[4] One day he gave a man two hundred marks for presenting him with a basket of roses in winter which had blossomed by the heat from a stove. In front of him, his treasurer began writing down the transaction, and, as the words escaped from his pen, the Sultan observed as he wrote, *three hundred*. The Sultan said, "What are you doing?" The treasurer said, "Sire, I've made an error and I wish to correct it above." Then the Saladin spoke, "Don't correct it, but write, *four hundred*. What a misfortune it would be if your pen were more generous than I." This Saladin, during his Sultanate, ordered a truce between the Christians and himself, and he said that he would like to see our customs and, if they pleased him, he would become a Christian.[5] The truce was established. Saladin came in person to see the Christian customs.[6] He saw tables prepared for meals with pristine white tablecloths, and he praised them very much. And he saw the orderliness of the tables where the King of France[7] was eating, set apart from the others, and he praised them greatly. He saw the tables where the elders were eating, and he praised them greatly. He saw how the poor were humbly eating on the ground. He strongly

fecie tender suo padiglione assai ricco là dove mangiavano, et in terra fecie coprir di tapeti i quali erano tutti lavorati a croci spessissime. I Cristiani stolti entrarono dentro andando con li piedi su per quelle Croci sputandovi suso siccome in terra. Allora parlò il Soldano e ripreselli forte. Voi predicate la Crocie e spreggiatella tanto? Così pare ke voi amiate vostro Iddio in sembianti di parole ma non in opera. Vostra maniera e vostra guisa non mi piacie. Ruppessi la triegua erricominciossi la guerra.

Novella XXVI.

Qui conta d'uno Borghese di Francia.

Uno Borghese di Francia avea una sua moglie molto bella. Un giorno era a una festa con altre donne della villa. Et avevavi una molto bella donna la quale era molto sguardata dalle genti ella moglie del Borghese dicieva infrasse medesima. Se io avessi così bella cotta[a] com'ella io sarei altresì sguardata come ella. Perk'io sono altresì bella come sia ella. Tornò a casa al suo marito. E mostrolli cruccioso sembiante. Il marito la domandava sovente perkè ella stava crucciata. Ella donna rispose, perk'io non sono vestita sì ke io possa dimorare con l'altre donne. Kè a cotale festa l'altre donne kennon sono così belle com'io, erano sguardate et io no, per mia laida cotta. Allora suo marito le promise del primo guadangnio ke prendesse di farle una bella cotta. Poki giorni dimorò ke venne allui un Borghese e domandolli dieci marki in prestanza. Et offersellinе duo marki di guadangnio a cierto termine. Il marito rispose, io nonne farò neente. Però kell'anima mia ne sarrebbe obbrigata allo'nferno. Ella moglie rispose, ai disleale traditore tul fai per non farmi la mia cotta. Allora il Borghese per la puntura della moglie prestò l'argento a duo marki di guidardone e fecie la cotta a sua mogliera. La moglie andò al monistero con l'altre donne. In quella stagione v'era Merlino. Et uno parlò e disse. Per San Iani quella è bellissima Dama e Merlino il saggio profeta parlò e disse. Veramente è bella se i nemici di Dio non avessero parte in sua cotta. Ella Dama si volse e disse. Ditemmi come i nemici di iddio anno parte in mia cotta. Rispose. Dama io lo vi dirò. Membravi quando voi foste a cotal festa dove l'altre donne erano sguardate più ke voi per vostra laida cotta? E tornaste e mostraste cruccio a vostro marito? Et elli impromise di farvi una cotta del primo guadangnio ke prendesse? E da ivi a poki giorni venne un Borghese per dieci marki in presto a due marki di guadangnio, onde voi v'induceste vostro marito? E di sì malvagio guadangnio è vostra cotta. Ditemmi Dama se io fallo di neente. Cierto Sire no, rispose la Dama. E non piaccia addio nostro Sire kessì malvagia cotta stea forme. E veggente tutta la gente lassi spogliò. E pregò Merlino kella prendesse a diliverare di sì malvagio periglio.

reprimanded them and greatly criticized the fact that the friends of their Lord were forced to eat in such a vile and base manner.[8] Then the Christians went to see their customs. They saw the Saracens eating on the very filthy ground. The Sultan had an elaborate pavilion erected where they could eat, and had the ground covered with carpets, all intricately worked and densely decorated with crosses. The foolish Christians entered, walking all over those crosses and spitting on them as if they were on bare ground. Then the Sultan spoke and he strongly reprimanded them. "You preach the cross, yet you treat it with such scorn? As such, it seems that you love your God in words but not in deeds.[9] I do not like your manners nor your methods." He broke the truce and the war began once again.

Novella XXVI.

Here is told of a townsman[1] *of France.*

A townsman of France had a very pretty wife. One day she went to a celebration with other women from the village. And there was a very pretty woman present whom everyone stared at intently and the wife of the townsman said to herself, "If I had a long dress as pretty as hers, I would be stared at as much as she, because I am just as pretty." She returned home to her husband with an irritated look upon her face. Her husband asked her repeatedly why she was so irritated. The woman replied, "Because I am not dressed in a manner which allows me to stay with all the other women; because at that celebration the other women, who are not as pretty as I, were stared at and not me, all because of my ugly dress." Then her husband promised her that he would use his next earnings to have a pretty dress made for her. A few days later another townsman came to him asking for a loan of ten marks.[2] And he offered two marks in interest to be paid after a determined period of time. The husband replied, "I will do no such thing that would oblige my soul to hell."[3] And his wife replied, "Oh, disloyal traitor, you're doing this to get out of having my dress made." Then the townsman, because of his wife's stinging words, lent the silver for the two marks recompense and had his wife's dress made. His wife went to a monastery with the other women. During that time, Merlin[4] was there. And a man spoke to him and said, "By Saint John, that is a beautiful lady," and Merlin the wise prophet spoke and said, "She truly is beautiful; if only the enemies of God had not had a hand in making her dress." And the lady turned to him and said, "Tell me how the enemies of God had a part in making my dress." He replied, "Lady, I will tell you how. Remember when you went to that celebration where the other women were being stared at more than you because of your ugly dress? And you returned to your husband displaying such irritation? And he promised to have a dress made for you from his next earnings? And a few days later a townsman came to him asking for a loan of ten marks, offering two marks in interest, which you pressed your husband to accept? From these evil earnings came your dress. Tell me, lady, if I err in any way?" "Certainly not, Sire," replied the lady, "And it cannot be pleasing to Our Lord that such an evil dress stay on my body." And she stripped the frock off, for all present to see. And she begged Merlin to take it and deliver her from such an evil danger.

Novella XXVII.

Qui conta d'uno grande Moaddo[a] *a cui fu detta villania.*

Uno grande Moaddo andò ad Alexandro et andava un giorno per sue bisogne per la terra, et un altro li venia di dietro e dicievalli molta villania e molto lo spregiava e quelli non facieva niuno motto. Et uno lissi fecie dinanzi e disse. O kè non rispose a colui ke tanta villania ti dicie. E quelli sofferente rispose e disse a colui kelli diciea ke rispondesse. Io non rispondo perk'io non odo cosa kemmi piaccia.

Novella XXVIII.

Qui conta della costuma ke era nello Reame di Francia.

Costuma era nel Reame di Francia kell'uomo ke era dengnio d'esser disonorato e giustitiato si andava in sullo carro. E s'avenisse ke campasse la morte mai non trovava ki volesse usare nè stare con lui per niuna cagione. Lancialotto quand'elli venne forsennato per amore della Reina Ginevra si andò in sulla carretta e feciessi tirare per molte luogora e da quello giorno innazi non si spregiò più la carretta kelle donne elli cavalieri di gran paraggio vi vanno ora su a solazzo. Oi mondo errante et uomini sconoscenti di poca cortesia quanto fu maggiore lo singniore nostro ke fecie il Cielo ella Terra, kennon fu Lancialotto ke fu un cavaliere di scudo e mutò errivolse così grande costuma nel Reame di Francia ke era Reame altrui. E Giesù Cristo nostro singniore non poteo perdonando a' suoi offenditori fare ke niuno uomo perdoni. E questo volle e fecie nel Reame suo a' quelli kello puosero in crocie a coloro perdonò e pregò il suo padre per loro.

Novella XXIX.

Qui conta come i savi Astrologi disputavano del cielo Impireo.

Grandissimi savi stavano in una scuola a Parigi e diputavano del ciel Impereo e molto ne parlavano disiderosamente. E come stava di sopra li altri cieli. Contavano il cielo dove Giuppiter Saturno e Mars, e quel del Sole e di Mercurio e della Luna. E come sopra tutti stava lo'mpireo cielo. E sopra quello sta Dio padre in maestade sua. Così parlando venne un matto, e disse loro. Singniori e sopra il capo di quel Singniore ke a? L'uno rispose a gabbo. Avvi un capello. El matto se n'andò, e' savi rimasero. Disse l'uno, tu credi al matto un capello aver dato. Ma elli è rimaso a noi. Or diciamo sopra capo ke a. Assai ciercaro loro scientie. Non trovaro neente allora dissero. Matto è

Novella XXVII.

Here is told of a great Mu'addib[1] to whom many insults were directed.

A great Mu'addib went to Alexander,[2] and one day was going about his business throughout the land when another man began following him everywhere, insulting him greatly and treating him with much disdain; yet the man answered not a word. And another man came before him and said, "Why do you not respond to this man who is saying such insulting things about you?" And this long-suffering man answered this one who told him to reply, "I do not respond because I hear nothing which pleases me."

Novella XXVIII.

Here is told of a custom that was held in the kingdom of France.

There was a custom in the kingdom of France, whereby any man who was deserving of dishonor or execution was led about on a cart.[1] And if it happened that he survived death, he would never again find anyone who would make use of him or stay with him for any reason. Lancelot,[2] when he went insane for the love of Guenevere,[3] traveled about on a cart and had himself carried to many different places.[4] And from that day on, no one held the cart in disdain anymore; in fact, ladies and knights from illustrious families now travel about on them for pleasure. Oh wayward world and stupid, discourteous men, how much greater was Our Lord, who made heaven and earth, than Lancelot, who was but a knight of the sword, and yet he changed and overturned such a great custom in the kingdom of France, which was the kingdom of others. And Jesus Christ, Our Lord, could not, while pardoning those who offended him, find any man to pardon him. And this he desired and did, in his own kingdom, for those who placed him on the cross. And he pardoned them and prayed to His Father for them.

Novella XXIX.

Here is told how wise astrologers discussed the heaven of the Empyrean.[1]

There were great wise men[2] at a school in Paris[3] who were discussing the heavenly Empyrean, and about this they spoke most willingly. And they stated that it was above all the other heavens. They spoke of the heavens of Jupiter, Saturn and Mars, and those of the Sun and Mercury and the moon.[4] And how above all these was the heavenly Empyrean. And above this was God the Father in all his majesty. While discussing these matters, a crazy man appeared and said to them, "Gentlemen, and above the head of God, what is there?" One sage replied jokingly, "Why his hat of course." And then the crazy man went away, while the wise men remained. One man said, "You think that you have pulled the crazy man's hat over his eyes, but it is he who has done

colui ke è sì ardito kella mente mette di fuor del tondo. E via più matto e forsennato è colui ke pena e pensa di sapere il suo principio. È sanza veruno senno ki vuole sapere li suoi profondissimi pensieri.

Novella XXX.

Qui conta come uno cavaliere di Lombardia dispese il suo.

Uno cavaliere di Lombardia era molto amico dello'mperadore Federigo et avea nome .G. il quale non avea reda niuna bene avea gente di suo lengniaggio. Puosessi in quore di voler tutto dispendere alla vita sua sìke non rimanesse il suo dopo lui. Istimò quanto potesse vivere, e soprapuosessi bene anni dieci. Ma tanto non si soprapuose ke dispendendo e scialacquando il suo li anni sopravennero e soperchiolli tempo errimase povero kè avea tutto dispeso. Puosessi mente nel povero stato suo erricordossi dello'mperadore Federigo ke grande amistade avea collui e nella sua corte molto avea dispeso e donato. Propuosessi de andare allui credendo kell'accogliesse a grandissimo amore. Andò allo'mperadore e fu dinanzi dallui. Domandò ki e' fosse tutto ke bene lo conoscea. Quelli li racontò suo nome. Domandò di suo stato. Contò lo cavaliere come li era incontrato. E come il tempo li era soperchiato. Lo'mperadore rispose. Esci di mia corte e sotto pena della vita non venire in mia forza impero kettusse' quelli ke non volei ke dopo i tuoi anni niuno avesse bene.

Novella XXXI.

Qui conta d'uno Novellatore di Messere Azzolino.

Messere Azzolino avea uno suo Novellatore il quale faciea favolare quando erano le notti grandi di verno. Una notte avenne kel favolatore avea grande talento[a] di dormire. Et Azzolino il pregava ke favolasse. Il favolator incominciò addire una favola d'uno villano k'avea suoi cento bisanti. Il quale andò a uno mercato a comperare berbici[b] et ebbene due per bisante. Tornando con le sue pecore. Uno fiume k'avea passato era molto cresciuto per una grande pioggia ke venuta era. Stando alla riva vide uno pescator povero con uno suo burchiello[c] adismisura picciollino sì kennon vi capea sennon il Villano et una pecora per volta. Allora il Villano cominciò a passare con una berbicie e

so to us. Now let us discuss what really is found above the head of God." They began to search diligently through their science, but found nothing that spoke to the question, and so they said, "Crazy is he who is so presumptuous as to occupy his mind outside its reach. And even crazier and more insane is he who toils after and desires to know the original principle of existence. For he who wishes to know these most profound thoughts is truly lacking all intelligence."[5]

Novella XXX.

Here is told how a knight of Lombardy[1] dispensed of his possessions.

A knight of Lombardy, whose name was G.,[2] was a very good friend of the Emperor Frederick.[3] This man had no heirs, although he did have many other family relations. Somehow the desire settled in his heart to spend all he was worth during his lifetime so that nothing would remain after him. He estimated how long he might live and then added another ten years to this figure. But he did not add enough years, for, as he was recklessly spending and wasting his riches, the years came and went, and he lived beyond the expected time, and thus remained poor for having spent everything. In his mind he began to dwell on his poor circumstances and remembered the Emperor Frederick, who was such a grand friend to him, and who had given and dispensed much bounty from his court. He decided to go to him, thinking that he would be received with the greatest love. He went to the Emperor and appeared before him. The Emperor asked who he was, although he had recognized the knight well enough. The knight pronounced his name for him. The Emperor asked after his personal circumstances. The knight explained the agreement he had made with himself, and how the expected time had been surpassed. The Emperor replied, "Leave my court and, under penalty of death, do not venture again into this Empire which is under my authority; for you are one of those who wishes well on no one after your years have ended."

Novella XXXI.

Here is told of a story-teller of Master Azzolino.[1]

Master Azzolino had a story-teller whom he had narrate tales during the long winter nights. One night it happened that the story-teller had a great yearning to sleep. Yet Azzolino begged him to tell a tale. The story-teller began to relate a story of a peasant who had one hundred bezants.[2] The man went to a market to buy sheep, which he obtained at two sheep per bezant. Returning with his sheep, he found a river he had crossed greatly swollen because of a heavy rain which had occurred. Standing on the bank, he saw a poor fisherman in a wherry so small that it could only carry one sheep and the peasant at a time. So the peasant began to carry across each sheep, rowing across the wide river. He rowed and crossed. And here the story-teller ceased speaking. And

cominciò a vogare[d] lo fiume era largo. Voga e passa. Ello favolatore restò di favolare. Et Azzolino disse, Va oltre. Ello favolatore rispose, lasciate passare le pecore e poi racconterò il fatto, kelle pecore non sarebbeno passare in uno anno sì ke in tanto puote ben adagio dormire.

Novella XXXII.

Delle belle valentie di Riccar Loghercio del Illa.

Riccar Loghercio fu Singniore de Illa, e fu grande gentiluomo di Provenza e di grande ardir e prodezza a dismisura. E quando i Saracini vennero a combattere la Spangnia. Elli fu in quella battaglia kessi chiamò la Spangniata, e fulla più perigliosa battaglia ke fosse dallo tempo di quella di Troiani e di Greci in qua. Allora erano li Saracini in grandissima moltitudine e con molte generationi di stormenti[a] sì ke Riccar Loghercio fu il conducitor[b] della prima battaglia. E per cagione kelli cavalli non si poteano mettere avanti per lo sovento delli stormenti comandò a tutta sua gente ke volgessero tutte le groppe de' cavalli alli nemici, e tanto ricularo ke furo intra nemici. E poi quando furo intra i nemici così riculando ebbe la battaglia dinanzi e veniano uccidendo a destra et a sinestra sì ke misero i nemici a destruttione.

[c]E quando il Conte di Tolosa si combattea col conte di Provenza altra stagione si dismontò del destriere Riccar Loghercio e montò in su uno Mulo, et il Conte disse, ke è ciò Riccar? Messere io vo mostrare ke io non ci sono per cacciare nè per fuggire. Qui dimostrò la sua grande franchezza la quale era nella sua persona oltre gli altri cavalieri.

Novella XXXIII.

Qui conta una novella de Messere Imberal del Balzo.[a]

Messere Imberal del Balzo grande castellano di Provenza vivea molto ad algura[b] a guisa Spangniuola et uno filosofo k'ebbe nome Pitagora fu di Spangnia e fecie una tavola per istorlomia[c] nella quale secondo i dodici sengniali erano molte singnificationi d'animali. Quando li uccelli s'azzuffano. Quando l'uomo trova la donola nella via. Quando lo fuoco sona, e delle Giandaie e delle Gazze. E delle cornacchie e così di molti animali molte singnificationi secondo la luna. E così Messer Imberal cavalcando un giorno con sua compagnia andavassi prendendo guardia di questi uccelli perk'essi temea d'incontrare algure. Trovò una femina in cammino e domandolla e disse. Dimmi donna settu ai trovati o veduti in questa matina di questi uccelli siccome Corbi Cornille[d] o Gazze? Ella donna rispose. Sengnior ie[e] vit una Cornacchia in uno cieppo di salicie. Or mi di' donna verso qual parte teneva volta sua coda? Ella donna rispose. Sengnior ella avea volta verso il cul. Allora Messer Imberal temeo l'algura e disse alla sua compagnia.

Azzolino said, "Keep going." And the story-teller replied, "Let the sheep cross over and then I'll tell the rest of the tale, and since it will take more than a year for all the sheep to cross, in the mean time you might as well take it easy and go to sleep."[3]

Novella XXXII.

Concerning the fine abilities of Richard Loghercio of Ille.[1]

Richard Loghercio was the lord of Ille and he was a grand gentleman of Provence, one of great daring and bravery beyond measure. And when the Saracens came to war against Spain, he took part in that battle now known as the Spangniata,[2] which was the most perilous battle that was ever fought, from the time of the battle of the Trojans and the Greeks. At that time, the Saracens had arrived in great numbers, bringing with them many war machines which they had engineered. Richard Loghercio was in charge of the first battle. And because he could not get his horses to move forward, since they feared such strange war machines, he ordered all his men to turn their horses around, so that, arses first, they advanced into the ranks of their enemies. And then, when they were immersed in the enemy ranks, in this way, with arses forward, he conducted the battle, killing Saracens left and right, completely destroying his enemy.

And another time, when the Count of Toulouse[3] came to wage war[4] against the Count of Provence,[5] Richard Loghercio jumped down from his steed and mounted a mule. And the Count said, "What is this, Richard?" "Sir, I wish to show you that I am not one to be cast out or to flee." This demonstrated the great candor which resided in his person, far greater than that found in any other knight.

Novella XXXIII.

Here is told a tale about Master Imberal of Balzo.[1]

Master Imberal of Balzo was a great lord of a castle in Provence, who lived much of his life, following the Spanish way,[2] according to augury. And he had a philosopher from Spain, named Pythagoras,[3] who fashioned a table, based on astronomy,[4] on which the twelve signs[5] were represented by many animals;[6] such as, when birds battle one another, when a man encounters a weasel in the road,[7] and when fire sings. There were signs with jays[8] and magpies,[9] and with crows,[10] and so on, representing many animals signifying many things, according to the moon.[11] And so, one day, Master Imberal went riding with some companions, intent on observing these birds, for he feared an encounter with evil augury. He met a woman walking along, and asked her,[12] "Tell me, lady, if you have found or seen this morning any birds, like ravens,[13] crows, or magpies?" And the lady replied, "Sire, I saw a crow on a willow stump." "Now, lady, tell me, towards what part was its tail pointing?" And the lady replied, "Sire, it was pointing towards its arse." Then Master Imberal became frightened of this augury and said to his companions, "It

Covenga dieu ie non cavalkerai nì uoi[f] nì doman a questa algura. E molto si contò poi la novella in Provenza per novissima risposta k'avea fatto sanza pensare quella femina.

Novella XXXIIII.

Come due Nobili Cavalieri s'amavano di buono amore.

Due Nobili Cavalieri s'amavano di grande amore l'uno avea nome Messer .G. ell'altro Messere .S. Questi due Cavalieri s'aveano lungamente amato l'uno di questi si mise a pensare e disse così. Messere .G.[a] a uno bello palafreno se io li le keggio darebbelmelli? E così pensando faciea il partito nel pensiero diciendo, sì darebbe. E così tral sì el no vinse il partito kennon li le darebbe. Il Cavaliere fu turbato. E cominciò a venire col sembiante strano contro all'amico suo. E ciasuno giorno in pensare crescieva errinovellava il cruccio. Lasciolli di parlar e volgeasi quando elli passava in altra parte. Le genti si maravigliavano et elli medesimo si maravigliava forte. Uno giorno avenne ke Messere .S. il Cavaliere il quale avea il palafreno non poteo più sofferire andò allui e disse. Compangnio mio, perkè non mi parli tu? Perkè settu cruciato? Elli rispose, perk'io ti chiesi lo palafreno tuo, e tullo mi negasti. E quelli rispose, questo non fu già mai. Non può essere. Lo palafreno ella persona si è tua k'io t'amo come me medesimo. Allora lo Cavaliere si ricconciliò e tornò in sull'amistade usata erriconobbe ke non avea ben pensato.

Novella XXXV.

Qui conta del Maestro Taddeo di Bolongnia.

Maestro Taddeo leggiendo a' suoi scolari in medicina trovò ke ki continovo mangiasse nove dì petronciano[a] diverebbe matto. E provavallo secondo la Fisica. Uno suo scolaro udendo quel capitolo propuosessi di volerlo provare. Prese a mangiare de' petronciani et in capo di nove dì venne dinanzi al Maestro e disse. Maestro il cotale capitolo ke leggieste non è vero, però k'io l'oe provato e non sono matto. E pur alzossi, e mostrolli il culo. Scrivete, disse il Maestro, ke tutto questo è del petronciano e provato è. E facciassene nova chiosa.

is the will of God, according to this augury, that I not ride today or tomorrow." And afterward this tale was often told in Provence, because of the peculiar response that the woman, without thinking, had given.

Novella XXXIIII.

How two noble knights loved one another with a fine love.

Two noble knights loved one another with a very great love. One was called Master G. and the other Master S.[1] After these two had loved each other for a long time, one of them, while mulling over their relationship, said to himself, "Master S. has a beautiful palfrey; if I ask him, would he give it to me?" And, thinking in this manner, he began to debate within himself, wondering if his friend would give the horse to him. And so, amid this yes and no inner discussion, eventually the negative prevailed. The knight became angry. And he began to wear a strange look on his face, against his friend. And as each day passed, as he revisited the situation in his mind, his vexation grew. He ceased talking to his friend and would turn his back and cross the street when his friend passed by. Everyone was amazed and his friend was especially amazed. One day it happened that Master S., the knight who owned the palfrey, could not stand it any longer, and went to him and said, "Comrade of mine, why will you not speak to me? Why are you so angry?" And the other replied, "Because I asked you for your palfrey and you refused me." And the first knight answered, "Such a thing never happened. This cannot be, for both the palfrey and its owner are yours, for I love you as much as I love myself." Then the knight was reconciled and returned to his old friendly manner, recognizing the error of his thoughts.

Novella XXXV.

Here is told of Master Thaddeus of Bologna.[1]

While reading medicine to his students, Master Thaddeus came across a passage which stated that anyone who ate eggplant for nine consecutive days would go mad.[2] And this was proven according to the laws of physics. After hearing this chapter, one of his students proposed to put it to the test. He began eating eggplant and immediately after nine days he presented himself to his master, and said, "Master, that chapter which you read to us is not true, for I have tried it and I have not gone mad." He then rose to his feet, and revealed his arse for all to see. "Write," said the master, "that all that has been said about eggplant has been proven here." And he then proceeded to construct a new gloss about it.

Novella XXXVI.

Qui conta come uno Re crudele perseguitava i Cristiani.

Fue uno Re molto crudele il quale perseguita il popolo di Dio et era la sua grandissima potenza e neente poteva acquistare contro a quel popolo però ke Dio l'amava. Quel Re ragionò con Balaam profeta, e disse. Dimmi Balaam ke è ciò delli miei nemici? Sono assai io più poderoso dilloro e non posso loro tenere niuno danno? E Balaam rispose. Messere però ke sono popolo di Dio. Ma io farò così ke io andrò sopra loro e maladicierolli ettu darai la battaglia et averai sopra loro vittoria. Salio questo Balaam in su uno Asino et andò su a uno monte il popolo era quasi ke giù al piano. E quelli andava per maladirli dissù il monte. Allora l'Angelo di Dio lissi fecie dinanzi e non lo lasciava passare. Et elli pungea l'Asino credendo ke ombrasse e quelli parlò, non mi battere ke veggio qui l'Angelo di Dio con una Spada di fuoco in mano ke non mi lascia andare. Allora lo Profeta Balaam guardò e vide l'Angelo. Ell'Angelo parlò, Ke è ciò kettu vai a male dire il popolo di Dio? Incontanente lo benedi settu non vuoli morire, come tul volevi maladire. Andò il Profeta e benediciea lo popolo di Dio ello Re diciea, ke fai? Questo non è maladire e que' rispose, non può essere altro perokell'Angelo di Dio il mi comandò. Onde fa così. Tu ai di belle femine elli n'anno diskesta. To'ne una quantità e vestille riccamente e poni loro da petto una mosca d'oro o d'ariento cioè una boccola[a] con un fibbiaglio[b] nella quale sia intagliata l'Idola kettu adori, ke adorava la statua di Mars, e dirai così loro kelle non consentano se non promettano di adorar quella statua e figura di Mars. E poi quando averanno peccato io avrò balia di maladirli, ello Re così fecie. Tolsero di belle femine in quello modo e mandolle nel campo li uomini ne erano vogliosi consentivano et addoravano l'Idole poi peccavano con loro. Allora lo Profeta andò e maladisse il popolo di Dio, e Dio non li atoe.[c] E quello Re diede battaglia e sconfiselli tutti. Onde li giusti patiro la pena d'alquanti ke peccaro. Ravidersi e feciero penitentia, e cacciaro le femine, e riconciliarsi con Dio e tornaro nella loro libertade.

Novella XXXVII.

Qui conta d'una battaglia ke fu tra due Re di Grecia.

Due Re furo nelle parti di Grecia e l'uno era più poderoso dell'altro furo insieme a battaglia, lo più poderoso perdeo, tornò et andò in una camera maravigliandossi siccome avesse songniato, et al postutto non credeva avere combattuto intanto l'Angelo di Dio venne allui e disse. Come stai? Ke pensi? Tu non ai songniato anzi combattuto essei isconfitto. Ello Re guardò l'Angelo e disse, come può essere? Io avea tre cotante genti dillui. Ell'Angelo rispose. Però te avenuto kettusse' nemico di Dio. Allora lo Re rispose, o è lo nemico mio sì amico di Dio ke però m'abbia vinto? No, disse l'Angelo, ke

Novella XXXVI.

Here is told how a cruel king[1] persecuted the Christians.[2]

There once was a very cruel king who persecuted the people of God and, although he was immensely powerful, he could not acquire anything against those people because God loved them. The king discussed the situation with the prophet Balaam,[3] and said, "Tell me, Balaam, what is it about my enemies? I am so much more powerful than they, and yet I cannot inflict any damage upon them?" And Balaam replied, "Sire, it is because they are the people of God. But I will do the following. I will go and position myself above them and curse them; meanwhile you engage them in battle and victory will be yours." This Balaam mounted an ass[4] and journeyed up a mountain,[5] so that the people were almost below him on the plain. And he was going in order to curse them from the mountain top. Then the angel of God appeared in front of him and blocked his path. And he spurred his ass, suspecting it had become skittish. And the ass spoke to him, "Don't beat me, for here I see the angel of God, with a flaming sword in his hand, who won't let me pass." Then the prophet Balaam looked and saw the angel. And the angel spoke to him, "What is this, that you are going to curse the people of God? Quickly, bless these people, if you don't wish to die, in the same way you wanted to curse them." The prophet went on and blessed the people of God. And the king said, "What are you doing? This is not a curse." And he replied, "I cannot do otherwise, for the angel of God has commanded me so.[6] But you do the following.[7] You have many beautiful women who are longing for many things. Take some fabric and richly dress them, and place necklaces[8] of gold or silver on their breasts; that is, jewelry with clasps incised with the idol you worship," for he worshiped the statue of Mars.[9] "And tell them not to give themselves to the men unless they agree to worship the statue and image of Mars. And then, when they have sinned, they will be at the mercy of my curses." And the king did these things. He took and dressed some beautiful women in the manner described, and sent them onto the field. The men desired them, and agreed and worshipped the idol, and then they sinned with the women. Then the prophet went and cursed the people of God, and God did not help them. And the king attacked and defeated them all, whereby the just suffered punishment with the sinners. The people realized their crime and repented, and they drove out the women and reconciled themselves with God, who returned them to a state of freedom.

Novella XXXVII.

Here is told of a battle fought between two kings of Greece.[1]

There once were two kings somewhere in Greece, and one was more powerful than the other. They battled each other and the more powerful one lost. He went away and entered a room in a state of wonder, as if he were dreaming, for above all, he could

Dio fa vendetta del nemico suo col nemico suo. Vattu coll'oste tua da capo. Ettu lo sconfigerai come elli a fatto te. Allora questi andò erriccombatte col nemico suo e sconfisello e presello siccome l'Angelo avea detto.

Novella XXXVIII.

D'uno Strologo k'ebbe nome Melisus ke fu ripreso da una donna.

Uno lo quale ebbe nome Melisus grandissimo Savio in molte scientie. E spetialmente in istrologia secondo kessi leggie in libro sesto de' civitate dei. E conta ke questo Savio albergò una notte in una casetta di una feminella. Quando andò la sera alletto disse a quella feminella. Vedi donna l'uscio mi lascierai aperto sta notte perk'io sono costumato di levare a proveder le stelle. La femina lasciò l'uscio aperto. La notte piovve e dinanzi avea una fossa et empiessi d'acqua. Quando elli si levò sivvi cadde dentro quelli cominciò a cridare aiutorio. La femina domandò, ke ai? Que' rispose. Io sono caduto in una fossa. Oi cattivo, disse la femina. Or tu badi nel cielo e non ti sai tenere mente a' piedi. Levossi questa femina et aiutollo ke periva in una fossatella d'acqua per poca e per cattiva provedenza.

Novella XXXIX.

Qui conta del Vescovo Aldrobandino[a] come fu skernito da uno Frate.

Quando il Vescovo Aldrobandino vivea al vescovado suo d'Orbivieto[b] stando uno giorno al vescovado a tavola ov'erano Frati minori a mangiare et eravene uno ke mangiava una cipolla molto savorosamente e con fine appetito il Vescovo guardandollo disse a uno donzello.[c] Vammi a quello Frate e dilli ke volontieri li accambierei a stomaco. Lo donzello andò e disselile. Ello Frate rispose, va' di' a Messere ke ben credo kemm'accambierebbe a stomaco ma non a vescovado.

Novella XL.

D'uno uomo di Corte[a] ke avea nome Saladino.

Saladino lo quale era uomo di corte. Essendo in Cicilia un giorno ad una tavola per mangiare con molti cavalieri davassi l'acqua et uno cavaliere disse. Lava la bocca e

not believe that he had done battle. Meanwhile, an angel of God came to him and said, "How are you? What are you thinking? You have not been dreaming for you did do battle and were defeated." And the king looked at the angel and said, "How can this be? I have three times the men that he has?" And the angel replied, "This has happened because you are an enemy of God." Then the king replied, "Oh, and my enemy is God's friend, and for this reason he has won?" "No," said the angel, "for God avenges Himself on His enemies with His enemies. Return once again with your army, and you will defeat him as he did you." And so he went and once again fought his enemy and he defeated him and took him prisoner, just as the angel had foretold.

Novella XXXVIII.

Concerning an astrologer named Melisus[1] who was reprimanded by a woman.

There was a certain man named Melisus who was extremely learned in many sciences,and especially in astronomy, as one reads in the sixth book of *The City of God*.[2] And it is told that one night this wise man lodged in the cottage of a little woman. That evening, when he went to bed, he said to that little woman, "Lady, tonight see that you leave the front door open, for I am accustomed to rising to examine the stars." The woman left the front door open. It rained that night and a ditch in front of the door filled with water. When he arose, he fell into the ditch and began to scream for help. The woman asked, "What's wrong?" He replied, "I've fallen in a ditch." "Oh, you evil man," said the woman, "You're so intent on the heavens that you can't keep your mind on your feet." This woman arose and helped the man who, as bad luck would have it, had nearly perished in a silly, water-filled, little ditch.[3]

Novella XXXIX.

Here is told how the Bishop Aldobrandino[1] was mocked by a friar.

One day, when the Bishop Aldobrandino was living in his bishopric in Orvieto, he was at table, eating with some minor friars.[2] And there was one, whom the bishop watched, eating an onion with such zest and gusto that he said to a young squire, "Go to that friar for me, and tell him that I would gladly exchange stomachs with him." The young squire went and said this to him. And the friar replied, "Go and tell my lord that I am sure he would exhange stomachs with me, but not bishoprics."

Novella XL.

Concerning a minstrel named Saladino.[1]

One day, while he was in Sicily at table eating with many knights, Saladino, who was a minstrel, began to pour water over his hands, when one knight said to him, "Wash

non le mani. E Saladino rispose. Messer io non parlai oggi di voi. Poi quando piazzeggiavano[b] così riposando in sul mangiare fue domandato il Saladino per uno altro cavaliere così diciendo. Dimmi Saladino s'io volesse dire una mia novella[c] a cui la dico per lo più savio di noi. Il Saladino rispose. Messere ditella a kiunque vi pare il più matto. I cavalieri mettendollo in quistione pregarollo ke aprisse sua risposta. Il Saladino rispose. Alli matti ogni matto pare savio per la sua somiglianza. Adunque quando al matto sembrerà uomo più matto sia quel cotale più savio, però kel savere è contrario della mattezza. Ad ogni matto li savi paiono matti. Siccome a' savi i matti paiono veramente matti e di stoltitia pieni.

Novella XLI.

Una Novella di Messer Polo Traversaro.

Messer Polo Traversaro fu di Romangnia e fu lo più nobile uomo di tutta Romangnia e tutta quasi la singnoreggiava a keto. Avea tre cavalieri molto leggiadri e non parea loro ken tutta Romangnia avesse uomo ke potesse sedere con loro in quarto. E però là ove elli teneano corte aveano una panca di tre e più non ve ne capeano e niuno era ardito di sedervi per temenza della loro leggiadria. E tutto ke Messere Polo fosse loro maggiore, et ellino nell'altre cose l'ubbidiano. Ma pure in quello luogo leggiadro non usava sedere tutto ke confessavano ke elli era lo migliore uomo di Romangnia el più presso da essere il quarto ke niuno altro. Ke feciero i tre cavalieri vedendo ke Messer Polo li seguitava troppo, rimuraro un uscio d'un loro palagio perkè non vi entrasse. L'uomo era molto grosso di persona non potendovi entrare spogliossi et entrovvi in camiscia. Quelli quando il sentiro entraro nelle letta, e feciersi copri come malati. Messere Polo li credeva trovare a tavola trovolli nelle letta confortolli e domandolli dillor mala voglia, et avidessene bene e chiese conmiato e partissi dalloro. Quelli cavalieri dissero, questo non è giuoco. Andaro ad una Villa dell'uno ove avea bello castelletto con fosse e ponte levatoio puosersi in quore di fare quivi il verno. Un die v'andò Messer Polo con buona compangnia e quando ellino vollono entrare dentro elli levaro il ponte. Assai puote dire kenno vi entraro. Ritornaro indietro. Passato il verno ritornaro alla cittade. Messer Polo quando elli tornaro non si levò, e que' ristettero, ell'uno disse. O Messer per mala ventura ke cortesie sono le vostre quando i forestieri giungono a città voi non fate onore loro? E Messer Polo rispose, perdonatemmi Messere ke io non mi levo sennon per lo ponte kessi levò per me. Allora li cavalieri ne feciero grande festa. Morio l'uno de' cavalieri e quelli segaro la sua terza parte della panca ove sedeano quando il terzo fu morto, perkè non trovaro in tutta Romangnia niuno cavaliere ke fosse dengnio di sedere in suo luogo.

your mouth and not your hands." And Saladino replied, "But Sir, I have not spoken about you today." Then, while they were strolling about the town square, relaxing after having eaten their fill, Saladino was questioned by another knight who said, "Tell me, Saladino, if I wish to relate one of my tales, to whom would I direct myself as the wisest man among us?" Saladino replied, "Sir, tell your tale to whoever seems the maddest to you." The knights began to discuss this answer, and begged him to elaborate on his response. Saladino replied, "To madmen, every madman, because he resembles them, appears wise. Therefore, when, to a madman a man appears even madder than he, that man is probably much wiser, since wisdom is the opposite of madness. To every madman, the wise appear mad; just as, to the wise, the mad appear truly mad and full of stupidity."

Novella XLI.

A Tale concerning Master Polo Traversaro.[1]

Master Polo Traversaro was from Romagna and was considered the noblest man in all of Romagna. And he peacefully held dominion over almost all of the province. He had three very attractive knights who believed that in all of Romagna there could not be found a fourth knight worthy to sit with them. However, where they held court, there was a bench which could only accommodate three, and no one else dared to sit on it, for fear of their charms. And, although Master Polo was their superior, and in all other things they obliged him, still he was not allowed to sit in that place of distinction, even though the knights confessed that he was the best man in all of Romagna and worthier than any other to stand as a fourth with them. What did these three knights do when they saw Master Polo constantly following them? They walled up the entrance to one of their palaces so that he could not enter. The man was so very large in figure that, not being able to enter, he stripped off his clothes and entered in his undershirt. When the knights heard him, they took to their beds and covered themselves, feigning illness. Master Polo thought he would find them at table, but finding them in bed, he comforted them and asked after their ailments. When at last he realized the situation, he asked to take his leave, and left them. The knights said, "This is no longer a game." They went to a village where one knight had a lovely little castle with a moat and a drawbridge. They all earnestly desired to winter there. One day Master Polo happened by with a group of fine companions and, when they sought admittance, the knights raised the bridge. Suffice it to say that they could not enter and so they turned back. Winter having passed, the knights returned to the city. When they arrived, Master Polo did not rise from his seat and they remained standing and one said, "Oh Sire, by God, what kind of courtesy is this, that you do not honor strangers when they arrive in your city?" And Master Polo replied, "Pardon me, Sir, if I do not rise as the draw-bridge rose for me." The knights were greatly amused by this answer. One of the knights died, and the others sawed off that third of the bench where he used to sit before he died, for, in all of Romagna, they found no knight worthy of sitting in his place.

Novella XLII.

Qui conta bellissima novella di Guglielmo di Bergdam di Provenza.

Guglielmo di Bergdam fue nobile Cavaliere di Provenza al tempo del Conte Raimondo Berlinghieri. Uno giorno avenne ke' cavalieri si vantavano e Guglielmo si vantò kennon avea niuno nobile uomo in Provenza kennon li avesse fatto votare la sella e giacciuto con sua mogliera, e questo disse in udienza del Conte. El Conte rispose. Or mee? Guglielmo disse. Voi Singnior io lo vi dirò. Fecie venire suo destriere sellato e cinghiato bene li sproni in pie' mise il pie' nella staffa e quando fu ammannato parlò al Conte e disse. Voi Singniore nè metto nè traggo.[a] E monta a cavallo e sprona va via.[b] Il Conte s'adiroe molto que non venia a corte. Un giorno si ragunaro[c] donne a uno nobile convito, mandaro per Guglielmo di Bergdam ella Contessa vi fu e dissero. Or ci di' Guglielmo perkè ai tu così onite le donne di Provenza. Cara la comperrai. Katuna avea uno mattero[d] sotto. Quella ke parlava disse. Vedi Guglielmo ke per la tua follia ti convien morire. E Guglielmo parlò e disse vedendo kelli si era sorpreso, di una cosa vi prego donne per amore kemmi facciate un dono. Le donne risposero, domanda salvo kennon domandi tua scampa. Allora Guglielmo parlò e disse. Donne io vi prego per amore ke qual di voi èlla più putta mi dea in prima. Allora l'una riguardò l'altra non si trovò ki prima li volesse dare, e così scampò a questa volta.

Novella XLIII.

Qui conta di Messer Giacopino Rangone come elli fecie a un giullare.

Messere Giacopino Rangone nobile cavaliere di Lombardia stando un giorno a una tavola avea due inguistare[a] di finissimo vino bianco innanzi e vermiglio. Un Giucolare[b] stava a questa tavola e non s'ardiva chiedere di quel vino avendone grandissima voglia. Levossi sue e prese un miuolo[c] a lavollo di vantaggio. E poi kell'ebbe così lavato molto girò la mano. E disse, messere io lavato l'oe. E Messer Giacopino diede della mano nella guastada[d] e disse. Tu il pettinerai[e] altrove kennon qui. Il Giullare si rimase così e non ebbe del vino.

Novella XLIIII.

D'una quistione ke fu posta ad un uomo di corte.[a]

Marco Lombardo fue nobil uomo di corte e savio molto. Fu a uno Natale ad una cittade dove si donavano molte robbe e non ebbe niuna. Trovò un altro uomo di corte lo quale era nesciente appo lui et avea avuto robbe di questo nacque una bella sententia

Novella XLII.

Here is told a wonderful tale of William of Bergdam from Provence.[1]

William of Bergdam was a noble knight from Provence during the time of Count Raymond Berengar.[2] One day it happened, while the knights were all boasting, that William claimed that there was no knight in all of Provence that he had not unsaddled or with whose wife he had not lain. And this he said within hearing of the Count. And the Count replied, "And me too?" William said, "You, lord, now I will tell you." He had his steed brought, saddled and well-cinched, and with spurs on his feet, he placed his foot in the stirrup and readied himself. He then spoke to the Count as said, "You, Sire, I neither include nor exclude." He mounted his horse and spurred it away. The Count's rage was so fierce that he prohibited William from coming to court. One day many ladies were assembled at a noble banquet. They sent for William of Bergdam, and the Countess was there and the ladies said, "Now, tell us, William, why you find the women of Provence so onerous. Dearly you will pay for this." Each woman had a rolling-pin hidden under her skirts. She who was speaking said, "You see, William, because of your foolishness, you deserve to die." And William spoke and, seeing that he had been taken by surprise, said, "Ladies, in the name of love, I beg one thing of you, that you grant me one request." The ladies answered, "Ask anything, as long as you do not ask to be released." Then William spoke and said, "Ladies, in the name of love, I ask that she who is the biggest whore among you be the first to strike me." Then the ladies looked at one another, and not one was found willing to strike the first blow. And in this way William escaped; this time!

Novella XLIII.

Here is told what Master Giacopino Rangone[1] *did to a jester.*[2]

One day while at table, Master Giacopino Rangone, a noble knight of Lombardy, had two carafes of the finest white and red wines set before him. A juggler[3] was at the table who did not dare to ask for any wine, although he greatly desired some. He rose to his feet and took a cup and washed it meticulously. And then, after he had washed it so, he began to turn it in his hand. And he said, "Sire, I have washed this cup." And Master Giacopino picked up the water pitcher and said, "You will guzzle your fill elsewhere, but not here." The jester remained standing and had none of the wine.

Novella XLIIII.

Concerning a question posed to a minstrel.

Marco Lombardo,[1] a noble minstrel, was very wise indeed. One Christmas he found himself in a city which freely gave gifts of clothing, yet he received nothing. He met another minstrel, who was an ignoramus in comparison to Marco, yet this man had

ke quello giullare disse a Marco. Ke è ciò Marco? Ke io o avuto sette robbe ettu niuna. Essi settu troppo migliore e più savio di me. Quale è la cagione? E Marco rispose. Non è per altro sennon kettu trovasti più de' tuoi k'io non trovai de' miei.

Novella XLV.

Come Lancialotto si combattè a una fontana.

Messere Lancialotto si combattea un giorno a una fontana con uno cavaliere di Sansongnia lo quale avea nome .A. et combattevansi aspramente alle spade, dismontati delloro cavalli. E quando presero lena[a] domandò l'uno del nome del l'altro. Messere Lancialotto rispose. Dapoi kettu disideri mio nome, or sappi k'io o nome Lancialotto. Allora si cominciò la meslea[b] ello cavaliere parlò a Lancialotto e disse, più mi nuoce tuo nome kella tua prodezza. Perkè saputo il cavaliere era Lancialotto cominciò a dottare[c] la bontà sua.

Novella XLVI.

Qui conta come Narcis s'innamorò dell'ombra sua.

Narcis fu molto buono e bellissimo cavaliere. Un giorno avenne k'elli si riposava sopra una bellisima fontana. E dentro l'acqua vide l'ombra sua molto bellissima. E cominciò a riguardarla errallegravassi sopra alla fonte. E così credeva ke quella ombra avesse vita ke stesse nell'acqua e non si accorgeva ke fosse l'ombra sua. Cominciò ad amare et innamorare sì forte kella volle pigliare. Ell'acqua si turbò ell'ombra spario onde elli incominciò a piangere. E l'acqua schiarando vide l'ombra ke piangea. Allora elli si lasciò cadere nella fontana sì ke annegò. Il tempo era di prima vera. Donne si veniano a diportare alla fontana videro il bello Narcis affogato con grandissimo pianto lo trassero della fonte e così ritto l'appoggiaro alle sponde. Onde dinanzi allo Dio d'amore andò la novella. Onde lo Dio d'amore ne fecie nobilissimo mandorlo molto verde e molto bene stante, e fu et è il primo albero ke prima fa frutto errinovella Amore.

Novella XLVII.

Qui conta come uno Cavaliere richiese una donna de amore.

Uno Cavaliere pregava un giorno una Donna d'amore e diciealle intrall'altre parole k'elli era gentile e ricco e bello adismisura. El vostro marito è così laido come voi sapete. E quel cotal marito era dopo la parete della camera. Parlò e disse. Messer per

received gifts of clothing. From this was born an interesting discussion, whereby the minstrel said to Marco, "What is this, Marco, that I have received seven new suits of clothing and you nothing? For if you are so much better and wiser than me, what is the reason for this?" And Marco replied, "It is obviously because you have found more people like yourself than I have found like myself."

Novella XLV.

How Lancelot[1] fought at a fountain.

One day Master Lancelot fought at a fountain with a knight from Saxony whose name was A.[2] Alighting from their horses, the knights fiercely fought with swords. And during a period of respite, one asked the other for his name. Master Lancelot replied, "Since you wish to learn my name, know that I am called Lancelot." Then the contest resumed, and the knight spoke to Lancelot and said, "Your name inflicts more harm on me than your talent." For once he realized that his adversary was Lancelot, the knight began to fear his abilities.

Novella XLVI.

Here is told how Narcissus[1] fell in love with his own shadow.

Narcissus was a very fine and extremely handsome knight.[2] It happened one day that he was resting above a very lovely fountain. And in the water he saw his own very beautiful shadow. And he began to contemplate it and to enjoy himself there above the fountain, believing that the shadow was a living being underneath the water, never realizing that it was his own image. He began to love the shadow, and to fall in love so strongly that he wished to hold it. And in doing so he disturbed the water and the shadow vanished. Narcissus began to cry and when the water cleared, he saw his own shadow crying. Then he let himself fall into the water and he drowned.[3] It was spring time, when ladies would come to enjoy themselves by the fountain. They saw the beautiful Narcissus drowned, and amid great tears, they dragged him out of the fountain and laid him down on the river bank. And from here the news reached the god of love,[4] who transformed him into a most noble almond tree,[5] very green and very rich, and it was and is the first tree to bear fruit and to renew love.

Novella XLVII.

Here is told how a knight asked a lady for her love.

One day a knight beseeched a lady for love and, among his many words, he said that he was a gentleman, rich and handsome beyond measure. "And your husband is exceedingly ugly, as you well know." And that husband had stationed himself outside one of the room's walls. He spoke and said, "Sir, speak well of your own merits, but please

cortesia acconciate li fatti vostri e non isconciate li altrui. Messere Licio di Val Buona fu il laido. E Messere Rinieri da Calvoli fu l'altro.

Novella XLVIII.

Qui conta del Re Curado padre di Curadino.

Leggiessi del Re Curado ke quando era garzone si avea in compangnia dodici garzoni di sua etade. Quando lo Re Curado fallava li maestri kelli erano dati a guardia non lo batteano. Ma batteano questi garzoni suoi compangni. E que' diciea. Perchè battete voi costoro? Rispondeano li Maestri, per li falli tuoi. E que' diciea. Perkennon battete voi me, ke mia èlla colpa? Elli Maestri rispondeano, perkettu se' nostro singniore. Ma noi battiamo costoro per te. Onde assai ti dee dolere settu ai gentil quore, k'altri porti pena delle tue colpe. Et perciò si dicie kello Re Curado si guardava molto di fallire per la pietà di coloro.

Novella XLIX.

Qui conta d'uno Medico di Tolosa come tolse per moglie una nepote dell'Arcivescovo di Tolosa.

Uno Medico di Tolosa tolse per moglie una gentile Donna di Tolosa nepote dell'Arcivescovo. Menolla. In due mesi fecie una fanciulla. Il Medico non mostrò nullo cruccio. Anzi consolava la donna e mostravalle ragioni secondo fisica ke ben poteva esser sua di ragione. E con quelle parole, e con belli sembianti feciesi kella donna nolla puote traviare.[a] Molto onoroe la donna nel parto. Dopo il parto sille disse. Madonna io vi o onorata quant'io o potuto priegovi per amore di me ke voi ritorniate omai a casa di vostro padre. Ella vostra figliuola io terrò a grande onore. Tanto andaro le cose innanzi kell'Arcivescovo sentì kel Medico avea dato conmiato alla nepote. Mandò per lui et acciò ke era grande uomo parlò sopra lui molto grandi parole mischiate con superbia e con minnacie. E quando ebbe assai parlato. Il Medico rispose. E disse così. Messer io tolsi vostra nepote per moglie credendomi della mia rikezza poter fornire e pasciere[b] la mia famiglia e fu mia intentione d'avere un figliuolo l'anno e non più. Onde la donna a cominciato a fare figliuoli in duo mesi. Per la qual cosa io non sono sì agiato sel fatto dee così andare kelli potessi notricare e voi non farebbe onore ke vostro lengnaggio andasse a povertade. Perk'io vi keggio merciede ke voi la diate a uno più ricco uomo k'io non sono sì ke a voi non sia disinore.

don't denigrate those of others." The ugly man was Master Licio of Val Buona.[1] And the other was Master Rinieri of Calvoli.[2]

Novella XLVIII.

Here is told of King Conrad,[1] the father of Conradin.[2]

It is written[3] concerning King Conrad that when he was a boy he kept company with twelve boys of his own age. When King Conrad made a mistake, the teachers, who had been entrusted as his guardians, did not beat him. Instead they beat these boys who were his companions. And he would say, "Why do you beat them?" The teachers replied, "For your mistakes." And he would say, "Why do you not beat me, since it is all my fault?" And the teachers replied, "Because you are our lord. But we beat them in your place. And this must cause you great pain, if you have a gentle heart, to have others bear the pain for your faults." And because of this, it is said that King Conrad earnestly attempted not to make any mistakes, for the pity he felt for these other boys.

Novella XLIX.

Here is told of a doctor from Toulouse and how he took for a wife the niece of the Archbishop of Toulouse.

A doctor from Toulouse took for his wife a gentle woman of Toulouse, the niece of the Archbishop. He brought her home and two months later she gave birth to an infant girl. The doctor showed no signs of anger; instead, he consoled his lady and presented many reasons, according to the laws of physics, which logically proved the child could be his. And with these words and with pleasant looks, he convinced the lady not to arrest the pregnancy.[1] He greatly honored the lady during her labor. After the birth, he said to her, "My lady, I have treated you with as much respect as I could; now, in the name of any love you might have for me, return to your father's house. I will keep your daughter and treat her with the greatest respect." Things went forward in this manner, until the Archbishop heard that the doctor had asked his niece to leave. He sent for the doctor and, since he was a great man, he lectured him using grand words, mingled with arrogance and threats. And after he had spoken at great length, the doctor replied as follows, "Sire, I took your niece for my wife believing that my resources would be enough to provide for and nurture[2] my family. And it was my intention to have one child a year, and no more. However, the lady began by producing a child in two months. But I am not wealthy enough for such a thing, nor could I provide adequately if things continued in this manner, and it would be no honor to you if your lineage were reduced to poverty. For this reason I mercifully ask that you give her to a man richer than myself, so no dishonor befalls you."

Novella L.

Qui conta di Maestro Franciesco figliuolo di Maestro Accorso da Bolongnia.

Maestro Franciesco figliuolo di Maestro Accorso della città di Bolongnia quando ritornò de' Inghilterra dove era stato lungamente fecie una così fatta proposta dinanzi al commune di Bolongnia e disse così. Un padre d'una fameglia si partì di suo paese per povertade e lasciò i suoi figliuoli et andonne in lontane provincie. Stando uno tempo et elli vide uomini di sua terra. Lo amore de' figliuoli lo strinse a domandaro dilloro. E quelli risposero. Messere vostri figliuoli anno guadangniato e sono ricchi. E quelli udendo così propuose di ritornare e tornò in sua terra. Trovoe li figliuoli ricchi. Addomandoe a' suoi figliuoli kel rimettessero in sulle possessioni siccome padre e sengniore. I figliuoli negaro diciendo così. Padre noi il ci avemo guadangniato non ci ai ke fare sì ke ne nacque piato.[a] Onde la leggie volle kel padre fusse al postutto Singniore di quello k'aveano guadangniato i figliuoli. E così addomando io al commune di Bolongnia. Kelle possessioni di miei figliuoli siano a mia singnioria cioè de' miei scolari. Li quali sono grandi maestri divenuti et anno molto guadangniato poi ke io mi partì dalloro. Piaccia al communale di Bolongnia poi k'io sono tornato ke io sia singniore e padre siccome commanda la leggie ke parla del padre della fameglia.

Novella LI.

Qui conta d'una Guasca come si richiamò allo Re di Cipri.

Era una Guasca in Cipri alla quale fu fatta un dì molta villania et onta tale kennon la poteo sofferire. Mossessi et andonne al Re di Cipri e disse. Messer a voi son già fatti dieci mila disinori et amme ne è fatto pur uno, priegovi ke voi ke tanti n'avete sofferti m'insengniate sofferire il mio uno. Lo Re si vergongniò e cominciò a vendicare li suoi et a non volere più sofferire.

Novella LII.

D'una Campana ke si ordinò al tempo del Re Giovanni.

Al tempo del Re Giovanni d'Atri fue ordinata una Campana ke chiunque ricievea un gran torto sill'andava a sonare el Re ragunava i savi acciò ordinati acciokè ragione fosse fatta. Avenne kella Campana era molto tempo durata kella fune era venuta meno sì ke una Vitalba v'era legata. Or'avenne ke uno Cavaliere d'Atri avea uno suo nobile destriere lo quale era invecchiato sì ke sua bontà era tutta venuta meno, si ke per non

Novella L.

Here is told of Master Francesco,[1] the son of Master Accorso of Bologna.[2]

Master Francesco was the son of Master Accorso from the city of Bologna. When he returned from England, where he had sojourned for a long while, he made the following proposal in front of the Commune of Bologna. He said the following, "A father of a family was forced by poverty to depart from his country and left his children and went to far off lands. Having been away awhile, he saw some men from his native land. The love he bore his children pressed him to ask after them. And these men replied, 'Sir, your children have earned much and are rich.' Having heard this he decided to return and headed for home. He found his children rich. He asked his children to place all their possessions in his hands, as is the right of a father and lord. The children refused, saying, 'Father, we have earned all this by ourselves; you have had nothing to do with it.' And from this litigation was born, whereby the law wishes a father, above all else, to lord over all that his children have earned. And so, I ask the Commune of Bologna that the possessions of my children be placed under my jurisdiction, likewise those of my students, who have become great teachers and who have earned much since I left them. May it please the Commune of Bologna, since I have returned, to declare me lord and father as the law commands when it speaks of the father of a family."

Novella LI.

Here is told how a Gascon lady appealed to the King of Cyprus.[1]

There was a Gascon lady in Cyprus to whom so much rudeness and so many insults were directed in just one day that she could not stand it any longer. She decided to act and went to the King of Cyprus and said, "Sire, at least ten thousand shameful things have already been done to you, and to me only one. I pray you, who have suffered so many, teach me how to endure my one." The king felt much shame and began to avenge the insults to him, willing to suffer them no longer.

Novella LII.

Concerning a bell purchased during the time of King John.

During the time of King John of Atri,[1] a bell was purchased so that anyone who suffered a great wrong could go and ring this bell. And then, the king would call to council his wise men, as arranged, so that a decision could be reached. It happened that the bell had endured such a long time that its rope became frayed, and so a clematis was fastened to it. Now, it happened that a knight from Atri had a most noble steed[2] that had grown so old that its faculties had lessened. The knight, so as not to be required to feed

darli mangiare il lasciava andare per la terra. Lo cavallo per la fame aggiunse con la bocca a questa Vitalba per rodegarla.[a] Tirando la Campana sonò. Li Giudici si adunaro, e videro la petitione del cavallo ke parea ke domandasse ragione. Giudicaro kel Cavaliere cui elli avea servito da giovane il pasciesse da vecchio. Il Re lo constrinse e comandò sotto gran pena.

Novella LIII.

Qui conta d'una gratia kello'mperadore fecie a un suo Barone.

Lo'mperadore donò una gratia a uno suo Barone ke qualunque uomo passasse per sua terra kelli togliesse d'ongni magangnia evidente un danaio[a] di passaggio. Il Barone mise alla porta un suo passaggiere[b] arricogliere il passaggio. Un giorno avenne ke uno ke avea meno uno piede venne alla porta il pedagiere[c] li domandò un danaio. Quelli si contese azzuffandosi con lui. Il pedagiere il prese. Quelli difendendossi trasse fuori uno suo monkerino k'avea meno l'una mano. Allora il pedagiere il vide disse. Tu me ne darai due l'uno per la mano ell'altro per lo piede. Allora furo alla zuffa il Capello li cadde di capo. Quelli avea meno l'uno occhio disse il pedagiere, tu me ne darai tre. Pigliarsi a' capelli lo passaggier li puose mano in capo. Quelli era tingniosi. Disse lo passaggiere, tu me ne darai ora quattro. Così convenne a colui ke potea sanza lite passare per uno pagasse quattro.

Novella LIIII.

Qui conta come il Piovano Porcellino fu accusato.

Uno Piovano il quale avea nome il Piovano Porcellino al tempo del Vescovo Mangiadore fu accusato dinanzi dal Vescovo k'elli guidava male la pieve per cagione di femine. Il Vescovo faciendo sopra lui inquisitione trovollo molto colpevole. E stando in Vescovado attendendo l'altro dì d'esser disposto. La famiglia volendolli bene l'insengniaro campare. Nascoserlo la notte sotto il letto del Vescovo. Et in quella notte il Vescovo v'avea fatto venire una sua amica et essendo entro il letto volendolla toccare l'amica non si lasciava diciendo, molte impromesse m'avete fatte e non me ne attenere neente. Il Vescovo rispose, vita mia io lotti prometto e giuro. Non disse quella, io voglio li danari in mano. Il Vescovo levandossi per andare per danari per donarli all'amica. Il Piovano uscì di sotto il letto e disse, Messere a cotesto colgono elle me. Or chi potrebbe fare altro. Il Vescovo si vergongniò e perdonolli. Ma molte minaccie li fecie dinanzi alli altri Kerici.

it, allowed the horse to wander across the land. Out of hunger, the horse attached its mouth to that clematis and began to chew on it. And doing so, it pulled on the bell which began to ring. The judges gathered together and saw the petition of this horse which seemed to be appealing for justice. They decreed that the knight, whom the horse had served from its youth, should provide for it in old age. The king compelled him to do so under penalty of great pain.

Novella LIII.

Here is told of a right which the Emperor granted to one of his barons.[1]

The Emperor granted the right to one of his barons to collect one dinar[2] for each and every obvious physical defect exhibited by anyone passing through his territory. The baron positioned at the gate one of his toll-collectors to collect payment for passage. It happened one day that a man missing a foot arrived at the gate. The toll-collector demanded one dinar from him. The man contested and the two came to blows. The toll-collector grabbed the man, who, while defending himself revealed a stump where he had lost a hand. When the toll-collector saw this, he said, "You now owe me two dinars, one for your hand and the other for your foot." Then, during the brawl, the man's hat fell off his head. The man had an eye missing. The toll-collector said, "Now you owe me three." The toll-collector grabbed him by the hair, placing his hand on the man's head. The man's scalp was full of ringworm. The toll-collector said, "Now you owe me four." And so it happened that one who could have passed through, without a fight, paying one; now paid four.

Novella LIIII.

Here is told how the parish priest Porcellino[1] *was accused.*

A parish priest named Pastor Porcellino, during the time of Bishop Mangiadore,[2] was accused in front of the bishop of poorly guiding his parish because of his love of women. Having investigated the situation, the bishop found him quite guilty. The next day, while awaiting deliberation in the bishopric, some relatives, who cared very much for him, taught the priest how to save himself. That night they hid him under the bishop's bed. And during the night the bishop had a lady friend come to him, and when they both were in his bed, he felt a great desire to touch her. But she would not allow him, saying, "You have made so many promises to me, but you have kept none of them." The bishop replied, "On my life, I promise and I swear I will give you money." But she would only reply, "I want the money in hand." The bishop arose to go for the money to give to his lady friend. The parish priest came out from under the bed and said, "Sire, this is exactly how they got me." Now who could do anything else? The bishop was full of shame and pardoned him, but, in front of all the other clerics he continued his terrible threats.

Novella LV.

Qui conta d'una novella di uno uomo di corte[a] ke avea nome Marco.

Marco Lombardo savissimo più ke niuno di suo mestiero fu un dì domandato da un povero orrevole[b] uomo e leggiadro il quale prendea i danari in sagreto da buona gente, ma non prendea robbe. Era a guisa di morditore[c] et avea nome Paolino fecie a Marco una così fatta quistione, credendo ke Marco non vi potesse rispondere. Marco, disse elli. Tusse' lo più savio uomo di tutta Italia esse' povero e disdengni lo chiedere, perkennon ti provedestitu sì kettu fossi sì ricco ke non ti bisongniasse di chiedere? E Marco si volse d'intorno poi disse così. Altri non vede ora noi e non ci ode. Et tu come ai fatto? El morditore rispose, o fatto sì k'io sono povero. E Marco disse, tiello credenza amme et io atte.

Novella LVI.

Come uno della Marca[a] andò a studiare a Bolongnia.

Uno della Marca andò a studiare a Bolongnia. Vennerli meno le spese. Piangea. Un altro il vide e seppe perkè piangea disselli così. Io ti fornirò lo studio ettu m'imprometti kettu mi darai mille livre[b] al primo piato[c] kettu vincerai. Lo Scolaio studiò e tornò in sua terra. Quelli li tenne dietro per lo prezzo. Lo Scolaio per paura di dare il prezzo si stava e non avogadava e così avea perduto l'uno ell'altro l'uno il senno ell'altro i danari. Or ke pensò quelli de' danari richiamossi dillui e dielli un libello[d] di due mila livre e disselli così. O vuoli vinciere o vuoli perdere. Settu vinci tu mi pagherai la promessione. Settu perdi tu m'adempierai il libello. Allora lo Scolaio il pagò e non volle piatir con lui.

Novella LVII.

Di Madonna Angniesina di Bolongnia.

Madonna Angniesina di Bolongnia istando un giorno in una corte[a] da sollazzo et era donna dell'altre intralle quali avea una sposa novella alla quale volea fare dire come ella fecie la prima notte. Cominciossi Madonna Angniesina alle più sfacciate. E domandò in prima loro l'una dicieva, io il presi con le due mani, ell'altre dicieano in altro sfacciato modo. Domandò la sposa novella. Ettu come faciesti? E quella disse molto vergongniosamente con gli occhi kinati, io il presi con le due dita. Madonna Angniesina rispose e disse. Dhe caggiù ti fossello.

Novella LV.

Here a tale is told of a minstrel named Marco.[1]

Marco Lombardo was the wisest of men in his profession. One day he was asked a question by a poor but handsome man from an honorable family who secretly took money but not things from good people. He was known as a gossip and was called Paolino. He asked the following question of Marco, believing that Marco would not be able to respond. "Marco," he said, "You are the wisest man in all of Italy, and yet you are poor and despise asking for things. Why do you not provide for yourself so that you become so rich that you need never ask for anything?" And Marco looked about and then said, "No one can see or hear us now. So, why have you done certain things?" And the gossip replied, "I have done so because I am poor." And Marco replied, "You keep my secret and I will keep yours."

Novella LVI.

How a man from the country[1] *went to study in Bologna.*[2]

A man from the country went to study in Bologna. When he had run through all his money, he began to cry. Another man saw this and realized why the man was crying, and he said the following, "I will provide for you while you study but you must promise me one thousand lire[3] from the first case that you win." The scholar completed his studies and returned home. The man followed him, concerned for his money. For fear of having to return the money, the scholar refrained from practicing law. And in this way both men lost, one the use of his learning and the other his money. Now what did the man who lent the money think to do? He appealed to the courts and sued the scholar for two thousand lire. Then he said the following, "Do you wish to win or lose this case? If you win, then you must pay me the previously promised amount. If you lose, then you must meet the requirements of the suit." Then the scholar paid him, wishing never again to litigate with him.

Novella LVII.

Concerning Lady Agnesina of Bologna.

One day Lady Agnesina of Bologna was relaxing in her courtyard playing hostess to some other ladies, and among them was a new bride whom she wanted to force to describe the details of her first night of married life. Lady Agnesina began by questioning the more shameless ladies. The first among them whom she questioned said, "I grabbed it with both my hands." And others related accounts just as shameless. Then she asked the new bride, "And what did you do?" And she said, quite embarrassed with her eyes lowered, "I held it with the tips of two fingers." Lady Agnesina replied by saying, "Ah! He couldn't keep it up for you."

Novella LVIII.

Di Messer Beriuolo Cavaliere di Corte.

Uno Cavaliere di Corte k'ebbe nome Messere Beriuolo era in Gienova venne a rampongnie con uno donzello,[a] Quello donzello li fecie la fica[b] quasi in fino all'occhio diciendolli villania. Messere Barancadoria[c] il vide. Seppelli reo. Venne a quello Cavaliere di Corte. Confortollo ke rispondesse. E faciesse la fica a colui kella faciea allui. Ma dio, rispose quelli, non farò k'io non li farei una delle mie per ciento delle sue.

Novella LIX.

Qui conta d'un gentiluomo kello'mperadore fecie impendere.

Federigo Imperadore fecie impendere un giorno un grande gentil uomo per certo misfatto. E per fare riluciere la giustitia sil faciea guardare ad uno grande Cavaliere con comandamento di gran pena kennollo lasciasse spiccare, sì ke questi non guardando bene lo'mpiccato fu portato via. Sì ke quando quelli senn'avide prese consiglio dassè medesimo per paura di perdere la testa. Et istando così pensoso in quella notte si prese ad andare ad una Badia, ke era ivi presso per sapere se potesse trovare alcuno ke fosse novellamente morto acciò kel potesse mettere alle forke in colui scambio. Giunto alla Badia la notte medesima sivvi trovò una Donna in pianto scapigliata e scinta forte lamentando et era molto sconsolata e piangea un suo caro marito lo quale era morto lo giorno. Il Cavaliere la domandò dolcemente, Madonna ke modo è questo? Ella Donna rispose. Io l'amava tanto ke mai non voglio essere più consolata, ma in pianto voglio finire li miei dì. Allora il Cavaliere le disse. Madonna ke savere è questo? Volete voi morire quì di dolore? Ke per pianto nè per lagrime non si po' recare a vita il corpo morto. Onde ke mattezza è quella ke voi fate? Ma fate così prendete me a marito kennon o donna e campatemmi la persona perk'io ne sono in periglio. E non so la dove mi nasconda ke io per comandamento del mio Singniore guardava un Cavaliere impenduto per la gola li uomini del suo lengniaggio il m'anno tolto insengniatemmi campare ke potete. Et io sarò vostro marito. E terrovvi onorevolemente. Allora la donna udendo questo s'innamorò di questo Cavaliere e disse. Io farò ciò kettummi comandarai tanto è l'amore k'io ti porto. Prendiamo questo mio marito e traiamlo fuori della sepoltura et impichiamlo in luogo di quello ke v'è tolto, e lasciò suo pianto. Et atò[a] trarre il marito del sepolcro. Et atollo[b] impendere per la gola così morto. Il Cavaliere disse, Madonna elli avea meno un dente della bocca et o paura kesse fosse rivenuto a rivedere ke io non avesse disinore. Et ella udendo questo li ruppe un dente di bocca. Ess'altro vi fosse bisongniato a quel fatto sill'avrebbe fatto. Allora il Cavaliere vedendo quello ke ella avea fatto di suo marito disse. Madonna sì come poco v'è caluto[c] di costui ke tanto mostravate d'amare così vi carrebbe[d] vie meno di me. Allora si partì dallei et andossi per li fatti suoi et ella rimase con gran vergongnia.

Novella LVIII.

Concerning Master Beriuolo,[1] knight of the court.

A knight of the court named Master Beriuolo, while in Genova, was forced to reprimand a squire. The squire flipped him the finger,[2] right in his face, while saying the rudest of things. Master Branca Doria[3] saw this and realized how wicked it was. He went to the knight and advised him to respond by giving the finger in return. "By God," he replied, "That I will not do, for I would not give one of mine for one hundred of his."

Novella LIX.

Here is told how the Emperor had a gentleman hanged.[1]

One day the Emperor Frederick[2] had a great gentleman hanged for certain misdeeds. And, in order to reinforce the law, he commanded a great knight, under penalty of much pain, to make sure no one removed the body from the gallows. But this knight did not keep watch very well and the hanged man was carried away. And when he saw what had happened, fearing the loss of his own head, he began to search in his mind for a remedy. That night, consumed in thought, he made his way to a nearby abbey to see if he could find some recently dead body to place on the gallows in exchange for the one removed. That same night, when he arrived at the abbey, he found a woman weeping and lamenting strongly; disheveled, with her robes ungirt, who was quite despondent over the death of her husband that day. The knight asked her sweetly, "My lady, what fashion is this?" And the lady replied, "I loved him so that I never wish to be consoled, but simply to end my days in tears." Then the knight replied, "My lady, what manner of reasoning is this? You wish to die, here and now, of your pain? You must know that neither cries nor tears can return a dead body to life. Now, what manner of insanity is this that you are doing? No, do this instead: take me for a husband, as I have no woman, and save my person for I am in danger. And I don't know where to hide myself, for my lord commanded me to guard the body of a knight hanged by the throat, but his relatives came and took him from me. Teach me the way to survive; I know you can, and I will become your husband and hold you in the highest esteem." Then the woman, hearing this, fell in love with this knight and said, "I will do what you ask, so great is my love for you. Let's take my husband and drag him from his grave and hang him up in place of the body removed." Then she ceased her weeping and helped drag her husband from the grave and hang him, dead as he was, by the throat. The knight said, "My lady, the hanged man had a tooth missing from his mouth, and I fear, if the Emperor returns to review the body, I can still be dishonored." And she, hearing this, yanked a tooth from her dead husband's mouth; and if anything else needed to be done, she certainly would have done so. Then the knight, seeing what she had done to her husband said, "My lady, how little time it took for the great love you showed for this man to subside; it would take even less for your love for me to dwindle." Then he left her and went about his business, while she remained greatly ashamed.

Novella LX.

Qui conta come Carlo Mangnio amò per amore.

Carlo nobile Re di Cicilia e di Gierusalem quando era Conte d'Angiò si amoe per amore la bella Contessa di Teti la quale amava medesimamente il Conte d'Universa. In quel tempo il Re di Francia avea difeso sotto pena del quore ke niuno torneasse. Il Conte d'Angiò volendo provare qual meglio valesse d'arme trallui el Conte d'Universa sissi provide e fu con grandissime preghiere a Messer Allardo de' Valleri e manifestolli dove elli amava e kessi era posto in quore di provarsi in campo col Conte d'Universa pregandollo per amore ke acattasse la parola dal Re ke solo un torneamento faciesse con sua licentia. Quelli domandò cagione. Il Conte d'Angiò l'insengniò in questa guisa. Il Re si è quasi beghino e per la grande bontade di vostra persona elli spera di fare prendere a voi drappi di religione per aver la vostra compangnia. Onde in questa domanda sia per voi kesto in gratia ke uno solo torneamento lascia a voi fedire. E voi farete quanto ke allui piacierà. E Messere Allardo rispose. Or mi di' Conte perderò io la compangnia de' Cavalieri per uno torneamento? El Conte rispose. Io vi prometto lealmente k'io ve ne diliberrò. Essì fecie elli in tale maniera come io vi conterò. Messer Allardo senn'andò al Re di Francia e disse. Messere quando io presi arme il giorno di vostro coronamento allora portaro arme tutti li migliori Cavalieri del monde onde io per amor di voi volendo in tutto lasciare il mondo e vestirmi di drappi di religione piaccia a voi di donarmi una nobile gratia cioè ke un torneamento feggia là dove s'armi la nobiltà de' Cavalieri sì kelle mie arme si lascino in grande festa come si presero. Allora lo Re l'ottiò. Ordinossi un torneamento. Dall'una parte fu il Conte d'Universa. E dall'altra il Conte d'Angiò. La Reina con Contesse Dame e Damigelle di gran paraggio furo alle loggie ella Contessa di Teti vi fue. In quel giorno portaro arme li fiori de' Cavalieri del mondo dall'una parte e dall'altra. Dopo molto torneare il Conte d'Angiò e quello d'Universa feciero diliverare l'arringo ell'uno incontrò all'altro si mosse alla forza de' poderosi destieri con grosse aste in mano. Or avenne ke nel mezzo dell'arringo il destriere del Conte d'Universa cadde col Conte in un monte onde le donne discesero delle loggie e portarlone in braccio molto soavemente. Ella Contessa di Teti vi fue. Il Conte d'Angiò si lamentava fortemente diciendo. Lasso perkè non cadde mio cavallo siccome quello del Conte d'Universa kella Contessa mi fosse tanto di presso quanto fu allui. Partito il torneamento il Conte d'Angiò fu alla Reina e chiesselle mercie ke ella per amore de' nobili Cavalieri di Francia dovesse mostrare cruccio al Re poi nella pacie li domandasse un dono el dono fosse di questa maniera ke al Re dovesse piaciere ke' giovani Cavalieri di Francia non perdessero sì nobile compangnia come era quella di Messere Allardo di Valleri. La Reina così fecie. Crucciò col Re e nella pacie li domandò quello ke ella volea. El Re le promise il dono.

Novella LX.

Here is told how Charles the Great[1] fell madly in love.

Charles, noble King of Sicily and Jerusalem,[2] when he was the Count of Anjou,[3] fell madly in love with the lovely Countess of Teti,[4] who, at the same time, was in love with the Count of Universa.[5] At that time, the King of France[6] had outlawed, under pain of death, all tournaments. The Count of Anjou, wishing to prove who was the worthier in arms, himself or the Count of Universa, provided himself the opportunity by earnestly imploring Master Allardo de' Valleri[7] and revealing to him whom he loved and how he was determined to prove himself on the field against the Count of Universa. The count did so by pleading with him, in the name of love, to beg the king for his word to permit just one tournament to take place.[8] Master Allardo asked what justification he could give. The Count of Anjou instructed him in this way, "The king has practically become a beghard[9] and, because of your great personal goodness, he hopes to convince you to don the habit[10] in order to retain the pleasure of your company. Now, concerning this question, ask him to grant for you that one more tournament be permitted to take place. And then you will do whatsoever pleases him." And Master Allardo replied, "Now tell me, Count, am I to lose the company of knights for the sake of a tournament?" And the Count replied, "In faith, I promise that I will free you from your pledge." And he did these things in the manner I will now relate. Master Allardo went to the King of France and said, "Sire, when I took up arms the day of your coronation, at that time all the world's greatest knights carried arms. Now for the love I bear you, I wish above all else to leave this world and take the religious habit. I ask, if it pleases you, to grant me one noble wish. Let a tournament be staged where the noblest knights may take up arms, so that I may renounce my arms amid grand festivities reminiscent of when I first assumed them." The king conceded and ordered a tournament to take place. On one side presided the Count of Universa and on the other, the Count of Anjou. The queen[11] sat in the loggia amid noble countesses, ladies and damsels. And the Countess of Teti was there. On that day, the flower of knighthood from all over the world took up arms. After much jousting, the Counts of Anjou and Universa had the field cleared, each moved to clash with the other, lances in hand, on the backs of mighty steeds. Now it happened that the Count of Universa and his steed fell in a great heap in the center of the field, whereby the ladies descended from the loggia and carried him away, ever so gently, in their arms. And the Countess of Teti was there. The Count of Anjou loudly lamented, saying, "Oh God, why could not my horse have fallen, like the Count of Universa's, so that the countess would have been as near to me as she was to him?" The tournament abruptly ended. The Count of Anjou went to the queen and mercifully begged her, for love of the noble knights of France, to quarrel with the king. And then, while making peace, she should request a kindness, and it should consist of the following; that, should it please the king, the noble knights of France not lose such a noble companion as Master Allardo de' Valleri. The queen did as requested. She became angry at the king and, to

E fu diliberato Messer Allardo di ciò k'avea promesso e rimase con gli altri nobili Cavalieri torneando e faciendo d'arme siccome la rinomea per lo mondo si corre sovente di grande bontade d'oltre maravigliose prodezze.

Novella LXI.

Qui conta di Socrate Filosofo come rispose a' Greci.

Socrate fu nobile Filosofo di Roma et al suo tempo mandaro e[a] Greci nobile e grandissima Ambascieria ai Romani. Ella forma della loro Ambasciata sì fu per difendersi da' Romani del tributo ka davano loro con ragione. E fue loro così imposto dal Soldano.[b] Andrete et usarete ragione. Esse vi bisongnia usarete moneta. Li Ambasciadori giunsero a Roma. Propuosessi la forma della loro Ambasciata nel consiglio di Roma. Il consiglio di Roma provide la risposta della domanda de' Greci kessi dovessa fare per Socrate Filosopho sanza niuno altro tenore. Riformando il consiglio ke in Roma stesse acciokè per Socrate fosse risposto. Li Ambasciadori andaro colà dove Socrate abitava molto di lungi da Roma per opporre le loro ragioni dinanzi dallui. Giunsero alla casa sua la quale era di non gran vista. Trovaro lui ke cogliea erbetta. Avisarollo da lungi. L'uomo era di non grande apparenza. Parlaro insieme confideranti tutte le soprascritte cose. E dissero intra loro. Di costui avremo noi grande mercato acciokè sembiava loro anzi povero ke ricco. Giunsero e dissero, Dio ti salvi uomo di grande sapientia la quale non può essere picciola poi kelli Romani t'anno conmessa così alta risposta kente è questa. Mostrarli la informagione[c] di Roma e dissero allui. Proporremo dinanzi datte le nostre ragionevoli ragioni le quali sono molte. Il senno tuo provederà il nostro diritto. E sappi ke siamo di ricco Singniore prenderai questi perperi[d] e quai sono molti et al nostro singniore è neente, et atte può essere molto utile. E Socrate rispose alli Ambasciadori e disse. Voi pranzerete innanzi e poi intenderemo a vostri bisongni. Tennero lo invito e pranzaro assai cattivamente sanza molto rilevo. Dopo il pranzo parlò Socrate alli Ambasciadori e disse. Singniori qual'è meglio tra una cosa o due. Li Ambasciadori rispose, le due. E que' disse. Or andate ad ubbidire a' Romani con le persone ke se 'l commune di Roma avrà le persone de' Greci, elli avrà le persone ello avere. Ess'io togliesse l'oro i Romani perderebbeno la loro intentione. Allora li Ambasciadori si partiro dal Filosofo assai vergongniosi et ubbidiro a' Romani.

restore peace, she asked for that which she wished. The king agreed to grant her wish. And so Master Allardo was freed from his promise and remained with the other noble knights, jousting and fighting, so that tales of his great goodness and bravery beyond wonder coursed constantly throughout the world.

Novella LXI.

Here is told how Socrates the philosopher replied to the Greeks.

Socrates was a noble Roman philosopher[1] and during his time the Greeks sent a very great and noble embassy to the Romans. And the mission of their embassy was to reasonably argue against the tribute they were required to give to the Romans. And the Sultan[2] charged them as follows, "Go and use your powers of reason, and if need be, use money." The ambassadors arrived in Rome and proposed the intent of their mission to the Council of Rome. The Council of Rome provided this reply to the petition of the Greeks, that there was no other way; the answer must come from the philosopher Socrates. The Council proclaimed that Rome would abide by whatever Socrates replied. The ambassadors went where Socrates was living, very far from Rome, to present their arguments before him. They arrived at his house, which was nothing very grand to see. They found him gathering herbs.[3] They observed him for quite a while. He seemed quite modest in appearance.[4] They spoke among themselves, considering all the above written things. And they said among themselves, "We should be able to buy this one quite cheaply," since he seemed to them quite poor rather than rich. They went up to him and said, "God keep you, man of great wisdom, which cannot be small since the Romans have entrusted you with such an important response as this one." They showed him the Roman decree and said to him, "We will propose before you our reasonable arguments, which are many. Your wisdom will provide us with justice. And understand that we come from a rich lord. Take these perperi,[5] which are many and could be most useful to you, but to our lord are nothing." And Socrates replied to the ambassadors and said, "First you will dine, then we will listen to your needs." They accepted the invitation and ate an exceedingly unappetizing meal of meager portions. After dinner Socrates spoke to the ambassadors and said, "Gentlemen, what is better, to have one thing or two?" The ambassadors replied, "Two." And then he said, "Now, go and tell your people to obey the Romans, for if the Commune of Rome takes the people of Greece, it will have its people and their possessions. And if I take this gold from them, the Romans might forget their original intentions." Then the ambassadors, much embarrassed, left the philosopher and obeyed the Romans.

Novella LXII.

Qui conta una novella di Messer Roberto.

Arimini monte[a] si è in Borgongnia et avvi un Sire kessi chiama Messer Roberto et è contado grande. La Contessa antica e sue Cameriere si aveano un Portiere Milenso[b] et era molto grande della persona et avea nome Baligante. L'una delle cameriere cominciò a giaciere con lui, poi il manifestò a un'altra tanto ke così andò fino alla Contessa. Sentendo la Contessa k'elli era a gran misura giacque con lui. Il Sire lo spiò. Feciello amazzare e del quore fe' fare una torta e presentolla alla Contessa et alle sue Cameriere e mangiaronla. Dopo il mangiare venne il Singniore a corteare e domandò kente fulla torta. Tutte risposero, bona. Allora rispose il Sire, ciò non è maraviglia ke Baligante v'è piaciuto vivo s'elli vi piace di morto. Ella Contessa elle Cameriere quando intesero il fatto si vergongniaro e videro bene k'elle aveano perduto l'onore di questo mondo. Arrendersi monake e feciero un monistero kessi chiamava il monistero delle Nonane[c] di Rimino monte. La casa crebbe assai e divenne molto ricca. E questo si conta in novella ke è vera. Ke v'è que' costume ke quando elli vi passasse alcuno Gentiluomo con molti arnesi et elle il facieano invitare e facieanlli grandissimo onore. Ella Badessa. Elle suore li veniano incontro. Et in sul donneare[d] quella ke più li piaciesse quella il servia et accompangniava a tavola et alletto. La mattina sissi levava trovavalli l'acqua e tovaglia e quando era lavato et ella li apparecchiava un ago vuoto et un filo di seta e covenia ke s'elli si volea affibbiar da mano, kelli mettesse lo filo nella cruna dell'ago e s'alle tre volte avisasse kennon lo vi mettesse silli toglieano le donne tutto suo arnese e non li rendeano neente. Esse mettea il filo alle tre volte nell'ago silli rendeano l'arnese suo e donavalli di belli gioielli.

Novella LXIII.

Del buon Re Meliadus e del Cavaliere sanza paura.

Il buono Re Meliadus el Cavaliere sanza paura si erano nemici mortali in campo. Andando un giorno questo Cavaliere sanza paura a guisa d'errante cavaliere disconosciutamente trovò suoi sergienti che molto l'amavano ma nollo conoscievano. E dissero, dinne cavaliere errante per onore di cavaleria qual'è miglior cavalier tral buon Cavalier sanza paura ol buon Re Meliadus? El cavalier rispose, se Dio mi dea buona ventura lo Re Meliadus èllo miglior cavalier ke in sella cavalki. Allora li sergienti ke voleano male al Re Meliadus per amore dilloro singniore si sorpresero questo lor Singniore attragione[a] e così armato lo levaro da destrieri e miserollo attraverso d'uno ronzino e dicieano communemente kel voleano impendere. Tenendo lor camino trovaro il Re Meliadus trovarollo a guisa di cavaliere errante ke andava a uno torneamento e domandò i vasalli perk'elli menavano quello cavaliere così villanamente. Et elli risposero. Messer però k'elli a bene morte servita, esse voi il sapeste, voi il menareste più tosto di

Novella LXII.

Here is told a tale of Master Roberto.[1]

Mount Arimini[2] is in Burgundy,[3] where there was a lord of a very large territory called Master Roberto. The old countess and her maids had a great big oaf of a porter called Baligante.[4] One of the maids began to lay with him. This she revealed to another, and so it went until the news reached the countess. Hearing that he was heavily hung, the countess lay with him. The lord spied on them. He had Baligante murdered and had a pie prepared from his heart, which he presented to the countess and her maids, who promptly ate it. After they ate, the lord went to spend some time with his ladies and he asked about the pie. They all replied, "Good." Then the lord replied, "This comes as no surprise, since you enjoyed Baligante so much alive, that you should enjoy him dead." When they heard this, the countess and her maids were mortified and understood quite well that they had lost all honor in this world.[5] They resigned themselves to the veil and established a monastery called the monastery of the nuns of Mount Rimino. The holy house grew very large and became quite wealthy. And in a tale it is said to be true that there developed this custom that when some man passed by the house well attired, they would invite him in and treat him most honorably. And then the abbess and her sisters would gather about him. And concerning women, she who pleased him the most would serve him and accompany him from the table to the bed.[6] In the morning, upon rising, he would find ready water and a towel, and when he had washed, an empty needle and a silk thread would be placed before him. He would need to thread the needle in order to fasten his cuffs.[7] And, if after three attempts, he did not succeed in doing so, the ladies would remove his apparel and leave him with nothing. But if he succeeded in threading the needle in his three tries, they would return his apparel to him, and bestow upon him many lovely jewels.

Novella LXIII.

Concerning good King Meliadus[1] *and the Fearless Knight.*[2]

Good King Meliadus and the Fearless Knight were mortal enemies in the field. One day this Fearless Knight was traveling about disguised as a knight errant when he encountered his soldiers,[3] who loved him very much, but did not recognize him. And they said, "Tell us, knight errant, by the honor of all knighthood, between the Fearless Knight and good King Meliadus, who is the better knight?" And the knight replied, "May God grant me favor, King Meliadus is the best knight who ever rode in a saddle." Then these soldiers, who hated King Meliadus, for love of their own lord, treacherously surprised this man who was their lord and, armed as he was, they ousted him from his steed and pitched him across an old nag, saying, in chorus, that they wished to hang him. Along the road they met King Meliadus, whom they found also dressed as a knight errant

noi. Addomandatello di suo misfatto. Il Re Meliadus si trasse avanti e disse, Cavaliere ke ai tu misfatto a costoro ketti menano così laidamente? El Cavaliere rispose, niuna cosa. Nè misfatto o fatto loro sennon ke io volea mettere il vero avanti. Disse il Re Meliadus, ciò non può essere, contatemmi più vostro misfatto. Et elli rispose. Sire volentieri. Io sì tenea mio cammino a guisa d'errante cavaliere trovai questi sergienti e que' mi domandaro per la verità di cavaleria ke io diciessi qual fosse miglior cavaliere tral buon Re Meliadus, ol Cavalier sanza paura. Et io siccome io dissi di prima per mettere il vero avanti dissi kel Re Meliadus era migliore e nol dissi sennon per verità dire, ancora kel Re Meliadus sia mio mortal nemico e mortalmente il disamò. Io non volea mentire. Altro non o misfatto. E però subitamente mi fanno onta. Allora il Re Meliadus cominciò ad abbattere i servi e feciello sciogliere e donolli un ricco destriere con la insengnia sua coperta e pregollo kennon la levasse insino a suo ostello e, partirossi e ciascuno andò a suo cammino. Il Re Meliadus e' sergienti el Cavaliere giunsero la sera all'ostello. Levò la coverta della sella. Trovò l'arme del Re Meliadus kelli avea fatta sì bella diliberanza e donolli et era suo mortal nemico.

Novella LXIIII.

D'una Novella k'avenne in Provenza alla Corte del Po.

Alla corte del Po, di nostra donna in Provenza s'ordinò una nobile Corte quando il figliuolo del Conte Raimondo si fecie cavalier et invitò tutta buona gente. E tanta ve ne venne per amore kelle robbe ell'argento fallio. E convenne ke disvestisse de' cavalieri di sua terra e donasse a' cavalieri di corte. Tali rifiutaro. E tali consentiro. In quello giorno ordinaro la festa e poneassi un sparviere di muda in su un'asta. Or venia kissi sentia sì poderoso d'avere e di coraggio e levavasi il detto sparaviere in pungnio. Convenia ke quel cotale fornisse la corte in quello anno. I cavalieri e donzelli ke erano giulivi e gai si facieano di belle canzoni el suono el motto e quattro approvatori[a] erano stabiliti ke quelle ke aveano valore facieano mettere in conto. Ell'altre a kill'avea fatte dicieano kelle migliorasse. Or dimoraro e dicieano molto bene di loro singniore. Elli loro figliuoli furo nobili cavalieri e costumati. Or avenne ke uno di quelli cavalieri pongniamli nome Messer Alamano uomo di gran prodezza e bontade amava una molto bella donna di Provenza la quale avea nome madonna Grigia et amavalla sì cielamente ke niuno li le potea fare palesare. Avenne kelli Donzelli del Po si puosero insieme d'ingannarlo e di farlo vantare. Dissero così a cierti cavalieri e baroni. Noi vi pregamo kal primo torneare kessi farà kella gente si vanti. E pensaro così. Messere cotale è prodissimo d'arme e farà bene quel giorno del torneamento e scalderassi d'allegrezza, li cavalieri si vanteranno. Et elli non potrà tenere kennon si vanti di sua Dama. Così ordinaro. Il torneamento fedio.[b] Il Cavalier ebbe il pregio dell'arme. Scaldossi

on his way to a tournament. And he asked the vassals why they were carrying this knight in such an uncivil manner. And they replied, "Sir, because he well deserves to die. And if you knew why, you, rather than we, would be carrying him in this way. Ask him yourself about his crime." King Meliadus strode forward and said, "Knight, what crime have you committed against these men that they treat you in such a vile manner?" And the knight replied, "I have done nothing, nor have I committed any crime against them, except that I wished to put the truth forward." King Meliadus said, "This cannot be. Tell me more about your crime." And he replied, "Most willingly, Sire. I was traveling about, in the manner of a knight errant, when I happened upon these soldiers, and they asked me to tell them, by the verity of chivalry, who might the better knight be between good King Meliadus and the Fearless Knight. And I, as I stated previously, putting truth before all else, said that King Meliadus was better. And I only said this to state the truth, since King Meliadus is my mortal enemy and one I mortally hate. But I had no desire to lie, nor did I commit any other crime. Afterwards, however, these men immediately molested me." Then the king began to rebuke the servants and made them release the knight. Then he gave him a splendid horse, covering his coat of arms with a blanket. And he asked him not to uncover it until he reached his inn. And then they parted, each taking his own road. King Meliadus, the soldiers and the knight all arrived at the inn that evening. The knight removed the blanket from his saddle and found the coat of arms of King Meliadus, who had liberated him in such a wonderful way and had bestowed gifts upon him, even though he was his mortal enemy.

Novella LXIIII.

Concerning a tale from Provence at the court of Puy.

At the court of Puy-of-Our-Lady-in-Provence,[1] a noble court feast was ordered, to which all the good people were invited, when the son of Count Raimondo[2] was made a knight. And so many came, for love of the count, that provisions and money ran short. And it became necessary to take from the knights of his land and give their things to knights arriving at court. Some refused and some agreed. On the day that the feast was ordered, a moulting sparrow-hawk was placed on a pole. Then it was decreed that whoever felt so strong and courageous as to remove said sparrow-hawk with his bare hands would be required to equip the court for that year. The knights and squires, who were so cheerful and gay, composed words and music to lovely songs, and four judges were appointed who were to record those of merit and to tell those who composed the others to better them. Now they all remained there and said many wonderful things about their lord. And their sons were polite and noble knights. Now it happened that one of these knights, let's call him Master Alamano,[3] a man of great goodness and skill, was in love with a most beautiful lady from Provence, named Lady Grigia.[4] He kept his love quite secret so that no one would expose it.[5] It happened that the squires of Puy together proposed to deceive him and force him to boast about his lady. They said the following to certain knights and barons, "During the next tournament we ask you to drive

d'allegrezza. Nel riposare la sera e' cavalieri si incominciaro avantare. Ki di bella giostra. Ki di bello castello. Ki di bello Astore. Ki di bella ventura. El Cavaliere non si potè tenere kennon si vantasse k'avea così bella Dama. Or avenne ke ritornò per prender gioia dillei com'era usato. Ella Dama l'acconmiatò. Il Cavaliere sbigottì tutto, e partissi dallei e dalla compangnia de' cavalieri, et andonne in una foresta errinchiusessi in uno romitaggio sì cielatamente ke niuno il seppe. Or ki avesse veduto il cruccio de' cavalieri e delle Dame e Donzelle kessi lamentavano sovente della perdita di così nobile Cavaliere assai n'avrebbe avuto pietade. Un giorno avenne ke i Donzelli del Po smarriro una caccia e capitaro al romitaggio detto. Domandolli se fossero del Po. Elli risposero di sì. Et elli domandò di novelle. Elli Donzelli li presero accontare come v'avea laide novelle ke per picciolo misfatto aveano perduto il fior de' cavalieri ke sua Dama li avea dato conmiato e niuno sapea kenne fosse adivenuto. Ma procianamente[c] un torneamento era gridato ove sarà molto buona gente e noi pensiamo k'elli a sì gentil quore ke dovunque elli sarà si verrà a torneare con noi. E noi avemo ordinate guardie di gran podere e di gran conoscenza ke incontanente lo riterranno. E così speramo di riguadangniare nostra gran perdita. Allora il Romito scrisse a un suo amico sacreto kel dì del torneamento li trammettesse arme e cavallo sacretamente. E rinviò i donzelli. Ell'amico fornì la rikesta del Romito kel giorno del torneamento li mandò cavallo et arme, e fu il giorno nella pressa de' cavalieri et ebbe il pregio del torneamento. Le guardie l'ebbero veduto. Avisarollo. Et incontanente lo levaro in palma di mano a gran festa. La gente rallegrandossi abbatterli la ventagia dinanzi dal viso e pregarlo per amore ke cantasse. Et elli rispose. Io non canteroe mai se io non o pacie da mia Dama. I nobili cavalieri sillasciarono ire dalla Dama, e richieselle con gran preghera kelli faciesse perdono. La Dama rispose. Ditelli così k'io non li perdonerò giamai sennon mi fa gridare mercie a ciento Baroni et a ciento Cavalieri et a ciento Dame et a ciento Donzelle ke tutti gridino a una bocie mercie, e non sappiano a cui lassi chiedere. Allora il Cavaliere il quale era di grande savere si pensò ke s'appressava la festa della candellara[d] kessi faciea gran festa al Po elle buone genti veniano al monistero. E penso mia Dama vi sarà e saravvi tanta buona gente quanto ella addomanda ke gridino mercie. Allora trovò una molto bella canzonetta. Ella mattina per tempo salio in sue lo pergamo e cominciò questa sua canzonetta quanto seppe il meglio ke molto lo sapea ben fare e diciea in cotal maniera.

all the people to boastfulness." For they thought as follows, "This gentleman is a very brave warrior and he will fare well on the day of the tournament, and then he will become quite excited in his joy. The knights will begin to boast among themselves and he will not be able to keep from boasting about his lady." And so the tournament was ordered. The knight was wounded and earned great renown with his arms. He became quite heated with joy. That night, while relaxing, the knights began to boast among themselves. Some spoke of remarkable jousts, others of beautiful castles; some spoke of admirable goshawks, and still others of marvelous adventures. And the knight could not refrain from boasting about his lovely lady. Then the time came for him to return and receive his accustomed, joyous favors from her; but the lady dismissed him. The knight became completely bewildered. He left her and the company of knights and went way into the forest and cloistered himself in a hermitage so hidden that no one could find him. Now, anyone who saw the sorrow of the knights and ladies and damsels, who constantly grieved the loss of such a noble knight, would have felt much pity for them. One day it happened that the squires of Puy lost their way while hunting and happened upon the already mentioned hermitage. He asked if they were from Puy and they replied, "Yes." Then he queried them for news. And the squires began by telling him that they had bad news, that, because of a minor mishap, they had lost the flower of knighthood, for his lady had dismissed him and no one knew where he had gone. "But a tournament has been heralded, to be held shortly, where many good people will be and we believe that such a gentle heart, wherever he may be, will come to tourney with us. And we have ordered guards of great strength, who know him well, to quickly restrain him. And in this way we hope to regain our great loss." Then, secretly the hermit wrote to a friend, asking him to obtain, in secret, arms and a horse for him the day of the tournament. Then he sent the squires on their way. And the friend furnished the hermit's request, so that on the day of the tournament he sent him a horse and arms. And that day he stayed among the knights and earned much praise at the tournament. The guards saw him and observed him. Then, quickly, they lifted him up on their shoulders[6] amid great glee. The participants began to clap their visors up and down in front of their faces, as a sign of their happiness, and they begged him, in the name of love, to grant them a song. And he replied, "I will never sing again until I have made peace with my lady." The noble knights left him and went to his lady, and asked her, amid much supplication, to pardon him. The lady replied, "Tell him that I will never pardon him until he can make one hundred barons and one hundred knights and one hundred ladies and one hundred damsels cry out for his mercy, and they all must cry out for mercy in unison, but they must not know to whom they are addressing themselves." Then the knight, who was very wise, realized that the feast of Candlemas[7] was fast approaching and that it was a great feast day in Puy, when all the good people came to the monastery. "And I believe my lady will be there and that there will be enough good people present to satisfy the number she deemed necessary to cry out for mercy." Then he composed a most beautiful little song[8] and that morning, for a time, he climbed into the pulpit and began to perform his little song, something he knew how to do better than most, and he recited it in this way.

Altresì come il Leo fante, Quando cade non si può levare, E li altri allor gridare, Di lor vocie il levan suso, E io voglio seguir quell'uso, kel mio misfatto è tan' greve e pesante, Kella corte del Po n'a gran burbanza. Esse il pregio di leali amanti, Non mi rilevan già mai non sarò suso, Ke dengniasser per me chiamar mercie, Là 've poggiarsi con ragion non val ren.

Esse io per li fini amanti, non posso ma gioia ricobrar, Per tos temps las mon cantar, Que de mi mon atent, Plus e vivrai sì con reclus, Sol sanza solaz, Car tal es mon talens, Ke m'inervia d'onor e plager, Kar'ei non sui della maniere d'ors, Ke qui batte non tien vile, Se mercie adorne engras, Et muluira or ven.

Ab rot le mon sui clautz, De mi trop parlar, Ess'io poghes finis contrefar, Ke non es mai c'uns que s'art, E poi resurte sus ieu m'arserei, Car sui tan malannaz, E mis fais dig, Messongier turanz, E sortir con spire et con plor, La giovenz e bietaz e valor, Es que non deu fallir un pauo di merses, La udieuasis tutt'altri bon.

Mia canzone e mio lamento, Va' là u ieu non os annar, De' miei occhi sguardar, Tanto sono forfatto e fallente. Ia ie non me n'escus, Nè nul fu miei di donna, Ke fu'n dietro du an, Or torno a voi doloroso e piangente, Sì come cierbo k'a fatto su lungo cors, Torn'al morir al grido delli cacciatori, Et io così torno alla vostra mercie, Ma voi non cal se d'amor no soven.

Allora tutta la gente quella ke era nella chiesa gridaro mercie e perdonolli la Donna. Erritornò in sua gratia come era di prima.

Novella LXV.

Qui conta della Reina Isotta e di Messere Tristano di Leonis.

Amando Messer Tristano di Cornovaglia Isotta la Bionda moglie del Re Marco si feciero tralloro un sengniale d'amore di cotal guisa ke quando Messer Tristano le volea parlare si andava ad un giardino del Re dove era una fontana et intorbidava il rigangniolo[a] ke faciea la fontana et andava questo rigangniolo per lo pallazzo dove stava la detta madonna Isotta. E quando ella vedeva l'acqua intorbidata si pensava ke Messere Tristano era alla Fonte. Or avenne k'uno mal aventurato Giardiniere senn'avide di guisa kelli due amanti neente il potea non credere. Quel Giardiniere andò allo Re Marco e contolli ogni cosa com'era. Lo Re Marco si diede a crederlo. Si ordinò una caccia e partissi da' suoi cavalieri siccome si smarisse dalloro. Li cavalieri lo ciercavano erranti per la foresta ello Re Marco n'andò insù il pino ke era sopra la fontana ove Messere Tristano parlava alla Reina. E dimorando la notte lo Re Marco sul pino e Messere Tristano venne alla fontana et intorbidolla. E poco tardante la Reina venne alla fontana. E da ventura le venne un bel pensero ke guardò il pino. E vide l'ombra più spessa kennon solea. Allora la Reina dottò[b] e dottando ristette e parlò con Tristano in questa maniera e disse. Disleale Cavaliere io t'o fatto qui venire per potermi compiangere di tuo gran misfatto ke già mai non fu in cavalier tanta dislealtade quanta tu ai per tue parole

[9]Just as the elephant,[10] when he falls and cannot rise, and all the others use their voices to raise him up,[11] so do I wish to follow their way, for my misdeed is so grave and heavy, that the Court of Puy has experienced great arrogance. And if the pleas of loyal friends don't raise me, I will never stand tall again. For if they are not worthy to beg for my mercy, then to depend upon reason matters nothing.

And if I, through faithful lovers, cannot recover my joy. I will leave my song for all time. And from me the world must expect nothing else, and I will go and live as a recluse, alone without solace for such is my desire, as in my life pain is my pleasure. For I am not like the bear who does not weaken when beaten mercilessly, but grows fat, and heals and is revived.[12]

In front of the entire world, I accuse myself of having spoken too much. If only I could imitate the Phoenix, of which there is but one, that burns itself and then comes to life again. Just so I would burn myself, so unhappy am I of my false words and treacherous lies. And I would resurrect from sighs and tears, there where beauty, youth and nobility reside, All that is needed is a bit of mercy from all the good people assembled here.

My song and my lament; go where I dare not, where my eyes won't see, so sinful and humbled am I that no one has pardoned me, nor has the Best-Among-Ladies during these two years past. Now I return to you sorrowful and weeping, like the deer after fleeing so long, turns toward the cries of the hunters to die. Just so, I turn toward your mercy, but you will not concede if you heed not love.

Then all the people who were in the church cried out for mercy, and the lady pardoned him. And he was returned to her good graces just as before.

Novella LXV.

Here is told of Queen Isotta[1] and Master Tristan of Lyonesse.[2]

Master Tristan of Cornwall[3] was in love with Isotta the Blond,[4] the wife of King Mark.[5] Between themselves, they devised a love signal in the following manner: when Master Tristan wished to speak to her, he would go to one of the king's gardens where there was a fountain and disturb the waters in the rivulet which flowed from the fountain.[6] And this rivulet coursed throughout the palace, including through the rooms of Lady Isotta. And whenever she saw the turbulent waters, she knew that Master Tristan was at the fountain. Now it happened that a spiteful gardener saw all of this, without the two lovers realizing his discovery. That gardener went to King Mark and related to him how things stood. King Mark lent credence to him. He organized a hunt and left his knights, intentionally separating himself from them. The knights searched the forest high and low for him, while King Mark had climbed up a pine tree that rose above the fountain where Master Tristan used to speak with the queen. And while the king was spending the night in the pine tree, Master Tristan came to the fountain and disturbed its waters. And a short time later, the queen came to the fountain. But, as luck would have

kemm'ai unita.[c] Ello tuo Zio Re Marco ke molto t'amava ke tusse' ito parlando di me intralli erranti cavalieri cose ke nello mio quore non poriano mai disciendere. Et innanzi darei me medesima al foco ke io unissi così nobile Re come Monsingnior lo Re Marco. Onde io ti disfido di tutta mia forza siccome disleale cavaliere sanza niuno altro rispetto. Tristano udendo queste parole dubitò forte e disse. Madonna se malvagi cavalieri di Cornovaglia parlan di me tutto primamente dico ke già mai io di queste cose non fui colpevole. Mercie donna per dio elli anno invidia di me ke io già mai non feci nè dissi cosa ke fosse disinore di voi nè del mio Zio Re Marco. Ma da ke vi pur piacie ubbidirò a' vostri comandamenti. Andronne in altre parti a finir li miei giorni. E forse avanti ke io mora li malvagi cavalieri di Cornovaglia avranno sofratta[d] di me siccome elli ebbero al tempo dello Amoroldo quando io diliverai loro e loro terre di vile e di laido servaggio. Allora si dipartiro sanza più dire. Ello Re Marco ke era sopra loro. Quando udì questo molto si rallegrò di grande allegrezza. Quando venne la mattina. Tristano. Fe' sembianti di cavalcare. Fe' ferrare cavalli e somieri. Valletti vengniono di giù e dissù. Ki porta freni, ki selle. Il tremuoto era grande. Il Re s'adirò forte del partire di Tristano e raunò Baroni e' suoi cavalieri e mandò comandando a Tristano kennon si partisse sotto pena del quore sanza suo conmiato. Tanto ordinò il Re Marco kella Reina ordinò e mandolli addire kennon si partisse. E così rimase Tristano a quel punto non si partì. E non fu sorpreso nè ingannato per lo savio avedimento k'ebbero intrallor due.

Novella LXVI.

Qui conta d'uno Filosofo lo quale era chiamato Diogene.

Fue uno Filosofo molto savio lo quale avea nome Diogene. Questo Filosofo era un giorno bangniato in una troscia[a] d'acqua stavassi in una grotta al sole. Alessandro di Maciedonia passava con grande cavaleria. Vide questo Filosofo parlò e disse. Dhe uomo di misera vita chiedimmi e darotti ciò kettu vorrai. El Filosofo rispose, priegotti ke mitti levi dal sole.

it, she thought to look at the pine and saw a shadow there larger than usual. Then the queen became frightened, and because of her fear, she restrained herself and spoke to Tristan in the following manner. She said, "Unfaithful knight, I have made you come here so I could complain of your great crime. For there has never been a knight so full of disloyalty as you have shown by your words which have disgraced me and your uncle, King Mark, who has loved you so. That you could go and talk about me among the knights errant, speaking of such things that would never enter into my head! Why, I would sooner give myself to the fiery stake than disgrace such a noble king as my lord King Mark. And so, I defy you with all my strength for the unfaithful and disrespectful knight that you are." Tristan, hearing these words, became highly suspicious, and said, "My lady, if the evil knights of Cornwall have spoken in such a way about me, first and foremost I must say that I am not guilty of these things. By God, have mercy, dear lady. They are envious of me, for I have never said or done anything that would bring dishonor to you or my uncle King Mark. But if it is your wish, I will obey your command and go far away to live out the remainder of my days. But, perhaps, before I die, these evil knights of Cornwall might have need of me, just as they did during the time of Amoroldo,[7] when I delivered them and their lands from vile and ugly servitude." He then left, saying no more. And when King Mark, who was above them, heared this he rejoiced in great happiness.[8] When morning came, Tristan pretended to prepare for a long ride. He had horses and donkeys shoed. Pages were constantly coming and going; some carried bridles, others saddles. The commotion was tremendous. The king was greatly enraged by Tristan's departure. He assembled his barons and knights and sent a message to Tristan commanding him not to leave, under pain of death, without his permission. King Mark's orders were so insistent that the queen herself sent an order telling him not to leave. And so, for this time, Tristan remained and did not depart. Nor was he surprised nor deceived, thanks to the shrewd understanding which had developed between the two of them.

Novella LXVI.

Here is told of a philosopher called Diogenes.[1]

There once was a very wise philosopher named Diogenes. One day this philosopher was soaked with the water from a puddle, and so he went and stood in the full sun in a grotto. Alexander of Macedonia[2] passed by with his great calvary. He saw this philosopher, spoke and said, "Oh man of such a pathetic life, ask me and I will give you whatever you wish." And the philosopher replied, "I beg you to remove yourself from the sun's rays."

Novella LXVII.

Qui conta di Papirio come il Padre lo menò a consiglio.

Papirio fu Romano uomo potentissimo e savio e dilettissimo molto in battaglia. E credeansi i Romani difendersi d'Alexandro confidandossi nella bontade di questo Papirio. Quando Papirio era fanciullo il padre lo menava seco al consiglio. Un giorno il consiglio si comandò credenza. Ella sua madre lo stimulava molto ke volea sapere di ke i Romani aveano tenuto consiglio. Papirio veggendo la volontà della madre si pensò una bella bugia e disse così. Li Romani tennero consiglio quale era meglio tra kelli uomini avessero due mogli olle Donne due mariti acciò kella gente moltipilicasse perkè terre si rubellavano da Roma, onde il consiglio stabilio ke era meglio e più convenevole kel l'uomo abbia due mogli. La Madre kelli avea promesso di tenere credenza il manifestò a un'altra donna e quella a un'altra. Tanto andò d'una in altra ke tutta Roma il sentì. Ragunarossi le donne et andaronne a' Senatori e doleansi molto. Et elli temettero di maggior novità. Udendo la cagione diedero cortesemente loro conmiato e comendaro Papirio di grande savere per innanzi. Et allora lo commune di Roma stabilio ke niuno padre dovesse menare suo figliuolo a consiglio.

Novella LXVIII.

D'una quistione ke fecie un giovane ad Aristotile.

Aristotile fue grande Filosofo un giorno venne allui un giovane con una nuova domanda diciendo così, e maestro Io o veduto cosa ke molto mi dispiacie all'animo mio k'io vidi un vecchio di grandissimo tempo fare laide mattezze. Onde sella vecchiezza n'a colpa io m'accordo di voler morire giovane anzi ke invecchiare e matteggiare. Onde per Dio mettetecci consiglio se essere po'. Aristotile rispose, io non posso consigliare ke invecchiando la natura non muti in debolezza il buon calore naturale e non venga meno la virtù ragionevole e manca. Ma per la tua bella provedenza io t'apprenderò come io potrò. Farai così kennella tua giovanezza tu usarai tutte le belle e piacievoli et oneste cose e d'allor contra Dio ti guarderai al postutto e quando sarai vecchio non per natura nè per ragione viverai con nettezza ma per la tua bella e piacievole e lunga usanza k'avrai fatta.

Novella LXVII.

Here is told how Papirius'[1] father led him to Council.[2]

Papirius was a very powerful and wise Roman man who delighted very much in battle. And the Romans believed they could defend themselves against Alexander by entrusting themselves to the skills of this Papirius.[3] When Papirius was but a young boy, his father would take him to council. One day the council imposed an order of secrecy. But his mother pestered him greatly because she wished to know why the Romans had held council. Papirius, seeing his mother's desire, fabricated a wonderful lie and said, "The Romans debated whether it was better for men to have two wives or for women to have two husbands, in order to multiply the populace, since lands were rebelling against Rome. And so the council decreed that it was better and more suitable for a man to have two wives." His mother, who had sworn herself to secrecy, revealed this to another woman, and she, in turn, to another. The story went about from one woman to another until all of Rome had heard it. The women gathered together and went and complained bitterly to the senators. And the men feared this new major turn of events. Listening to their reasons, they graciously dismissed them, and commended Papirius for his great wisdom. And from that day forward, the Commune of Rome decreed that no father should bring his son to council.

Novella LXVIII.

Concerning a question that a young man asked of Aristotle.[1]

Aristotle was a great philosopher. One day a young man came to him with an original question, saying this, "Teacher, I have seen something that has caused great sadness in my soul. I saw an old man, of very advanced years, act like a crazy, dirty old man. Now, if old age is responsible, then I have come to the conclusion that I wish to die young, rather than become old and act insanely. For the love of God, if you can, put forth your council on this issue." Aristotle replied, "I can not deny, that while growing old, nature does not weaken the natural healthy warmth of the body, nor can I say that the ability to reason does not decrease. But because of your wonderful foresight, I will teach you as best I can. Act in the following manner. In youth, use all the lovely, pleasing and honest things; and be on your guard, above all else, not to act contrary to God. Then, when you grow old, it will not be because of nature or reason that you will live a clean, orderly life, but because of the lovely and pleasant habits to which you have long accustomed yourself."[2]

Novella LXIX.

Qui conta della gran giustitia di Traiano imperadore.

Lo'mperadore Traiano fu molto giustissimo singniore. Andando un giorno con la sua grande cavaleria contra suoi nemici. Una femina vedova lissi fecie dinanzi presello per la staffa e disse. Messer fammi diritto di quelli k'attorto m'anno morto il mio figliuolo. Ello'mperadore disse, io ti sodisfarò quando io tornarò. Et ella disse. Settu non torni? Et elli rispose, sodisfaratti lo mio successore. E sel tuo successore mi vien meno tummissei debitore. E pongniamo ke pure mi sodisfaciesse. L'altrui giustitia non libera la tua colpa. Bene averrae al tuo successore selli liberra se medesimo. Allora lo'mperadore smontò da cavallo e fecie giustitia di coloro k'aveano morto il figliuolo di colei e poi cavalcò e sconfise i suoi nemici. E dopo non molto tempo dopo la sua morte venne il beato San Grigoro papa e trovando la sua giustitia andò alla statua sua. E con lagrime l'onorò di gran lode e feciello disepelire trovaro ke tutto era tornato alla terra salvo kell'ossa ella lingua. Ecciò dimostrava come era suto giustissimo uomo e giustamente avea parlato. E Santo Grigoro orò per lui addio. E diciessi per evidente miracolo ke per li preghi di questo santo papa l'anima di questo Imperadore fu liberata dalle pene dell'inferno, et andonne in vita eterna et era stato pagano.

Novella LXX.

Qui conta d'Ercules come n'andò alla foresta.

Ercules fu uomo fortissimo oltre li altri uomini et avea una sua moglie la quale li dava molta travaglia. Partisse un dì di subito et andonne per una gran foresta e trovava orsi e leoni. Et assai fiere pessime tutte le squarciava et uccidea con la sua forza. E non trovò niuna bestia sì forte ke dallui si difendesse. E stette in questa foresta gran tempo poi tornò a casa alla moglie co' panni tutti squarciati con pelli di leoni addosso. La moglie lissi fecie incontro con gran festa e cominciò addire, ben vengniate singnior mio ke novelle? Et Ercules rispose, io vengnio dalla foresta tutte le fiere o trovate più umili di te. Ke tutte quelle k'io o trovate o soggiogate salvo kette. Anzi tu ai soggiogato me. Dunque se'ttu la più forte femina ke io mai trovassi k'ai vinto colui ke tutte l'altre cose a vinto.

Novella LXIX.

Here is told of the great justice of the Emperor Trajan.[1]

The Emperor Trajan was a very just lord. One day, while traveling with his great cavalry to engage the enemy, a widow came before him, and grasping his stirrup, she said, "Sire, grant me justice against those who have wronged me by the death of my son." And the emperor said, "I will give you satisfaction upon my return." And she said, "And if you do not return?" And he replied, "My successor will give you satisfaction." "And if your successor falls short, it is you who are indebted to me. And let us suppose that he does satisfy my request. Justice performed by others does not relieve you from your obligation. All good will go to your successor for discharging the debt himself." Then the emperor dismounted and dispensed justice against those who had killed the woman's son. Then he galloped away and defeated his enemies. And not long after he died, the Blessed Pope, Saint Gregory[2] came and, learning of his love of justice, went to his statue. And with tears, he honored Trajan with lavish praise and had his body exhumed. He found it completely returned to the earth, except his bones and tongue. And this proved that he had been a very just man who had always spoken justly. And Saint Gregory prayed to God for him. And because of this obvious miracle, it is said that the soul of this emperor was freed from the pains of hell through the prayers of this Sainted Pope, and went to live life everlasting, even though he had been a pagan.

Novella LXX.

Here is told how Hercules[1] *went into the forest.*

Hercules was stronger than all other men, but he had a wife[2] who gave him quite a lot of trouble. He left quickly one day and went into a great forest where he found lions and bears, and many even more dangerous beasts, all of which he tore apart and killed using his great strength. And he found no beast strong enough to defend itself from him. And he spent a long time in this forest, then he returned home to his wife, with his clothes all torn, wearing lion skins. His wife greeted him with great revelry, and began to say, "Welcome my lord, what news do you bring?" And Hercules replied, "I come from the forest where all the beasts I found were humbler than you. For I have vanquished all those I have encountered, except you. Moreover, it is you who have vanquished me. And so, you are the strongest woman I have ever known, for you have beaten him who has beaten all other things."

Novella LXXI.

Qui conta come Seneca consolò una donna a cui era morto uno suo figliuolo.

Volendo Seneca consolare una donna a cui era morto uno suo figliuolo siccome si leggie nel libro di consolatione disse cotali parole. Settu fossi femina siccome l'altre io non ti parlerei com'io farò. Ma però ke tusse' femina et ai intelletto d'uomo sitti dirò così. Due donne furo in Roma a ciascuna morì il figliuolo l'uno era de' cari figliuoli del mondo. Ell'atro era vie più caro. L'una si diede a ricievere consolatione e piacquelle essere consolata ell'altra si mise in un canto della casa errifiutò ogni consolatione e diessi tutta in pianto. Quale di queste due è il meglio? Settu dirai quella ke vuole essere consolata dirai il vero. Dunque perkè piangi? Se mi di', piango il figliuolo mio perkè la sua bontà mi faciea onorare. Dico kennon pianghi il danno tuo onde tu piangi te medesima, et assai è laida cosa piangere altri sè stesso. Essettu vuoli dire, il quor mio piange perkè tanto l'amava. Non è vero ke meno l'ami tu morto ke quando era vivo. Esse per amore fosse tuo pianto perkè nol piangevi tu quando era vivo, sapiendo ke dovea morire? Onde non ti scusare to' ti dal pianto. Sel tuo figliuolo è morto altro non può essere. Morto è secondo natura dunque per convenevole modo lo quale è di necessitade a tutti. E così consoloe colei.

Ancora si leggie di Seneca k'essendo Maestro di Nerone sillo batteo quando era giovane come suo scolaio e quando Nerone fu fatto Imperadore ricordossi delle battiture di Seneca sillo fecie pigliare. E giudicollo a morte. Ma cotanto li fecie di gratia kelli disse ke eleggiesse di qual morte elli volesse morire. E Seneca chiese di farsi aprire tutte le vene in un bangnio caldo. Ella moglie sil piangea e diciea, de' Singnior mio ke doglia m'è kettu mori sanza colpa? E Seneca rispose, meglio m'è ke io moia sanza colpa ke con colpa. Così sarrebbe dunque scusato colui, ke m'uccide attorto.

Novella LXXII.

Qui conta come Cato si lamentava contra alla ventura.

Cato Filosofo uomo grandissimo di Roma standо in pregione et in povertade parlava colla ventura e doleassi molto e diciea, perkè m'ai tu tanto tolto? Poi si rispondea in luogo della ventura e diciea così. Figliuolo mio quanto dilicatamente t'o allevato e nodrito e tutto ciò kemm'ai kesto t'o dato. La Singnioria di Roma t'o data. Singniore t'o fatto di molte dilitie, di gran palazzi, di molto oro, gran cavalli, molti arnesi. O figliuolo mio perketti ramaraki tue? Perk'io mi parta datte? E Cato rispondea, sì ramarico. Ella ventura rispondea. Figliuolo mio tusse' molto savio. Or non pensi tu k'io o figliuoli picciolini li quali mi convien nodricare, vuo'tu k'io li abbandoni? Non farebbe ragione.

Novella LXXI.

Here is told how Seneca[1] *consoled a lady over the death of her son.*

Seneca, wishing to console a lady over the death of her son, as is read in the book of consolation,[2] pronounced the following words, "If you were a woman as all others, I would not speak to you as I do. For, although you are a woman, you have a man's intelligence, and so I will speak to you as follows. There were two women in Rome, and each had lost her son. One son was one of the sweetest boys in the whole world, and the other was even sweeter. One woman accepted condolences and was heartened to be consoled. The other immured herself in a corner of her house, refusing all consoling gestures, giving herself over completely to tears. Which of these is the better mother? If you say she who wished to be consoled, then you speak the truth. So, why do you weep? If you say to me, `I weep for my son whose goodness brought me so much honor.' Then I would say to you; don't cry for your own loss, for you will be crying only for yourself, and it is a most repugnant thing to weep for yourself. And if you wish to say, `My heart weeps for it loved him so.' But it cannot be true that you love him any less dead than you did alive. And if your tears were for love; why then did you not weep when he was alive, knowing that some day he would have to die? And so, you have no excuse, so cease your weeping. If your son is dead, nothing can change that. Death is a component of nature. Therefore, it is an inevitable state which will necessarily come to everyone." And in this way he consoled her.

One also reads[3] that Seneca, having been the teacher of Nero,[4] beat him when he was his young student. And when Nero became emperor, he remembered those beatings and had Seneca seized. And he condemned him to death. But so many begged him for mercy that he said that Seneca could elect his own method of dying. And Seneca asked to have all his veins opened in a hot bath. And his wife wept and said, "My lord, it gives me such pain to have you die without blame." And Seneca replied, "It is better for me to die blameless, rather than with blame. For the latter would excuse him who wrongly had me killed."

Novella LXXII.

Here is told how Cato[1] *complained against Fortune.*[2]

Cato, the philosopher, was a very great Roman. While in prison and reduced to poverty, he spoke to Fortune and, complaining bitterly, said, "For what possible reason have you taken so much from me?" Then he himself replied, in Fortune's place, and said the following, "My son, how gently have I raised and nurtured you; and everything you ever asked of me I gave to you. I gave you the Seignory of Rome. I made you lord over many wonderful things, great buildings, much gold, powerful horses and many

Ai quanti piccioli figliuoli o a nutricare. Figliuol mio non posso star più teco. Non ti ramaricare. K'io non ti o tolto neente. Kecciò ke tu ai perduto non era tuo. Perciò kecciò kessi può perdere non è propio. Ecciò ke non è propio non è tuo.

Novella LXXIII.

Come il Soldano avendo bisongnio di moneta volle coglier cagione a un Giudeo.

Il Soldano avendo bisongnio di moneta fu consigliato ke cogliesse cagione a un ricco Giudeo k'era in sua terra e poi li togliesse il mobole[a] suo k'era grande oltra numero. Il Soldano mandò per questo Giudeo e domandolli quale fosse la migliore fede. Pensando, selli dirà la Giudea io li dirò kelli pecca contra la mia. Esse dirà la Saracina, et io dirò dunque perkè tieni la Giudea? Il Giudeo udendo la domanda del Singniore rispose così. Messer elli fu un padre k'avea tre figliuoli et avea un suo anello con una pietra pretiosa la miglior del mondo ciascuno di costoro pregava il padre k'alla sua fine li lasciasse questo anello. Il padre vedendo ke catuno il volea. Mandò per un fine Orafo e disse, Maestro fammi due anella così appunto come questo e metti in ciascuno una pietra ke somigli questa. Lo Maestro fecie l'anella così appunto ke nessuno conosciea il fine[b] altro kel padre. Mandò per li figliuoli ad uno ad uno et a catuno diede il suo in sacreto e catuno si credea aver il fine e niuno ne sapea il vero altri kel padre loro. E così ti dico delle fedi ke sono tre il padre disopra sa la migliore elli figliuoli ciò siamo noi, ciascuno si crede avere la buona. Allora il Soldano udendo costui così riscuotersi non seppe kessi dire di coglierli cagione sillo lasciò andare.

Novella LXXIIII.

Qui conta una Novella d'uno Fedele[a] e d'uno Singniore.

Uno Fedele d'uno Singniore ke tenea sua terra. Essendo a una stagione i fiki novelli il Singniore passando per la contrada vide in sulla cima d'un fico un bello fico maturo fecielsi cogliere. Il Fedele si pensò, da' kelli piacciano io li guarderò per lui. Sissi pensò d'imprunarlo[b] e di guardarli. Quando furo maturi silliene portò una soma[c] credendo venire in sua gratia. Ma quando li recò la stagione era passata ke n'erano tanti ke quasi si davano a' porci. Il Singniore veggendo questi fiki sissi tenne bene scornato e comandò a' fanti[d] suoi kel legassero e togliessero que' fiki et a uno a uno li le gittassero entro il volto. E quando il fico li venia presso all'occhio e quelli gridava, Domine ti lodo. Li fanti per la nuova cosa l'andaro addire al Singniore. Il Singnior disse, perk'elli dicieva

furnishings. Oh my son, why do you complain so? Is it because I have left you?" And Cato replied, "Yes, that is why I complain." And Fortune responded, "My son, you are very wise. Now, don't you think that I have many little children whom I must nurture? Do you wish me to abandon them? That would make no sense. Oh, how many little children do I have to nurture. My son, I cannot tarry any longer with you. Complain no more, for I have taken nothing from you. For that which you have lost was never truly yours, because the things a man can lose never truly belonged to him. And, the things that do not belong to you are not yours."

Novella LXXIII.

How the Sultan,[1] in need of money, wished to take advantage of a Jew.[2]

The Sultan, in need of money, was counseled to take advantage of a rich Jew who was in his land, and then to confiscate all his possessions that numbered well beyond counting. The Sultan sent for this Jew and asked him which was the best religion, thinking, "If he answers Judaism, then I will say that he sins against my religion. And if he says Islam, I will say, `Then why do you remain a Jew?'" The Jew, hearing his lord's question, answered in the following manner, "Sire, there once was a father who had three sons and he owned a ring with a precious stone that was the best in all the world. Each of his sons begged the father, upon his death, to leave him this ring. The father, seeing that each one wanted it, sent for a fine goldsmith and said, `Master, make me two rings just like this one, and put a stone in each that resembles this one.' The master goldsmith made exact copies, so that no one, except the father, could identify the original.[3] He sent for his sons, and one by one, gave to each one, in secret, his own ring. And each believed that he possessed the original, and no one, except their father, knew the truth. And so I say to you, concerning religion, that there are three, and Our Father above knows which is the best. We are his children, each one of us believes he practices the true one." Then, the Sultan, hearing this man recover himself in such a way, knew not what to say in order to gain the advantage over him. And so he let him go.

Novella LXXIIII.

Here is told a tale of a vassal and a lord.[1]

There was a vassal who maintained his lord's lands. During the season of new figs, the lord was passing through the countryside, when he saw a beautiful, mature fig at the top of a fig tree and had it picked. The vassal thought, "Since he likes them so much, I will keep an eye on them for him." And so he fenced them in with thorn-bushes and kept watch over them. When they ripened, he brought a chest of them to his lord, thinking in this way to win his favor. But when he picked them, the season had already passed, so that there were so many that they were practically feeding them to the pigs. The lord, seeing these figs, was highly insulted and ordered his servants to bind and strip

cosi? E quelli rispose. Messere perkè io fu incorato di recare pesche kess'io l'avessi recate io sare' ora cieco. Allora il Singniore incominciò a ridere e feciello sciogliere e vestire di nuovo e donolli per la nuova cosa k'avea detta.

Novella LXXV.

Qui conta come Domenedio s'accompangniò con uno Giullare.[a]

Domenedio s'accompangniò una volta con uno Giullare. Or venne un dì ke s'era bandito[b] una corte di nozze e bandissi uno ricco uomo k'era morto. Disse il Giullare, io andrò alle nozze ettu al morto. Domenedio andò al morto e guadangniò kel risuscito ciento bizanti.[c] Il Giullare andò alle nozze e satollossi e redì[d] a casa e trovò il compangnio suo k'avea guadangniato. Fecielli onore. Quelli era digiuno. Il Giullare si fe' dare danari e comperò un grosso cavretto et arostillo et arostendollo sinne trasse li ernioni[e] e mangiolli. Quando il compangnio l'ebbe innanzi domandò delli ernioni. Il Giullare rispose, e non anno ernioni quelli di questo paese. Or venne un'altra volta kessi bandiro nozze et un altro ricco uomo k'era morto. Et iddio disse, io voglio ora andare alle nozze ettu va' al morto. Et io t'insengniarò come tul risusciterai. Sengnierailo e comandaraili kessi levi suso et elli si leverà. Ma fatti fare l'impromessione dinanzi. Disse il Giullare, Benlo farò. Andò e promise di suscitarlo e non si levò per suo sengniare. Il morto era figliuolo di gran singniore. Il padre s'addiroe veggendo ke questi faciea beffe dillui. Mandollo ad impendere per la gola. Domenedio lissi parò dinanzi e disse, non temere k'io lo suscitarò. Ma dimmi per tua fe' ki mangiò li ernioni del cavretto? Il Giullare rispose, per quel santo secolo dove io debbo andare compangnio mio ke io non li mangiai. Domenedio veggendo kennon li le potea far dire increbbelli[f] dillui. Andò e suscitò il morto. E questi fu dilibero et ebbe la promessione kelli era fatta. Tornaro a casa disse Domenedio. Compangnio mio io mi voglio partir datte perk'io non t'o trovato leale com'io credeva. Quelli vedendo ke altro non poteva essere disse. Piaciemmi divedete et io piglierò. Domenedio fecie tre parti de' danari. Il Giullare disse, ke fai noi non semo sennon due, disse Domenedio, bene è vero ma questa una parte sia di colui ke mangiò li ernioni ell'altre, sia l'una tua ell'altra mia. Allora disse il Giullare, per mia fede da ke tu di' così, ben ti dico ke io li mangiai io sono di tanto tempo k'io non debbo omai dir bugia. E così si provano tali cose per danari le quali dicie l'uomo kennon le direbbe per iscampare da morte a vita.

the vassal, and, one by one, they threw those figs in the vassal's face. And when a fig struck near his eyes, the vassal screamed, "May the Lord be praised." Because of this strange reply, the servants went to relate it to their lord. The lord said, "Why did you say such a thing?" And he replied, "Sire, because I had been encouraged to pick peaches instead; and if I had picked them, I'd be blind by now." Then the lord began to laugh and had him untied and dressed once again. And he bestowed gifts on the vassal for the novelty of what he had said.

Novella LXXV.

Here is told how God was accompanied by a minstrel.[1]

God was once accompanied by a minstrel. Now, one day it happened that a nuptial feast and the death of a rich man were publicly proclaimed. The minstrel said, "I will go to the wedding, and you to the wake."[2] God went to the wake and earned a hundred bezants[3] for raising the corpse from the dead. The minstrel went to the wedding where he sated himself completely. Then he returned home and learned that his companion had made some money. The minstrel praised God who had been fasting. The minstrel had God give him some money and he bought a fatted kid and roasted it. And while it was roasting, he extracted the kidneys and ate them. When his companion had the food before him, he asked after the kidneys. The minstrel replied, "Oh, goats in this country don't have kidneys." Then, once again it happened that a nuptial feast and the death of another rich man were publicly proclaimed. And God said, "Now I want to go to the wedding and you go to the wake. And I will teach you how to raise him from the dead. Make the sign of the cross over him and then command him to rise, and he will arise. But make them promise your reward before hand." The minstrel said, "Fine, I'll do it." He went and promised to raise the man from the dead, but the man did not arise after the minstrel's sign of the cross. The dead man was the son of a very great lord. The father became angry when he saw this minstrel making a fool of him. He sent him to be hung by the neck. God appeared before him and said, "Have no fear, for I will raise him. But tell me, on your honor, who ate the kid kidneys?" The minstrel replied, "I swear on that holy place where I must spend eternity, my friend; I did not eat them." God, seeing that he could not make him tell the truth, became annoyed with him. He went and raised the dead man. And the minstrel was freed, and God received the promised reward that had been made. After returning home, God said, "My friend, I want to leave you because I have not found you to be loyal, as I once thought." The other one, seeing there was nothing more to be had, said, "It's fine with me, divide the money and I'll take my part." God divided the money into three portions. The minstrel said, "What are you doing? There are only two of us." God said, "This may all be well and true, but this part is for him who ate the kidneys; and the others, one is yours and the other mine." Then the minstrel said, "On my honor, since you put it that way, very well, I tell you that I ate them. I have arrived at an age when I should not tell lies any longer." And so it is proven that man will admit to certain things for money which he would not admit to even to save his life from death.

Novella LXXVI.

Qui conta della grande uccisione ke fecie il Re Ricciardo.

Il buono Re Ricciardo d'Inghilterra passò una volta oltre mare con Baroni Conti e Cavalieri prodi e valenti e passaro in nave sanza cavalli et arrivoe nelle terre del Soldano. E così a pie' ordinò sua Battaglia e fecie de' Saracini sì grandi uccisioni kelle balie de' fanciulli dicono quando elli piangono. Ecco il Re Ricciardo acciò ke come la morte fu temuto. Diciessi kel Soldano veggendo fuggire la gente sua domandò quanti Cristiani sono quelli ke fanno questa uccisione? Fulli risposto. Messere èllo Re Ricciardo solamente con sua gente. El Re cioè il Soldano disse. Non voglia il mio iddio ke così nobile uomo come il Re Ricciardo vada a piede. Prese un nobile destriere e mandollile. Il messaggio il menò e disse. Messere Il Soldano vi manda questo acciokè voi non siate a piede. Lo Re fu savio fecievvi montare su un suo scudiere acciokel provasse. Il Fante così fecie. Il cavallo era nodrito. Il Fante non potendollo tenere sissi drizzò verso il padiglione del Soldano a sua forza. Il Soldano aspettava il Re Ricciardo ma non li venne fatto. E così nelli amikevoli modi de' nemici non si dee uomo fidare.

Novella LXXVII.

Qui conta di Messer Rinieri cavaliere di Corte.

Messer Rinieri da Monte Nero cavaliere di Corte si passò in Sardengnia e stette col Donno[a] d'Alborea et innamorovvi d'una Sarda k'era molto bella. Giacque con lei. Il marito li trovò non li offese ma andossenne dinanzi al Donno e lamentosse forte. Il Singnore amava questo Sardo. Mandò per Messer Rinieri disselli molte parole di gran minaccie. E Messer Rinieri scusandossi disse ke mandasse per la donna e domandassella secciò ke fecie fu altro ke per amore. Le gabbe[b] non piacquero al Singniore. Comandolli ke sgombrasse il paese sotto pena della persona. E non avendollo ancora meritato di suo stallo[c] Messere Rinieri disse, piacciavvi di mandare in Pisa al Siniscalco vostro kemmi proveggia. Il Donno disse, cotesto farò io volentieri. Fecielli una lettera e dielille. Or giunse in Pisa e fu al detto Siniscalco et essendo con la nobile gente a tavola contò il fatto come era stato, e poi die questa lettera al Siniscalco. Quelli la lesse e trovò k'elli dovesse donare un paio di calze line a staffetta[d] cioè sanza peduli, e non altro. Et innanzi a tutti i cavallieri ke v'erano sille volle. Avendolle ebbevvi gran risa e solazzo. Di ciò non s'adirò punto perciò k'era molto gentil cavaliere. Ora avenne k'entrò in una Barca con un suo cavallo e con un suo fante e tornò in Sardengnia. Un giorno andando il Donno a solazzo con altri cavalieri e Messere Rinieri era grande della persona et avea le

Novella LXXVI.

Here is told of the great slaughter performed by King Richard.[1]

One time good King Richard of England traveled beyond the sea with his brave and valiant barons, counts and knights.[2] And they traveled in ships, without horses, and arrived in the lands of the Sultan.[3] And so he prepared to do battle on foot where he slaughtered so many Saracens that the nannies of their children still say to them when they cry, "Here comes King Richard, he who is as feared as death itself." It is said that the Sultan, seeing his people flee, asked, "How many Christians are involved in this slaughter?" And the reply was, "Sire, it is only King Richard with his men." And the king, that is the Sultan, said, "My God does not want a man as noble as King Richard to travel on foot."[4] He took a noble steed and sent it to him. A messenger brought it and said, "My lord the Sultan sends this to you so that you do not remain on foot." The king was a wise man. In order to test the horse, he had one of his squire's mount it. The servant did as he was told. The horse had been well nurtured. The servant was not able to control the horse, and so it went straight away, on its own steam, toward the Sultan's tent. The Sultan was expecting King Richard, but he, in fact, did not appear. And so, man should not place faith in the friendly advances of his enemies.

Novella LXXVII.

Here is told of Master Rinieri, knight of the court.

Master Rinieri da Monte Nero,[1] knight of the court, traveled to Sardinia and stayed with Lord[2] D'Alborea,[3] where he fell in love with a Sardinian woman who was very beautiful. He lay with her. Her husband happened upon them but did them no harm, instead he went before his lord and complained bitterly. The lord loved this Sardinian. He sent for Master Rinieri, addressing him with many threatening words. And Master Rinieri excused himself by asking the lord to send for the woman and to ask her if she had acted in such a way for any reason except love. Jokes were not pleasing to this lord. He ordered Master Rinieri to quit his country under pain of death. And not yet having earned anything from his stay, Master Rinieri said, "If it please you, send me to Pisa[4] where your seneschal[5] might provide for me." The lord said, "This I will do most willingly." He prepared a letter and gave it to him. Now, when he arrived in Pisa he went to the above mentioned seneschal, who was at table with many noble people, and related the facts to him as they stood, and then he gave this letter to the seneschal. He read it and learned that he was to give this man a pair of stirruped-linen hose, without stocking-padded feet, and nothing else. And he wished to receive his gifts in front of all the knights who were present. After having received them, they all laughed long and hard. He betrayed no anger, precisely because he was such a gentlemanly knight. Then it happened that, with his horse and servant, he boarded a boat and returned to Sardinia. One day, while the lord was traveling about, enjoying himself with some other knights,

gambe lunghe et era su un magro Ronzino et avea queste calze line in gamba. Il Donno il conobbe e con adiroso animo il fe' venire dinanzi dassè e disse. Ke è ciò Messer Rinieri ke voi non siete partito di Sardengnia? Certo, disse Messere Rinieri, sì sono ma sono tornato per li scappini[e] delle calze. Stese le gambe mostrò i piedi. Allora il Donno si rallegrò e rise e perdonolli e donolli la robba k'avea indosso e disse, Messere Rinieri tu ai saputo più dime e più ke io non t'insengniai. E que' disse. Messere Elli è al vostro onore.

Novella LXXVIII.

Qui conta d'uno Filosofo molto cortese di volgarizzare[a] la scientia.

Fue uno Filosofo lo quale era molto cortese di volgarizzare la scientia per cortesia a' singniori et altre genti. Una notte li venne in visione kelle dee della scientia a guisa di belle donne stavano al bordello. Et elli vedendo questo si maravigliò molto e disse, ke è questo non siete voi le dee della scientia? Et elle risposero, cierto sì. Come è ciò ke voi siete al bordello? Et elle risposero, bene è vero perkettusse' quelli ke vicci fai stare. Isvegliossi e pensossi ke volgarezzar la scientia si era menomar[b] la deitade. Rimasessenne e pentessi fortemente. E sappiate ke tutte le cose non sono licite a ongni persona.

Novella LXXVIIII.

Qui conta d'uno Giullare[a] k'adorava un Sengniore.

E fue un Singniore k'avea uno Giullare in sua corte e questo Giullare l'adorava siccome un suo iddio. Un altro Giullare vedendo questo sillie ne disse male. E disse. Or cui chiami tu iddio? Elli non è mai neuno. E quelli a baldanza[b] del Singniore sil batteo villanamente. E quelli così tristo non potendossi difendere andossenne arrichiamare al Singniore e disselli tutto il fatto. Il Singniore senne fecie gabbo.[c] Quelli si partì e stava molto tristo intra poveri perkennon ardiva di stare intra buone persone sill'avea quelli concio.[d] Or avenne kel Singniore fu di ciò molto ripreso sì kessi dispose di dare conmiato a questo suo Giullare a modo di confini et avea cotale uso in sua corte. Ke cui elli presentasse sissi intendea aver conmiato di sua corte. Or tolse il Singnior molti danari d'oro e fecielli mettere in una torta e quand'ella li venne dinanzi silla presentò a questo suo Giullare. E disse infrasse. Da poi k'elli mi convien donare conmiato io voglio kessia ricco uomo. Quando questo Giullare vide la torta fu tristo. Pensossi e disse. Io o mangiato serberolla e darolla all'oste mia. Andandonne con essa all'albergo trovò colui cui elli avea così battuto misero e cattivo, preselliene pietade, andò in verso

Master Rinieri, who was a very large person with long legs, came riding along on a skinny old nag, wearing those linen hose. The lord recognized him and, with an angry heart, had him brought before him and said, "What is this Master Rinieri, I thought you had left Sardinia?" "Why certainly I did," said Master Rinieri, "but I have returned for the foot pieces to my hose." He elongated his legs and exposed his bare feet. Then the lord cheered up, laughed and forgave him, and furnished Master Rinieri with the clothes off his own back. And he said, "Master Rinieri, you understand more than I, and have learned more than I ever taught you. And he replied, "All this is in your honor, lord."

Novella LXXVIII.

Here is told of a philosopher who most courteously undertook the translation[1] *of the sciences.*

There was a philosopher who was so courteous that he translated the sciences as a kindness to the gentry and other people. One night a vision came to him, where the goddesses of the sciences, in the guise of beautiful women, were living in a bordello. And he, seeing this, was flabbergasted and said, "What is this, are you not the goddesses of the sciences?" And they replied, "Why certainly." "How then do you find yourselves in a bordello?" And they replied, "Well, this is true because it is you who forces us to remain here." He awoke and realized that to translate the sciences was to belittle the gods. He remained there, thinking it over, and strongly repented his actions. And know that everyone is not entitled to every thing.[2]

Novella LXXVIIII.

Here is told of a minstrel who worshipped his lord.

And there was a lord who had a minstrel at his court and this minstrel worshipped him as if he were God. Another minstrel, seeing this, chided him about it. And he said, "Now, who are you calling God, when there is but one?" And the first one, encouraged by his lord's support, brutally beat him. The other, finding himself in such a sorry state and unable to defend himself, went and complained to the lord, telling him everything that had transpired. The lord made light of the situation. And so this minstrel left the court and remained in a most unhappy state among the poor, because he no longer dared to live among the good people, who had treated him so poorly. Now it happened that the lord was greatly criticized for this, to such an extent that he resolved to dismiss his minstrel and send him into exile. At his court there was a custom whereby whoever was presented with a gift by the lord, should understand it to mean expulsion from his court. Now this lord took a great many golden coins and had them placed inside a tart. And when his minstrel next came before him, the lord presented it to him. And the lord said to himself, "Since I must send him into exile, at least I wish him to go a rich man." When

lui e dielli quella torta. Quelli la prese andossenne con essa. Ben fu ristorato di quello k'ebbe dallui. E tornando al Singniore per isconmiatarsi dallui. Il Singniore disse. Or sei tu ancor qui non avestu la torta? Messersì ebbi. Or kenne faciesti? Messere io avea allora mangiato diedilla a un povero Giullare kemmi dicieva male per k'io vi chiamava mio iddio. Allora disse il Singniore. Va' con la mala ventura ke bene è miglior il suo iddio kel tuo e disselli il fatto della torta. Questo Giullare si tenne morto non sapea kessi fare. Partissi dal Singniore e non ebbe nulla dallui. Et andò kaendo[e] colui a cui l'avea data. Non fu vero ke mai lo trovasse.

Novella LXXX.

Qui conta una novella ke disse Messer Migliore delli Abbati di Firenze.

Messere Migliore Abbati di Firenze si andò in Cicilia al re Carlo per impetrar[a] gratia ke sue case non fossero disfatte. Il Cavaliere era molto bene costumato. E ben seppe cantare e seppe il Provenzale oltre misura ben proferere. Cavalieri novelli di Cicilia feciero per amore dillui un gran corredo.[b] Or venne ke furo levate le tavole. Menarollo a donneare.[c] Mostrarolli loro gioielli e loro camere. Intra quali li mostraro palle di Rame stampate nelle quali ardeano Aloe et Ambra e del fumo ke n'uscía oloravano le camere. In questo parlò Messere Migliore e disse. Questo ke diletto vi rende? L'uno parloe e disse. Quello perkè elle erano. Messere Migliore disse. Singniori male avete fatto. Questo non è diletto. Li cavalieri li feciero cerchio intorno. Domandaro il perkè e quando elli li vide affisati ad udire e que' disse. Singniori ogni cosa tratta della sua natura ma tutta è perduta. E que' domandaro, come? Et elli disse kel fumo dell'Aloe e dell'Ambra da loro perduto il buono odore naturale. Kella femina non vale neente se di lei non viene come di luccio[d] passetto.[e] Allora i cavalieri cominciaro affar gran solazzo e gran festa del parlare di Messer Migliore.

the minstrel saw the tart, he became extremely sad. Thinking to himself he said, "I have already eaten, I'll keep this tart and give it to my landlady." He took it to his lodgings, and there encountered the man whom he had beaten, still miserable and unhappy. He felt pity for him, went up to him and gave him the tart. The man took it and went on his way with it. He certainly was well compensated for all that he had endured on account of the court minstrel. Then the other minstrel returned to his lord to formally take his leave. His lord said, "You're still here? Didn't you receive a tart?" "Sire, I had it." "What did you do with it?" "Sire, I had already eaten and so I gave it to that poor minstrel who chided me for calling you my god." Then the lord said, "May misfortune follow you, for it is true that his god is better than yours." And then he told him all about the tart. This minstrel was dumb struck and knew not what to do. He left his lord and received nothing from him. And he went in search of the man to whom he had given the tart. Nor was it true that he ever found him again.

Novella LXXX.

Here is told a tale related by Master Migliore delli Abbati of Florence.[1]

Master Migliore Abbati of Florence went to King Charles in Sicily,[2] hoping to court his favor so that none of his properties would be destroyed. The knight was very well mannered. And he knew how to recite poetry well[3] and was extremely well versed in the Provençal idiom. All the new Sicilian knights prepared a grand banquet in honor of their love for him. Now, the time came to leave the table, and they led him away to where he could meet the ladies. They showed him their ladies' jewels and their bedchambers. Among the many things displayed were engraved copper balls in which aloe and amber were burning, and the smoke which escaped from them scented their bedchambers.[4] Master Migliore spoke concerning these balls, and said, "What pleasure does this give you?" And one spoke and said, "We do this because this is where women were." Master Migliore said, "Gentlemen, you have done wrong, for this can give no pleasure." The knights encircled him and asked for an explanation, and when he saw them intent on hearing his words, he said, "Gentlemen, everything operates according to its own nature; but here all this rule implies is lost." And they asked, "How so?" And he said that, because of the women, the smoke issuing from the aloe and amber had lost its fine, natural odor; "since a woman is worthless unless she smells like a pike past its prime."[5] Then the knights began to laugh mightily, most heartily welcoming the words of Master Migliore.

Novella LXXXI.

Qui disotto conta il consiglio ke tennero i Figliuoli del Re Priamo di Troia.

Quando i Figliuoli del Re Priamo ebbero rifatto Troia kell'aveano i Greci disfatta et avevano menato Talamone et Agamennon la loro suora Ensiona. I Figliuoli di Priamo si feciero ragunanza dilloro grande amistade e parlaro così intralli amici. Be' Singniori i Greci n'anno fatta grande onta. La gente nostra uccisero. La città disfeciero, e nostra suora ne menaro, E noi avemo riffatta la cittade e rafforzata, l'amistà nostra è grande. Del tesoro avemo raunato assai. Onde mandiamo alloro kecci facciano l'amenda. Kecci rendano Talamone et Ensiona e questo parloe Parigi. Allora il buono Ettorre ke passò in quel tempo di prodezza tutta la cavaleria a quello tempo parlò così. Singniori la guerra non mi piacie e non la consiglio perkelli Greci sono più poderosi di noi. Essi anno la prodezza, il tesoro, el savere, sikè non siamo noi da poter guerreggiare colloro per la loro gran potenzia e questo k'io dico io nol dico per viltade. Kesse la guerra sarae kennon possa rimanere io difenderò mia partita siccome un altro. E portaro il peso della battaglia. E questo è contra li arditi cominciatori. Or la guerra pur fue. Ettorre fu nella battaglia coi Troiani insieme elli era prode come un leone. Et uccise di sua mano duo mila cavalieri de' Greci. Ettorre uccidea li Greci e sostenea i Troiani e scampavalli da morte. Ma pur alla perfine fu morto Ettorre e i Troiani perdero ogni difesa. Kelli arditi cominciatori vennero meno nelle loro arditezze e Troia fu anke disfatta da' Greci e soprastettero loro.

Novella LXXXII.

Qui conta come la Damigiella di Scalot morì per amore di Lancialotto Dellac.

Una figliuola d'un grande Varvaso Re si amò Lancialotto Dellac oltre misura ma elli non le voleva donare suo amore imperciokè elli l'avea donato alla Reina Ginevra. Tanto amò costei Lancialotto k'ella ne venne alla morte e comandò ke quando sua anima fosse partita dal corpo ke fosse arredata una ricca navicella coperta d'uno vermiglio sciamito[a] con un ricco letto ivi entrò con ricche e nobili coverture di seta ornato di ricche pietre pretiose. E fosse il suo corpo messo in questo letto vestita di suoi più nobili vestimenti e con bella corona in capo ricca di molto oro e di molte ricche pietre pretiose e con ricca cintura e borsa. Et in quella borsa avea una lettera ke era dello infrascritto tenore. Ma imprima diciamo di ciò ke va innanzi la lettera. La Damigiella morì di mal d'amore e fu fatto di lei ciò ke disse. La navicella sanza vela fu messa in mare colla donna. Il mare la guidò a Camalot erristete alla riva. Il grido fu per la corte. I cavalieri e' Baroni dismontaro de' palazzi ello nobile Re Artù vi venne e maravigliavassi forte k'era sanza niuna guida. Il Re intrò dentro vide la Damigiella ell'arnese. Fe' apprire la borsa.

Novella LXXXI.

Here below is told of the council held by the sons of King Priam of Troy.[1]

When the sons of King Priam had rebuilt Troy, after the Greeks had destroyed it,[2] and Telamon[3] and Agamemnon[4] had led away their sister Hesione,[5] they called together their mighty allies and spoke among their friends in the following manner, "Well, gentlemen, the Greeks have committed a great outrage against us. They murdered our people, destroyed our city and led our sister away. And now we have rebuilt and reinforced the city. Our allies are mighty and we have more than restored our treasury. So, let us send a message to them demanding that they make restitution and return Telamon and Hesione to us." And this was spoken by Paris.[6] Then good Hector,[7] who in those times surpassed all of chivalry in valor, spoke in the following manner, "Gentlemen, I don't like war, and I do not advise it, since the Greeks are much more powerful than we. They have the power, the wealth and the knowledge, so much so that we are not able to engage them in battle because of their great power. And that which I say, is not said out of cowardice, for, if war comes and it cannot be avoided, I will defend my country like any other man. And I will carry my weight in battle." And this was directed against those who were so fired up to begin the battle. Now, war inevitably came. Hector went to battle with the Trojans and acted as bravely as a lion. And by his own hand, he slew two thousand Greek knights. Hector killed the Greeks and bolstered the Trojans, saving them from death. But, alas, in the end Hector was killed and the Trojans lost all possibility of defense, for those who at first were so fired up, began to wane in enthusiasm. And Troy was once again destroyed by the Greeks and controlled by them.

Novella LXXXII.

Here is told how the Lady of Shalott[1] *died for the love of Lancelot of the Lake.*[2]

A daughter of a great Vavasour King fell in love, beyond all measure, with Lancelot of the Lake; but he did not wish to return her love because he had already given his to Queen Guenevere.[3] This woman loved Lancelot so much that death came to her. And she decreed that, when her soul departed from her body, a sumptuous ship be furbished, covered by a vermilion brocade with a lavish bed underneath, bedecked in rich and regal silk bed covers, embellished with rich, precious stones. And her body was to be placed on this bed, garbed in her most elegant clothes, with a beautiful crown on her head, laden with much gold and many precious stones, and her body richly cinched with a purse attached. And in this purse there was a letter which read as is written below. But first let us tell what came before the letter. The lady died of love sickness and her instructions were executed exactly as she had said. The ship was put to sea without sails, with the lady aboard. The sea guided it to Camelot,[4] where it beached on the shore. A cry went up throughout the court. The knights and barons emptied their castles and

Trovaro quella lettera. Feciella leggiere e diciea così. A tutti i cavalieri della tavola ritonda manda salute questa Damigiella di Scalot siccome alla miglior gente del mondo. Esse voi volete sapere per k'io a mio fine sono venuta sì è per lo migliore cavaliere del mondo e per lo più villano cioè Monsingniore Messer Lancialotto Dellac ke già nel seppi tanto pregare d'amore k'elli avesse di me merciede. E così lassa sono morta per bene amare come voi potere vedere.

Novella LXXXIII.

Come Cristo andando un giorno co' disciepoli suoi per un foresto luogo videro molto grande tesoro.

Andando un giorno Cristo co' disciepoli suoi per un foresto luogo nel quale i disciepoli ke veniano dietro videro luciere da una parte piastre d'oro fine. Onde essi chiamando Cristo maravigliandossi perkè non era ristato ad esso sì dissero. Singniore prendiamo quello oro kecci consolerà di molte bisongnie. E Cristo si volse erripreselli e disse. Voi volete quelle cose ke togliono al rengnio nostro la maggior parte dell'anime. E ke ciò sia vero alla tornata n'udirete l'assempro[a] e passaro oltre. Poco stante due cari compangni lo trovaro, onde furo molti lieti et in concordia andaro alla più presso villa per menare uno mulo ell'altro rimase a guardia. Ma udite opere ree kenne seguiro poscia[b] de' pensieri rei kel nemico die loro. Quelli tornò col mulo e disse al compangnio, io o mangiato alla villa ettu dei avere fame mangia questi duo pani così belli e poi carikeremo. Quelli rispose, io non o gran talento di mangiare ora e però carichiamo prima. Allora presero a caricare. E quando ebbero presso ke caricato quelli k'andò per lo mulo si kinò per legare la soma ell'altro li corse di dietro a tradimento con uno appuntato coltello et uccisello. Poscia prese l'uno di que' pani e diello al mulo. Ell'altro mangiò elli. Il pane era attoscato cadde morto elli el mulo inanzi ke movessero di quel luogo ell'oro rimase libero come di prima. Il nostro Singnior passò indi con suoi disciepoli nel detto giorno e mostrò loro l'assempro ke detto avea.

Novella LXXXIIII.

Come Messere Azzolino fecie bandire[a] una grande pietanza.

Messere Azzolino Romano fecie bandire una volta nel suo distretto et altrove ne fecie invitata ke volea fare una grande limosina. E però tutti i poveri bisongniosi uomini come femine. Et a cierto die fossero nel prato suo et a catuno darebbe nuova gonella e

noble King Arthur[5] came and was quite startled by this ship without a pilot. The king went aboard and saw the lady and all her trappings. He had her purse opened and found the letter. He had it read and it said the following, "To all the knights of the Round Table, this Lady of Shalott sends you greetings, for you are the best people in all the world. And if you wish to know how I came to such an end, it is for the best knight in the entire world, and the cruelest one, My Lord Master Lancelot of the Lake, to whom I knew not how to beg for love so that he would take pity on me. And so, alas, I died for love, as you can plainly see."

Novella LXXXIII.

How Christ was walking one day with his disciples through a wooded place when they saw a very great treasure.

One day Christ was walking with his disciples through a wooded place when those bringing up the rear saw, off to one side, light reflecting off slabs of pure gold. And these men called to Christ and were amazed that such news did not even cause him to break his stride. And they said, "Lord, let's take this gold, for it will satisfy many of our needs." And Christ turned to them, chastised them and said, "You wish for those things which ousted the majority of souls from our kingdom. And to prove this, on the return trip, you will hear an example of this." And then they walked on. A short time later, two dear companions came upon the gold, a find which made them quite happy. And they agreed completely that one should make for the nearest house and bring back a mule, while the other should remain on guard. But now listen to the wicked deeds that followed, and then the wicked thoughts given to them by the Evil One. The man returned with the mule and said to his companion, "I have eaten at that house, but you must be hungry. Eat these two very nice loaves of bread and then we'll load the mule." The other replied, "Right now I'm not very hungry, so first let's load the mule." Then they set to work loading the mule. And when they were almost done loading, the man who had brought the mule bent down to fasten the cargo, when the other ran up behind him and, with a pointed knife, treacherously murdered him. Then he took one of the loaves of bread and gave it to the mule, and the other he ate himself. The bread had been laced with poison. Both he and the mule fell dead before they could move from that very spot. And so the gold remained free, exactly as it had been before. On the prescribed day, Our Lord passed by once again with his disciples and showed them the example, just as he had said he would.

Novella LXXXIIII.

How Master Azzolino[1] had a great feast proclaimed.

One time, Master Azzolino Romano had proclaimed throughout his district, and extended invitations elsewhere, that he wished to perform a great charity. And all the

molto da mangiare. La novella si sparse. Trasservi d'ongni parte. Quando venne il giorno dell'agunanza. I Sescalchi[b] suoi furo tralloro con le gonelle e con la vivanda et a uno a uno li faciea spogliare e scalzare tutto igniudo e poi lo rivestia di panni nuovi e davalli mangiare. Quelli rivoleano i loro stracci ma neente valse ke tutti li mise in un monte e cacciovvi entro fuoco. Poi vi trovò tanto oro e tanto argento ke valse più ke tutta la spesa, e poi li rimandò con dio.

Et al suo tempo lissi richiamò un villano d'un suo vicino k'elli avea imbolato[c] ciriegie. Compario l'accusato e disse, mandate a sapere secciò può essere perciò kel ciriegio e finemente imprunato.[d] Allora Messere Azzolino ne fecie prova ell'accusatore condannò in quantità di moneta però kessi fidò più nelli pruni ke nella sua singnioria. Ell'altro diliberrò.

Per tema della sua tirannia una li portò un sacco di noci le quali non si trovaro somiglianti. Et essendossi il meglio acconcia[e] k'ella poteo giunse colà dove elli era co' suoi cavalieri e disse, Messer Dio vi dea lunga vita. Et elli sospecciò e disse, perkè diciesti così? Et ella rispose. Perkè secciò sarà noi staremo in lungo riposo. E quelli rise e fecielle mettere un bel sottano il quale le dava a ginocchio e feciellavvi cingere su e tutte le noci fecie versare per la sala e poi a una a una li le faciea ricoglier errimettere nel sacco, e poi la meritò grandemente.

In Lombardia e nella Marca si chiamano le Pentole, *ole*. La sua famiglia avevano un dì preso un pentolaio per malleveria[f] e menandollo a giudicie. Messer Azzolino era nella sala disse, ki è costui? Uno rispose. Messer è un olaro. Andalo ad impendere. Come Messere ke è un olaro. Et io però dico ke voi l'andiate ad impendere. Messere noi diciamo k'elli è uno olaro. Et ancor dico io ke voi l'andate ad impendere. Allora il giudicie senn'accorse. Fecielne inteso ma non valse ke perkè avea detto tre volte convenne ke fosse impeso.

Addire come fu temuto sarrebbe gran tela[g] e molte persone il sanno. Ma si ramenterrò come essendo elli un giorno con lo'mperadore a cavallo con tutta lor gente s'ingaggiaro ki avesse più bella spada sotto. Lo'mperadore trasse la sua del fodero k'era maravigliosamente fornita d'oro e di pietre. Allora disse Messere Azzolino, molto è bella ma la mia è assai più bella. Ettrassella fuori. Allora seicento cavalieri k'erano con lui trassero tutti mano alle loro. Quando lo'mperadore vide le spade disse ke ben'era la più bella. Poi fu Azzolino preso in battaglia in un luogo kessi chiama Casciano percosse tanto il capo al feristo[h] del padiglione overa legato kessi uccise.

needy poor, men as well as women, on a certain day were to assemble in his field, and each person would be given a new robe and much to eat. The news spread and traveled everywhere. When the day of the gathering arrived, his Seneschals[2] moved among the people with robes and food. And, one by one, they made each person strip off his clothes and remove his shoes, until each was completely naked, and then each was dressed in new clothes and given food to eat. The people wanted their rags returned to them, but since they were worthless, Azzolino had them gathered into a pile and set aflame. Afterwards, he found amid the ashes,[3] huge amounts of gold and silver, worth more than all he had spent. And so, in God's name, he sent them on their way.

And during Azzolino's time, a peasant of one of his neighbors was accused of having stolen some cherries. The accused appeared before him and said, "Send word to learn if this is possible, since the cherry tree is surrounded by a dense, thorny hedge." Then Master Azzolino had this substantiated and sentenced the accuser to pay a sum of money, because he had placed his trust in thorns rather than in the power of his lord. And the other man was set free.

Fearing his tyranny, a woman brought Master Azzolino a sack of nuts, the likes of which were not to be found in those parts. And, having fixed herself up as best she could, she arrived in that place where he was with his knights, and she said, "Sire, may God grant you long life." And he became suspicious and said, "Why did you say such a thing?" And she replied, "Because if such were to come to pass, we would be in for a nice long rest." And then he laughed and had her dressed in a lovely skirt which reached her knees. And he had her cinch it up about her waist, while he had all the nuts spilled throughout the hall. And then, one by one he had her gather them up and replace them in the sack. Afterwards he rewarded her grandly.

In Lombardy and in the Marches pots are called *ole*. One day his relatives arrested a potter and, to determine his bail, they brought him before a judge. Master Azzolino was in the courtroom. He said, "Who is this man?" And one replied, "Sire, he is a potter [thief]."[4] "Go and hang him." "What, Sire, because he is a potter [thief]? "You should go and hang him, I say." "But, Sire, we have said that he is a potter [thief]." "And again I say that you should go and hang him." Then the judge realized what was happening and explained the misunderstanding to him, but to no avail; since he had said it three times, it was necessary to have him hung.

As many people know, it would be an enormous undertaking to tell how much he was feared. But it was remembered how, one day, while riding with the emperor[5] and all his men, the two began to argue about who had the more beautiful sword under his cloak. The emperor unsheathed his sword from its scabbard. It was marvelously embellished with gold and gems. Then Master Azzolino said, "It is very lovely, but mine is lovelier still." And he unsheathed his sword. At the same time, six hundred knights who were with him, all put their hands to their swords. When the emperor saw their swords he said that truly Azzolino had the lovelier one.

Then Azzolino was taken in battle, in a place called Casciano, and he beat his head against the iron pole of a pavilion where he had been bound and killed himself.[6]

Novella LXXXV.

D'una grande carestia ke fu una volta in Gienova.

In Gienova fu un tempo gran caro[a] ellà si trovavano più ribaldi sempre ke in niuna altra terra. Tolsero alquante Galee. E tolsero conducitori e pagarli e mandaro il bando[b] ke tutti li poveri andassero alla riva et avrebbero del pane del commune. Andarvene tanti ke maraviglia fu, ecciò fu perkè molti ke non erano bisongniosi si travisaro[c] elli ufficiali dissero così. Tutti questi non si potrebbero ciernire[d] ma vadano li citadini su questo lengnio e' forestieri nell'altro. Elle femine co' fanciulli in quelli altri sì ke tutti v'andaro suso. I conducitori furo presti diedero de' remi in acqua et apportarli in Sardengnia. Ellà li lasciaro ke v'era dovitia[e] et in Gienova ciessò il caro.

Novella LXXXVI.

Qui conta d'uno k'era ben fornito adismisura.

Fu uno k'avea sì grande naturale ke non trovava neuno ke fosse sì grande ad assai. Or avenne ke un giorno si trovò con una putta ke non era molto giovane et avengnia ke molto fosse orrevole[a] e ricca molti n'avea veduti e provati. Quando furo in camera et elli lo mostrò. E per grande letitia la Donna rise. Que' disse, ke venne pare? Ella Donna rispose.*

Novella LXXXVII.

Come uno s'andò a confessare.

Uno s'andò a confessare al prete suo et intrall'altre cose disse, io o una mia congniata el mio fratello è lontano e quando io ritorno a casa per grande domistikezza[a] ella missi pone a sedere in grembo come debbo fare? Rispose il prete, a me il faciesse ella k'io la ne pagherei bene.

Novella LXXXVIII.

Qui conta di Messer Castellano da Cafferi di Mantova.

Messere Castellano da Mantova essendo Podestà di Firenze si nacque una quistione tra Messere Pepo Alemanni e Messer Cante Caponsacchi tale kenne furo a gran minaccie. Onde la Podestà per ciessar quella briga[a] silli mandoe a' confini. Messer Pepo

Novella LXXXV.

Concerning a great famine that occurred in Genoa.[1]

In Genoa there was once a great famine.[2] And one always found there more scoundrels than in any other land. They brought out some galleys and sailors whom they paid. Then they sent out a proclamation directing all the poor to go down to the shore where they would receive bread from the Commune. It was incredible how many people came there. And this was because many who were not in need disguised themselves as such. And the officials said the following, "One could never separate the truly needy from all these people. So make all the citizens board this boat and foreigners on the other. And women and children on those other boats, until everyone is aboard." The sailors were quick to dip their oars into the water and brought them to Sardinia. And there they left them where there was plenty, and the famine ceased in Genoa.

Novella LXXXVI.

Here is told of a man who was well endowed beyond all measure.

There was a man whom nature had endowed so grandly that no one larger could be found anywhere. Now it happened one day that he found himself with a whore who was not very young but who happened to be rich and from an honorable family, and who had been seen and tried by many. When they were in her bedroom, he showed it to her. And in her great joy, the lady laughed. The man said, "So, what do you think of it?" And the lady replied, [*1].

Novella LXXXVII.

How a man went to confession.

A man went to confess himself to his priest, and among other things, he said, "I have a sister-in-law, and my brother is far away, and when I return home, with great intimacy, she seats herself on my lap. What am I to do?" The priest replied, "If she would only do that to me, I'd pay her well for it."

Novella LXXXVIII.

Here is told of Master Castellano da Cafferi from Mantua.[1]

While Master Castellano from Mantua was the podesta[2] of Florence, such an argument was born between Master Pepo Alemanni[3] and Master Cante Caponsacchi[4] that escalated into serious threats. Whereby the podesta, in order to arrest this trouble, sent

mandò in cierta parte, e Messere Cante perk'era grande suo amico sil mandò a Mantova. Erraccomandollo a' suoi, e Messere Cante li le ne rendeo tal guidardone kessi giaciea con la moglie.

Novella LXXXIX.

Qui conta d'un uomo di Corte[a] ke cominciò una Novella ke non venia meno.

Brigata de' Cavalieri cienavano una sera in una gran casa Fiorentina et aveavi un uomo di Corte il quale era grandissimo favellatore. Quando ebbero cienato cominciò una Novella kennon ne venia meno. Uno Donzello[b] della casa ke servia e forse non era troppo satollo lo chiamò per nome e disse. Quelli kett'insengniò cotesta Novella non latt'insengniò tutta. Et elli rispose, perkè no? Et elli rispose, perkè non t'insengniò l'arrestata. Onde quelli si vergongniò e ristette.

Novella XC.

Qui conta come lo'mperadore Federigo uccise un suo falcone.

Lo'mperadore Federigo andava una volta a falcone et avevane uno molto sovrano kell'avea caro più d'una cittade. Lasciollo a una Grua quella montò alta. Il falcone si mise alto molto sopra lei. Videssi sotto una Guglia[a] giovane percossella a terra e tanto la tenne kell'uccise, Lo'mperadore corse credendo ke fosse una Grua trovò come era. Allora con ira chiamò il Giustitiere[b] e comandò kal falcone fosse tagliato il capo perkè avea morto lo suo Singniore.

Novella XCI.

Come uno si confessò da un frate.

Uno si confessò da un frate e disse ke essendo elli una volta alla ruba di una casa con assai gente, il mio intendimento si era trovare in una cassa ciento fiorini d'oro et io la trovai vota onde io nonne credo avere peccato. Il Frate rispose, cierto sì ai come settu li avessi avuti. Questi si mostrò molto crucciato e disse, per dio consigliatemmi. El Frate rispose, io non ti posso consigliare settu nolli rendi. E que' rispose, io lo fo volentieri ma non so a cui. Et il Frate rispose, recalli amme et io li darò per dio. Questi li promise e partissi e prese tanta contezza kevvi tornò l'altra mattina. E ragionando collui disse k'elli era suto mandato uno bello storione[a] e ke li le volea mandare a disinare. Ello Frate li rende molte gratie. Partissi questi e non li le mandò. Ell'altro dì tornò al Frate con

them both into exile. He sent Master Pepo off to certain parts, and Master Cante, because he was a good friend of his, he sent to Mantua, entrusting him to his family's care. And Master Cante repayed this kindness by laying with his wife.

Novella LXXXIX.

Here is told of a man of the court[1] who began a tale that never seemed to end.

One evening a group of knights were dining in a great Florentine house, and with them was a man of the court who was a very great storyteller. When they had finished dining, he began a tale that never seemed to end. A page of the household, who was serving them and who probably had not eaten his fill, called to him by name and said, "He who taught you this tale did not teach you all of it." And he replied, "Why not?" And the other replied, "Because he did not teach you the ending." Whereby the man became ashamed and ceased speaking.[2]

Novella XC.

Here is told how the Emperor Frederick[1] killed one of his falcons.

Once the Emperor Frederick went falconing and he had with him a most regal bird that he held dearer than an entire city. He loosed it after a crane that had flown on high. The falcon positioned itself much higher, over the crane. Below, it espied a young eagle which it struck to the ground and held tightly until it was killed. The emperor ran to the scene, expecting to see a crane; instead he found things as they were. Then, greatly angered, he called his executioner and commanded him to cut off the falcon's head because he had killed his own lord.[2]

Novella XCI.

How a man confessed himself to a friar.

A man confessed himself to a friar and said that he had once gone to rob a house with many other people. "It was my understanding that we were to find one hundred golden florins[1] in a safe, but I found it empty; therefore, I believe I have committed no sin." The friar replied, "Of course you have, just as if you had gotten them." The man looked quite disturbed and said, "In the name of God, advise me." And the friar replied, "I can not advise you unless you return the money." And he replied, "I would do so willingly, but I don't know to whom." And the friar replied, "Give it to me and I will give it away in the name of God." The man promised to do so and left, completely understanding the situation so that the next morning he returned there. And while freely conversing with the friar, he said that he had been sent a fine sturgeon and he wished to

allegra ciera.[b] El Frate disse. Perkè mi faciesti tanto aspettare? E que' rispose, o credevatello voi avere? Cierto sì. E non l'aveste? No. Dico ke è altrettale come se voi l'aveste avuto.

Novella XCII.

Qui conta d'una buona femina k'avea fatta una fine crostata.[a]

Fue una femina k'avea fatta una fine crostata da riguille[b] et avevalla messa nella madia. Vide entrare uno topo per la fenestrella ke trasse all'odore. Quella allettò la gatta e missella nella madia perkè lo pigliasse. Il topo si nascose tralla farina ella gatta si mangiò la crostata e quando ella aperse il topo ne saltò fuori. Ella gatta perk'era sattolla non lo prese.

Novella XCIII.

Qui conta d'uno Villano kess'andò a confessare.

Un Villano s'andò un giorno a confessare e pigliò dell'acqua benedetta e vide il Prete ke lavorava nel colto[a] chiamollo e disse, o Sere io mi vorrei confessare. Rispose il Prete, ofessastititu[b] anno? E que' rispose, sì. Or metti un danaio[c] nel colombaio,[d] e quella medesima ragione ti fo uguanno[e] ke anno.

Novella XCIIII.

Qui conta della volpe e del mulo.

La volpe andando per un bosco si trovò un mulo e non avea mai più veduti. Ebbe gran paura e fuggì e così fuggiendo trovò il lupo disse come avea trovata una novissima bestia e non sapea suo nome. Il lupo disse, andiamvi. Furo giunti allui. Al lupo parve vie più nuova. La volpe il domandò. Il mulo rispose, cierto io non l'o bene a mente ma settu sai leggiere io l'o scritto nel pie' diritto di dietro. La volpe rispose, lassa k'io non so leggiere ke molto lo sapre' volentieri. Rispose il lupo, lascia fare amme ke molto lo so ben fare. Il mulo silli mostrò il pie' diritto sì kelli chiovi pareano lettere. Disse il lupo, io non le veggio bene. Rispose il mulo, fatti più presso perokè sono minute. Il lupo si fecie sotto e guardava fiso. Il mulo trasse e dielli un calcie tale kell'uccise. Allora la volpe senn'andò e disse, ongni uomo kessa lettera non è savio.

send it to him for supper. And the friar thanked him heartily. The man left, but did not send it to him. And the next day, with a smile on his face, he returned to the friar. And the friar said, "Why did you make me wait so long?" And he replied, "Oh, did you really think that you would have it?" "Of course." "And did you have it?" "No." "Then, I say that it is the same as if you had gotten it."

Novella XCII.

Here is told of a good woman who had baked a fine tart.

There was a woman who had baked a fine eel tart and had placed it in the cupboard. She saw a mouse enter by a window, drawn by its aroma. She beckoned to her cat and placed it in the cupboard to grab the mouse. The mouse hid itself in some flour, and the cat ate the tart. And when she opened the door, the mouse jumped out, but the cat did not catch it because its belly was full.

Novella XCIII.

Here is told of a peasant who went to confess himself.

One day a peasant went to confess himself and, while taking some holy water, he saw the priest working in his garden. He called to him and said, "Oh Father, I wish to confess myself." The priest replied, "Did you confess your offences last year?" And he replied, "Yes." "Then put a coin in the poor box, and the lecture I gave you last year applies to this year as well."

Novella XCIIII.

Here is told of the vixen and the mule.[1]

While traveling through a wood, a vixen came across a mule, the likes of which she had never seen before. She became quite frightened and fled, and while fleeing she met a wolf and told him how she had found a new kind of animal and didn't know its name. The wolf said, "Let's go back there." They went back to the mule. To the wolf it truly seemed something new. The vixen asked its name. The mule replied, "Why, I most certainly don't have it on the tip of my tongue, but if you know how to read, I wrote it on my right, back hoof." The vixen replied, "Oh dear, I don't know how to read, but I'd be most willing to learn." The wolf replied, "Leave it to me, for I know how to read very well." The mule showed him his right hoof, where the shoe nails seemed to form letters. The wolf said, "I can't see them very well." The mule replied, "Come closer because the letters are quite small." The wolf bent down closer and stared intently. The mule drew back his hoof and gave him such a kick that it killed him. Then the vixen ran away and said, "Not every man who knows his letters is wise."

Novella XCV.

Qui conta d'uno Martore[a] di villa[b] k'andava a cittade.

Uno Martore di villa venia a Firenze per comperare uno farsetto.[c] Domandò a una bottega ove era. Il Maestro, non v'era. Uno disciepolo disse. Io sono il Maestro ke vuoli? Voglio uno farsetto. Questi ne trovò uno. Provollile. Furo a mercato.[d] Questi non avea il quarto de' danari. Il disciepolo mostrandossi d'acconciarlo[e] da piede silli appuntò la camiscia col farsetto e poi disse, tralti. Quelli lossi trasse. Rimase ingnudo. Li altri disciepoli furo intenti colle correggie.[f] Lo scoparo per tutta la contrada.

Novella XCVI.

Qui conta di Bito e di Ser Frulli di Firenze da San Giorgio.[a]

Bito fu Fiorentino e fu bello uomo di corte[b] e dimorava a San Giorgio Oltr'arno. Avea un vecchio k'avea nome Ser Frulli et avea un suo podere di sopra a San Giorgio molto bello sì ke quasi tutto l'anno vi dimorava con la famiglia sua et ongni mattina mandava la Fante[c] sua a vender frutta o kamangiare[d] alla Piazza del Ponte.[e] Et era sì iscarsissimo[f] e sfidato ke facieva i mazzi del kamangiare et annoveravalli alla Fante e facieva ragione ke pigliava. Il maggiore ammonimento kelle dava sì era kennon si posasse in San Giorgio perokè v'aveva femine ladre. Una mattina passava la detta Fante con uno paniere di cavoli Bito ke prima l'avea pensato s'avea messa la più ricco robba di vaio[g] k'avea et essendo in sulla panca di fuori chiamò la Fante et ella venne allui incontanente e molte femine l'aveano chiamata prima non vi volle ire. Buona femina come dai questi cavoli? Messere due mazzi al danaio.[h] Cierto questa è buona derrata.[i] Ma dicotti ke io non ci sono sennon io ella Fante mia kè tutta la famiglia mia è in villa[j] sì ke troppo mi sarrebbe una derrata. Et io li amo più volentieri freski. Usavansi allora le medaglie[k] in Firenze kelle due valevano uno danaio però disse Bito. Dammene ora una medaglia. Dammi un danaio ette una medaglia et un'altra volta torrò l'altro mazzo. Allei parve ke diciesse bene e così fecie. E poi andò a vendere li altri a quella ragione kel Singnior l'avea data. E tornò a casa e diede a Ser Frulli la moneta. Quelli annoverando più volte pur trovava meno un danaio. Dissello alla Fante. Ella rispose, non può essere. Quelli riscaldandossi collei, domandolla sess'era posata a San Giorgio. Quella volle negare ma tanto la scalzò[l] k'ella disse, sì posai a un bel cavaliere e pagommi finemente. E dicovvi ke io li debbo dare ancora un mazzo di cavoli. Rispose Ser Frulli, dunque ci avrebbe ora meno un danaio e mezzo. Pensovvi suso avidessi dello'nganno e disse alla Fante molta villania e domandolla dove quelli stava ella li le disse appunto. Avidessi

Novella XCV.

Here is told of a village oaf who went to the city.

A village oaf came to Florence to buy a doublet. He entered a store and demanded to see the proprietor. He was not there. An apprentice said, "I am the proprietor, what do you want?" "I want a doublet." This man found one for him. He tried it on and they began to discuss price. The oaf did not have a quarter of the money needed. The apprentice, feigning to fit him from his feet on up, sewed his shirt to the doublet, and then he said, "Take it off." The oaf took it off and remained completely naked. The other clerks were waiting with leather straps and they whipped him across the entire countryside.

Novella XCVI.

Here is told of Bito[1] and Master Frulli[2] of Florence from San Giorgio.[3]

Bito was a Florentine, and a very handsome minstrel he was, who lived in San Giorgio beyond the Arno.[4] There was an old man named Master Frulli who worked his farm above San Giorgio that was so lovely that he and his family lived there almost the whole year long. And each morning he would send his maidservant to Bridge Square[5] to sell fruits and greens. And he was such a terrible miser and so distrusting that he would make up the bunches of greens himself and count them in front of the maidservant, instructing her how much money she was to receive for them. The strongest warning he gave her was not to dally in San Giorgio where there were many women thieves. One morning this maidservant, with a basket of cabbage greens, passed by Bito who, beforehand, had thought to dress in his finest robes of rich vair. And, sitting on a bench outside, he called to the maidservant who quickly came to him, although she had not wanted to join the many women who had called to her earlier. "Good woman, how much for these cabbage greens?" "Sir, two bunches a penny." "This is certainly a good buy. But I must tell you that I am now all alone with my maidservant since my entire family is at our country estate. And so, an entire portion would be too much; and yet, I do love them so much more when they are fresh." In those days the Florentines used the *medaglia* as currency, two of which were worth a penny. Then Bito said, Now you give me a *medaglia*. Give me a penny and I'll return a *medaglia* to you, then some other time I'll take my other bunch." His words seemed fitting to her and so she complied. And then she left to sell the other bunches as instructed by her master. She returned home and gave the money to Master Frulli. He counted it many times, always finding one penny missing. He told this to his maidservant who replied, "This can't be." He became furious with her, asking if she had dallied in San Giorgio. She wanted to deny it, but he pressed her so strongly, that she said, "Yes, I lingered by a handsome knight who paid me well. In fact, I tell you that I still owe him one bunch of cabbage greens."

k'era Bito ke molte beffe li avea già fatte riscaldato d'ira la mattina per tempo si levò e misessi sotto le pelli una spada ruginosa e venne in capo del ponte ellà trovò Bito ke sedea con molta buona gente. Alza[m] questa spada e fedito[n] l'avrebbe se non fosse uno kello tenne per lo braccio. Le genti vi trassero smemorate credendo ke fosse altro. E Bito ebbe gran paura. Ma poi ricordandossi com'era incominciò a sorridere. Le genti ke erano intorno a Ser Frulli domandarlo com'era quelli il disse con tanta ambascia[o] k'appena poteva. Bito fecie ciessare le genti e disse, Ser Frulli io mi voglio conciare[p] con voi. Non ci abbia più parole. Rendete il danaio mio e tenete la medaglia vostra. Et abbiatevvi il mazzo de' cavoli con la malitione d'iddio. Ser Frulli rispose, ben mi piacie. Esse così avessi detto imprima tutto questo non ci sarebbe stato. E non accorgendossi della beffa silli die un danaio e tolse una medaglia et andonne consolato. Le rise vi furo grandissime.

Novella XCVII.

Qui conta come uno Mercatante portò vino oltre mare in botti a due palcora[a] e come intervenne.

Un Mercatante portò vino oltre mare in botti a due palcora. Di sotto e di sopra avea vino e nel mezzo acqua tanto kella metà era vino ella metà acqua. Di sotto e di sopra avea squilletto[b] e nel mezzo no. Vendero l'acqua per vino e raddoppiaro i danari sopra tutto lo guadangnio e tosto ke furo pagati si montaro in su un lengnio con questa moneta. E per sentenza di Dio apparve in quella nave un grande scimmio e prese il tasketto[c] di questa moneta et andonne in cima dell'albero. Quelli per paura k'elli nol gittasse in mare andaro con esso per via dillusinghe. Il Bertuccio[d] si pose a sedere e sciolse il tasketto con bocca e toglieva i danari dell'oro ad uno ad uno. L'uno gittava in mare ell'altro lasciava cadere nella nave. E tanto fecie kell'una metà si trovò nella nave col guadangnio ke fare senne dovea.

Novella XCVIII.

Qui conta d'un Mercatante ke comperò berette.

Uno Mercatante ke recava berette silli bangniaro et avendolle tese sivvi appariro molte scimmie e catuna senne mise una in capo e fuggivano su per li alberi. A costui ne parve male. Tornò indietro e comperò calzari[a] e preselle e feciene buon guadangnio.

Master Frulli replied, "In that case we're now one and a half pennies shy." Mulling it over, he uncovered the deception and ranted and raved at the maidservant, and then he asked her where the man lived and she told him exactly. He realized it was Bito, who had already played many tricks on him. Heated with rage, the next morning he arose early, placing a rusty sword under his robes. And he went to the top of the bridge, where he found Bito sitting with many good people. He lifted his sword and would have wounded him, if a man had not stayed his arm. Struck with fear, thinking something more sinister had occurred, they carried him away. And Bito was quite frightened, until he remembered what had happened and began to smile. The people around Master Frulli asked him what had happened, and he, breathless from fear, told them as soon as he was able. But Bito silenced the people and said, "Master Frulli, I wish to make amends. Let's have no more words between us. Give me back my penny, and take your *medaglia*. And keep your bunch of cabbage greens; God damn you." Master Frulli replied, " I like this well enough; and if you had said so before, none of this would have happened." And he did not realize the joke; he gave him the penny, took the *medaglia*, and went on his way quite contented. The laughter this produced was hysterical.

Novella XCVII.

Here is told how a merchant carried wine beyond the sea in barrels divided by two slats and what happened afterwards.

A merchant carried wine beyond the sea in barrels divided by two slats. The above and below compartments contained wine, while the center was filled with water, so that half was wine and half water. The above and below compartments had spigots while the middle one did not. He sold water as wine and so doubled the money he earned on the entire shipment, and immediately after being paid, he boarded a ship with this money. And by God's decree, a huge monkey[1] appeared on that ship and took the purse holding this money and climbed to the top of the mast.[2] The merchant, fearing the monkey would throw the purse into the sea, followed it, attempting to entice it down. The ape sat down, opened the purse with its mouth and took out the golden coins one by one. One he would drop into the sea and the next he would allow to fall onto the ship. And he did this until half of the money was found on the ship, an amount equal to the earnings the man should have made.

Novella XCVIII.

Here is told of a merchant who bought berets.

A merchant who dealt in berets found them wet one day and, after hanging them out to dry, there appeared many monkeys, and each one put on a beret and fled up the trees. This was a terrible thing for the merchant. He turned back and bought shoes instead and captured the monkeys.[1] After which he earned a fine living.

Novella XCIX.

Qui conta una bella novella d'amore.

Un giovane di Firenze amava carnalmente una gentile pulzella.[a] La quale non amava neente lui ma amava adismisura un altro giovane lo quale amava anke lei ma non tanto ad assai quanto costui. Ecciò si parea ke costui n'avea lasciato ongni altra cosa e consumavassi come smemorato. E spetialmente il giorno k'elli non la vedea. A un suo compangnio ne'ncrebbe. Fecie tanto kello menò a un suo bellissimo luogo. Ellà tranquillaro quindeci dì. In quel mezzo la fanciulla si crucciò con la madre. Mandò la Fante[b] e fecie parlare a colui cui amava kenne voleva andar con lui. Quelli fu molto lieto. La Fante disse. Ella vuole ke voi vengniate a cavallo già quando sia notte ferma ella farà vista di sciendere nella ciella[c] apparecchiato sarete all'uscio e gittaravvissi in groppa ella è leggiera e sa ben cavalcare. Elli rispose, ben mi piacie. Quando ebbero così ordinato fecie grandemente apparecchiare a un suo luogo. Et ebbevvi suoi compangni a cavallo a fecielli stare alla porta perkè non fosse serrata. E mossessi con un fine ronzone[d] e passò dalla casa. Ella non era ancora potuta venire perkè la madre la guardava troppo. Questi andò oltre per tornare a' compangni. Ma quelli ke consumato era in villa non trovava luogo. Era salito a cavallo. El compangnio suo nol seppe tanto pregare kel potesse ritenere e non volle la sua compangnia. Giunse quella sera alle mura tutte le porte erano serrate ma tanto accierchiò ke s'abbattè a quella porta ove erano coloro. Entrò dentro andonne verso la magione[e] di colei non per intendimento di trovarla nè di vederla, ma solo per vedere la contrada. Essendo ristato dirimpetto[f] alla casa di poco era passato l'altro. La fanciulla disserrò l'uscio, e chiamollo sotto bocie[g] e disse ke accostasse il cavallo. Questi non fu lento accostossi. Et ella lissi gittò giustamente in groppa et andaro via. Quando furo alla porta li compangni dell'altro non li diedero briga[h] ke nol conobbero. Perokè se fosse stato colui cui elli aspettavano sarebbe ristato colloro. Questi cavalcaro ben dieci miglia tanto ke furo in un bel prato intorniato di grandissimi abeti. Smontaro e legaro il cavallo a un albero e prese a baciarla. Quella il conobbe. Accorsessi della disaventura. Cominciò a piangiere duramente. Ma questi la prese a confortare lagrimando et arenderle tanto onore k'ella lasciò il piangiere e preselle a voler bene veggiendo kella ventura era pur di costui et abbracciollo. Quell'altro cavalcò poi più volte tanto ke udì il padre ella madre fare romore nell'agio[i] et intese dalla Fante come ella n'era andata in cotal modo. Questi sbigottì. Tornò a' compangni e dissello loro. E que' risposero, ben lo vedemmo passar collei ma nol conosciemmo et è tanto ke puote bene essere allungato et andarne per cotal strada. Misersi incontanente a tenere loro dietro. Cavalcaro tanto kelli trovaro dormire così abbracciati e miravanli per lo lume della luna k'era apparito. Allora ne'ncrebbe loro disturbarli e dissero, aspettiamo tanto k'elli si sveglieranno e poi faremo quello k'avemo affare, e così stettero tanto kel sonno

Novella XCIX.

Here is told a lovely love story.

A young Florentine fell madly in love with a gentle maid who did not love him at all, but instead loved another young man beyond all measure. And he loved her too, but not nearly as much as the first young man. And because of his love, it seemed that he had abandoned all other things and was so consumed with love that he could think of nothing else, especially on those days that he did not see his beloved. One of his friends took such pity on him that he led him away to a most beautiful place and there he remained in tranquil surroundings for fifteen days. Meanwhile, the young maid quarreled with her mother. She sent her maidservant to speak with the man she loved, saying that she wished to go away with him. He was most happy. The maidservant said, "She wants you to come on horseback in the dead of night and she will pretend to go down to the cellar. You must be ready at the door and she will jump onto the saddle. She is slight and rides quite well." He replied, "I like this very much." When everything was organized, he had one of his residences lavishly prepared for her. And he had his companions wait on horseback at one of the city's gates so it would not be locked shut. Then he rode off on a fine stallion and passed by her house. But she had not been able to appear yet, because her mother was watching her so closely. And so he continued on, intending to return to his companions. Meanwhile the young man consumed by love found the country no place of peace. He jumped on his horse and his friend knew no manner of entreaty that could restrain him; nor did he want his friend's company. That night he reached the walls of the city but the gates were all locked; still he circled for so long that finally he happened upon the gate where the other man's companions were waiting. He entered and went to the gentle maid's residence, not because he expected to find her, or even see her, but simply to see the neighborhood where she lived. He stopped opposite her house, minutes after the other man had left. The young girl unlocked the door and called softly to him, telling him to bring the horse near. He was not reluctant in complying. And she jumped perfectly onto the saddle and off they went. When they arrived at the gate, the other man's companions did not hinder them since they knew them nought. For if it had been the man they were awaiting, he would have stayed awhile with them. They galloped for at least ten miles until they came upon a lovely field surrounded by huge fir trees. They dismounted and tied the horse to a tree, and then he began to kiss her. At this point she recognized him and realized her misfortune. She began to weep violently, but he took her in his arms and comforted her, crying and exhibiting so much honor towards her that she quit her tears and began to fall in love with him, realizing that fortune was on his side. And then she embraced him. Meanwhile the other man rode past her house many times, until he heard her mother and father making a ruckus inside, and he learned from the maidservant what had taken place. He was mortified, returned to his companions and told them all. They replied, "We did see them pass, but we didn't know them. It was so long ago, they must be far away by now.

giunse e furo tutti addormentati. Coloro si svegliaro in questo mezzo e trovaro ciò k'era. Maravigliarsi. E disse il giovane. Costoro ci anno fatta tanta cortesia kennon piaccia addio kennoi li offendiamo. Ma salio questi a cavallo et ella si gittò in su un altro de' migliori ke v'erano et andaro via. Quelli si destaro e feciero gran corotto[j] perkè più non li potevano ir ciercando.

Novella C.

Come lo'mperadore Federigo andò alla Montangnia del Veglio.[a]

Lo'mperadore Federigo andò una volta infino alla Montangnia del Veglio e fulli fatto grande onore. Il Veglio per mostrarli come era temuto guardò in alto e vide in sulla torre due assassini. Presessi la gran barba, quelli senne gittaro in terra e moriro incontanente.

Lo'mperadore medesimo volle provare la moglie però k'elli era detto k'uno suo barone giacieva con lei. Levossi una notte et andò allei nella camera. E quella disse, voi ci foste pur ora un'altra volta.

This is the road they took." Quickly they set out after them. They traveled very far, until they found them asleep, wrapped in each others' arms, and they observed them by the light of the moon that had appeared. They were reluctant to disturb them and said, "Let's wait until they awaken and then we'll do what we came to do." But they waited for so long that weariness came upon them and they all fell asleep. The lovers awoke to this scene and found things as they stood. Amazed at the sight, the young man said, "These men have been so courteous to us that it would displease God if we were to offend them." So he mounted his horse and she leapt onto one of the finest of their steeds and off they went. When the others awoke, they bellowed with grief because they could no longer continue the chase.

Novella C.

How the Emperor Frederick[1] went to the Old Man of the Mountain.[2]

The Emperor Frederick once went all the way to the Old Man of the Mountain and was received with great honor. The Old Man, to demonstrate how greatly he was feared, looked up and saw two assassins[3] on top of a tower. He tugged on his great beard[4] and they threw themselves down to the earth and died immediately.

This same emperor wished to test his wife, for he had been told that one of his barons was laying with her. One night he arose and went to her in her chamber. And she said, "What, back again; but you were just here."[5]

NOTES TO THE TEXT AND TRANSLATION

Novella I.

[1] Luke 6:45 "...For a man's words flow out of what fills his heart."

Novella II.

[a] *ingenerationi*: ingeneramento.
[b] *gradora*: gradini (not in the *Crusca*).

[1] The first mention in the West of an oriental Christian king (albeit Nestorian) named John who conquered the Persians and the Medes, but was obstructed by the Tigris from moving on to Jerusalem, is found in the words of Bishop Hugh of Jubala (1145) as they were recorded by Otto, Bishop of Freising (d. 1158) in his famous *Chronicle*, also known as *The Two Cities*. From its initial appearance in the West, the legend of Prester (Presbyter) John combined fact, wish and myth, claiming the potentate to be a direct descendant of one of the Magi, and somehow affiliated with Saint Thomas. Around 1165 a letter, supposedly written by Prester John and addressed to Manuel Comnenus, Emperor of Byzantium (1120-1180), began to circulate throughout the Christian West. The original epistle (although no extant copies exist today) invited the Emperor to visit John's mythical theocracy, whose description includes fabulous beasts, waterless seas, magical stones, wondrous citizens and a mystical palace. The apocryphal epistle attained immediate popularity and was quickly translated into many languages, its fantasy consistently heightened and amplified. Subsequent renditions included or substituted the Holy Roman Emperor, Frederick Barbarossa (1121-1190) as the addressee. By the 14th century, at least four distinct interpolations (A-D) had appeared; the third, interpolation C from around 1221, contained similar information to that found in this novella, suggesting that the tale might have appeared as a logical consequence of this apocryphal epistolary tradition.

[2] The Emperor Frederick is by far the most popular character in *The Novellino*, appearing in no less than seven novellas; including the first (after the introductory novella) and the last. Surprisingly, the anonymous author of the collection never distinguishes one Frederick from another. Many editors of *The Novellino*, including some modern ones like Lo Nigro and Pia Piccoli Addoli, as well as the "Broadway Translation" by Edward Storer, identify this character as Frederick II, Holy Roman Emperor and King of Sicily (1194-1250). Given that the novella is directly related to the legend of the letter of Prester John, it seems logical that the figure in question is actually the above named Frederick's grandfather, Frederick I, Holy Roman Emperor, more commonly known as Frederick Barbarossa (1121-1190).

[3] The apocryphal Letter of Prester John to Manuel I Comnenus states, "Our land is divided into four parts, for there are so many Indias. In Greater India lies the body of the Apostle Saint Thomas... (Slessarev 68)."

[4] These words seem to mirror the description of another Frederick, the second Duke of Swabia; Frederick Barbarossa's father, in Otto of Freising's *The Deeds of Frederick Barbarossa* (p. 45). "The aforesaid duke was brave in battle, shrewd in his business dealings, calm in appearance and in spirit, courteous in speech, and so generous of gifts..."

The description of Frederick II given by the Florentine chronicler Giovanni Villani (d. 1348) indicates that similar attributes were used to describe the Holy Roman Emperor. "This Frederick reigned as Emperor for thirty years, and was a man of great enterprise and valor, learned in literature, and naturally intelligent, knowledgeable in all things. He knew the Latin language, and our vulgate, German, and French, Greek, and Arabic, and copiously endowed with all virtues, generous and courteous in giving gifts, courageous and wise in combat, and feared by many [*my translation*] (Villani V.1 76)." It is no wonder that he came to be known as *stupor mundi*.

[5] Many studies have been done documenting the attribution of special and magical powers (virtues), in the Middle Ages, to jewels and precious stones. "The lapidaries of the Middle Ages shew, however, how constant was the belief in the magical virtues of gems, and the evidence of literature and the inventories of the period proves that this belief was not merely theoretical, but played a real part in everyday life (Evans 111)."

[6] "Therefore let the princes of the earth, who are set in the highest places, learn to observe moderation by holding before their minds their Creator, who is the highest of all; so that, as Cicero says [*De officiis* I.xxvi], the greater they are, the more humbly they may conduct themselves (Otto of Freising 31)."

[7] seneschal - meaning "old servant," in the Middle Ages signified a household official who advised the lord and managed his estates, as well as a provincial administrator. The position became increasingly important; "gradually he [seneschal] emerged as the most important political administrator after the king himself, his power extending not simply to a general supervisory role, but also to the administration of justice and (with the constable) to command of the feudal army (*Dictionary of the Middle Ages*. V.11 159-61)."

[8] lapidarian, a person, often attached to a royal court, versed in the knowledge of stones.

[9] Although the first Letter of Prester John does not mention any such stone, "according to Interpolation C, there are certain stones known as *midriosi*, which eagles seek and take to their nests; these greatly sharpen the vision, can restore the blind to sight, and, with the appropriate spells, have the power of making a person invisible (Silverberg 67-68)."

The *heliotrope* was another stone with similar attributes, made famous by Boccaccio in *Decameron* VIII,3. In the *Lapidario estense* (p. 94), "The heliotrope is a green stone with azure and green droplets, like emeralds, and it has sparse blood-like veins. And it possesses this virtue, that whoever carries it about with him encased in gold with an herb called heliotrope under it, cannot be seen by anyone [*my translation*]."

Many medieval lapidaries attribute the power to render one invisible to a stone named *acate*. The Sloane Lapidary, which is a free translation of a mid-13th-century Anglo-Norman lapidary, describes the acate as such: "It is fowned in ye cast in the fleume caled Acate. It is of many divers things, for one is black and it is gird with white lynes. It tempereth a man's thirst, it comforteth men of age, and the men that holdeth him close in his fist, he shall be invisible (Serjeantson 129)."

Novella III.

[a] *vermine*: Si dice propriamente a piccolo animaluzzo, che vada con la pancia per terra, generato, per lo più, di putredine.
[b] *pistore*: fornaio.

[1] If one accepts the premise that the novellas in *The Novellino* are intentionally positioned; and since the next novella concerns Alexander the Great, then one can surmise that the Philip here in question is his father, Philip II of Macedonia; however, the novella relates no specifics that confirm this supposition.
[2] While the novella gives no hint or suggestion as to the specific identity of this jailed "wise Greek," one may recall how things Greek were held in high esteem during this period by "Hellenized barbarians." It was during the rule of Philip II of Macedonia that the concept of "professional philosophers" developed, numbering among its authorities Plato and his *Academia* perfection of formal logic and rationalistic criticism, and Aristotle and his systematic philosophical specializations and categorizations (Gay 179-80).
[3] One should remember that Philip employed Aristotle as tutor to his son, Alexander (Plutarchus 805).
[4] Dialogue and the perfection of question and answer techniques were preferred pedagogical methods employed by Plato and other "professional philosophers" (Gay 179-80).

Novella IIII.

[a] *giullare*: buffone. Lo giullare si è quel che conversa con le genti, con riso, e con giuoco, e fa beffe di se, e della moglie e de' figliuoli, e non solamente di loro, ma eziando degli altri huomini.
[b] *Giadre*: Gaza [*Giadre* is most probably an Italianized version of *Gadres*, from the canto "Fuers de Gadres," from the 12th-century *Li Romans D'Alixandre* (Lambert Li Tors 459). Immediately preceding Strabo's discussion of Gaza in his famous *Geography*, which mentions its conquest by Alexander, is an entry for a surprisingly similar sounding city, "Gadara" (Strabo V.3 175-76).
[c] *uomo di corte*: vale trattenitore [da trattenere; cioè, far passare il tempo gradevolmente], e huomo piacevole.
[d] *marco*: una certa quantità di moneta.
[e] *stantio*: Ciò che per troppo tempo ha perduto sua perfezione [cioè, troppo a lungo].
[f] *giucollare*: giocolare: che giuocola, buffone, bagattelliere.

[1] The word *giullare* can mean jester, buffoon, minstrel, or even troubadour; but in this case, the first interpretation seems most appropriate, given the action of the novella.
[2] Alexander the Great (356-323 BC); son of Philip of Macedonia, the most likely protagonist of the previous novella, and Olympias, a princess of Epirus. Alexander was King of Macedonia and conqueror of the Persian Empire. He is considered one of the greatest military geniuses of all time, most noted for his brilliance as a tactician, troop leader and for his ability to travel great distances with much speed and efficiency. Aristotle was his tutor and trained him in rhetoric and literature, as well as science, medicine and philosophy. During the Middle Ages, Alexander became a favorite figure in myth and legend.
[3] For discussions concerning Alexander's campaign against the city of Gaza, ruled by the eunuch Batis, see: O'Brien 84-86 and Arrian 144-47.

[4] "[F]rom the twelfth century until the fourteenth Alexander enjoyed a proverbial reputation for liberality, and the work which contributed most to the establishment of that reputation was the *Roman d'Alexandre*, with its emphasis upon Alexander as a generous giver. This reputation disappeared during the fourteenth and fifteenth centuries when the indiscriminate largesse which supported it fell into disrepute, and was replaced by a reputation for valour such as is emphasized in the *Triomphe des Neuf Preux*. This broad statement has been accepted by all subsequent writers as the fundamental fact of Alexander's secular reputation (Cary 209)."

[5] Man of the court is often used to mean minstrel or jester, who often served at a variety of courts.

[6] Historians usually describe Alexander as being found in the thick of battle, but reports of the siege of Gaza show him acting atypically. While sacrificing before the battle, "a bird reportedly flew and dropped a stone on the king's head. Alexander asked Aristander what this signified, and was told that the city would be taken, but he must take precautions regarding his own safety (O'Brien 85)." Watching at a distance, Alexander could not control himself and rushed into battle. He was hit by a catapult shot, and when his wound began to bleed profusely, "He collapsed and was taken back to the camp to recuperate (O'Brien 85)." History, thus provides the setting for the meeting of Alexander with the knight and the jester under his pavilion.

[7] Historians tell us that the citizens of Gaza did not cede so graciously to their conquest by Alexander. "The defenders, though the town (Gaza) was taken, still stood shoulder to shoulder and fought to the last. Every one of them was killed at his post. Their women and children were sold as slaves (Arrian 147)." "Curtius recounts the unusually cruel punishment inflicted on Batis, who remained defiantly silent when brought before his adversary... The captive's feet, we are told, were pierced and thongs were inserted through openings. His body was then attached to Alexander's chariot, and he was dragged behind until he was dead (O'Brien 85-86)."

[8] marks: "marc (Fr. and Ital.) money of account. The French under Philip I in 1060 had substituted the marc for the livre as money of account, and in 1093 nine marcs of silver were given to the king to rebuild a burned church (Broughton 324)."

[9] The knight demeans the jester by calling him a juggler, a more pedestrian label. This conforms with the medieval concept of liberality, "that the worth of the recipient was also appreciated as an ingredient of true liberality (Cary 214)."

Novella V.

[a] *fantilitade*: infanzia.

[b] *bambolitade*: fatto, o azion di bamboli.

[1] humors: "[A] rigid system of medical care evolved, combining the knowledge of astrology with Galen's teaching of the bodily `humours' and `elements' or `qualities'. Medieval medicine was profoundly influenced by this combination which, simply put, involved the hypothesis that health depended upon an equilibrium being established between the four bodily qualities, earth, fire, air and water, and the corresponding four humours, melancholia, cholera, blood and phlegm. Earth was regarded as cold and dry, fire as hot and dry, air as hot and moist and water as cold and moist. Thus the melancholic patient was cold and dry, the choleric, hot and dry, the sanguine, hot and moist and the phlegmatic, cold and moist. Disease, therefore, was thought to be caused by an excess of one of the four humours which treatment was expected to reduce (Rubin 191)."

Specific instances of the medical study of the humors in Bologna and Florence, during the time of the writing of *The Novellino* can be found in writings concerning Taddeo Alderotti (d.1295) (Siraisi 130, 180, 251, 255, 261, 287, 326-28).

Novella VI.

[1] David, first king of Israel (1030?-965?BC)
[2] The novella follows closely, although not exactly, the text of the *Bible*, found in 2 Samuel 24:1-17.
[3] 1 Samuel 16:10-13. "Jesse presented his seven sons to Samuel, but Samuel said to Jesse, 'Are these all the sons you have?' He answered, 'There is still one left, the youngest; he is out looking after the sheep'. Then Samuel said to Jesse, 'Send for him; we will not sit down to eat until he comes'. Jesse had him sent for, a boy of fresh complexion, with fine eyes and pleasant bearing. Yahweh said, 'Come, anoint him, for he is the one'."
[4] The Biblical account does not specifically state the sin which David committed, since it was Yahweh who "incited David" to take the census. There is, however, a note in *The Jerusalem Bible* which states, "In those days a census was considered impious because it usurped the prerogative of God to whom alone it belonged to give increase to family and nation (p. 415)."

Novella VII.

[a] *pusture*: postura - Per deliberazion segreta, e fraudolente.

[1] Solomon was the second king of Israel, the son of David (d.972 BC).
[2] 1 Kings 11:1-8. "King Solomon loved many foreign women: not only Pharaoh's daughter but Moabites, Edomites, Sidonians and Hittites, from those people whom Yahweh had said to the Israelites, 'You are not to go to them nor they to you, or they will surely sway your hearts to their own gods'.... Solomon became a follower of Astarte, the goddess of the Sidonians, and of Milcom, the Ammonite abomination. He did what was displeasing to Yahweh, and was not a wholehearted follower of Yahweh, as his father David had been. Then it was that Solomon built a high place for Chemosh the god of Moab on the mountain east of Jerusalem, and to Milcom the god of the Ammonites. He did the same for all his foreign wives, who offered incense and sacrifice to their gods."
[3] 1 Kings 11:9-13. "Yahweh was angry with Solomon because his heart had turned from Yahweh the God of Israel who had twice appeared before him and who had then forbidden him to follow other gods; but he did not carry out Yahweh's order. Yahweh therefore said to Solomon, 'Since you behave like this and do not keep my covenant or the laws I laid down for you, I will most surely tear the kingdom away from you and give it to one of your servants. For your father David's sake, however, I will not do this during your lifetime, but will tear it out of your son's hands'."
[4] 1 Kings 11:3. "He [Solomon] had seven hundred wives of royal rank and three hundred concubines."
[5] Roboam, or Rehoboam, the son of Solomon who succeeded him as king of Israel.
[6] This is known as the Assembly at Shechem. The novella follows the Biblical account where Roboam foolishly follows the severe advice of the young men, rather than the compassionate advice of the elders (1 Kings 12:1-16).
[7] 1 Kings 9:15. "This is an account of the forced labour King Solomon levied for the building of the Temple of Jahweh, his own palace, the Millo and the wall of Jerusalem, Kazor, Megiddo, Gezer."

[8] 1 Kings 12:16-19. "When all Israel saw that the king took no notice of their wishes, they gave him this answer:

> `What share have we in David?
> We have no inheritance in the son of Jesse.
> To your tents, Israel!
> Henceforth look after your own house, David!'

And Israel went off to their tents. Rehoboam, however reigned over those sons of Israel who lived in the towns of Judah. King Rehoboam sent Adoram who was in charge of forced labour, but the Israelites stoned him to death; whereupon King Rehoboam was obliged to mount his chariot and escape to Jerusalem. And Israel has been separated from the House of David until the present day."

Novella VIII.

[a] *fattione*: fazione - statura, effigie, fattezze, cera, aria.
[b] *peritosa*: che si perita; cioè, esser timido.

[1] Aulix: seems to have no historical counterpart.
[2] The seven liberal arts: grammar, rhetoric, dialectic [trivium], arithmetic, geometry, music and astronomy [quadrivium]. For a brief discussion of the seven liberal arts in the Middle Ages, see Curtius 36-39.

Novella IX.

[a] *ruga*: Per istrada.
[b] *derrata*: tutto quello, che si contratta in vendita.

[1] C. Segre suggests, in his edition of *The Novellino* that *Romania* stands for the Levant in general.
[2] The twelve cities founded by Alexander before he died are described in more detail in the didactic allegorical poem, *L'Intelligenza (late 13th to early 14th century)*, attributed by some to Dino Compagni; specifically in stanzas 238-39. The text, however, gives the name Alexandria to the last two cities alone.

> "And there are twelve cities in all,
> established during the March before he died
> by Alexander, and they are full of bounty:
> The first is named Prosineasse
>
> ...
>
> the eleventh is Alexandria proper, what
> a noble city, beautifully adorned;
> the twelfth is Alexandria of Egypt."
> [*my translation*] (Fubini 479)

[3] A sultan is a Muslim ruler, the most famous during the Middle Ages being, "Saladin, a Kurdish-born officer of the Zangid dynasty of Syria, [who] rose to power in Egypt in 1169 (Gay 277)."

Saladin, or Salah ad-Din Yusuf ibn Ayyub (1137/38-1193) was a Muslim leader famous for his victory over the Crusaders and his recovery of Jerusalem, and later for his struggle against the Third Crusade.

Novella X.

[a] *Romeaggio*: pellegrinaggio.
[b] *bisante*: moneta antica, nella quale, a principio, erano improntati due santi.

[1] The Slave of Bari was not, in fact, a judge, but an early 13th-century minstrel and composer of moral *sirventesi* and proverbs. He most probably acquired a judicial reputation from his proverbs which are highly judicious and moral in nature. Seventy-seven of these have been published by the Bologna Commission for Language Texts, edited by A. Penna in 1968.

Around the time of the printing of *The Novellino* editio princeps, Monsignor Sabba da Castiglione wrote his *Ricordi*, in which he paraphrased this novella and described the Slave of Bari as, "an idiot man, without letters and without learning, but possessed of an acute intellect, discreet judgment and much experience [*my translation*] (Sabba da Castiglione 64)."

[2] Borghese, during the Middle Ages, technically meant one who dwells in a particular area; usually a neighborhood, quarter or village.

[3] bezants: "coins of the Byzantine Empire and their imitations (Broughton 62)."

[4] Medieval and Renaissance Italian city-states run by a lord (*signore*) who replaced republican institutions, were called seignory or signoria. Communes, such as Florence, used the term to refer to the city's executive council.

Novella XI.

[1] The Lo Nigro and Segre editions identify *The Treatises of Farriery Attributed to Hippocrates Translated from the Arabic into Latin by Master Moisé da Palermo and Translated into Italian in the Thirteenth Century (Trattati di mascalcia attribuiti ad Ippocrate Tradotti dall'arabo in latino da Maestro Moisé da Palermo volgarizzato nel secolo XIII.)* as the source for this tale. The original identifies the protagonist as Hippocrates and not Giordano. The story comes from the book's introduction. While *The Novellino* ends on a negative note, the original continues, describing Hippocrates as becoming extremely proficient in the care of horses which results in his re-establishing himself in the good graces of the king, fictitiously called Condisio, by curing the ailments of his stable of horses. In the end, the king asks Hippocrates to prepare a "brief book" on the care of horses, which results in the above-mentioned treatises (Moisé da Palermo 203-05).

Novella XII.

[a] *conducitore*: uno che conduce; menare, guidare, essere scorta.
[b] *dottare*: temere, aver paura.

[1] Aminadab: Aminadab, or Aminadap, is erroneously placed in this novella. He was, in fact, a figure from *Li Romans D'Alixandre*, identified as King of the Greeks [rois d'Elenie] (Lambert Li Tors 309).

[2] The story is taken from the *Bible*, 2 Samuel 12:26-31. There are some discrepancies in *The Novellino* version, for the *Old Testament* account attributes the victory to Joab, not Aminadab; and the city conquered was not a Philistine city, but rather the Ammonite city of Rabbah.

Novella XIII.

[a] Antinogo: misspelling of Antigono.
[b] *conducitore*: see *note* for *Novella XII, a.*

[1] Antigonus: Antigonus I, also known as *The Cyclops*, due to the loss of an eye, was a general in the army of Alexander the Great who gained much land at the death of Alexander (323 BC). At one time (306 BC) he was the self-proclaimed King of Asia. Antigonus died in battle at Ipsus in 301 BC.

The Storer translation describes Antigonus as "teacher". Historically, the man was anything but a teacher and should be viewed in the novella as a staunch military man enraged by Alexander's frivolous delight in music.

[2] Alexander: see *note* for *Novella IIII, 2.*

[3] Moral anecdotes concerning Alexander were popular in the Middle Ages. Cary cites the tale concerning "self-control" of "Antigonus, Alexander's tutor, reproving him for playing the lyre," as coming from the *Policraticus* of John of Salisbury (Cary 96).

[4] The cithara is an ancient musical instrument resembling the lyre, precursor of the zither.

[5] Porus was the Indian king who fought and was defeated by Alexander on the banks of the Hydaspes. Alexander was so impressed by his valor and dignity that afterwards they became allies (Arrian 266-86; Plutarchus 844-45).

Novella XIIII.

[1] This novella paraphrases a story found in chapter 30 of *Barlaam and Ioasaph* as told by St. John Damascene. *The Novellino* tale maintains all significant aspects of the original, only replacing the number of years spent in shadows from twelve to ten (John Damascene 451-53).

[2] The story gains notoriety in Italy when Boccaccio includes it as the meta-novella of Filippo Balducci and his son, found in the Introduction to Day IV of *The Decameron*. Boccaccio replaces John's regal environment with more pedestrian personages, lightens the tale by substituting the summit of "Ass Mountain" as the isolating locale, and minimizes the misogynistic appelation of "demons" with a still belittling gaggle of "geese" (Boccaccio 287-90).

Novella XV.

[1] Valerius Maximus, who lived during the reign of Tiberius, was the author of a collection of historical anecdotes, around 31 A.D. He was purported to be a professional rhetorician from a poor family.

[2] *Nine Books of Memorable Facts and Sayings (Factorum et dictorum memorabilium libri novem)*. Book six is concerned with good moral qualities.

[3] Valerius Maximus identifies Zaleucus, not Calogno, as the protagonist of the tale. Zaleucus was a law-giver of the Epizephyrian Locrians, around 660 B.C., who produced the first collection of written laws, described as a severe code, possessed by the Greeks (Smith, W. 317).

Novella XVI.

[1] Saint Paulinus of Nola was born in Bordeaux around 353 A.D. and educated by Ausonius. While in Nola he became a devotee of the cult of Saint Felix. Eventually he withdrew from all

worldly pursuits, accompanied by his wife, Theresia. He became famous for his personal asceticism and his liberality toward the poor. Toward the end of his life, he settled once again in Nola, where he distributed his vast wealth to poor pilgrims, for the debts of the poor, and for the construction of public works and cathedrals. He became the Bishop of Nola in 409 A.D. He died in 431 A.D. and his feast day is celebrated by the Roman Catholic Church on June 22nd.

[2] *The Novellino* tale is but an incomplete rubric of the actual story of Paulinus found in the Prologue to Dialogue III of *The Dialogues* of Saint Gregory the Great. The original continues: after Paulinus replaces the young man in prison, as the slave of an African king, he works marvelously as a gardener. Eventually he gains the respect of the king and his son-in-law, foretells the old man's death, reveals his status as a Bishop, and is rewarded with his freedom and that of other Christians held in captivity in the African king's domain (Gregorius 111-14).

Novella XVII.

[a] *tavoliere*: Modern Italian editions (Lo Nigro, Segre) describe this term as meaning banker. Given; however, the miserly attitude desired, I have chosen money-lender as a more appropriate modern derivative.

[1] *The Novellino* tale is but a sketch of the more ample description of the story of Peter the Tax-Gatherer imbedded in the story of Saint John the Almoner (January 23) of *The Golden Legend* (Jacobus de Voragine 118-20).

Novella XVIII.

[a] *generatione*: per ispezie.
[b] *trono*: da *tronare*, lo stesso che *tonare*: lo strepitar che fanno le nugole.

[1] Charlemagne or Charles the Great (b. 742), eldest son of King Pepin the Short and Bertrada, became King of the Franks and later, Roman Emperor. His reign extended over the entire Christian West, except for Britain and parts of Spain and Southern Italy, and continued until his death in 814.

[2] An earlier version of the story is found in Chapter VII of the *Historia Karoli Magni et Rotholandi*, commonly known as the *Pseudo-Turpin* (mid-12th century). While the action takes place during Charlemagne's attack of the Basque city of Bayonne, the protagonist is not Charlemagne himself, but rather a man named Romaricus. The English synopsis reads:

"While Charles and his army are at the Basque city of Bayonne, one Romaricus on his deathbed bequeaths a horse to a kinsman with the injunction that he sell it and give the money to clerics and to the poor. But the kinsman, after selling the horse, spends the money on himself for food and drink and other necessities. When thirty days have passed, the dead man appears in a nocturnal vision before his kinsman and tells him that, though his own sins have now been forgiven, the kinsman's dereliction has caused him to be delayed in the underworld; the dead man proceeds now to peace, but the kinsman will on the morrow be suffering in hell. In the morning the guilty man talks openly about his vision, and while the warriors are discussing it a host of demons, howling like wild animals, snatch him aloft (Smyser 23)."

Novella XIX.

[a] *uomo di corte*: see *note* for *Novella IIII, c.*

[b] *marco*: see note for *Novella IIII, d.*

[1] The "Young King" is Henry Court Mantel (d. 1183), son of Henry II, Plantagenet, King of England (1154-1189). The *senhal* must have been quite common in Italy during the Middle Ages, since Dante identifies him as "re giovane (the Young King)," in *The Divina Commedia* (*Inf.* XXVIII, 135).

[2] Bertran de Born (ca. 1140-ca. 1215), born in Salagnac, was one of the best-known troubadours, a writer of political *sirventes* and an infamous conspirator. For familial reasons, he developed a fierce hatred for Henry II, King of England, and allied himself with his son Henry, known as the "Young King," convincing him to war against his father. His bellicose disposition and racketeering abilities earned him a place in Dante's *Inferno* XXVIII, among the sowers of discord.

"And so that thou may carry news of me
Know that Bertram de Born am I, the same
Who gave to the Young King the evil comfort.
I made the father and the son rebellious;
Achitophel not more with Absalom
And David did with his accursed goadings.
Because I parted persons so united,
Parted do I now bear my brains, alas!
From its beginning, which is in this trunk.
Thus is observed in me the counterpoise."

(Dante 149)

[3] "And Bertran de Born (Beltram in the text) used to boast that he was of such worth that he did not think he would ever need all his wit (*Vidas* 19)."

[4] marks: *see* note for *Novella IIII, 8.*

[5] This episode is virtually the same as the one encountered in "The Tale of The Young King ("Conto del re giovane)," chapter 18 of *The Tales of Ancient Knights* (*Conti di antichi cavalieri*) (*Conti* 143).

[6] seneschal: *see* note for *Novella II, 7.*

Novella XX.

[1] King of England: *see* note for *Novella XIX, 1.*

[2] While this incident does not appear in the *Conti di antichi cavalieri* or in the troubadour *Vidas*, it does exemplify a statement of the Young King's found in Chapter 17 of the *Conti* (p.141). "The greatest shame of all is acquired by not giving to one who is in need [*my translation*]."

[3] The word cloak is implied in the text.

[4] seneschal: *see* note for *Novella II, 7.*

[5] The old king is Henry II, Plantagenet, King of England (1154-1189).

[6] This "yes and no" is taken directly from the *Vidas* where Bertran calls the old king (albeit erroneously), "Oc e No" (*Vidas* 19).

[7] Bertran de Born: *see* note for *Novella XIX, 2.*

[8] "[F]inally the Young King was killed by an arrow in a castle of Bertran de Born (*Vidas* 19)."

[9] Payment by the old king for the release of his son's soul constitutes the text of chapter 20 of *Conti di antichi cavalieri* (*Conti* 147).

[10] This final episode between Bertran and the old king is found in chapter 17 of the *Vidas* (p. 19).

Novella XXI.

[a] *schiavina*: vesta lunga da panno grosso, propriamente da schiavo, e le portano anche i pellegrini, e i romiti.

[1] The term necromancy is incorrectly used here, since the magic employed by the masters is in no way concerned with the dead. The use of such a strange term, however, adds an element of the exotic to the atmosphere of the tale which complements medieval Italy's attitude towards Sicilian society which, to them, "appeared more exotic in western eyes than even the crusader kingdom of Jerusalem (Smith, D. Mack 26)."

[2] Frederick II: *see* note for *Novella II, 2*. Frederick was considered too "secular and rational" for his Western counterparts and the Roman curia. "Popes referred to him as a baptised Sultan (Smith, D. Mack 60)." This great leader's "boyhood was spent in the exotic world of the royal palace in Palermo (Smith, D. Mack 51)."

[3] *see* note for *Novella II, 4.*

[4] The Albigensian Crusade (1209) gave the Northern Franks the opportunity to attack, decimate and occupy the rich and cultured cities of the Languedoc, resulting in "the Provençal Muse [being] silenced in Provence (Briffault 160)." Many troubadours, accused of Catharism, were executed, others fled to foreign lands. "To the Italians we owe the survival of most - one might say all - of the texts of the troubadour lyrics which we possess (Briffault 160)." "The court of the great emperor [Frederick II],...placed as it was, like Provence, under the ban of the Church, offered the most obvious refuge to the exiled poets who fled before the terror of the French Inquisition (Briffault 163)."

[5] Graf's retelling of the story states that "they began to pour water over their hands [*my translation*] (Graf V.2 263)," a cleansing act that was performed before the partaking of a repast.

[6] Pilgrims' robes were long gowns made of course cloth, appropriate for slaves, but also worn by pilgrims and hermits [*my translation*] (Accademia 762).

[7] This is a retelling of a tale concerning Michael Scot (c.1190 - c.1250), astrologer to the court of Frederick II. Arturo Graf's paraphrase shows the original to consist of only two magicians who select a count named Ulfo to accompany them, whom they detain for twenty years. At the end of the tale, Michael and his companion disappear, much to the chagrin of the Emperor (Graf V.2 263-64).

Michael Scot was a famous translator, linguist, scientist and philosopher, who taught in Bologna and Paris, and eventually became the court astrologer for Frederick II. While his writings occasionally concern themselves with astrology and magic, even demonology and necromancy, one could not call him a magician (Thorndike Chapters 10-12). Legends, however grew up around him, purporting him to be a man endowed with frightening magical powers. He appears in Boccaccio's *Decameron*, in VIII,9, described as "a great master in necromancy (Boccaccio 618)." Dante hurls him into the fourth *malabolgia* of the eighth circle of the *Inferno* (XX 115-17) among the other soothsayers, magicians and sorcerers.

"The next, who is so slender in the flanks,
Was Michael Scot, who of a verity
Of magical illusions knew the game."
(Dante 111)

[8] Count Richard of San Bonifacio was podestà of Mantua, which fell to Frederick in October of 1237 (Kantorowicz 435).

Novella XXII.

[a] *podestà*: autorevol potere. Quegli ch'è constituto in podestà, ed ha imperio sopra colore, che gli son dati in governo.

[1] Birds of prey were particularly precious to Frederick II. Not only was the Sicilian emperor an avid, expert falconer, but he was also an accomplished scholar who compiled a treatise on the subject entitled, *The Art of Falconery* (*De arti venandi cum avibus*).
[2] Frederick II: *see* note for *Novella II, 2.*
[3] Frederick laid siege to Milan twice during his reign; once in 1237 when he defeated the Lombard League, and again in 1247-48 (Kantorowicz 475, 649).
[4] A podesta was a chief magistrate elected annually in medieval Italian towns and republics with judicial functions and almost unlimited power.
[5] Frederick is alluding to the fact that, "when almshouses raised funds by sending their inmates on begging rounds, authorities supplemented but also regulated this practice by supplying uniforms (*Dictionary of the Middle Ages.* V.6 490.)"

Novella XXIII.

[a] *poltrone*: Da poco, pauroso, d'animo vile, e dimesso, infingardo. Qui uomo di bassa condizione.
[b] *barlione*: lo stesso che *barletto*: picciolissimo barile da portare a cintola.
[c] *tamericie*: qui vaso fatto dall'albero tamerice.
[d] *mazzero*: baston pannocchiuto.
[e] *corno*: grandi corna, che son buone per sonare e per portar vino.

[1] Frederick II: *see* note for *Novella II, 2.*
[2] The term *poltrone* can also mean a person of low condition, or a coward.
[3] Frederick himself describes the ideal hunting attire as follows: "The skirts of his garments must be short, so that they do not hamper his movement, and of a single color, preferably beige or an earthen tint, and of such material as peasants wear (Frederick II 280)."
[4] Frederick was a man particularly concerned with personal hygiene. *Novella XXI* shows the washing of hands at the Emperor's table before the partaking of a repast. Historians relate that he had public baths built, and encouraged their use by the populace.

"Even his regular use of baths scandalised many westerners as too strange for comprehension (Smith, D. Mack 61)."

Novella XXIIII.

[1] The Holy Roman Emperor Frederick Barbarossa: *see* note for *Novella II, 1.*
[2] The story is based on the legal proceedings which the Emperor held at the Assemby of Roncaglia, on November 11, 1158, where, "He listened attentively to complaints and appeals of rich and poor alike. He had four judges, namely, Bulgar, Martin, James and Hugo (Otto of Freising 237)."
[3] "Bulgaro of Alberto Bulgari, noble Bolognese, was born in 1140. He was a disciple of Guarnerio, called Irnerio, and after him gave the best interpretation and explanations of the Law. This Bulgaro was a most famous doctor, and one of the first glossators of the Law, and because of his knowledge he was called Golden Mouth, as is told by Odofredo. His opinions were so

reasonably consonant with the law that they were followed by the School of the Citramontani Doctors, of which he was the founder. And because of his contrary opinions, these doctors did not accept the teachings of Martino Gosio.

In 1166 he was one of the counsellors to the Emperor and his Vicar. Behind the School was his house and a courtyard, called the Court of the Bulgari, where many inconsistencies in the law, using his opinions, were put to rest. These opinions obtained universal approbation and the power of law; such as, the *L. Dos à patre, C. solut. matr.* and the *Autentica hoc locum, C. si secundo nup. mul.* and others, as attested to by Odofredo and other Doctors from these places. He published the *Commentarij sopra Tit. Digestis de Regulis Iuris*, and some *Sommarij* of other titles of the *Digesti*, placed in the *Somma d'Azone*, and his glosses are found in the texts. He died in 1196 and was buried in San Procolo [*my translation*] (Alidosi 39)."

[4] "Martino Gosio, or Gosiano was born in 1150. He was a most noble and excellent Doctor, and a disciple of Imerio. He was one of the first glossators and illuminators of Civil Law. He was a counsellor to the Emperor Frederick and a contemporary of Bulgaro, with whose opinions he almost always disagreed. These two were like Captains who divided the opinions of the other doctors. And those who held to his opinions were called *Gosiani*, as is attested to by Cino, who tells us that his household was expelled from the land for siding with the Ghibellines. His glosses were published [*my translation*] (Alidosi 166)."

[5] While modern history has relegated these two Bolognese doctors to virtual oblivion, the original audience for *The Novellino* would have been well versed in the oppositional antics of these two antagonistic academics. The placement of the two counsellors on opposite sides of the Emperor structurally heightens the comic quality of the situation.

[6] The question proposed by the Emperor, concerning his legal rights in relation to his subjects, is taken from an opinion expressed by the Archbishop of Milan during the Assembly of Roncaglia. "Know, therefore, that all authority in establishing laws for the people is vested in you. Your will is law, in accordance with the statement: `What pleases the prince has the force of law, as the people have yielded and granted to him all their authority and power. For whatever the emperor has established by letter, or taken cognizance of and decreed, or enjoined by an edict, that is accepted as law.' `It is natural that the profits should acrue to him on whom the losses fall,' so you who bear the burden of care for all of us ought to rule us all (Otto of Freising 236-37)."

[7] It is interesting to note that the author of *The Novellino* restricts the addressing of the participants in the debate to pronomial forms without nominal referents, leaving it to the reader to determine who exactly won the debate.

Novella XXV.

[1] Sultan, originally an Arabic title, denoted political authority. It eventually took on the significance of supreme political authority.

[2] marks: *see* note for *Novella IV, 8.*

[3] *see* note for *Novella IX, 3.*

[4] "He [Saladin] was as good an example of the Noble Enemy as could be found. He was considered so noble and chivalrous that it was popularly supposed by the French that he had a French mother or grandmother. The English thought she must have been English. He became Christendom's favorite Moslem. He had been knighted according to the European ritual, or so it was believed, and he left money to Christian foundations (Newby 13)."

"Saladin's famous generosity was an important factor in ensuring loyalty; it was welcomed for the material advantages it brought but also regarded admiringly as evidence of greatness of character (Newby 73)."

[5] The tale is taken from Chapters 12 and 13 from the *Historia Karoli Magni et Rotholandi*, commonly known as the *Pseudo-Turpin* (mid-12th century), except that the original story is about the Saracen, Aigolandus, at the table of Charlemagne. The *Historia* ending differs, for "When Charles realizes that his lack of charity has cost him his converts, he causes the poor in his army to be sought out and copiously provided for. Let this be a lesson to all Christians to be ever mindful of the needy. Faith without good works is like a body without a soul (Smyser 31)."

[6] It was not uncommon during truces and ceasefires for the Crusaders and the Moslems to invite their enemies to banquets. "When the Franks saw virtues in a Moslem, as they did in Saladin, they thought that he had European blood in his veins, and was a Christian knight at heart (Newby 129)."

[7] Philip (Augustus) II, King of France, 1165-1223.

[8] Luke 6:20 "'How happy are you who are poor: yours is the kingdom of God.'"

[9] Saladin, at least in his mature years, was considered a religious and sober man of high "moral stature, a man who chose to remain outside Christianity yet whose life exemplified the Christian virtues (Newby 199)." It is for these reasons that Dante grants him a place among the virtuous pagans in the First Circle of Hell (*Inf.* I, 129).

The symbol of the cross takes on a heightened significance when one remembers that the Crusades were considered religious wars by both sides. The Moslems called them *jihad* or Holy War. The Crusaders, a term which means warriors of the cross, were fighting for the return of the Holy Lands (Jerusalem), as well as to recapture the relic of the True Cross.

Novella XXVI.

[a] *cotta*: propriamente toga, vesta lunga, sopravvesta.

[1] borghese: *see* note for *Novella X, 2.*

[2] marks: *see* note for *Novella IIII, 8.*

[3] "Usury, in the vocabulary of medieval theologians and canonists, meant any return received or demanded on a loan in addition to the loaned property itself. Usury in this sense was both a sin, for which penance had to be done, and a canonical crime, for which church courts might impose penalties."

"During the twelfth and thirteenth centuries popes and councils enacted ever more rigorous penalties for those who took interest on loans. The practice was forbidden to both clerics and laymen and was prohibited even if the ultimate purpose was pious, as for example loans made to redeem prisoners from captivity. The mere intention of charging interest on a loan, whether fulfilled or not, violated the law. The Third Lateran Council (1179) declared that usurers were excommunicate, that if they died without repenting this sin they could not be buried in consecrated ground, and that churches must refuse any gifts from usurers (*Dictionary of the Middle Ages*. V.12 335, 337.)"

[4] Merlin is best known as the legendary magician at the court of King Arthur. Many of the early works concerning Merlin minimize or eliminate Arthur from the text. Geoffrey of Monmouth's *Vita Merlini* (c.1150) describes him as such; "Merlin the Briton was famous throughout the world as king and prophet (Geoffrey 53)."

This novella is a concentrated version of Chapter 238, entitled "Concerning Merlin and the Well-Dressed Lady ("De Merlin et de la dame bien ecesmee")," from *Les prophecies de Merlin*

(Paton V.1 276-77). This collection of over three hundred prophecies attributed to the famous seer was written sometime in the 1270s, although some manuscripts state that they were composed around 1228 by Maistre Richart d'Irlande, for a historical figure very important to *The Novellino*, The Holy Roman Emperor, Frederick II (Paton V.2 4).

Novella XXVII.

[a] *Moaddo*: Many Italian editors agree that the term is an attempt at phonetically transcribing the Arabic word, *Mu'addib*, meaning teacher or learned one, into Italian.

[1] Mu'addib: *see* note for *Novella XXVII, a.*
[2] Alexander: *see* note for *Novella IIII, 2.*

Novella XXVIII.

[1] During the Middle Ages, especially in England and France, criminals were put in a cart and paraded through the streets to the jeers and threats of the populace. An eighteenth-century English dictionary defines "carting" as "the punishment formerly inflicted on bawds, who were placed in a tumbrel or cart, and led through a town that their persons might be known (Grose n.p.)." The term eventually led to the coining of a slang expression, "in the cart," meaning "wrong, or in the wrong." Its provenance is described as "Perhaps going back to the cart in which criminals were taken to execution (Partridge 130)."

[2] Lancelot was "The famed lover of Queen Guenevere. Lancelot is the central figure of three medieval romances...and plays a prominent role in several others (Lacy 323)."

"Lancelot or Launcelot du Lac. The most famous of the knights of King Arthur's Round Table. He was the son of King Ban of Brittany but as a babe was stolen by Vivien, the Lady of the Lake, who presented him, when grown up, to Arthur. He twice caught sight of the Grail. Though a model of chivalry, his adulterous love for Guinevere caused the disruption of the Round Table and Arthur's death. Lancelot was the father of Sir Galahad. He died as a repentant hermit (Bulfinch 920)."

[3] Guenevere was "the wife of King Arthur and mistress of Lancelot du Lac. Geoffrey of Monmouth's *Historia* (ca. 1135) identifies Guenevere as a noble Roman whom Arthur married for her surpassing beauty and whom his nephew, Modred, also married after usurping his uncle's throne (Lacy 262)."

"Guinevere. In Arthurian legend, the wife of King Arthur. She was the daughter of Leodegraunce, king of Camelyard. She entertained a guilty passion for Sir Lancelot of the Lake, but during Arthur's absence she was seduced by Modred. Later she took the veil at Almesbury, where she died, and was buried at Glastonbury (Bulfinch 910)."

Lancelot's descent into insanity as a result of his love for Guenevere is encountered in Chrétien de Troyes' *Lancelot*: "The cart knight brooded at some length,/a man without defense or strength/ against Love and her tyranny./His thoughts were of such quality,/no feeling of himself persisted,/he did not know if he existed,/could not remember his own name,/where he was bound, from whence he came,/or whether he was armed or not./Except for one thing, he forgot all others totally, and all/but her were lost beyond recall./He thought so much of her alone, things went unseen, unheard, unknown (Chrétien 20-21)."

[4] The novella is referring to the many adventures encountered by Lancelot in his quest to save King Arthur's Queen Guenevere from the unsavory desires of her abductor, Meleagant, as found in the source poem by Chrétien de Troyes, *Lancelot or the Knight of the Cart.*

Novella XXIX.

[1] "In the Middle Ages all [this] was united with the special conceptions of ancient astronomy, which had taken its rise amongst the great Greek astronomers of the third century before Christ, and was systematized mainly by the Alexandrian Ptolemy in the second century of the Christian era, further details being added by Arabian scholars, especially under the Sassanid dynasty in Spain...Right down into the sixteenth century the conviction remained unshaken that the earth was fixed at the middle point of the universe. All the heavenly spheres circled round it as their centre." "Beyond it [the ninth heaven] lies the eternal, unchanging peace of God, to which the Christian astronomers assigned a tenth heaven, the Empyrean, `the heaven that is pure light; light intellectual full of love, love of the good full of joy, joy that transcends all sweetness (Dante *Paradiso* XXX, 39)'(Dinsmore 232, 235)."

[2] Many great and wise men taught or attended the schools of Paris in the twelfth century; these included, Peter Abelard, William of Champeaux, John of Salisbury, Hugh of Saint Victor, Gilbert of Poitiers and Peter Lombard (Ferruolo 22, 43).

[3] While Bologna had formed a "university of students" which excelled in Canon Law by 1193, Paris established a "university of masters" by 1215 which exceeded all others in the study of theology and dialectic. The earliest schools of Paris included the Cathedral School of Notre Dame, as well as the monastery schools of St. Germain des Prés, St. Maur des Fossés, St. Denis, St. Geneviève and the abbey school of St. Victor (Ferruolo 3, 17, 27-44).

[4] "Far beyond the sphere of fire came the seven planets, each of which had a heaven to itself, the moon counting as the undermost of the planets. The sun was in the middle, between the three inner and outer planets...Beyond Saturn (the most distant planet known till the year 1781) lay the heaven of the fixed stars. (Dinsmore 233)."

"But Heaven too, is an organized whole, with degrees and distinctions, according to the particular qualities for which each spirit was conspicuous...A separate company of the blessed is assigned to each; those who vowed themselves to God are in the chaste moon; in Mercury are those who strove after intellectual perfection; in Venus (not mentioned in the novella), those who were inflamed with heavenly love; in the sun, the source of all light, the theologians who sank deep into the light of God; in Mars, those who fought for Christ; in Jupiter, the source of all justice according to the Ancients, the righteous rulers; and finally, the holy hermits in Saturn, who pursues his slow course far removed from the other planets (Dinsmore 242-43)."

[5] The lesson exemplified by this novella follows the pedagogical philosophy of Hugh of St. Victor who, as scholasticus of St. Victor (1124-41), advocated a liberal arts education and disapproved of scholarly specialization. Hugh "lashes out first against the proud and overly ambitious scholars who, having studied under great masters, publicly advance opinions on the most profound matters. Even more vehement is Hugh's criticism of those whom he calls "triflers" (*nugigeruli*), scholars with inflated egos who condemn great masters as simple-minded, deny the value of their teaching, and claim to be able to interpret the mysteries of Scripture by personal ingenuity alone." "Hugh was also, apparently, the first to complain that many scholars choose to study the insignificant subtleties of the philosophers only because they fail to understand the complexities of Scripture...`They wish to search obscure matters and know new things, to learn much and do nothing' (Ferruolo 38-39)."

Novella XXX.

[1] Lo Nigro, in his Italian edition, informs us that Lombard in the thirteenth century was used to describe all of Northern Italy.
[2] The novella does not give sufficient information to accurately identify *G.* in a historical context.
[3] Since both Frederick II and Frederick Barbarossa had dealings with Lombardy and were noted for their liberality, it is impossible to determine with any degree of accuracy which one is the actual protagonist of this tale.

Novella XXXI.

[a] *talento*: voglia, disiderio.
[b] *berbice*: pecora.
[c] *burchiello*: diminutivo di *burchio*: barca da remo coperta.
[d] *vogare*: remare.

[1] Azzolino is Ezzelino III da Romano, born 1194 and died in 1259. Ezzelino was the Lord of Verona, Vicenza and Padova. He took the side of the Emperor Frederick II against the Papacy, was wounded and captured near Blancanuga. He died a few days later, having never reconciled his differences with the Church (*Enciclopedia Italiana, V.14 692-93)*. Dante places him in *Inferno XII* among the violent. See also the *note* for *Novella LXXXIIII, 1*.
[2] bezant: *see* note for *Novella X, 3*.
[3] The novella is originally found in Petrus Alfonsi's *Disciplina clericalis*, chapter 12, entitled "The King and His Story-Teller (Petrus Alfonsi 123-24)." The author of *The Novellino* chose to replace the generic "king" with Ezzelino as protagonist.

Novella XXXII.

[a] *stromento*: strumento, ordigno.
[b] *conducitor*: see *note* for *Novella XII, a*.
[c] This paragraph separation is the first actually found in the *editio princeps*.

[1] Riccar Loghercio to date has not been identified with a historical figure.
[2] Battle of La Spangniata: "The [Spanish] army left Toledo on 20 June 1212, and after some victories in the course of its march southward--at Malagón, Calatrava, Alarcos, Piedrabuena, and other places--the Christian troops crossed the Sierra Morena by the pass of Muradal. On the other side, at Las Navas de Tolosa, there awaited them the army of the Almohades led by their emperor himself. The battle took place on 16 July and resulted in a complete victory for the Christians, who secured enormous booty. The road to the south now being clear, the army proceeded to take the castles and towns of Vilches, Ferral, Baños, Tolosa, Ubeda and Baeza. This triumphant advance towards southern Andalusia was only arrested by the plague, which broke out among the troops; but the Muslim forces had been sufficiently enfeebled by this decisive action (*The Cambridge Medieval History*. V.6 409-10)."
[3] Raymond VII, the last Count of Toulouse, was born around 1197 and died in 1249 (*Nouvelle* V.41 748-51).
[4] "In 1226 Louis VIII mustered an army at Lyons in imperial territory and marched against the imperial town of Avignon, which capitulated after a three months' siege. The feud between

Raymond VII of Toulouse and Raymond Berengar IV of Provence, who was supported by his son-in-law Louis IX, led in 1239 to a further weakening of the imperial and a corresponding strengthening of the French influence. Then in 1246 the decisive blow fell. Raymond Berengar died in 1245 leaving no sons, but four daughters (*The Cambridge Medieval History*. V.6 126-26)."

[5] Raymond Berengar (IV), Count of Provence from 1209 to 1245. He married in 1220 Beatrice, the daughter of Thomas, Count of Savoy. Nostradamus affirms that he saw the count's poetic productions in the private library of Count Robert II (*Nouvelle* V.5 471).

Novella XXXIII.

[a] *Imberal del Balzo*: Barral de Baux. The *Im* is actually an honorific prefix used in Provençal to denote the title "Sir."

[b] *algura*: *agura*: lo stesso che *agurio*: si dice generalmente a ogni segno, indizio, o presagio di cosa futura, che comunemente gli antichi lo predavano dal cantar degli uccelli.

[c] *storlomia*: e *strolomia*: astronomia.

[d] *cornille*: deriva dal provenzale *cornilha* o *cornalha* che significa *cornacchia.*

[e] *ie*: deriva dal provenzale *ieu* che significa *io.*

[f] *uoi*: è provenzale per *oggi*.

[1] Imberal del Balzo is an Italianized form for Barral de Baux. Born around 1210, Barral allied himself with Raymond VII, Count of Toulouse, against Raymond Berengar, Count of Provence. Politically astute, Barral engaged in a variety of political and military exploits in Provence and became the podesta of both Avignon and Arles. Eventually he accompanied Charles of Anjou to Naples and was named podesta of that city in 1265 (*Dictionnaire*, V.5 967).

[2] Spain was known throughout the medieval world as a center for the translation of Arabic, Hebrew and Latin texts, many of which were concerned with astrology and astronomy.

[3] Once again the author of *The Novellino* displays an ignorance of ancient history. Pythagoras was not a medieval Spaniard, but "a Samian aristocrat who had imigrated to Southern Italy about 530 B.C., had turned in a new direction. He conceived of philosophy as a way of life to be realized in a private society. Men who rejected the standards of the world need not resign themselves, like Psalmists, to converse only with God. He founded a brotherhood to practice the spiritual life and reform the rest of society. Within a century revolutions destroyed his brotherhood, but in the new world, with its growth of private life, its political exiles and *déracinés*, his idea lived on. It inspired Plato and a line of later imitators, through monasticism, to the present day (Gay 169)."

[4] "Astronomy and astrology. In the Middle Ages, the two terms were synonymous (Kay 1)."

[5] "You should know that the stars we can identify and distinguish clearly in the firmament number 1,200, according to what we find in the book of Almagestes which good King Ptolemy made. Among the others there are twelve which are called the twelve signs of the zodiac. These are: Aries, Taurus, Gemini, Cancer, Leo, Virgo, Libra, Scorpio, Sagittarius, Capricorn, Aquarius and Pisces (Latini 73)."

[6] Sometime around 1282, Ristoro D'Arezzo wrote a medieval scientific treatise entitled, *The Composition of the World* (*La composizione del mondo*). Chapter IV of Book I, entitled "Concerning the Discovery of the Twelve Signs of Heaven (Del trovamento de li dodici segni del cielo)," identifies the animals associated with each of the zodiac signs (D'Arezzo 989-91).

[7] While medieval bestiaries describe the odd sexual and procreative habits of weasels which render it unpalatable, none describes the animal as the source of evil omen. Mercatante's *Encyclopedia*

of World Mythology and Legend, however, states "For the ancient Greeks the weasel was a symbol of evil. If one appeared at a meeting, the group would disperse (Mercatante 671)."

[8] Jays seem to have no augurial significance in medieval bestiaries.

[9] "Magpies or pies might be called poets, because they can speak words with different sounds, like men...The magpie is called `Picus', after Saturn's son, because he used them in foretelling the future. It is said that this bird has something divine about it (*Bestiary* 153)."

Brunetto Latini's *The Book of the Treasure* has no entry for the magpie.

[10] "The crow is a bird which lives to a great age. Its name is the same in Greek as in Latin: `cornix'. They say that it can reveal the purpose of men's actions: it can disclose the whereabouts of an ambush, and predict the future (*Bestiary* 160)."

"The crow is a long-lived bird. The ancients said that it could tell the future, and showed it to man by its cry and by many other signs, so that if man can master the technique, he can learn what will happen to him in the future (Latini 120)."

[11] The moon represents the effects of astrology, in general, on man. "The Sun and the Moon were only the most obvious celestial agents (Grant 577)." The Middle Ages believed that the moon directly influenced many human psychological attributes. For a detailed discussion of the effects of the moon as portrayed in Dante's *Divina Commedia, see*: Kay 17-37.

[12] The author accentuates the Provençal atmosphere of the text, particularly in passages of direct discourse, with the inclusion of Provençal words and desinences.

[13] "The raven signifies the blackness of sinners...the raven is the blackness of sin or unfaithfulness (*Bestiary* 159)."

Latini's entry for the raven in *The Book of the Treasure* is purely descriptive and attributes no augurial significance to its appearance.

Novella XXXIIII.

[a] The Gualteruzzi edition confused the initials and mistakenly wrote *G* when the text obviously required *S*.

[1] The identities of the two knights, to date, have not been historically identified.

Novella XXXV.

[a] *petronciano*: Frutta d'erba di qualità di zucca grossa più d'una comuna pera, e di color *paonazzo*: colore tra azzurro, e nero, forse detto dal colore delle penne del paone.

[1] Taddeo Alderotti, also known as Thaddaeus Florentinus, was born in Florence in 1223. He began his studies in medicine late in life, but quickly rose to prominence as a professor of medicine at the University of Bologna. He was one of the first to annotate Hyppocrates and Galen, and to translate Aristotle's *Ethics*. Dante placed him among the illustrious teachers in *Par.* XII, 83. Taddeo was held in the highest esteem by the Bolognese, and was called to the Vatican to attend to Pope Onorius IV, during his last malady. He died in Bologna in 1295 (*Dizionario Biografico*, V.2 85).

[2] Alderotti is famous for his *Booklet on the Conservation of Health* (*Libello per conservare la sanità*) which discusses in detail which foods are good and which are bad for one's health and during which seasons they should be ingested. The eggplant is never mentioned in the text. The

humor of the tale is heightened when one remembers that the patron saint of Bologna is Saint Petronius.

Novella XXXVI.

[a] *boccola*: Italian editions have interpreted this word as meaning *monile* or necklace. Modern Italian translates it specifically as earrings. Since it seems improbable contextually to use the modern significance, I have opted to translate the word generically as jewelry. The term does not appear in the *Vocabolario* of the Accademia della Crusca.
[b] *fibbiaglio*: fermaglio.
[c] *atare*: aiutare.

[1] Balak, son of Zippor, King of Moab (Numbers 22:2).
[2] While the novella correctly identifies the persecuted as "the people of God," that is, the Israelites, the rubric mistakenly translates this into "Christians," leading one to remember that the two were in fact not originally composed by the same person(s).
[3] Balaam was the son of Beor, a soothsayer from the Euphrates.
[4] While the Italian indicates a male animal, the Biblical story identifies it as a she-donkey, which was "considered a princely mount in the second millennium B.C. (Numbers 22:21 *note d*)."
[5] The summit of Peor (Numbers 23:29).
[6] The text, to this point, follows Numbers 22 and 23:1-10.
[7] The remainder of the novella is an elaboration of the description of the debauchery of Israel with the daughters of Moab (Numbers 25:1-3). In the end, it was Moses who chided the Israelites for sparing the lives of the Midian women.

"Why have you spared the life of all the women?
These were the very ones who, on Balaam's advice,
perverted the sons of Israel and made them
renounce Yahweh in the affair at Peor."

(Numbers 31:15-17)

The Israelites followed the orders of Moses, purified themselves and "kill[ed] all the women who had slept with man (Numbers 31:18)." There is no mention in the Biblical account of the adornment of the women.
[8] I have translated *mosca* as a variation of *nusca*, which means a clasp necklace. Some early editions suggest a literal translation of *mosca* as fly; to be interpreted as meaning a necklace with an incised fly medallion, much like the scarab jewels found in ancient Egypt.
[9] Mars: The Roman god of war, naturally plays no part in the Biblical account from which the novella is derived. In the Biblical narration, Yahweh is angry with the Israelites who were perverted by the Midian women into renouncing Him and committing to the "Baal of Peor (Numbers 26:3; 31:16)."

Novella XXXVII.

[1] The tale functions as *exemplum*, the nature of the tale becoming even more indistinct if one accepts the identification with Greece here to mean the East in general.

Novella XXXVIII.

[1] "Thales of Miletus, who initiated the Ionian School, was one of the celebrated Seven Wise Men. While the remaining six were distinguished by balanced lives and moral teachings, Thales took up the study of nature and committed the results of his researches to writing. He won particular applause by his mastery of astronomical calculations and by his predictions of solar and lunar eclipses (Augustine, St. 145)."

"Melissus, the son of Ithaegenes, was a native of Samos. He was a pupil of Parmenides... In his view the universe was unlimited, unchangeable and immovable, and was one, uniform and full of matter. There was no real, but only apparent, motion. Moreover he said that we ought not to make any statements about the gods, for it was impossible to have knowledge of them. According to Apollodorus, he flourished in the 84th Olympiad [444-440 B.C.] (Diogenes Laertius 433-35)."

[2] Actually Thales of Miletus is discussed in Book VIII, Chapter 2 of *The City of God*.

[3] The comic elements of the novella are significantly enhanced for those who were conversant with the account of Melissus in Diogenes Laertius' *Lives of Eminent Philosophers*, where this man who almost drowns in a little puddle of water is described as a man who "was elected admiral and won more admiration than ever through his own merit (Diogenes Laertius 433)."

Novella XXXIX.

[a] *Aldrobandino* is a misspelling for Aldobrandino.
[b] *Orbivieto* is an ancient form of Orvieto.
[c] *donzello*: Giovane senza moglie.

[1] Aldobrandino Cavalcanti was born into the famous Florentine family around 1217. It is believed that he was Prior of Santa Maria Novella from 1244-53, and again from 1262-65. He became Bishop of Orvieto sometime around 1273. He died in 1279 (*Dizionario Biografico*, V.22 601-03).

[2] Minor friars is a term used for Franciscan friars. For a detailed account of *frati minori*: see *Enciclopedia Cattolica*, V.5, 1722-1743. It is interesting to note that Bishop Aldobrandino was a Dominican.

Novella XL.

[a] *uomo di corte*: see *note* for *Novella IIII, c.*
[b] *piazzeggiare*: andare a spasso per le piazze.
[c] *novella*: narrazion favolosa, favola.

[1] Monaci tells us that Saladino was not an uncommon name in medieval records from Northern Italy. While this figure cannot be unquestionably identified, a Saladino of Pavia, or of Acqui, does appear as a poet in certain medieval manuscripts. This figure; however, is described as a notary. One ballata by Saladino, entitled *Tanto di fino amore son gaudente* (I am made so merry by courtly love) is found in Monaci's *Crestomazia* (p. 239-40).

Novella XLI.

[1] The Traversari was a Ravenna family which reached its zenith from the ninth to the thirteenth centuries. They were administrators of the vast resources of the bishoprics and monasteries of Ravenna. They were always primarily involved in the military and political affairs of the city. Paolo (Polo), son and successor to Pietro, joined with the Pope and his intervention as chief of the Ravenna military was decisive in the battle against the Ghibellines of Romagna, and in retaking Ferrara from the Salinguerra and giving it back to the Este family. His death (10 August 1240) resulted in the decline of the family [*my translation*] (*Enciclopedia italiana*, V.34 238)."

Novella XLII.

[a] *traggo*: da *traggere*, forma di *trarre*.
[b] The author(s) mistakenly remains in the direct address present tense instead of switching back to the descriptive past.
[c] *ragunaro*: adunare.
[d] *mattero*: matterello.

[1] "Guillem de Berguedan was a noble baron of Catalonia, viscount of Berguedan, lord of Madorna and of Reichs, a good knight and a good warrior." "He composed good *sirventes*, in which he slandered some and praised others, and he boasted of all the ladies who permitted him to love them. He had many adventures in arms and in gallantry, and great misadventures. Later he was killed by a foot-soldier (*Vidas* 52)."

"Berédan (Guillaume) Spanish troubadour, from the ancient house of his name in Catalonia. He lived during the last half of the twelfth century. He became famous for his excesses and fits of passion. He murdered by treachery one of his enemies. As punishment for this crime, the King of Aragon stripped him of all his possessions. His poetry wallows in obscene subject matter [*my translation*] (*Nouvelle* V.5 493)."
[2] This Raymond Berengar, given the dates of the protagonist, is most likely the third (III), Count of Barcelona from 1131 to 1162 (*see*: note in the Lo Nigro edition 128).

Novella XLIII.

[a] *inguistara*: guastada.
[b] *giucolare*: *see* note for *Novella IIII, f.*
[c] *miuolo*: bicchiere.
[d] *guastada*: Vaso di vetro corpacciuto, con piede, e collo stretto, nel quale, comunalmente, si tiene l'acqua, per annacquare il vino. By using both *inguistare* and *guastada* in the same, short tale, it seems obvious that the author(s) intended them to signify slightly different objects.
[e] *pettinare*: Per mangiare presto, e durare assai. Pettinare col pettine, e col cardo, Si dice di chi mangia, e chi beve assai: modi bassi.

[1] "Rangoni, a noble Modenese family still in existence today... Iacopino, brother of Gherardo, after having been podesta of Todi in 1234, Siena in 1237, Bologna in 1259, commanded the Florentine Guelph army at the rock of Monteaperti (4 September 1260). From these held positions the Guelph leanings of the family already appeared; these became completely affirmed when Iacopino, with other Modenese nobles, left the Imperial field in Parma in 1247 and, by forming the Aigoni party

in direct opposition to the Modenese Ghibellines, called Grasolfi, he went to Bologna and contributed to the victory of Fossalta (1249), and the establishment of a mixed regime in Modena which ceased in 1264 with the expulsion of the Ghibellines [*my translation*] (*Enciclopedia Italiana*, V.28 824)."

[2] The reasons for translating *giullare* as *jester* here are the same as those found in the note for *Novella IIII, 1*.

[3] See note for *Novella IIII, 9*.

Novella XLIIII.

[a] *uomo di corte*: see *note* for *Novella IIII, c*.

[1] "Marco Lombardo lived around the middle of the thirteenth century. He was a noble soul, trustworthy, dignified and astute; a pungent minstrel, one of the wisest but one of the least fortunate of his age. He was endowed with moral virtue, chivalrous, intellectual and an expert of things concerning the world. Marco drifted from court to court (he was most probably called *lombardo* because he frequented most the courts of Northern Italy, rather than it being his place of birth). He led a bitter, wanderer's life. While mocked for his poverty, Marco was always upright and magnanimous. Nothing about him is certain, not his age, his place of birth, not even the facts concerning his life. Upheld by contemporaries as one of the great champions of his class and his art, a series of legends evolved around him [*my translation*] (Siebzehner-Vivanti 354)."

"Lombardo was I, and I was Marco called;
The world I knew, and love that excellence,
At which has each one now unbent his bow."
(*Purg.* XVI, 46-48)

Dante honors Marco Lombardo with a Purgatorial place among those who, "the knot of anger go unloosening (*Purg.* XVI, 24)." Marco instructs Dante on the nature of free will, the limited powers of the astral spheres, and places at least part of the blame for contemporary moral decline on a lack of temporal direction, resulting from the loss of the balance of power between the Church (Pope) and the State (Emperor).

Novella XLV.

[a] *lena*: respirazione.

[b] *meslea*: forma di *mislea*: Combattimento di Spada.

[c] *dottare*: see *note* for *Novella XII, b*.

[1] *Lancelot*: see *note* for *Novella XXVIII, 2*.

[2] The knight designated by *A*. "was Alibon, the son of the vavasor of the Queen's Ford." Many Italian editions identify *The Vulgate Version of the Arthurian Romances* as the source of this tale, and indeed many instances are similar. In *The Vulgate*, however, Alibon does not learn the name of "the knight who carried white arms and rode a white horse" during their fracas (*Vulgate* V.3, pt.1, 140-42).

Novella XLVI.

[1] "Narcissus, the son of Cephisus; a beautiful youth who saw his reflection in a fountain, and thought it the presiding nymph of the place. He gradually pined away for love of this unattainable spirit, and nothing remained but a flower which the nymphs called by his name. He was beloved by Echo and his fate was a punishment for his cruel indifference to her passion (Bulfinch 929)."
[2] The use of *knight* as descriptor removes the tale from its classical origins and attempts to create a contemporary atmosphere.
[3] In the original Ovidian tale, Narcissus eventually realized that the reflection in the pond was his own, "Alas! I am myself the boy I see. I know it: my own reflection does not deceive me. I am on fire with love for my own self (Ovid 93)." Ovid does not have Narcissus drowned in the pool; but instead "he was worn and wasted away with love, and slowly consumed by its hidden fire (Ovid 94)."
[4] Cupid. The god of love in Roman mythology, identified with the Greek Eros, son of Mercury and Venus. He is represented as a winged boy, carrying a bow and arrows. One legend says that he wets with blood the grindstone on which he sharpens his arrows (Bulfinch 897)."
[5] In mythology Narcissus is changed into "a flower with a circle of white petals round a yellow centre (Ovid 94)," rather than an almond tree.

Novella XLVII.

[1] "Lizio, a Guelph gentleman of Valbuona in Romagna, from the feudal family which dominated the lands that now constitute the Commune of Bagno. He was a man of noble habits and liberal in hospitality; a large, curial man of great courtesy, said Lana; so much so that in order to prepare a dinner for his friends, he once sold half of a sendal blanket, as narrated by Ottimo. In 1260, the year of Monteaperti, he was in the service of Guido Novello, then podesta of Florence. He helped Rinieri de' Calboli against the Ghibellines of Forlì and in 1279 swore a peace treaty with him. He was born circa 1230 and died in 1280 [*my translation*] (Siebzehner-Vivanti 337)."
[2] "Rinieri de' Paolucci from Calboli, land in the Mantone valley, center of a small fief, today corresponding to the territory of the Commune of Rocco San Casciano (Forlì). From a noble family, he was a captain of the Guelphs and took part in the turbulent battles which consumed the Romagna of the 13th century. In the war of 1276 he rebelled against the Commune of Forlì, helped by the Bolognese and Florentine Guelphs. He eventually gave in to Guido of Montefeltro. He was podesta of Parma and in various central Italian cities from 1247 to 1282. He made peace with the Church in 1291, along with Malatesta of Verruccio he was among the guarantors of the pact with the Pontifical rector of Romagna. Exiled from Forlì in 1294, he was later able to return, but shortly afterwards (1296), he was killed by adversarial Ghibellines while defending the city against them [*my translation*] (Siebzehner-Vivanti 517)."

Novella XLVIII.

[1] "Conrad IV (b. April 25, 1228, Andria, Italy--d. May 21, 1254, Lavello), German king from 1237 and King of Sicily from 1251. The son of Emperor Frederick II and his second wife Isabella (Yolande) de Brienne. Conrad was heir to the Kingdom of Jerusalem through his mother; he was also invested by his father as Duke of Swabia 1235. At Vienna in February of 1237 he was elected King of the Romans in place of half-brother Henry VII, who rebelled against the Emperor in 1235...On Dec. 12, 1250, Frederick II died. Troubles in Sicily and the rising strength of the papal

party in Germany...forced Conrad to abandon Germany for Sicily late in 1251, when he took the title of King of Sicily. Conrad's position in Sicily was secured by his capture of Naples in October 1253, but his efforts to reach an understanding with the papacy failed (*New Encyclopaedia Britannica: Micropaedia* V.3 546)."

[2] "Conradin, also called Conrad V (b. March 24, 1252, Wolfstein, Swabia--d. Oct. 29, 1268, Naples, Italy), the last of the German Hohenstaufen dynasty, Duke of Swabia, King of the Romans, and claimant to the throne of Sicily. The leading hope of the antipapal Italian ghibellines, he led an expedition into Italy in 1267 in an unsuccessful attempt to regain Sicily from Charles of Anjou.

Son of the Emperor Conrad IV and grandson of the emperor Frederick II, Conradin claimed inheritance of the Kingdom of Sicily and the Kingdom of Jerusalem. His uncle Manfred, an illegitimate son of Frederick II, however, usurped the Sicilian throne in 1258. Conradin contented himself with regaining what remained of the Duchy of Swabia.

When Manfred fell, Conradin was enthusiastically greeted by the Italians. He set out for Sicily and was unexpectedly defeated by Charles at Tagliacozza on August 23, 1268. He was tried before Charles' jury in Naples and beheaded in the public marketplace (*New Encyclopaedia Britannica: Micropaedia* V.3 549)."

[3] The literal translation is, "here one reads."

Novella XLIX.

[a] *traviare*: Cavar di via, allontanare, uscir di proposito.

[b] *pasciere*: E proprio il tagliar, che fanno le bestie co' denti l'erba, o altra verzura, per mangiare. Per dar mangiare.

[1] The term used to indicate abortion actually means, "to extract from the road, to interrupt, to break."

[2] The term used actually means "to graze," suggesting the less than sophisticated behavior of his wife.

Novella L.

[a] *piato*: Il piatire. Lite davanti a magistrato.

[1] "Francesco, son of Accorso, but not inferior to his father, taught civil law at Bologna and in public debates vanquished his Bolognese doctor opponents, who were envious of his father's glosses and attempted to extinguish his fame. He was a pious defender of his father's name. He died in Bologna in the year of Our Lord 1309, at the age of sixty-eight and was buried with his father [*my translation*] (Villani V.2 433.)."

"Francesco Accursio, Doctor of Law, public lecturer in Toulouse and counsellor to King Richard of England, in whose memory he bought a quantity of land near Budrio Castle in the state of Bologna and named that place The Riccardina. His glosses were published by Leone in 1617-18. He wrote on the twenty-four *Digests*, on the *Codex* and on many questions concerning various authors. He prepared the additions to the glosses of his father, Accursio. He died in 1294 and was buried in Saint Francis in the beautiful vault of his father, where one finds the folowing letters: *Sepulc. Accursii Glosat. & Franc. Filii* [*my translation*] (Orlandi da Bologna 116)."

[2] "Accorso, glossator and commentator on civil law, born of rustic stock, but of very civil and delicate breeding, in the town of Bagnolo, opposite Montebuoni from the South, circa five miles

from Florence, where just a few years ago there still stood a house which, through the negligence of his successors was destroyed, was called Accorso Studio. There he lived a solitary life, spending long periods of time reading and commenting on the law, which to this day many attempt to debase. He died in the year of Our Lord 1265 at the age of seventy-eight. He was buried in Bologna in a raised tomb [*my translation*] (Villani V.2 431)."

"Accursio was a most famous glossator of Florentine origin. A citizen of Bologna and the founder of his house in Bologna. He prepared the last apparatus of glosses, concerning all texts and through his studies gathered together the glosses of all other writers, registered and compared them. For the space of thirty-four years he read at the Public Studio of Bologna...He died in the year 1260 and was buried in Saint Francis Cemetery [*my translation*] (Orlandi da Bologna 38)."

Novella LI.

[1] This tale became famous when Boccaccio chose to include an extended version of it in *The Decameron* (I,9). Since Boccaccio describes the king as "The First King of Cyprus;" subsequent editors of *The Novellino* have identified this character as King Guy of Lusignan, the first king of Jerusalem and Cyprus, who bought Cyprus from the Templars and the Lombards. He died in 1205. For an early account of this man, see: Makhairas V.1 17-28.

Novella LII.

[a] *rodegare*: the context suggests this to be a form of *rodere*.

[1] King John of Atri refers to "Jean de Brienne (ca. 1150-March 1237). Born to a family of the minor nobility in France, Jean de Brienne was a noted warrior and the husband of the heiress to the Kingdom of Jerusalem. He led the Fifth Crusade until he was ousted from command by his son-in-law Frederick II, the titular heir to Jerusalem, who crowned himself king in 1228...By the time Jean died, the Latin Kingdom consisted largely of the city of Constantinople and was in an extremely precarious state (*Dictionary of the Middle Ages*. V.7 52)."

He is called the King of *Atri* (other editions more correctly write *Acri*), because *Acre* acted for a time as the capital for the Latin Kingdom in the East. "The Third Crusade (1189-1192) quickly restored Acre in 1191, but not Jerusalem. For a century Acre functioned as the political and artistic capital of the Latin Kingdom (*Dictionary of the Middle Ages*. V.4 25)."

[2] Notes from the various Italian editions indicate that sources and variations on the story have the bell being tolled by a serpent in the Charlemagne legends and an Indian version where the toller is a cow. In keeping with medieval tradition, *The Novellino* author(s) selected a horse as the offended party; since this animal was considered most noble and devoted to its master.

"The horse is an animal of great knowledge, for since it always goes to live with men, this gives it some sense, so that it knows its master, and it often changes customs and habits when it changes masters." "There are some which recognize their master's enemies, for they bite them and strike them violently. There are some which will only carry their rightful master...And the horse of Craterus, the duke of Galatia, when his lord had died and King Antiochus mounted him to fight, ran down a great hill and stumbled in such a way that he killed himself and his lord, or, if you prefer, his rider." "It is a proven fact about many horses that they weep and shed tears because of the death of their lord, and there is no other animal that does this! (Latini 135)."

"Many [horses] recognise their masters, and become unmanageable if they change hands." "When the king of the Scythians was killed in single combat and his opponent tried to strip him of

his armour, his horse attacked him, kicking and biting him. When King Nicodemus was killed, his horse stopped eating and starved to death." "If their master is killed or dies, horses will weep. It is said that only horses will weep for men, and only they feel sorrow (*Bestiary* 102-03)."

Novella LIII.

[a] *danaio*: moneta di minor valuta.
[b] *passaggiere*: per gabelliere, o stradiere, cioè che sta a guardia del paese, per raccor gabella, o dazio.
[c] *pedagiere*: che ricoglie il pedaggio.

[1] This tale is a close adaptation of Tale VI, "The Hunchback and the Poet," found in the *Disciplina clericalis*. *The Novellino* omits the instructional, introductory remarks which, as is usual in the *Disciplina clericalis*, are found at the end of the previous tale.

"An Arab once said to his son: `If you find yourself in difficulty and you have the possibility of escaping from it with ease, do not dally, for if you wait for a better opportunity, you will find yourself in even greater straits. Never let what happened to the hunchback and the poet happen to you.' `What happened there?' asked the son. Then the father began (Petrus Alfonsi 116-7)."

[2] "*Dinar*, the Islamic unit of currency. The Arabic word *dinar* comes ultimately from the Latin *denarius*, which originally meant a silver coin but later became a common term for the Roman-Byzantine gold solidus."

"Medieval documents and texts discriminate among dozens of different kinds of dinars, which are identified by issuing authority, by geographic origin, or by some special feature of appearance. In addition to the many different Muslim dinars, Christians in England, Spain, Sicily, and the crusader states imitated dinars or struck their own with distinctive Arabic legends (*Dictionary of the Middle Ages*. V.4 187)."

Novella LIIII.

[1] In Italian, the pastor's name signifies "piggy" or "piglet;" thus the tale is about "Pastor Piggy."
[2] Giovanni Mangiadore was Bishop of Florence from 1251 to 1273. "He knew how to abstain from openly taking sides in a period when there were violent conflicts between the Guelphs and the Ghibellines [*my translation*] (Antonetti 206)."

The author's selection of this historical figure adds to the humor of the tale, since his name translates as "glutton" or "big eater," or coarsely put, "pig," and so we have the tale of Pastor Piggy and Bishop Pig.

Novella LV.

[a] *uomo di corte*: see *note* for *Novella IIII, c.*
[b] *orrevole*: sincopa d'*onorevole*.
[c] *morditore*: Che morde. Qui maledico, riprensore.

[1] Marco Lombardo: see *note* for *Novella XLIIII, 1.*

Novella LVI.

[a] *Marca*: paese, contrada.
[b] *livre*: "French money of account which in the time of Charlemagne (768-814) equalled one pound of silver, but in time its value lessened (Broughton 311)."
[c] *piato*: see *note* for *Novella L, a.*
[d] *libello*: domanda giudiciaria, fatta per iscrittura.

[1] The word *marca* in the Middle Ages, according to the *Crusca*, could mean countryside. Some editors have chosen to define it as the geographical location; "The Marche, mountainous region of central Italy, comprising the provinces of Ancona, Ascoli Piceno, Macerata, and Pesaro-Urbino; pop. (1981) 1,412,404; area 9,692 sq. km.; extends between the rivers Foglia and Tronto down the east slopes of the Appino Umbro-Marchigiano to the Adriatic Sea (*Chambers* 395)."
[2]Legends concerning the foundation of the University of Bologna go as far back as the reconstruction of the city by Theodosius II in 423. The school's earliest records, dating from the eleventh century, affirm its prominence in legal studies, which flourished and became famous under the tutelage of Irnerius (born c. 1055). "Irnerius is the immortal man who revives, represents and brings to light Roman Law resuscitating it from its ashes [*my translation*] (Sorbelli V.1 35)."

"By the second half of the twelfth century Bologna became the center of legal studies, thanks to the presence of famous masters, among them Irnerius (*ca.*1055 - *ca.*1130), Martinus, Bulgarus, Jacobus and Hugh, advisers of Emperor Frederick Barbarossa, all legists and Gracian canonists (*Dictionary of the Middle Ages*. V.12 283-84)."
[3] Livre actually refers to an earlier French coin, which seems inappropriate for this text. I have, therefore, chosen to follow the consensus of Italian editors who interpret it as a variation on the term *lire*.

Novella LVII.

[a] *corte*: serraglio o chiusura, che si fa nelle ville.

Novella LVIII.

[a] *donzello*: see *note* for *Novella XXXIX, c.*
[b] *fica*: parte vergognosa della femmina, che anche si dice potta. E da questa, per qualche similitudine, si chiama fica quell'atto, che con le mani si fa, in dispregio altrui messo il dito grosso tra l'indice, e'l medio: onde Far le fiche.
[c] *Barancadoria* è Branca Doria.

[1] Messer Beriuolo is a character found in a minor work which appeared around the same time as *The Novellino*, entitled *Libro di motti* (*Book of Sayings*), which the critic Guido Biagi believes has much in common with *The Novellino*. In his introduction to the text, Biagi states, "The name of the author is not registered at the beginning or at the end, but more than once in the text, and his name is Messer Vanni Giudice. He cites an infinite number of times a certain Messer Beriuolo, his friend, as a man of great fame in clever replies [*my translation*] (*Studii* 431)."

[2] The young squire in the text makes a vulgar gesture which, in medieval Italy, crudely represented female genitalia by inserting the thumb between the index and the middle fingers. The action corresponds roughly to the raising of the middle finger today.

[3] Brancaleone (Branca) Doria was born in Genoa to a well-known family around 1235. He is mentioned numerous times in the civil records of Genoa as owning land in Genoa and Sardinia. Doria was known as a "citizen merchant." He died around 1325 [*my translation*] (from *Dizionario biografico* V.41 299-305).

Novella LIX.

[a] *atare*: aiutare.
[b] *atare*: aiutare.
[c] *calere*: curarsi.
[d] *calere*: curarsi.

[1] The tale is an adaptation of the story demonstrating "the fickleness of women," concerning the widow of Ephesus, found in Petronius' *Satyricon* (Petronius 117-20). Italian editors are correct in suggesting that *The Novellino*'s immediate source was the medieval adaptation found in *Il Libro dei Sette Savi di Roma* (*The Book of the Seven Sages of Rome*), of a tenth-century Indian collection which circulated throughout Europe, probably by way of a late thirteenth-century Spanish adaptation. Our author(s), however, minimizes the misogynistic violence present in the *Libro*, where the Roman widow enthusiastically drags her husband from his tomb and strings him up on the gallows herself, then slashes his skull with a sword and bashes in his front teeth with a stone (*Il Libro dei Sette Savi* 34-37).

[2] *The Novellino* author(s) once again shows his predilection for the Emperor Frederick by transferring the action to his court.

Novella LX.

[1] Charles I, or Charles of Anjou (1226-1285) was the Angevin King of Naples and Sicily, a great but brief empire. An ally of the church, Charles was convinced by the French Pope, Urban IV, to depose Manfred for his decadent lifestyle, and to usurp his Sicilian crown. Historians describe Charles as a great leader. "Charles of Anjou by sheer ability made himself the greatest potentate in Europe (Smith, D. Mack 67)." Villani recounts his feats in great detail and describes him as "Charles, Count of Anjou and Provence, son of the King of France (Louis VIII) and brother of Good King Louis (IX), was the most accomplished prince in the use of arms and was graced with all the virtues of his age. He came from a powerful house, that of France, was a champion of the Holy Church, King of Sicily and Puglia, recapturing the kingdom from Manfred, who held it by illicit force and who was an excommunicant and damned [*my translation*] (Villani V.1 108)."

Charles fought alongside his brother in the Holy Lands. His preference for Naples over Sicily, compounded by his strict orthodoxy, stringent laws and excessive taxes, inevitably caused the Sicilian revolt of 1282, now known as The Sicilian Vespers, which resulted in his loss of the Island to Peter of Aragon. (*See*: Smith, D. Mack 65-75. Michele Fuiano has also published a collection of historical essays in Italian on Charles of Anjou).

[2] In 1277 he became heir to the Kingdom of Jerusalem.

[3] see *note* for *Novella LX, 1.*

[4] To date no historical Countess of Teti has been found.

[5] Italian editors are correct in their identification of the Count of Universa as the Count of Nevers. This confusion, on the part of our author(s), is most probably the result of errors in phonetic transcription, producing d'[U]nivers[a] from de Nevers. This particular Count was Jean Tristan, son of King Louis IX, who died of plague in Tunis, like his father, in 1270 (Joinville 119, 252, 266; De Lespinasse 251-68, 298).

[6] "Louis IX of France (St. Louis) 25 April 1214-25 August 1270) became King of France in 1226 at the age of twelve." "In penitential recollection for his failure as a crusader, the returned king became what many of his contemporaries considered a model prince: he reintroduced the *enquêteurs* as a permanent element of government; he overhauled provincial officialdom, concentrating on the bailiffs and the seneschals; he investigated and reformed municipal (communal) administration as well as administration in Paris; he undertook a not altogether unsuccessful program providing incentives for the voluntary conversion of Jews, and he became remarkably considerate of the poor, widows, orphans and the sick, founding and endowing a score of hospitals, and alms for lepers. He was, in short, a serious, hard-working prince, and one constantly on the move because of his interest in provincial government." "Louis IX again took the cross in 1267. Already in poor health, he departed France in 1270 after three years of careful preparations. He died of natural causes soon after landings and skirmishes in Tunisia. He was succeeded by his son, Philip III, during whose reign the first efforts were made for his canonization. These efforts were brought to fruition during the reign of his grandson, Philip IV, in 1297. The feast of St. Louis Confessor is celebrated on 24 August (*Dictionary of the Middle Ages*. V.7 674-76)." For a contemporary account of Louis IX, see the work of Joinville.

[7] *Allardo de' Valleri*: "Erard de Valéry, counselor to Charles of Anjou, who assisted him in the battle of Tagliacozzo, which resulted in the defeat of Conradin and the end of the rule of the House of Swabia [*my translation*] (Siebzehner-Vivanti 16)."

[8] Louis IX enacted a number of ordinances; most important are those of 1254, 1261 and 1269, intended to "eliminate from his kingdom all sins offensive to divine majesty, heresy and usury." "The ordinance of 1261 prohibited "battles," substituting proof by witnesses." In this way Louis attempted to suppress the feudal custom of "judicial duel," whereby a knight proved the truth of his statement by defeating his accusor in hand to hand combat (Richard 155, 174-75)."

[9] "Beguines and beghards were urban women and men of continental northern Europe who led lives of chastity, poverty and religious devotion without joining an approved order. Beguines first appeared in the Low Countries at the end of the twelfth century. Beghards, their male counterparts, appeared soon afterward, but there were always many more beguines than beghards." "The likelihood that both *beguinus* (with feminine *begina*) and *beghardus* were originally pejorative terms is strengthened by the certainty that beguines and beghards were regarded by many with suspicion and hostility throughout the thirteenth century. One reason for this was that religious traditionalists and members of the secular clergy were often hostile to the "apostolic" movement with which the early beguines and beghards were associated (*Dictionary of the Middle Ages*. V.2 157-62)."

Ernest McDonnell, in his definitive work on the beguines and beghards, discusses Louis IX's patronage of these groups. "However much Louis IX was interested in every manifestation of religious and extraregular life, even showing good will to congregations which failed to meet the approval of the second council of Lyons (1274) a scant four years after his death, the feminine religious movement and the mendicant orders appear to have received consistently preferential treatment. As `father consoler of the poor,' the king founded the well-known beguine house in Paris near the gate Barbeel in the parish of St. Paul. According to the

investigation conducted on behalf of the Ghent beguines in the spring of 1328 St. Louis had visited them; expressing pleasure over their earnestness and fervor, he secured from the bishop of Tournai a church for the community and obtained for their benefit privileges and immunities. It was in imitation of this institution that the king then proceeded to establish and endow the Paris community as well as 'several others in different places' (McDonnell 224)."

[10] "Louis' policies and religious devotions did not lack critics. His deep affection for the friars (expressed in his adoption of a mendicant-style tunic in personal dress, endowments of mendicant convents, and employment of friars as *enquêteurs*) was viewed with vehement opprobrium." "His desire to wear a hairshirt was reproved by his own confessor (*Dictionary of the Middle Ages*. V.7 675)."

Joinville describes the king as follows: "After that the King was come back from beyond the seas, he bare himself so devoutly that never again did he wear ermine or minever, or scarlet, or gilded stirrups or spurs. His robes were of grogram or of watchet cloth; the furs of his coverlets and of his robes were of wild goat, or hare's legs or lamb (Joinville 203)."

[11] "In 1234 Louis married Marguerite of Provence (1221-1295), daughter of Raymond Berenger IV, by whom he had eleven children (*Dictionary of the Middle Ages*. V.7 675)."

Novella LXI.

[a] The author mistakenly uses *e* for *i*.
[b] *Soldano*: Titolo di Principato.
[c] *informagione*: ragguaglio, notizia.
[d] *perpero*: sorta di moneta.

[1] Once again our author(s) demonstrates his ignorance of classical history. Socrates was, of course, not a Roman, but an Athenian, born around 470 BC. and "drank the hemlock" in 399 BC. The fact that he wrote nothing, thereby leaving no primary documents to posterity, must have contributed greatly to the emergence of fables and legends concerning his life.

[2] The use of the word Sultan is an inappropriate title for a Greek leader.

[3] While the presentation of Socrates in the novella might surprise some modern readers, history has described him as "outwardly grotesque." He, in fact, cut quite a strange figure in many tales during the Middle Ages. Socrates appears in the *Fiore di filosofi e di molti savi* (*The Flower of Philosophers and Other Wise Men*), which appeared in Italy shortly before *The Novellino* and is considered a source for at least three of its novellas. In the *Fiore*, Socrates is found quarreling, in a slap-stick manner, with his two wives, who eventually get the better of him. "And he got up and ran away and they followed right behind, with clubs and beat him so hard that they left him for dead. After which he fled with some of his disciples and went to live in a place in the country, far from people, in order to better study, and there he wrote many books [*my translation*] (*Fiore* 6)."

[4] The description of Socrates in *The Novellino* is actually quite tame when compared to his treatment in other medieval works. "Socrates was a very great philosopher at that time, and he was extremely ugly to look at, he was ridiculously little, with a face full of hair, a large pug-nose, a bald cavernous pate, hairy neck and armpits, and skinny bow legs [*my translation*] (*Fiore* 5)."

[5] The *Vocabolario degli Accademici della Crusca* defines *perpero* as simply "a type of money."

Novella LXII.

[a] Arimini monte is actually Remiremont.
[b] *milenso*: sciocco; scimunito, senza garbo; con un certo modo, quasi lezioso.
[c] *nonane*: Italianized form of the French *nonne* (or *nonnaine*) for *nun*.
[d] *donneare*: da donna, fare all'amore con le donne, e conversar con esse per trattenersi.

[1] Roberto seems not to have been an historical figure.
[2] Mount Arimini is actually Remiremont.
[3] Remiremont is actually north of Burgundy, located in the region of Vosges, between Alsace and the Lorraine plateau.
[4] Baligant is a great Paynim character, the Emir of Babylon, from *The Song of Roland*. He appears in the second half of the poem, coming to the aid of Marsilion, who has killed Roland and Oliver and is being pursued by Charlemagne. Although never described in such intimate detail as found in this novella, in *The Song of Roland*, Baligant is described as admirably "great" in both courage and physical appearance.

"Stalwart is he, capacious in the fork,
Large in the ribs, lean in the flanks and small;
Broad is his breast and beautifully formed,
His shoulders wide, his colour fresh withal,
Warlike his bearing, his curling locks unshorn
White as a flower upon a summer's morn,
His valour proved in battle o'er and o'er;
Were he but Christian, God! what a warrior!"
(*The Song of Roland* l.3157-64)

[5] The motif of serving the heart of a lover to a faithless wife comes from the *Vida* of Guillem de Cabestaing who took as a lover Lady Soremonda, the wife of Raimon de Castel Roussillon. Upon learning of his wife's betrayal, he killed Guillem, "took the heart out of his body, and had it taken to a squire in his house, and had it cooked and peppered, and gave it to his wife to eat (*Vidas* 53)." The story obtained immortal acclaim in its retelling by Boccaccio in *Decameron* IV, 9 (*Boccaccio* 350-53).
[6] The Abbey of Remiremont has a long and complicated history. Originally an abbey for men, it shifted to a women's abbey sometime around 900. At some point the abbey became involved in wars between the Holy Roman Emperor and the Duchy of Lorraine, which resulted in many secular women, even princesses of the empire, being named abbess. In the eleventh century, Pope Eugenius III wrote a papal bull condemning the carnal practices of the "Noble Ladies of Remiremont," a fact which the town's chroniclers proclaim as false. In the twelfth century the Abbess Judith was accused of having an affair with her cousin Amédée, the Archbishop of Besançon. The amorous adventures of the religious ladies of Remiremont are the source of a poem written around 1160, entitled *Romaricimontis concilium* (*Remiremont* 32).
[7] "In *Guillaume de Dôle* the Emperor and his court go to the woods `manches décousues' to have greater freedom of action. When they have ended the chase and washed their hands at a spring the ladies sew up their sleeves with threads from the pouches that hang at their girdles." "*Jehan et Blonde*, c. 1280, shows that the fashion for tight sleeves which had to be sewn at the wrist continued until nearly the end of the century (Evans, *Dress* 14)."

Novella LXIII.

[a] *attragione*: colsero a tradimento (note from Segre edition).

[1] "*Palamedes*, a French prose romance of the thirteenth century, predating the cyclic version of the Prose *Tristan*. The work, which is anonymous (although attributed in the prologue to Elie, or Hélie, de Borron [c. 1240]), is preserved as part of the *Compilation* of Rusticiano da Pisa and, in fragmentary form, in several manuscripts. The full title of the work identifies its heroes as Palamedes, Meliadus (the father of Tristan) and Guiron le Courtois (Lacy 416)." Rusticiano da Pisa's work was available during the time of the writing of *The Novellino*. The later works concerning Tristan, such as those of Béroul and Bédier, identify his father as Rivalen of Lyonesse and not Meliadus.

[2] There are at least two French medieval romances named for Richard Sans Peur, or Richard the Fearless, third Duke of Normandy.

[3] The text specifically uses the term *sergeants* rather than *soldiers*.

Novella LXIIII.

[a] *approvatore*: maschile; che appruova, che giudica.
[b] *fedire*: ferire.
[c] *procianamante*: proccianamante, prossimamente.
[d] *candellara*: Candelora.

[1] "Puy-Notre-Dame is a borough of the province of Maine-et-Loire, a division of the Saumur district, circa six kilometers west-south-west of Montreuil-Bellay, in the rough plains that extend between Thouet and Layon, running to the left of the Loire, at an altitude of circa eighty-five meters [*my translation*] (Vivien 1000)."

Puy does not only refer to the geographical location, for in medieval Provence it signified poetic competitions. "We do know of Puys. The earliest known to us was that where the Monk of Montaudon acted as judge, but the event was a tournament, with competing poets in a minor role. It seems to have gone on for years, as other Troubadours refer to it. It was held in Vélay in the region under Robert I of Auvergne; he was a patron of Troubadours and may have founded it. Later on, as north France began imitating the Troubadours and the taste for their poems spread to the bourgeois, Puys were held in many towns: Arras, Amiens, Rouen, Abbeville, and so on (Lindsay 122)."

[2] Count Raimondo is most likely Raymond Berengar IV, since he was a count of Provence and reputed to be a poet in his own right. See *note* for *Novella XXXII, 5*.

[3] The pseudonym Messer Alamano could be translated as Master German, or the German master. The novella is a variation on the *razo* concerning the troubadour Rigaut de Berbezilh (1140-63? to 1170-1210?) (Hill V.1 90-94).

[4] The lady's *senhal* translates as Lady Grey, or the grey lady. The lady in the *razo* is identified as the wife of Jaufré of Tonai (Hill V.1 90).

[5] The need to conceal one's love from a jealous one, *gelos*, is a common theme in Provençal poetry and continues up to the screen lady in Dante's *Vita Nova*.

[6] The text actually states, "and they quickly raised him in the palms of their hands amid great glee."

[7] Candlemas is the Christian festival observed on February 2 in honor of the presentation of the Infant Christ in the Temple and the purification of the Virgin Mary. The Candlemas festival is believed to have been instituted in 541 or 542 by the Byzantine emperor Justinian I.
[8] *Canzonetta* is the diminutive form of *canzone*, "a short poem consisting of equal stanzas and an envoy of fewer lines than the stanza (Thrall 71)." The text is actually a Provençal *canso* where "love is the almost exclusive concern (*Encyclopedia of Poetry* 678)."
[9] The Knight's *canzone* is in fact a *canso* by Rigaut de Berbezilh. *The Novellino* text, however, is incomplete, reproducing stanzas one, two, four and five, of the original five. The original stanzas are composed of five heptameters and six decasyllables each. The tornadas are also omitted. The text reproduced in *The Novellino* is highly corrupt, fraught with errors in transcription and omissions, producing a hybrid text freely mixing Italian and pseudo-Provençal. This leads one to believe that the author(s) of *The Novellino* was not well acquainted with the Provençal language, and lends credence to the assertion that at least part of the text stems directly from the oral tradition. In order to prepare a coherent translation, I have compared *The Novellino* text to two editions of the original Rigaut *canso*, and, when absolutely necessary, I have reconstructed incoherent lines to proffer meaning in the translation. I have left the original pseudo-Provençal/Italian as transcribed in the Gualteruzzi edition. Both editions of Rigaut's work can be found in the "Bibliography to the Notes."
[10] The elephant might seem to contemporary readers a bizarre choice of symbol for love, yet medieval society viewed this distant, exotic creature as constant, faithful and representative of Adam and Eve (*Book of Beasts* 27).

"An elephant's nature is such that it does not know what it is to be in heat before thirteen years of age for females and fifteen for the males; and at the same time, they are so chaste that there is no fighting over females, but rather each elephant has its own mate which it remains attached to its whole life long, and if the male loses his mate or the female hers, they never link up with another, but instead they always go alone through the wilderness (Latini 137)."
[11] This strange passage is consistent with a bizarre belief regarding the elephant which was prevalent during the Middle Ages. "And those who have seen it say that the elephant, when it falls cannot get back up, even if it tries with all its might, because there are no knees in its legs; but nature, which watches over all animals, instructs it to cry out loud until all the other elephants in the country come, or at least twelve of them, and they all cry out together loudly and raise him up; but the very small elephants are of great help in raising him, for they put their snouts under him very forcefully (Latini 137)."
[12] This strange quality attributed to the bear is absent in many medieval bestiaries; however, the last line in Brunetto Latini's entry regarding bears states, "People say about the animal [the bear] that it gets fat and healthy from being beaten (Latini 142)."

Novella LXV.

[a] *rigangniolo*: picciol rivo.
[b] *dottare*: see *note* for *Novella XII, b*.
[c] *unita*: misspelling of the past participle for *onire*: *onta*: svergognare, fare onta.
[d] *sofratta* (*soffratta*): mancamente, necessità, carestia.

[1] Isotta, Isolde, Yseult or Iseult (the Blond, the Fair, or of the Hair of Gold) is the daughter of Anguish, King of Ireland, whose hand Tristan wins for his uncle, Mark, King of Cornwall. On

the way to the wedding, Tristan and Isotta drink a magic love potion. They become lovers and are eventually discovered, which leads to their tragic deaths (Lacy 575-78).

[2] Tristan is the son of Rivalin, King of Lyonesse and Blancheflor (or Meliadus and Elizabeth as they are called in the prose romances), sister to Mark, King of Cornwall. He and Isotta (see *note* above) accidentally drink a magic love potion and become lovers. They are eventually discovered, which leads to their tragic deaths (Lacy 575-78).

[3] Tristan is said to be of Cornwall here because he has left his father's realm and has become a knight in the service of his uncle, King Mark of Cornwall.

[4] Isotta is described as "the Blond" because in the story Tristan eventually meets and marries another Isotta of Brittany, called Isotta of the White Hands (Lacy 576). His love for Isotta the Blond never dies and his marriage is never consummated.

[5] "Mark, King of Cornwall, is the deceived husband in the triangle with Isolde of Ireland and his sister's son Tristan (Lacy 375)."

[6] In some versions of the tale, instead of disturbing the smooth flow of the waters, Tristan would float twigs on the rivulet for Isolde to see (Béroul 47).

[7] Tristan is referring to his single combat with Merholt of Ireland, uncle of Isolde, whom he defeated and killed in combat which resulted in the releasing of Cornwall from paying a tribute which "consisted of a number of young men and girls to be taken to Ireland as slaves (Béroul 40)."

[8] This scene is sometimes called "the tryst under the tree (Béroul 47-59).

Novella LXVI.

[a] *troscia*: stroscio.

[1] Diogenes (circa 412-323 B.C.), the famous Cynic philosopher, son of Icesias from Sinope in Pontus. After his father was condemned for counterfeiting coins, Diogenes fled to Athens. History proclaims him one of the great minimalists, "he denuded himself of all superfluous dress, furniture and even ideas (*Encyclopaedia Britannica* V.4 245)." Diogenes is famous for his witty apophthegms, which have been preserved in the work of Diogenes Laertius (V.2 23-85), one of the most famous being the interview with Alexander in Corinth related here. Concerning the novella, Cary writes (p.84), "These comments were often reproduced in the Middle Ages, sometimes with the anecdote (i.e. the tale) and sometimes independently. They point to a moral best expressed by Seneca, and typical of the Stoic treatment of Alexander's character. The world-conqueror, accustomed to boast that nobody could surpass him in liberality, was surprised by Diogenes, who, by his refusal to accept anything from him except what he could not give, proved himself richer in true riches, and a better man. The emphasis is therefore upon Alexander's making liberality a part of vanity, and on the rebuff which he receives from Diogenes, who asks him to give him back what he cannot give--the sunshine." Unfortunately, *The Novellino* omits Alexander's clever reply, "Had I not been Alexander, I should have liked to be Diogenes (Diogenes Laertius V.2 35)."

[2] Alexander the Great: see *note* for *Novella IIII,* 2.

Novella LXVII.

[1] "Lucius Papirius Cursor. Roman consul five times and dictator twice, hero of the Second Samnite War. As dictator he won over the Samnites in 309 B.C. His name became a byword for great strictness and severity (Avery 814)."

[2] The novella is virtually the same as the one concerning Papirius found in the *Fiore di filosofi e di molti savi* (pp.16-18).

[3] Papirius never encountered Alexander in battle.

Novella LXVIII.

[1] Aristotle (384-322 B.C.) was born in Macedonia (Stagira), studied under Plato and, with his teacher, became one of the most famous ancient philosophers. For a time, he was tutor to Alexander the Great. Later he established his own school (Lyceum) in Athens, which became known as the Peripatetic School, because of the pedagogical custom of strolling while learning. Aristotle's writings encompass a wide range of subjects; including, logic, science, metaphysics, ethics, poetics, rhetoric and politics.

[2] The novella produces a variation on the theme of *puer senex*, popular in the Middle Ages (Curtius 98-101).

The tale exemplifies the teachings of Aristotle from his *Ethics*, "We are now in a position to describe the happy man as `one who realizes in action a goodness that is complete and that is adequately furnished with external goods, and that not for some limited period but throughout a fully rounded life spent in that way (Aristotle 48).'"

Novella LXIX.

[1] Trajan or Marcus Ulpius Trajanus (53? - 117) was Roman Emperor from 98 to 117. Born in Italica (Spain), he became sole ruler of the Empire with the death of Nerva. He is most famous for his military exploits. He conquered the Dacians, for which the Trajan column was erected in Rome. On an expedition against the Parthians he died in Selinus. Trajan was succeeded by Hadrian.

The sequence of events in this novella is virtually the same as that found in the tale of Trajan from the *Fiore di filosofi* (pp. 58-61). The tale is also found in *The Golden Legend*, in the section concerning the Holy Day dedicated to Saint Gregory, March 12. In this rendition, however, it is stated that, "one of Trajan's sons, racing on horseback through the streets of the city, had run down and killed the son of a poor woman: whereupon the emperor had given his own son as a slave to the bereaved mother, and had begifted the woman munificently (Jacobus 184-85)." The section relating the exhumation of the emperor does not appear in this account.

[2] Saint Gregory, Gregory I was born around 540 and died in 604. He was pope from 590 to 604, and earned the title Gregory the Great. He is considered one of the four original Doctors of the Church. One of his most famous works, *The Dialogues*, is a collection of legends concerning the saints from his own time. The text mentions many famous individuals, but never the Emperor Trajan.

Novella LXX.

[1] "Hercules [was] a mighty Greek hero, son of Jupiter and Alcmena, who took part in the expedition of the Argonauts, and won immortality by accomplishing twelve feats, which are known as the Labors of Hercules. He was killed by Deianira, his wife, who gave him a fatal garment steeped in the blood of Nessus, which she thought to be a love-spell. After death, Hercules was placed among the stars. He was worshipped as the god of physical strength (Bulfinch 912)."

[2] "Deianira [was] a daughter of Oeneus and Althaea, sister of Meleager, wooed by Achilous but finally married to Hercules. She killed her husband inadvertently by causing him to wear the blood-steeped shirt of Nessus, the latter having told her that this action would assure her of Hercules' undying love. Deianira ended her life for grief (Bulfinch 898-99)."

Novella LXXI.

[1] Seneca the Younger (4? B.C. to 65 A.D.) was a leading intellectual at a time of sophisticated literary and artistic movements encouraged by imperial patronage. He became tutor to Nero and for eleven years held a position of unprecedented influence as imperial adviser. He was born rich and had become one of the wealthiest men in the world. From 62 A.D. Seneca began to lose his influence over Nero and rapidly fell into disfavor. Three years later he died by enforced suicide.

Seneca wrote constantly and diversely. As a professional philosopher he expounded the Stoic tradition in a large corpus of literature entitled *Stoic Ethics*. He also wrote moral and dialogue letters, satires and tragedies. Seneca's works were well known in the Middle Ages, where he was widely viewed as a martyr, a supposed friend of St. Paul, and the source of numerous anthologies of moral maxims (paraphrased from the work of Henry 807-08).

[2] The first part of the novella is directly inspired by *The Consolation of Marcia* (*Ad Marciam de Consolatione*) of Seneca. This consolatory letter, written to Marcia concerning the death of her son Metilius, argues the inevitability, the necessity, and the naturalness of death. Seneca attempts to dissuade Marcia from sustained, excessive, mourning; citing two types of grieving mothers, "a woman who abandons herself completely to the pain [i.e. Octavia at the death of her son Marcellus], and the other, a woman struck by the same tragedy who does not allow herself to be completely dominated for long by this evil, but quickly returns her spirit to its normal condition [i.e. Livia at the death of her son Drusus] [*my translation*] (Seneca 20-21)." Seneca examines the nature of grief and of death, demonstrating these as integral and therefore often laudatory elements of nature and life. The novella follows closely the structure of the source letter, creating an artificial dialogue between the mother and writer in order to have all possible exceptions philosophically remedied.

[3] This second story in the novella was quite well known in the Middle Ages and also appears in the *Fiore di filosofi*, which omits the final dialogue between Seneca and his wife. The *Fiore* account outlines in greater detail the cruel character of Nero: "He destroyed taverns, forced women, especially the wives of others...With his own mother he wished to lay carnally." "He wished to strangle his wife for being barren, and eventually killed her for adulterous reasons. His second wife he loved most tenderly; and when she was pregnant he kicked her in the stomach until she died. He had another woman killed for refusing him, and had his stepson drowned in the sea [*my translation*] (*Fiore* 38-39)."

[4] Nero (37-68) was the fifth emperor of Rome. He married Octavia, daughter of Claudius and was proclaimed emperor by the Praetorian guard at the age of seventeen. His first five years as emperor were perceived as full of moderation and clemency, due primarily to the influence of Burrus and his tutor, Seneca. The latter part of his reign was steeped in cruelty, including murders, forced suicides and Christian persecutions. While modern historians disagree, through the ages, Nero has been held responsible for the burning of Rome in 64.

Novella LXXII.

[1] "Cato (the Younger) of Utica (95 B.C.-46 B.C.), indomitable Roman figure of inflexible honesty, rigid personal habits and great military valor. To the end of his life, he fought strenuously in defense of Roman liberty. When he lost all hope in the fortune of the Republic (which constitutes the dialogue of this novella), rather than live to see the end of the Republic, he committed suicide (Siebzehner-Vivanti 100)."

[2] Earlier Italian critics are correct when they describe this novella as modeled after *The Consolation of Philosophy* by Boethius.

Novella LXXIII.

[a] *mobole*: mobile, facultà.

[b] *fine*: in estremo grado d'eccellenza.

[1] This story became one of the most celebrated in the Italian *novella* tradition with its inclusion by Boccaccio in *The Decameron* (*Dec.* I,3: Boccaccio 45-48). Boccaccio identifies the Sultan as Saladin (see *note* for *Novella IX, 3*).

[2] In *The Decameron* the Jew is identified as Melchizedek (Boccaccio 45-48).

[3] The Italian term *fine* actually means: that object which is of the finest quality of excellence.

Novella LXXIIII.

[a] *fedele*: suddito, vassallo, detto così dal giuramento di fedeltà, e d'ubbidienza al suo Signore.

[b] *imprunare*: mettere pruni sopra che che si sia, serrare, o turare i passi con pruni.

[c] *soma*: propriamente carico, che si pone a' giumenti.

[d] *fante*: servidore.

[1] The novella is based on a short tale told in the section concerning Tiberius found in *The Twelve Caesars* of Suetonius, where the figs are replaced by a mullet and the peaches by a crab. There is, however, a major discrepancy with the source tale where the outcome is not quite so jolly. "'Thank Heaven, I did not bring Caesar that huge crab I also caught!' Tiberius sent for the crab and had it used in the same way (Suetonius 143-44)."

Novella LXXV.

[a] *giullare*: see *note* for *Novella IIII, a*.

[b] *bandire*: pubblicare per bando.

[c] *bizante*: see *note* for *Novella X, b*.

[d] *redire*: *reddire*: ritornare.

[e] *ernione*: rognoni (not in the *Crusca*).
[f] *increscere*: rincrescere, venire a tedio, a noia, a fastidio.

[1] minstrel: see *note* for *Novella IIII, 1*.
[2] The Italian text literally says, "go to the dead man."
[3] *bezants*: see *note* for *Novella X, 3*.

Novella LXXVI.

[1] Richard I, King of England (1189-99), was call Lion-Hearted. He was the third son of Henry II and Eleanor of Aquitaine. His early years were spent in battle to protect his interests from his father, from which he earned the reputation of a great warrior. Richard accompanied Philip II of France on the Third Crusade, but the enterprise was doomed to failure due to constant conflicts between the two kings. Eventually Philip returned to France and Richard and Saladin agreed to a truce which left Jerusalem in the hands of Saladin. Richard was fatally wounded in a minor skirmish in 1199.
[2] Richard joined with Philip II on the Third Crusade in 1190 (Newby 150).
[3] The Sultan during the Third Crusade was Saladin: see *note* for *Novella IX, 3*.
[4] This magnanimous move by Saladin of providing King Richard with a horse is also found in Chapter XIV of *The Tales of Ancient Knights* (*Conti di antichi cavalieri*). This briefest of novellas, consisting of only two sentences states, "And King Richard's fighting on foot was revealed to Saladin, who immediately presented him with a steed, sending it to him stating that it was not proper for a king to fight on foot [*my translation*] (*Conti* 133)." Historians give a slightly different version. "This was the famous occasion when Richard's horse was killed and Saladin sent him two remounts so that, the story goes, he would be at no disadvantage (Newby 181)." Neither of these two other accounts mentions the less than honorable intentions of Saladin as related at the end of *The Novellino* tale.

Novella LXXVII.

[a] *Donno*: quasi domino, ed è il masculin di donna, in significato di Signora.
[b] *gabbare*: ingannare, giuntare, farsi beffe.
[c] *stallo*: lo stare, stanza, luogo dove si sta.
[d] *staffetta*: strumento, per lo più, di ferro appiccato alla sella, nel quale si mette il pie', sagliendo a cavallo, e cavalcando, vi si tien dentro.
[e] *scappini*: peduli.

[1] To date, no historical figure with this name has been discovered.
[2] Rulers of the Sardinian *giudicati* were not called *donno*, as stated in the novella, but rather *iudighe*. The selection of *donno* by our author(s) might stem from a misunderstanding of the term *donnicaliae* which referred to a type of territorial subdivision of the *giudicati* (Fois 89).

Donno could also be a derivative of the Latin, *dominus* (lord), since Dante describes the Sardinians in the *De Vulgari eloquentia* as, "They alone seem to be without any vulgar tongue of their own, imitating Latin as apes do men: for they say, `Domus nova' and `dominus meus' (Alighieri, *A Translation* 37)."
[3] "When documentation of medieval Sardinia once again appeared, one finds that the apparent unity of Sardinia has been fractured into four different states, called in the documentation

giudicati. By the second half of the eleventh century these *giudicati* already existed and were called: *The Giudicato of Calari* in the south, *The Giudicato of Arborea* in the central west, *The Giudicato of Torres* in the north, and *The Giudicato of Callura* in the north-east [*my translation*] (Fois 88-89)."

"Arborea: Name from the eleventh century which was given to one of the four *giudicati* of Sardinia. It comprised the mid-western section of the island, with its center at Oristano [*my translation*] (Gasca Queirazza 34)."

[4] Throughout the medieval period, Pisa and Genova were constantly fighting for control of the Sardinian *giudicati*. During the Middle Ages (from 900 - 1420) "the reign or *giudicato* of Arborea was almost always under the political and cultural influence of the powerful marine republic of Pisa [*my translation*] (Casula 48)."

[5] *seneschal*: see *note* for *Novella II, 7.*

Novella LXXVIII.

[a] *volgarizzare*: Il traslatar la scrittura di lingua morta, in quella, che si favella.
[b] *menomare*: diminuire.

[1] The term *volgarizzare* literally means, "to render into the vulgar tongue," and usually refers to translations from Latin or Greek.

[2] The "Question of Language (*Questione della lingua*);" that is, when and where to use Latin or the vulgate, was the source of continued debate throughout the Middle Ages and the Renaissance. Even Dante, in his famous fragmentary work, *De Vulgari eloquentia*, which praises the Italian vernacular as "illustrious, cardinal, courtly and curial (Alighieri, *A Translation* 55-56)," and the only proper means for expressing safety (i.e., prowess in arms), love and virtue (Alighieri, *A Translation* 71), exemplifies it solely as a poetical form. This treatise, praising the Italian language, is composed in Latin.

Novella LXXVIIII.

[a] *giullare*: see *note* for *Novella IIII, a.*
[b] *baldanza*: un certo apparente ardire in letizia, sicurtà d'animo, coraggio.
[c] *gabbare*: see *note* for *Novella LXXVII, b.*
[d] *concio*: mal trattato.
[e] *kaendo*: cercando.

Novella LXXX.

[a] *impetrar*: Ottener da altrui quel che si domanda.
[b] *corredo*: E per convito.
[c] *donneare*: see *note* for *Novella LXII, d.*
[d] *luccio*: pesce noto.
[e] *passetto* : some editions read the term as a misspelling for *passato*.

[1] The early twentieth-century critic Francesco Scandone identifies this character as a Florentine poet and, basing his findings on a letter written by Charles of Anjou on January 17, 1270, he asserts that "Migliore degli Abbati and two of his kinsmen had gone to the Kingdom of Sicily,

to the Court of King Charles; and in Capua had obtained favorable royal actions concerning himself and all his family [*my translation*] (Scandone 163)." One also learns from Scandone that Migliore was the son of a Messer Renaldo and that he was a knight from that time. Scandone believes the Abbati clan was most likely Ghibelline. Only one sonnet attributed to Migliore degli Abbati has survived, "Just as the Good Archer in Battle (Sì come il buono arciere a la battaglia) (*Poeti del Duecento* V.1 375)."

[2] Charles of Anjou: see *note* for *Novella LX, 1.*

[3] The text literally states that he knew how to "sing," referring to the fact that most *canzoni* were poetical constructs put to music.

[4] The *Crusca* defines *amber* as "a bitumen of a most precious aroma." *Aloe*, however, is described as "a most bitter medicinal herb." Interestingly, the herbal, *Herbolario Volgare*, lists among aloe's many medicinal properties, the ability to "modify melancholy (*Herbarium* V.2 prt.2 ch.1)," which suggests that its employment might have had the effect of intentionally keeping the ladies docile, as well as serving as a medieval air freshener.

[5] While this is the most obviously and blatantly misogynistic tale in the collection, there is no indication of Messere Abbati's distaste for women in documented sources.

Novella LXXXI.

[1] Priam was the son of King Laomedon and "King of Troy when that city was sacked by the Greeks, husband of Hecuba, and father of fifty sons and many daughters...When Hector was slain, the old king went to the tent of Achilles and made a successful plea for the body of his dead son. After the gates of Troy were thrown open by the Greeks concealed in the wooden horse, Pyrrhus, the son of Achilles, slew the aged Priam (Bulfinch 939)."

"King Laomedon had a certain son, borne to him by the queen, his wife. His name was Priam, a man of great valor and distinguished on account of his very wise counsel...He had a wife, a very noble lady named Hecuba, who had borne him five sons and three daughters. The first of his sons was called Hector, a knight of unheard-of valor, aggressive, courageous, whose many virtuous deeds are honored in continued remembrance and will, not without cause, be recounted for a long time. The second son was named Paris, also called Alexander, the most handsome of all young men, skilled above all others in the mastery of bow and arrows. The third was named Deiphobus, a valiant man, distinguished by the great intelligence of his counsels. The fourth was named Helenus, a man of great knowledge, for he was learned in the teachings of all sciences. The fifth and last was named Troilus, a young man as courageous as possible in war, about whose valor there are many tales which the present history does not omit later on (Guido delle Colonne 43)."

[2] When Jason left Thessaly with Hercules in search of the Golden Fleece, they inadvertently landed in Troy and were poorly received and asked to leave unceremoniously by King Laomedon. Hercules vowed revenge within three years for this affront against the customs of hospitality. He gathered together the Greek troops and, under the leadership of King Peleus, the Greeks attacked and destroyed Troy.

"The conquering Greeks were seizing, despoiling, and plundering. The Greeks were doing this with the greatest ease, since they were at their leisure to plunder for the space of a whole month. Finally, indeed when they had pulled down the high walls of the city itself, they destroyed the lofty palace and indiscriminately delivered the towering buildings to calamitous ruin. They destroyed everything completely, and when they had looted all the temples of the city in the manner of pirates, and delivered to the cruelest death whomever they found fleeing from

them, old men and children indiscriminately, and when they had delivered the buildings of the temple to ruin, they led away the young and beautiful girls they found as captive brides and conducted them to their ships, leading them into perpetual servitude (Guido delle Colonne 40-41)."

[3] Telamon was the "son of Aeacus, and father of Ajax. With his brother, Peleus, Jason and Nestor he took part in the Calydonian Hunt and the Argonautic expedition (Bulfinch 948)." Guido delle Colonne places him at the first destruction of Troy (p. 36).

[4] Agamemnon was "King of Mycenae, brother of Menelaus and leader of the Greek expedition against Troy (Bulfinch 879). The author(s) of *The Novellino* has mistakenly identified the character of Hercules as Agamemnon, who in fact was not present at the first destruction of Troy.

[5] "As they rushed into the palace of King Laomedon before they had destroyed it completely, on the very threshold of the donjon, they found Hesione, a young woman of marvelous beauty, the daughter of the said king--would that she had never been found or born! Hercules gave her to King Telamon as the reward of victory, for the reason that the same King Telamon was the first to enter that city as victor (Guido delle Colonne 41)."

[6] "Paris. The son of Priam, King of Troy and Hecuba; through his abduction of Helen, he is the cause of the Trojan War. It was he who awarded the Apple of Discord and the title of "Fairest" to Venus, who in return assisted him to carry off Helen, for whom he deserted his wife Oenone. At Troy, Paris earned the contempt of all by his cowardice; he killed Achilles with a poisoned arrow and suffered the same fate at the hands of Philoctetes when the city was taken (Bulfinch 935)."

The words of Paris and Hector found in the novella are quite similar to the extended monologues pronounced by these two characters in Book VI of *Historia Destructionis Troiae* (Guido delle Colonne 54-65).

[7] "Hector. Eldest son of Priam, the noblest of the Trojan chieftains in Homer's *Iliad*. After holding out for ten years, he was slain by Achilles who dragged the dead body thrice round the walls of Troy (Bulfinch 911)."

Notes LXXXII.

[a] *sciamito*: spezie di drappo di varie sorte, e colori.

[1] This is one of the earliest accounts of the death of the Lady of Shalott. The text differs significantly, especially in the details, from the popular version entitled, "The Fair Maid of Astolat," found in the works of Sir Thomas Malory (Malory V.3 1061-98). The critic L.S. Potwin has suggested that *The Novellino* tale is most likely one of the sources used by Tennyson for his 1832 poem, "The Lady of Shalott" (Potwin 473-77).

[2] Lancelot: see *note* for *Novella XXVIII, 2.*

[3] Guenevere: see *note* for *Novella XXVIII, 3.*

[4] "Camelot. Legendary place in England where Arthur's court and palace were located (Bulfinch 893)."

[5] "King Arthur. A semimythical British chieftain of the sixth century. He became the central figure of a great cycle of romance, in which he appears as living in state with his wife Guinevere at Caerleon on the Usk. He was fatally wounded in the battle of Camlan and was buried at Glastonbury (Bulfinch 919)."

Novella LXXXIII.

[a] *assempro*: esemplo.
[b] *poscia*: poi.

Novella LXXXIIII.

[a] *bandire*: see *note* for *Novella LXXV, b*.
[b] *sescalchi*: siniscalchi.
[c] *imbolare*: Lo stesso che rubare.
[d] *imprunare*: mettere pruni sopra che che si sia, serrare, o turare i passi con pruni.
[e] *acconciare*: per adornare, abbigliare.
[f] *malleveria*: promessa del *mallevadore*: quegli che promette per altrui, obligando se, e'l suo avere.
[g] *tela*: Per metafora; cioè cosa lunga.
[h] *feristo*: Forse lo stile, che regge li padiglioni da campo.

[1] The novella is actually a compilation of six anecdotes concerning Ezzelino III da Romano (see *note* for *Novella XXXI, 1*). While Ezzelino has been all but forgotten by modern historians, in the Middle Ages he was infamous for his cruelty and savagery. Although he is mentioned twenty-eight times in the *Chronicle* of Salimbene de Adam (written 1283-88), none of the accounts found in *The Novellino* is mentioned. Salimbene's description of Ezzelino is frightening indeed. "Ezzelino was feared more than the devil himself, for he would have men, women, and children killed for no reason at all, and would commit the most incredible atrocities. Not even those great tyrants, Nero, Domitian, Decius or Diocletian approach his like for cruelties...It would take too long to relate all his cruelties, for that would take a huge book. With full assurance, I believe that the son of God wanted to have one special friend like unto Himself (that is, St. Francis), so the devil had Ezzelino (Salimbene 186)."

The contemporary historian Orville Prescott does not dispute Salimbene's description. "Ezzelino's expression was habitually ferocious. People were terrified by his mere appearance, and also, of course, by the tales they had heard of his atrocities (Prescott 229)." At the end of his chapter on Ezzelino, entitled "The Man whom even the Demons Fear," Prescott labels Ezzelino "the most terrible tyrant in Italian history (Prescott 242)."

[2] seneschal: see *note* for *Novella II, 7*.
[3] The ashes are implied in the Italian original.
[4] The words *un olaro* have been misunderstood by Ezzelino to mean *uno la*[d]*ro*, in English signifying, a thief.
[5] History informs us that Ezzelino "switched sides, turned Ghibelline and became a feudal subordinate of the Emperor Frederick II (Prescott 226-27)."
[6] After unsuccessfully attacking Monza in 1259, Ezzelino "retreated to the bridge at Cassano over the Adda River." He "was wounded by an arrow through his foot and knocked off his horse by the blow of a club (some chroniclers say a reaping hook) on his head." Prescott paraphrases several chroniclers by saying "Ezzelino refused food and medicine and...committed suicide by ripping off his bandages and tearing open his wounds (Prescott 243-44)."

Novella LXXXV.

[a] *caro*: carestia: ma l'uno il distingue, e dice *caro*, quando la cosa è sconvenevol prezzo, e, *carestia*, quando non se ne truova par alcun prezzo.
[b] *bandire*: see *note* for *Novella LXXV, b.*
[c] *travisare*: travestirsi.
[d] *ciernire*: *cernire*: *cernere*: distinguere, e separare.
[e] *dovitia*: *dovizia*: *divizia*: copia, abbondanza.

[1] While the particulars might be suspect, the novella is based upon historical accuracy. In 1171 the Lombards instituted a blockade against grain shipments to Genoa which resulted in a terrible famine.

"Because this prohibition (of grain shipments) took place in areas beset with sterile crop yields, the price of a *mina* (430 grams) of grain rose as high as ten ducats, and this famine lasted for the space of six months. And during this year, four galleys were armed under the direction of Consul Otto di Caffaro who, together with many other gentlemen, brought King Barissone back to Sardinia, for he had already been detained in Genoa for six years because of accumulated debts he owed to the Commune [*my translation*] (Giustiniani V.1 248)."

[2] The novella uses *caro* and *carestia* interchangeably, although there is a slight difference between the two terms. *Carestia* refers to famine, whereas *caro* indicates a severe shortage.

Novella LXXXVI.

[a] *orrevole*: see *note* for *Novella LV, b.*

[1] Unfortunately the response of the woman, which must have been deliciously salacious, has been lost to posterity.

Novella LXXXVII.

[a] *domistikezza* usually means *familiarity*, but it can also signify intimacy.

Novella LXXXVIII.

[a] *briga*: Per lite, controversia, nimicizia.

[1] Italian editors (Lo Nigro and Segre) identify this figure as podesta of Florence in 1240.
[2] *podesta*: see *note* for *Novella XXII, 4.*
[3] To date, Pepo Alemanni has not been historically identified.
[4] The *Caponsacchi* was "one of the most illustrious ancient Florentine families whom Dante says came down from Fiesole (*Par.* XVI, 121) and were members of the ruling group who originated the Commune of Florence during the twelfth century [*my translation*] (*Dizionario biografico* V.18 665)."

Novella LXXXIX.

[a] *uomo di corte*: see *note* for *Novella IIII, c.*
[b] *donzello*: see *note* for *Novella XXXIX, c.*

[1] *man of the court*: see *note* for *Novella IIII, 5.*
[2] The theme of the boring, poorly-told tale reappears and becomes famous with Boccaccio's tale of Madonna Oretta, *Decameron VI, 1.*

Novella XC.

[a] *guglia*: most probably means *acquila*.
[b] *giustitiere*: *giustiziere*: Per giudici, e mantenitori della giustizia.

[1] The tale is most probably referring to Frederick II. See *note* for *Novella XXII, 1.*
[2] *The Dictionary of Medieval Knighthood and Chivalry* describes the eagle as "king of birds (Broughton 177)." While medieval bestiaries do not specifically define the eagle as "king," their descriptions of the bird are certainly regal and symbolic of the risen Christ. "You should know that the eagle lives for a long time because it renews itself and sheds its old age. Many say that it flies so high in the heat of the sun that its feathers burn, along with the darkness of its eyes, and that it lets itself fall into a spring of water and bathes itself three times, and right away it recovers the youth it had previously." "The eagle can eat whatever bird it wishes (Latini 112)."

Novella XCI.

[a] *storione*: pesce marino, che ama l'acqua dolce, ed è ottimo per mangiare.
[b] *ciera*: *cera*: per sembianza, e aria di volto, e, volto, semplicemente.

[1] "*Florin*: silver coin of Florence minted as early as the 12th century, depicting on the obverse the bust or the standing or seated figure of St. John the Baptist and on the reverse a lily (*fiorino*, Italian word for lily) and the arms of Florence which also was called the `Lily of the Arno'(Broughton 208)."

Novella XCII.

[a] *crostata*: torta, detta così delle croste, di pasta, che le si fanno sopra.
[b] *riguille*: most probably a misspelling of the French *anguille* or the Italian *anguilla* for *eel*.

Novella XCIII.

[a] *colto*: luogo coltivato.
[b] *ofessastititu* is most probably a misspelling of *confessasti tu*.
[c] *danaio*: moneta di minor valuta.
[d] *colombaio*: Lo Nigro defines it in his edition as "una specie di salvedenaio di terracotta che serviva per le offerte." The term is not defined in this way in the *Vocabolario della Crusca*.
[e] *uguanno*: questo anno.

Novella XCIIII.

[1] While the tale is obviously Aesopic in nature, it does not appear in Aesop collections consulted. Its absence from *The Medici Aesop* is most surprising.

The tale does resemble an episode found in two versions of the *Roman de Renard*. Richard Smith's *Type-Index* of the *Roman* describes it as "The Horse Kicks the Wolf in the Teeth." "Ysengrin invites Rainsent, the mare, to accompany him, promising her a much better life than that which she has with her master. The mare consents to go with him but first asks that he remove a thorn from her hoof. Ysengrin approaches to remove the thorn; the mare kicks him (Smith, Richard 10,38)."

Novella XCV.

[a] *martore*: sopranome, che, per ischerzo, si dava in quel tempo a' contadini.
[b] *villa*: Per città, alla francese.
[c] *farsetto*: vestimento del busto, come giubbone, e camiciuola.
[d] *a mercato*: per lo prezzo della cosa mercatata.
[e] *acconciare*: per apprestare, preparare, mettere in punto.
[f] *correggia*: cintura di cuoio.

Novella XCVI.

[a] *San Giorgio*: see *note* for *Novella XCVI,3.*
[b] *uomo di corte*: see *note* for *Novella IIII, c.*
[c] *La Fante*: see *note* for *Novella LXXIIII, d.*
[d] *kamangiare*: *camangiare*: ogni erba buona a mangiare, o cruda o cotta, erbaggio.
[e] *Piazza del Ponte*: see *note* for *Novella XCVI, 5.*
[f] *iscarsissimo*: *scarso*: Per tenace, misero, che spende a rilente.
[g] *vaio*: animale simile allo scoiattolo, col dorso di color bigio, e la pancia bianca, e dicesi *vaio* alla pelle, sì come all'animale.
[h] *danaio*: see *note* for *Novella XCIII, c.*
[i] *derrata*: see *note* for *Novella IX, b.*
[j] *villa*: Posessione con casa, e'l contado stesso.
[k] *medaglia*: Spezie di moneta.
[l] *scalzare*: Per sottrarre, e cavare altrui di bocca artatamente quello, che si vorrebbe sapere.
[m] *alza*: error for *alzò*.
[n] *fedito*: ferito.
[o] *ambascia*: difficultà di respirare, che nasce da soverchia fatica.
[p] *conciare*: *acconciare*: ridurre a bene essere, e mettere in sesto, e'n buon termine, il che diciamo anche, accomodare, contrario di guastare.

[1] Some Italian editors report the brief mentioning of a "Bito" in early Florentine archives; however, neither Bito nor Master Frulli has been associated with any significant historical event, nor have they been described in detail in any historical chronicles. The novella follows the traditional *beffa* or joke motif. Its urban, merchant environment where the sly, city con-man dupes his naive compatriot, however, suggests this tale is the immediate ancestor to the famous

slap-stick novellas of Calandrino, Bruno and Buffalmacco from Boccaccio's *Decameron* (VIII,3; VIII,6; IX,3; IX,5).

[2] See *note* for *Novella XCVI, 1*.

[3] There is no quarter or neighborhood in Florence proper called San Giorgio. The author could be referring to the area around the Church of the Spirito Santo, close to the Ponte Vecchio, where there is a street named Via della Costa San Giorgio. A remote possibility is the periphery area named San Giorgio in Colonica. This area, however, is found on the road to Pistoia which is on the wrong side of the Arno.

[4] Florence is divided in half by the Arno River. Beyond the Arno (Oltrarno) is the southeast side, away from the majority of cultural monuments. On this side one finds the Pitti Palace and the Boboli Gardens.

[5] There is no Bridge Square in Florence, in fact, city maps suggest squares were not constructed around the city's bridges. The author(s) might be referring to the Ponte Vecchio itself, which even today is one of the most crowded shopping districts in the city.

Novella XCVII.

[a] *palcora*: palco (divisa a tramezzi).
[b] *squilletto*: spillo, da spillare.
[c] *tasketto*: *taschetto*: sacchetto.
[d] *bertuccio*: scimia.

[1] Medieval bestiaries describe the monkey as an animal which mimics man. "The monkey is an animal which gladly imitates what it sees men doing (Latini 192)."

Just as the merchant gave his clients only half of what they paid for, so the monkey returns only half of what he stole.

[2] For mast the author(s) uses the word tree, suggesting the mast was made of wood and was as tall as a tree.

Novella XCVIII.

[a] *calzari*: scarpe o stivaletti.

[1] The novella is based upon a belief found in some medieval bestiaries concerning the incessant desire of monkeys to imitate the actions of man (see *note* for *Novella XCVII, 2*).

"And moreover, hunters who realize that they (monkeys) will willingly imitate anything that they see men do, go to those places frequented by monkeys and bring with them tiny shoes made to fit the feet of monkeys. Then they put on and take off their own shoes many times while the monkeys watch. Then the men depart and leave behind the tiny shoes, in plain view, and the monkeys watch and when they see that the men are gone, they climb down from the trees and put on the shoes, tying them tightly. Meanwhile the men have remained close by and emerge from hiding to capture them. The monkeys attempt to flee, but are not able to, and in this manner they are captured by men [*my translation*] (*Libro della natura degli animali* 303)."

Novella XCIX.

[a] *pulzella*: donzella, vergine, fanciulla.

[b] *La Fante*: see *note* for *Novella LXXIIII, d.*
[c] *ciella*: *cella*: propriamente stanza terrena, dove si tiene, per lo più, il vino.
[d] *ronzone*: caval grande, qui è preso per istallone.
[e] *magione*: abituro, abitazione.
[f] *dirimpetto*: rincontro, a petto, di rincontro, dal lato, opposto.
[g] *bocie*: voce.
[h] *briga*: see *note* for *LXXXVIII, a.*
[i] *agio*: E in vece di casa, e luogo da abitare.
[j] *corotto*: *corrotto*: pianto si fa a' morti.

Novella C.

[a] *La montagna del Veglio*: il veglio (o il vecchio) della montagna.

[1] *Frederick II*: see *note* for *Novella II, 2.*
[2] "Rashid al-Din Sinan, the famous leader of the Syrian Isma`ili sect in the second half of the xii[th] century, is better known to the world as Shaikh al-Djabal, or the "Old Man of the Mountain (*First Encyclopaedia of Islam* V.9 1123-24)."

Marco Polo describes the Old Man of the Mountain in his 1298 account of his travels to the east. "Mulehet, the name given to heretical Saracens, is also the name of the famous place where the Old Man of the Mountain used to live." According to Polo, the Old Man, also called Alaodin, constructed a garden between two mountains, so beautiful that people believed it to be Paradise. He would drug young men and carry them into the garden, where they delighted in believing that they had entered Paradise. Later, he would drug them again and remove them from the garden, promising they could return if they carried out murders he orchestrated. If they died for the Old Man, Paradise would immediately be achieved. And so, the *Assassins* of the Old Man of the Mountain came into being (Polo 37-39).

Legends surrounding Frederick II suggested that he had "a relationship to the assassins." One such legend recounts the emperor's visit to the Old Man as outlined in this novella.
"The Emperor had had intercourse--though very transitory--with this terrible sect whose daggers had laid low innumerable distinguished crusaders, and people told tales of a visit he was alleged to have paid to the "Old Man of the Mountain." To demonstrate the obedience of his people the Old Man had signalled to two who were standing at the top of a high tower; happy to attain Paradise so soon, they hurled themselves down at his bidding. A later version represents Frederick as rearing his own 'obedient stabbers' on similar lines (Kantorowicz 194)."
[3] The followers of the Old Man of the Mountain were called *assassins*. See also *note* for *Novella C, 2.*
[4] Tugging on his beard was obviously a signal.
[5] This final sketch in *The Novellino* will achieve maturity and fame later in Boccaccio's *Decameron III, 2*; the tale of the horsekeeper, King Agilulfo and his wife.

BIBLIOGRAPHY TO THE NOTES

Accademia della Crusca. *Vocabolario degli Accademici della Crusca*. Florence: Le Lettere, [1612] 1987.

Aesop. trans. Bernard McTigue. *The Medici Aesop*. New York: Abrams, 1989.

Alderotti, Taddeo. (anonymous translation into Italian) *Libello per conservare la sanità*. Florence: Tipografia del Vocabolario, 1863.

Alidosi, Gio. Nicolò Pasquali. *Li Dottori Bolognesi di legge canonica, e civile. Dal principio di essi per tutto l'anno 1619*. Bologna: Cochi, 1620.

Alighieri, Dante. trans. Henry Wadsworth Longfellow. *The Divine Comedy*. Boston: Houghton, Mifflin and Co., 1888, 3 Vols.

Alighieri, Dante. *A Translation of the Latin Works of Dante Alighieri*. London: Aldine, 1904.

Antonetti, Pierre. trans. Giuseppe Cafiero. *La vita quotidiana a Firenze ai tempi di Dante*. Milan: Rizzoli, 1983.

Aristotle. trans. J. A. K. Thomson. *The Ethics of Aristotle*. London: Penguin, 1955.

Arrian. trans. Aubrey de Sélincourt. *The Campaigns of Alexander*. New York: Dorset, 1971.

Augustine, Saint. trans. Gerald G. Walsh, Demetrius B. Zema, Grace Monahan, and Daniel J. Honan. *The City of God*. Garden City, N.Y.: Image, 1958.

Avery, Catherine (ed.). *The New Century Classical Handbook*. New York: Appleton-Century-Crofts, 1962.

Bèroul. trans. Alan S. Fedrick. *The Romance of Tristan*. Harmondsworth: Penguin, 1970.

Bestiary: Being an English Version of the Bodleian Library, Oxford M. S. 764. trans. Richard Barber. Woodbridge, Eng.: Boydell Press, 1993.

Boccaccio, Giovanni. trans. John Payne. ed. Charles S. Singleton. *The Decameron*. Berkeley: University of California Press, 1982.

The Book of Beasts: Being a Translation from a Latin Bestiary of the Twelfth Century. ed. T. H. White. New York: Putnam's Son, 1954.

Briffault, Robert S. *The Troubadours*. Bloomington, Indiana University Press, 1965.

Broughton, Bradford B. *Dictionary of Medieval Knighthood and Chivalry: Concepts and Terms*. New York: Greenwood, 1986.

Bulfinch, Thomas. *Bulfinch's Mythology*. New York: Avenel, 1979.

The Cambridge Medieval History. Volume VI. Victory of the Papacy. Planned by J. B. Bury. ed. J. R. Tanner, C. W. Previté-Orton, and Z. N. Brooke. New York: Macmillan. 1929.

Cary, George. *The Medieval Alexander*. Cambridge: Cambridge University Press, 1956 [1967].

Casula, Francesco Cesare. *La storia di Sardegna*. Sassari: Delfino, 1992.

Chambers World Gazetteer: An A-Z of Geographical Information. ed. David Munro. Cambridge: Chambers, 1988.

Chrétien de Troyes. trans. Ruth Harwood Cline. *Lancelot or the Knight of the Cart*. Athens: University of Georgia Press, 1990.

Conti di antichi cavalieri. ed. Alberto del Monte. Milan: Cisalpino-Goliardica, 1972.

Curtius, Ernst Robert. trans. Willard R. Trask. *European Literature and the Latin Middle Ages*. New York: Harper & Row, 1963.

D'Arezzo, Ristoro. *La composizione del mondo*. In *La prosa del Duecento*. ed. Cesare Segre and Mario Marti. Milan: Ricciardi, 1959, 981-1040.

De Lespinasse, René. *Le Nivernais et les Comtes de Nevers. II. Maisons De Donzy, De Bourbon, De Flandre*. Paris: Champion, 1911.

Dictionary of the Middle Ages. New York: Scribner's, 1989, 13 Vols.

Dictionnaire de Biographie Française. ed. M. Prevost and Roman D'Amat. Paris: Letouzey et Ané, 1951.

Dinsmore, Charles Allen. *Aids to the Study of Dante*. Boston: Houghton Mifflin, 1903.

Diogenes Laertius. trans. R. D. Hicks. *Lives of Eminent Philosophers*. Cambridge: Harvard University Press, 1979, 2 Vols.

Dizionario biografico degli Italiani. Rome: Istituto della Enciclopedia Italiana, 1979.

Enciclopedia cattolica. Vatican City: Ente per l'Enciclopedia Cattolica e per il libro cattolico, 1950.

Enciclopedia italiana di scienze, lettere ed arti. Milan: Treccani, 1932.

The Encyclopaedia Britannica. 9th ed. Chicago: Encyclopaedia Britannica, Inc., 1878.

Encyclopedia of Poetry and Poetics. ed. Alex Preminger. Princeton: Princeton University Press, 1965.

Evans, Joan. *Dress in Mediaeval France*. Oxford: Clarendon, 1952.

Evans, Joan. *Magical Jewels of the Middle Ages and Renaissance Particularly in England*. New York: Dover, 1976.

Ferruolo, Stephen C. *The Origins of the University: The Schools of Paris and Their Critics, 1100-1215*. Stanford: Stanford University Press, 1985.

Fiore di filosofi e di molti savi. Bologna: Commissione per i testi di lingua, 1968.

First Encyclopaedia of Islam 1913-1936. ed. M. Th. Houtsma, et al. Leiden: Brill, 1987.

Fois, Barbara. *Territorio e paesaggio agrario nella Sardegna medioevale*. Pisa: ETS, 1990.

Frederick II. Emperor of Germany, 1194-1250. *The Art of Falconery, Being the De arte venandi cum avibus of Frederick II of Hohenstaufen*. Translated and edited by Casey A. Wood and F. Marjorie Fyfe. Boston: Branford, 1943.

Fubini, Mario (ed.). *Poemetti del Duecento: Il Tesoretto, Il Fiore, L'Intelligenza.* Turin: UTET, 1951.

Fuiano, Michele. *Carlo I D'Angiò in Italia.* Naples: Liguori, 1974.

Gasca Queirazza, Giuliano. *Dizionario di toponomastica: storia e significato dei nomi geografici italiani.* Turin: UTET, 1990.

Gay, Peter, and John Garraty (ed.). *The Columbia History of the World.* New York: Harper & Row, 1972.

Geoffrey of Monmouth. trans. Basil Clarke. *Life of Merlin.* Cardiff: University of Wales Press, 1973.

Giustiniani, Agostino. *Annali della Repubblica di Genova.* Genoa: Canepa, 1854, 2 Vols.

Graf, Arturo. *Miti, leggende e superstizioni del Medio Evo.* Turin: Loescher, 1983, 2 Vols.

Grant, Edward. *Planets, Stars, and Orbs: The Medieval Cosmos, 1200-1687.* Cambridge: Cambridge University Press, 1994.

Gregorius I, the Great, Saint, Pope. *Dialogues.* New York: Fathers of the Church, 1959.

Grose, Francis. *A Classical Dictionary of the Vulgar Tongue.* London: Hooper, 1785.

Guido delle Colonne. trans. Mary Elizabeth Meek. *Historia Destructionis Troiae.* Bloomington: University of Indiana, 1974.

Henry, Elizabeth. "Seneca the Younger." *Ancient Writers: Greece and Rome.* ed. T. James Luce. New York: Scribners, 1982, 2 Vols.

Herbarium Apulei 1481. Herbolario Volgare 1522. Milan: Polifilo, 1979, 2 Vols.

Hill, R. T., and T. G. Bergin. *Anthology of the Provençal Troubadours.* New Haven: Yale University Press, 1972, 2 Vols.

Jacobus de Voragine. trans. Granger Ryan and Helmut Ripperger. *The Golden Legend.* New York: Arno, 1969.

The Jerusalem Bible. Garden City, NY: Doubleday, 1966.

John Damascene, St. trans. G.R. Woodward and H. Mattingly. *Barlaam and Ioasaph.* London: Heinemann, 1914.

Joinville, Jean Sire de. trans. Joan Evans. *The History of St. Louis.* London: Oxford, 1938.

Kantorowicz, Ernst. *Frederick the Second 1194 - 1250.* New York: Ungar, 1931.

Kay, Richard. *Dante's Christian Astrology.* Philadelphia: University of Pennsylvania, 1994.

Lacy, Norris J. (ed.) *The Arthurian Encyclopedia.* New York: Garland Publishing, 1986.

Lambert Li Tors and Alexandre De Bernay. ed. Heinrich Michelant. *Li Romans D'Alixandre.* Stuttgart: Bibliothek des Literarischen Vereins, 1846.

Latini, Brunetto. trans. Paul Barrette and Spurgeon Baldwin. *The Book of the Treasure.* New York: Garland Publishing, 1993.

Il Libro dei Sette Savi di Roma. ed. Antonio Cappelli. Bologna: Commissione per i testi di lingua, 1968.

Il libro della natura degli animali. In *La prosa del Duecento*. ed. Cesare Segre and Mario Marti. Milan: Ricciardi, 1959, 297-310.

Lindsay, Jack. *The Troubadours & Their World of the Twelfth and Thirteenth Centuries*. London: Muller, 1976.

Makhairas, Leontios. trans. R. M. Dawkins. *Recital Concerning the Sweet Land of Cyprus Entitled 'Chronicle'*. Oxford: Clarendon, 1932, 2 Vols.

Malory, Thomas, Sir. *The Works of Sir Thomas Malory*. Clarendon: Oxford, 1947, 3 Vols.

McDonnell, Ernest W. *The Beguines and Beghards in Medieval Culture*. New Brunswick: Rutgers University Press, 1954.

Mercatante, Anthony S. *The Facts on File Encyclopedia of World Mythology and Legend*. New York: Facts on File, 1982.

Moisè da Palermo. *Trattati di mascalcia attribuiti a Ippocrate tradotti dall'arabo in latino da Maestro Moisè da Palermo volgarizzato nel secolo XIII, messi in luce per cura di Pietro Delprato, corredati di due posteriori compilazioni in latino e in toscano e di note filologiche per cura di Luigi Barbieri*. Bologna: Romagnoli, 1865.

Monaci, Ernesto. *Crestomazia italiana dei primi secoli con prospetto grammaticale e glossario*. Rome: Società editrice Dante Alighieri, 1955.

The New Encyclopaedia Britannica. Chicago: Encyclopaedia Britannica Inc., 1994, 41 Vols.

Newby, P. H. *Saladin in His Time*. Boston: Faber and Faber, 1983.

Nouvelle Biographie Générale depuis Les Temps Les Plus Reculés Jusqu'a Nos Jours. dir. by De. M. Le Dr Hoefer. Paris: Firmin Didot Frères, 1855.

O'Brien, John Maxwell. *Alexander the Great: The Invisible Enemy. A Biography*. New York: Routledge, 1992.

Orlandi da Bologna, Fr. Pellegrino Antonio. *Notizie degli scrittori bolognesi e dell'opere loro stampate e manoscritte raccolte*. Bologna: Insegna di S. Michele, 1715.

Otto, Bishop of Freising. trans. Charles Christopher Mierow. *The Deeds of Frederick Barbarossa*. New York: Norton, 1953.

Ovid. trans. Mary M. Innes. *The Metamorphoses of Ovid*. London: Penguin, 1955.

Partridge, Eric. *A Dictionary of Slang and Unconventional English*. 6th edition. New York: Macmillan, 1967, 2 Vols.

Paton, Lucy Allen. *Les prophecies de Merlin*. New York: Heath, 1926, 2 Vols.

Petronius. trans. William Arrowsmith. *The Satyricon*. New York: New American Library, 1959.

Petrus Alfonsi. trans. Eberhard Hermes. *The "Disciplina Clericalis" of Petrus Alfonsi*. London: Routledge, 1977.

Plutarchus. trans. John Dryden. *The Lives of the Noble Grecians and Romans*. New York: Coronet. n.d.

Poeti del Duecento. Ed. Gianfranco Contini. Milan: Ricciardi, 1955, 2 Vols.

Polo, Marco. trans. Teresa Waugh. *The Travels of Marco Polo*. New York: Facts on File, 1984.

Potwin, L. S. "The Source of Tennyson's *The Lady of Shalott*." *Modern Language Notes*. 17 (1902): 473-77.

Prescott, Orville. *Lords of Italy: Portraits from the Middle Ages*. New York: Harper & Row, 1932.

Remiremont: Histoire de la Ville et de son Abbaye. ed. Jean-Claude Baumgartner. Basse-sur-le-Rupt: Gérard Louis, 1985.

Richard, Jean. *Saint Louis: Crusader King of France*. Cambridge: Cambridge University Press, 1992.

Rigaut de Berbezilh. ed. Alberto Varvaro. *Liriche*. Bari: Adriatica, 1960.

Rigaut de Berbezilh (Rigaut de Barbezieux). ed. Mauro Braccini. *Le Canzoni*. Florence: Olschki, 1960.

Rubin, Stanley. *Medieval English Medicine*. New York: Barnes & Noble, 1974.

Sabba da Castiglione. *Ricordi di Monsignor Sabba da Castiglione Cavalier Gierosolimitano*. Venice: Paolo Gerardo, 1560.

Salimbene, da Parma. trans. Joseph L. Baird et. al. *The Chronicle of Salimbene de Adam*. Binghamton: Medieval & Renaissance Text Studies, 1986.

Scandone, Francesco. "Notizie biografiche..." *Studi di letteratura italiana* 6 (1904-06): 161-

Schiavo di Bari. ed. A. Penna. *Dottrina dello Schiavo di Bari: Secondo la lezione di tre antichi testi*. Bologna: Commissione per i testi di lingua, 1968.

Seneca, L. Annaeus. *Ad Marciam de Consolatione*. Rome: Ateneo, 1965.

Serjeantson, Mary S., and Joan Evans. *English Medieval Lapidaries*. London: Oxford University Press, 1933.

Siebzehner-Vivanti, Giorgio. *Dizionario della Divina Commedia*. Milan: Feltrinelli, 1965.

Silverberg, Robert. *The Realm of Prester John*. Garden City, NY: Doubleday, 1972.

Siraisi, Nancy G. *Taddeo Alderotti and His Pupils*. Princeton: Princeton University Press, 1981.

Slessarev, Vsevolod. *Prester John: The Letter and the Legend*. Minneapolis: University of Minnesota Press, 1959.

Smith, Denis Mack. *A History of Sicily. Medieval Sicily 800 - 1713*. New York: Dorset, 1968.

Smith, Richard. *Type-Index and Motif-Index of the 'Roman de Renard.'* Uppsala: Uppsala University, 1980.

Smith, William, Sir. *The Classical Dictionary*. New York: Dutton, 1958.

Smyser, H. M. (ed.). *The Pseudo-Turpin: Edited from Bibliothèque Nationale, Fonds Latin, MS. 17656*. Cambridge, Mass.: The Medieval Academy of America, 1937.

The Song of Roland. trans. Dorothy L. Sayers. Baltimore: Penguin Books, 1957.

Sorbelli, Albano. *Storia della Università di Bologna*. Bologna: Zanichelli, 1944, 2 Vols.

Strabo. trans. H.C. Hamilton and W. Falconer. *The Geography of Strabo*. London: Bell, 1906.

Studii dedicati a Francesco Torraca nel XXXVI Anniversario della sua laurea. Naples: Perrella, 1912.

Suetonius Tranquillus, Gaius. trans. Robert Graves. *The Twelve Caesars*. Harmondsworth, Eng.: Penguin, 1979.

Thorndike, Lynn. *Michael Scot*. London: Nelson, 1965.

Thrall, William Flint, and Addison Hibbard. *A Handbook to Literature*. New York: Odyssey, 1960.

Tomasoni, Piera (ed.). *Lapidario estense*. Milan: Bompiani, 1990.

Valerius Maximus. *Factorum et dictorum memorabilium libri novem cum iulii paridis et ianuarii nepotiani epitomis*. Stuttgart: Teubner, 1982.

The Vidas of the Troubadours. trans. Margarita Egan. New York: Garland Publishing, 1984.

Villani, Giovanni. *Chroniche di Giovanni, Matteo e Filippo Villani, Secondo le miglior stampe e corredate di note filologiche e storiche*. Trieste: Lloyd Austrico, 1857-1858.

Vivien de Saint-Martin, Louis. *Nouveau Dictionnaire de Géographie Universelle*. Paris: Hachette, 1879-1895, 8 Vols.

The Vulgate Version of the Arthurian Romances. ed. H. Oskar Sommer. Washington: The Carnegie Institution of Washington, 1910, 5 Vols.

Index of Important People, Places and Things in the Translation

Garland Library of Medieval Literature

James J. Wilhelm and Lowry Nelson, Jr.

Series A (Texts and Translations)
Series B (Translations Only)

Bárdar Saga
Edited and translated by
Jón Skaptason and Phillip Pulsiano
Series A

The Poetry of Guido Guinizelli
Edited and translated by
Robert Edwards
Series A

Five Middle English Arthurian Romances
Translated by Valerie Krishna
Series B

The One Hundred New Tales (*Les Cent nouvelles nouvelles*)
Translated by Judith Bruskin Diner
Series B

Graelent and *Guingamor*
Two Breton Lays
Edited and translated by
Russell Weingartner
Series A

The Story of Meriadoc, King of Cambria (*Historia Meriadoci, Regis Cambrie*)
Edited and translated by
Mildred Leake Day
Series A

Guillaume de Machaut
The Fountain of Love (*La Fonteinne Amoureuse*) and Two Other Love Vision Poems
Edited and translated by
R. Barton Palmer
Series A

Der Stricker
Daniel of the Blossoming Valley (*Daniel von dem Blühenden Tal*)
Translated by Michael Resler
Series B

The Marvels of Rigomer
Translated by Thomas E. Vesce
Series B

The Song of Aspremont (*La Chanson d'Aspremont*)
Translated by Michael A. Newth
Series B

Chrétien de Troyes
The Story of the Grail (*Li Contes del Graal*), or *Perceval*
Edited by Rupert T. Pickens and translated by William W. Kibler
Series A

Romances of Alexander
Translated by Dennis M. Kratz
Series A

Guillaume de Machaut
Le Confort d'ami (*Comfort for a Friend*)
Edited and translated by
R. Barton Palmer
Series A

Moriz von Craûn
Edited and translated by
Stephanie Cain Van D'Elden
Series A

The Acts of Andrew in the Country of the Cannibals
Translations from the Greek, Latin and Old English
Translated by Robert Boenig
Series B

Francesco Petrarch
Rime Disperse
Edited, translated, and with an introduction by Joseph A. Barber
Series A

Renaut de Bâgé
Le Bel Inconnu (Li Biaus Descouneüs; The Fair Unknown)
Edited by Karen Fresco, translated by Colleen P. Donagher, music edited by Margaret P. Hasselman
Series A

Thomas of Britain
Tristran
Edited and translated by Stewart Gregory
Series A

Kudrun
Translated by Marion E. Gibbs and Sidney M. Johnson
Series B

A Thirteenth-Century Life of Charlemagne
Translated by Robert Levine
Series B

Penninc and Pieter Vostaert
Roman van Walewein
Edited and translated by David F. Johnson
Series A

Medieval Literature of Poland
An Anthology
Translated by Michael J. Mikós
Series B

Helyas or Lohengrin
Late Medieval Transformations of the Swan Knight Legend
Edited and translated by Salvatore Calomino
Series A

Kassia
The Legend, the Woman, and Her Work
Edited and translated by Antonía Tripolitis
Series A

The Song of Aliscans
Translated by Michael A. Newth
Series B

The Vows of the Heron (Les Voeux du héron)
A Middle French Vowing Poem
Edited by John Grigsby and Norris J. Lacy; translated by Norris J. Lacy
Series A

Medieval Galician-Portuguese Poetry
An Anthology
Edited and translated by Frede Jensen
Series A

Jaufre
An Occitan Arthurian Romance
Translated by Ross G. Arthur
Series B

Brunetto Latini
The Book of the Treasure (Li Livres dou Tresor)
Translated by Paul Barrette and Spurgeon Baldwin
Series B

The Pleier's Arthurian Romances
Garel of the Blooming Valley, Tandareis and Flordibel, Meleranz
Translated by J. W. Thomas
Series B

Jean Renart
The Romance of the Rose or of Guillaume de Dole (Roman de la Rose ou de Guillaume de Dole)
Edited and translated by Regina Psaki
Series A

Adam de la Halle
Le Jeu de Robin et Marion
Edited and translated by Shira I. Schwam-Baird
Series A

Amadas and Ydoine
Translated by Ross G. Arthur
Series B

JEAN FROISSART
La Prison Amoureuse (*The Prison of Love*)
Edited and translated by
Laurence de Looze
Series A

SONGS OF THE WOMEN TROUBADOURS
Edited and translated by
Matilda Tomaryn Bruckner,
Laurie Shepard, and Sarah White
Series A

THREE MEDIEVAL GREEK ROMANCES
Velthandros and Chrysandza, Kallimachos and Chrysorroi, Livistros and Rodamni
Translated by Gavin Betts
Series B

TUSCAN POETRY OF THE DUECENTO
An Anthology
Edited and translated by Frede Jensen
Series A

THE WRITINGS OF MEDIEVAL WOMEN
An Anthology
SECOND EDITION
Translations and introductions by
Marcelle Thiébaux
Series B

THE ROMANCE OF FLAMENCA
Edited and translated by E.D. Blodgett
Series A

THE PERILOUS CEMETERY
(*L'Atre Périlleux*)
Edited and translated by Nancy B. Black
Series A

THE NOVELLINO OR *ONE HUNDRED ANCIENT TALES*
An Edition and Translation based on the 1525 Gualteruzzi *editio princeps*
Edited and translated by
Joseph P. Consoli
Series A

For Product Safety Concerns and Information please contact our EU representative GPSR@taylorandfrancis.com
Taylor & Francis Verlag GmbH, Kaufingerstraße 24, 80331 München, Germany

www.ingramcontent.com/pod-product-compliance
Lightning Source LLC
Chambersburg PA
CBHW071401100726
47908CB00004B/1055

* 9 7 8 1 1 3 8 9 7 7 3 2 7 *